Soul Destruction: Unforgivable

Ruth Jacobs

**Fiction aimed at the heart
and the head...**

Published by Caffeine Nights Publishing 2013

Copyright © Ruth Jacobs 2013

Ruth Jacobs has asserted her right under the Copyright, Designs and Patents Act 1998 to be identified as the author of this work.

Published in Great Britain by Caffeine Nights Publishing.

www.caffeine-nights.com

British Library Cataloguing in Publication Data.
A CIP catalogue record for this book is available from the British Library.

ISBN: 978-1-907565-35-9

Cover design by
Mark (Wills) Williams

Everything else by
Default, Luck and Accident

Acknowledgements

I am eternally grateful for, and would like to thank, my brave and generous friends from the 1990s who, being call girls at the time, participated in my research into prostitution. To the many exited women and to the women currently in the sex trade I am in contact with and for whom I have much respect and admiration, I am sending you love. Yet we know this story is fiction, we also know how very real this is with many women in the life having suffered multiple rapes.

I owe so much to my Grandma Clara and my dear friend, Q, who are no longer alive, but who have played a large part in my writing this novel. To my wonderful sons, thank you for believing in me - sending you hugs. Thank you to my mother who was my very first reader, my father, and to my sister, Chloe, who told me I was writing a bestseller. For her never-ending care and encouragement, love and thanks to my mother-in-law (without a marriage), Elizabeth Sees. Thank you to my favourite Uncle David for never judging me and always loving me for who I am, and thank you to his fiancée, Bobie. Although no longer alive, I must thank my favourite Great Auntie Raie for her unconditional love, and my Grandpa Abe, and my Grandma Raie and my Grandpa Archie.

Massive thanks to Sharon Murphy who saved my life in my mid-twenties, and also to the many other special people who have pulled me from the wreckage in which I have found myself way too often. Thank you to Simon Birke for restoring me to sanity whenever I have lost it over the recent years. Huge thanks to Claire Meadows, Jane Frankland and Emma Roberts for their help, inspiration and support. Thank you to Estelle Longcroft, Natasha Sandy, Deborah Malyon, Jamie Easterman, Jayne Rogers, Laura Schulman and Avril Harker for their proofreading and encouragement. Thank you to Tabitha Rosen for always having my back and to Melanie Murphy-Fowle for always being there whenever I've needed her. To my friend, Katie Bridgit O'Brien, thank you for my very first radio interview on your show. Brian Parsons, thank you so much for allowing me to use your beautiful and powerful song, Just Us and Justice, for my trailer, and for making it for me too. Although I haven't known her long, I must thank Missy, who is an angel I hope stays in my life - from the US, she's managed to be an amazing support to me. Thank you to Pete Sortwell and Kat O'Dea - you both know how you've played a part in this. And thank you to

Clayton Dean for your excellent timing. For inside information, thank you to Richard Godly, and for her anecdotes, thanks to Jane Sibley. And a huge thank you to all my other friends, both new and old, who have helped and supported me so generously in numerous ways.

Thank you so much to Darren Laws at Caffeine Nights who believed in me and my debut novel, and special thanks to Sandra Mangan for editing, and Mark (Will) Williams for designing the cover.

For taking the time to help an aspiring novelist with research, thank you to Paula McColgan from The Lanesborough; James Kerman from Winkworth's, Ladbroke Grove; Lesley Atkinson from Holborn Library; The Magdala, Hampstead; Sandling Fireworks, Gloucestershire; UCAS; Metropolitan Police; Hertfordshire Police.

Soul Destruction: Unforgivable is dedicated to Q, the most beautiful soul and so impossible to forget. May she rest in peace, reunited with her babies in heaven.

Soul Destruction: Unforgivable

1. The Dead John

"There's only one kind of dead, the not moving and the not breathing kind, and that's the kind of dead he is." Despite her hysteria, Shelley Hansard tried to whisper on the phone from The Lanesborough.

"Not necessarily." Marianne's voice squeaked down the line. "Just because things seem a certain way, it doesn't mean they are."

"Sometimes it does. Sometimes things are exactly as they seem – and right now, this is one of those fucking times." Shelley sat rocking on the edge of the bed in the Regency-styled suite. "I'm telling you, he fucking died on me."

"You're not a doctor. You can't go around pronouncing people dead."

"If you don't believe me, get off the line and I'll call someone else."

"Don't you dare. You don't tell anyone. Do you understand? You come straight here." Marianne grunted. "Have you got the money?"

"What the fuck does that matter now?" A hot tear landed on Shelley's thigh.

"Get a grip, Kiki. Start acting like a professional."

Fighting the urge to look at the motionless body spread-eagled next to her, Shelley pushed herself up from the bed. Her neatly folded suit lay by her feet. She stood, staring down, burrowing her toes into the plush carpet. She knew she should get dressed, but clean clothes didn't belong on skin that felt unclean.

Taking a step towards the bathroom, she felt unbalanced. Her legs shuddered and her backside hit the floor. Reunited with her brown, pinstripe suit, she reached for her skirt. With trembling hands, she dragged it towards her. Shuffling on her back, she shimmied into it. Her fingers grappled with the hook and eye. Making a hasty exit was important, but making an exception to her rule was impossible. She couldn't do it.

She managed to stand but, stepping out of her skirt, she collapsed again. Pressing down on the carpet with her palms, she tried to lever herself back up. Her jolting arms gave way. The last limbs to surrender to the convulsionary rhythm that had overtaken the rest of her.

She didn't have control over her body. Instead, she had a helpless feeling of being completely powerless. The rush to leave the hotel and the corpse was over. As a periodic convulsionist, she knew the beat could monopolise her for hours. She just had to wait. She knew what to expect. Soon she'd be gone.

***

On regaining consciousness, her shaking had reduced. She staggered to the walnut bureau where earlier she'd left her handbag, took out her mobile and checked the time: nearly midnight. Two hours lost to another world.

Slipping the mobile back inside her cream handbag, she shut her eyes, realising what she'd done. She'd called Marianne from the phone in the hotel suite. Under the circumstances, that wasn't the phone she should have used.

After a shower, with hair wet, she dripped a track back to the bed. She dressed, trying not to look to her right but as she buttoned her jacket, she couldn't help it. She breathed in deeply, as if inhalation through her nose would draw the tears back through her ducts from whence they'd sprung.

Quietly, she said aloud, "God bless you."

What was his name? She tried to remember. She couldn't. She didn't know him, not in a real sense, only biblically. The last few hours they'd spent fornicating, high on a combination of crack and GHB. In the midst of proceedings, he'd complained of a chest pain. So, when he asked her to make him another pipe, she refused. On gently reminding her who was paying for the evening, and whose desires were to be met, he took the crack pipe from her hands and on the ash-covered foil, prepared himself a rock. The rock that would emerge to be the last ever smoked by the late, greying-blond john.

"Come to me, you...you...you nymph," he said, beckoning to her as he exhaled his final pipe. "Come over here and pleasure me— my penis. I mean, pleasure my penis. Would you, with your mouth, please?" The client reclined on the bed, unaware that his last words had just been spent on a bungled request for fellatio. And from a young woman whose name he didn't know – at least, not her real name.

Some time in, Shelley became aware that the penis in her mouth was lifeless. She stopped to look up and saw the fixed expression on his face. It wasn't changing. He wasn't moving. He looked like a waxwork from Madame Tussauds.

"What are you doing?" she asked, prodding his chest. "Stop fucking around," she shouted through the hairs in his ear.

After a vigorous shaking failed to extract even the slightest reaction, she put her fingers under his nostrils. He wasn't breathing. That was when she called Marianne.

***

From the console table, Shelley removed the remaining rocks. She wrapped them inside clingfilm then stashed them in her cigarette box. She dismantled the crack pipe. The smaller parts – elastic band, tin foil, broken biro – she put in her handbag. The abused mini Evian bottle, she put in her small suitcase.

Crouched down by the side of the mahogany bed, she methodically repacked her work paraphernalia. Two vibrators, one black strap-on dildo, handcuffs and another set of underwear were all she'd taken out her case.

Inside a crystal jar on the bathroom shelf, she found cotton wool. She wetted half a dozen pieces and, in the absence of eye makeup remover, added hand lotion. She scrubbed at the black around her eyes and the dark-grey lines that streaked her face. To stop her bloodshot eyeballs burning, she splashed them repeatedly with cold water.

Her face clean and dry, she evened the tone with powder foundation. On the blank canvas, she swirled pink blush on the cheeks, brushed black mascara through the blonde lashes and drew a line of black on the upper eyelids. To finish, she painted red on the lips, perfectly matching this week's manicure.

After drying her hair, she was ready to leave. She scanned the room, checking she hadn't left anything behind. Suddenly, she thought of fingerprints. She ran into the bathroom and grabbed a towel.

Keeping her head turned away from the dead john, she wiped down the telephone on the bedside table. Next to the phone stood a champagne flute – red lip prints on the rim – the one from which she'd drunk a Buck's Fizz. She picked it up inside the towel and polished it.

Flitting around the suite, she cleaned the bedside tables, the console table, the bureau, and everything else from the headboard to the ornaments in case she'd touched something unknowingly. In the bathroom, she wiped down the marble surfaces and glass shelves. Remembering the cotton wool in the bin, she fished out the blackened, wet balls and dropped them down the toilet. She flushed, watching them disappear. Then she flushed again to make certain they were gone. She wiped the cistern handle before throwing the towel in the bath.

Turning to leave, she looked in the mirror. The feeling that someone had put a stitch in her upper lip and was tugging at the thread looked as strange in her reflection as it felt on her face. This delayed after-effect didn't always occur but when it did, it always outlasted the shakes – sometimes by a day or a few, other times by months. However, on judging the catalytic incident – and considering the tsunami convulsion was already a weak breaker – there was a chance she'd be restored to an untwitching state in time for tomorrow night's dinner.

***

Shelley stood in the hallway, closing the hotel room door behind her. Waiting for the lift, she brushed her fingers through her thick, blonde hair. Though freshly washed and dried, that didn't stop its tendency to knot. Also knotted was her stomach. She pulled it in with a deep breath and raised her shoulders, standing straight, and taller than her natural five-foot and six-inches in her high stilettos.

Chameleon-like, she was adept at entering and exiting hotels at all times of the day and night without drawing attention. To blend in, she gave the impression of a guest, wearing business attire and carrying a case. She appeared to know the way to the lifts, and when she didn't, she could feign it.

Indelibly stamped in her memory was the floor plan of her exit, even though this was only her third visit to The Lanesborough. She hadn't had to rely on it as often as The Hilton, The Dorchester or The Four Seasons – the Park Lane hotels to which she was most often called – but The Lanesborough was stored with The Ritz, The Savoy, Claridges and numerous other London hotels she worked in less frequently.

With the air of confidence she'd mastered in faking, she strutted across the main hall. Tunnel vision for the grand exit. Her heart pounding so hard in her chest, as if preparing for its own escape, was disregarded.

She'd just made it into the drizzle outside when a low voice called out from behind her, "Good night, madam."

The uniformed porter startled her, but her calm exterior remained intact and she replied, "Good night," without a backward glance.

***

Approaching her Mercedes on Grosvnor Crescent, Shelley muddled through her handbag to find the key. She heard a banging noise. In fright, she looked up and down the street. It was devoid of people.

She opened the driver side door of her vintage 350SL. Keeping both feet on the pavement, she sat down sideways on the low seat. Then, with knees together, she lifted her legs, rotated her body ninety degrees and slipped her feet into the footwell. She believed this was the proper way for a lady to enter a sports car. Although she didn't feel like a lady, she maintained an outward appearance that was contrary to her internal turmoil.

Locked in, with her case and handbag on the passenger seat, she leant across to open the glove box. She took out a tatty, pink sponge meant for cleaning the windscreen. From a cavity inside the sponge, she drew out a white envelope. Sliding her hand underneath her skirt, she reached for her earnings tucked safely under the elasticated rim of her hold-ups. She counted out two-hundred pounds and put that in her purse. The remainder, she put in the white envelope, shoved the envelope back inside the sponge, and returned the sponge to its home in the glove box.

She looked out of her window. No one was there. She checked her rear view mirror. There was no one behind. Where were the voices coming from? Sometimes she heard voices in her head, but not these ones. There was one low and one higher pitched voice. The conversation was unintelligible, but something was funny. They were laughing. Now the voices were getting louder, getting closer. A screech pierced through her. Her head twisted brusquely to the side. Her neck felt whiplashed.

In the middle of a terrace, a young couple were kissing. The man was positioning the woman against the white-stuccoed wall of a townhouse. They didn't seem to notice Shelley in her car. Their Friday night was happening somewhere else. Another world. A world that Shelley no longer lived in, nor did she want to. Her experience of that world had propelled her into the one she inhabited now, and though she didn't care for her new world, she'd acclimatised to it. The emotional shutdown she'd acquired had brought her there and it left her stranded.

Robotically, she turned the key in the ignition, switched on the headlights, put the car into drive, checked her mirrors and pulled out of the tight space. She drove towards Chelsea, where Marianne lived off the King's Road, not far from The Lanesborough at Hyde Park Corner.

At the first set of red traffic lights, she dipped her hand into the side pocket of the door and blindly selected a CD. The Hue and Cry - *Bitter Suite* album calmed her for a moment, until she began worrying about her earlier mistake. What would Marianne say if she found out Shelley called her from the hotel phone and not her mobile? At twenty-one years of age, and after nearly three years of working, she should have known better.

2. An Alternative Reality

In less than five minutes, Shelley arrived in Cadogan Gardens. As usual, it was hard to park. She drove alongside the gated garden in the centre of the square and past Marianne's building before finding a space around the corner, a short walk away.

Sitting on the low seat, she swung her legs out of the black 350SL in the same fashion she'd swung them in. With her suitcase and handbag hanging over one arm, she walked to the rear and hid the suitcase out of sight in the boot.

Using the key fob, she activated the central locking. She heard it click but, not trusting her ears alone, she circled the car, checking the doors, windows and boot were secure with her eyes and her hands. Once she felt ready, she broke the cycle and walked around the corner to where Marianne lived – a duplex apartment on the fourth and fifth floors of an Edwardian mansion block.

At the top of the steps of the red-bricked building, Shelley called flat six on the intercom. Marianne told her to wait outside. She thought after what happened, she would at least be invited in, but Marianne was unpredictable like that. Sometimes Shelley would be allowed inside and other times not. Marianne would say she wanted to keep her business separate from her adult son – Matt – though occasionally she'd instruct Shelley to deliver her cut directly to Matt, so the excuse didn't float.

After a few minutes, Marianne came out wearing a leopard-print nightdress that was too short for a woman in her fifties unless she was a dwarf, and Marianne wasn't. She was closer to six-foot.

"Have you got the money?" Marianne asked, propping the front door open with her backside. She stood directly in the glare of the security light. Her face was the sort best illuminated by candle, and not the floodlight, which was exposing every line denoting the permanent scowl Shelley suspected time had carved into her constantly sullen face.

"He must've had a heart attack or something." Shelley took four fifty-pound notes from her purse and placed them in the empty palm in front of her.

"I'm sure he's fine."

"Why do you do this? I'm not gonna believe you. You weren't

there. You didn't see him."

Marianne sucked on what little remained of the super-thin cigarette she held to the centre of her mouth and the orifice morphed into an anus. "It was a crack job. What you saw wasn't what happened. It was what the drugs saw."

"It wasn't—"

"Look at the state of you." Marianne tossed her cigarette into the garden below. "You're tweaking, and the amount of time it's taken you to get here, I expect you stayed around to finish the crack."

"I would not have smoked crack in that room with a dead body."

"Stop doing that thing with your lip, it's repulsive. You better not do that in the company of my clients."

Shelley walked down a step to leave then changed her mind and turned around. "I'm gonna call the hotel and report it."

"Don't you dare," Marianne said through clenched teeth. "These things happen. You were unlucky. Now you need to forget about it and move on. I don't want to hear about this again. Is that clear?"

"What's to forget?" Shelley threw her hands in the air, unsteadying her balance on the narrow step. "What does it matter if I call the hotel? According to you, he's fine."

"You know what I meant."

"Don't I just?" Shelley muttered.

"Call me if you're working tomorrow. You should. It'll get you nowhere fast making something of this, believe me." Marianne stepped back inside the building and the door closed behind her.

***

Shelley had felt a modicum of guilt for taking home two-thousand eight-hundred pounds – substantially more than the four-hundred pounds Marianne believed was her share. However, after that compassionless exchange, the guilt left her. Initially, she'd been booked for two hours at a cost of six-hundred pounds. But less than an hour into the job, the client asked if she could stay for the night and, on telling him the fee, he completed the transaction with fresh-from-the-bank fifty-pound notes. She was supposed to give the madam a third of what she earned, but there was no doubt Marianne was undeserving. The crisp fifties were in their rightful place – her sponge.

Under the light rain, Shelley skulked back to her car. Considering the consequences of maintaining a miserable expression, she exercised her facial muscles with repetitions of smiles. Though awkward with a twitching upper lip, she didn't want her sadness engraved on her face as Marianne's bitterness had been marked on hers.

She set off homeward bound with the waxwork face revolving in her head. She wondered if anyone would have found him yet. No, it wouldn't be possible. The room was booked at least for the night. He may have booked it for days, if not a week or more, if he was staying in town. No one would know. The cleaner maybe. No, the sign for room cleaning wouldn't be on the door. Could she remember if it was? No, but it wouldn't be. Men don't engage hookers overnight and leave that sign out.

If she didn't alert the hotel, he could be there dead and alone for days. Who would be missing him? A family, if he had one. He probably did. If he was in London for business, there might be associates trying to reach him. Someone would miss him and report him. If not, the cleaner would find him. Oh, the poor cleaner! Perhaps she should stop at a payphone and make the call.

He wasn't a bad client and thankfully, he didn't have any strange requests. She despised some of her clients for their sick rhetoric, as well as the things they wanted her to say. As a call girl, she could refuse, and a few times in the past, she had done so, but when she was forced, there was little she could do. At five-foot and six-inches tall, and not quite eight stone, she wasn't a good match for the average-sized man.

It was a shame one of those sick perverts hadn't died on her. One of the clients who'd raped her or one who'd beaten her. The men that had done that to her gave the impression they didn't see anything wrong in their actions – flinging money at her after, or forcing her hands open to take it as she cried. As if that could justify their actions.

Shelley was used to Marianne's routine, the hard sell of an alternative reality. And when it didn't work, which it never did with Shelley, the advice that followed was always the same – forget about it and move on.

She'd been through that rigmarole after she was raped by the first client Marianne sent to her flat and again, when she was beaten by a film producer in his waterfront penthouse in Battersea. The film producer had said he thought she was acting – acting a part that he wanted. She was screaming, running from him, trying to get away. She was covered in blood, crying for him to stop, begging him to stop. He knew that wasn't an act. The scarring from that night ran deeper than the external welts and bruises that had pained her for weeks before they eventually healed. And those visible marks had faded rapidly, in contrast to what she knew was yet another eternal mar left on her psyche.

In total, there had been four attacks while she was working that could have been reported to the police, but none were declared. Although she would always get herself checked at the Praed Street Project, she would tell them as little as possible. What could they do? And as for the police – it was nonsensical talking to them. They would never believe a hooker over a wealthy professional or businessman. She wouldn't have told them what she did for a living, but after digging around – and she feared that's what would happen – they would realise she couldn't account for her standard of living: her flat in Hampstead, her car, her clothes. Although little money went in and out of her conventional bank and building society accounts, if there was ever a reason to search her flat, they'd surely find the cash that she kept hidden in her kitchen, inside the cold bank.

However much she wanted the justice that had eluded her, her experience proved it wasn't worth the risk. In Shelley's case, getting justice was as likely to happen as another chance to let her brother win a game of pool.

3. The Stranger, the Coke Can and the Futuristic Street Installation

Shelley found herself squatting on the dirty floor of a public toilet in Camden Town, trying to avoid the sparkling streams of urine under the dim light. Twenty minutes earlier, she'd plucked a young man from the street. He'd been sitting on the pavement by the Tube station, begging, appearing to be homeless. She had a knack for picking them – the junkies – and she was rarely wrong.

She entrusted him with one-hundred and twenty pounds to score sixty brown and sixty white. He both scored and brought back the drugs – the latter not being a given when strangers score for strangers, especially when buying heroin and crack. With that action, sadly, he proved more reliable and perhaps more deserving of her trust than the majority of people with whom she associated.

Although in her cigarette packet she still had the crack from The Lanesborough, she needed more. And she needed the heroin to come down, but before coming down, she wanted to get as high as she knew how. Speedballing. The superlative combination of heroin and crack. The transportation to Shangri-la.

None of her friends took heroin. The only two heroin dealers she knew – Jay and Ajay – weren't answering their phones. That was why she had to follow her usual Plan B, which she imagined was no more jeopardous than working.

The stranger had suggested shooting up in the toilet on Inverness Street. She didn't want to wait to walk back to her car so had accompanied him inside the futuristic street installation. Though the outside was modern, inside it was rank. One of the worst public conveniences Shelley had ever used for a hit. The stench of stale urine permeated every cell in the depths of her nasal cavities and from there, travelled down her throat like post-nasal drip. Even though she kept her mouth shut, she could taste it on her tongue. It was making her gag.

The spoon he cooked up in wasn't a spoon at all. Neither of them had one, so he used the bottom of a coke can as a substitute. Shelley hoped the boiling would sterilise the metal. She would have preferred her own clean spoon, but it was in her glove box.

She wondered if that was everything he owned, bundled into the small rucksack on his back. She didn't ask. She didn't say anything. And neither did he. Why was she dressed for the office when she was shooting up in a public toilet? Not that it would have been difficult to conjure an alternative to what happened at The Lanesborough, but she wasn't there for conversation. She was there to forget. In her own way. Not by the falsehoods Marianne tried to peddle.

She rolled up her sleeves to choose a vein. Her arms were clean. So far, she'd managed to evade the track marks, lumps, scabs, bruises and abscesses that would have been tantamount to commercial suicide. To charge upwards of two-hundred and fifty pounds an hour, her clients could never know she was an injector. So injecting had to be organised, alternating numerous veins in her arms, hands, legs and feet. If she was messy, she'd only be able to solicit clients on the street, and streetwalking came with far more risk and a far lower financial reward.

When the heroin had dissolved, she added a rock of crack. With the young man holding the can steady, she used the plunger end of her syringe to grind the white stone into the brown water. She hurried, craving to feel the warm safe-danger, her body pulsating, and her head pumping like it was pumping out every tormenting memory it stored. Soon, the relentless playback of those pictures and scenes would stop. She would have her reprieve. Her respite. And although earning the money to pay for it created new images, as abhorrent as they were, what she was originally escaping from was worse.

Shelley proffered her gold twenty-pack. He took a cigarette and, using his teeth, tore off a chunk of filter. He snatched it from his mouth with his thumb and index finger then dropped it into the concoction. Shelley noticed the scabs on his lips and the dirt under his fingernails. The filter wasn't clean. She needed the hit.

"You first." A gentleman, he held the can out in front of Shelley, letting her draw up her shot before him.

"Pass it here." Shelley positioned her filled syringe between her teeth and reached for the can to reciprocate.

Once his barrel was full, she delicately placed the empty can on what seemed like a dry area of the floor, saving the filter for the next fix. If she was taking one hit from the dirty filter, what difference would a second make?

She wrapped one hand around her wrist. She squeezed. On cue, her pulse thumped and the map of blue veins rose from the back of her hand. She let go, swiped the syringe from her mouth, removed the orange cap with her teeth and inserted the needle into a sinking vein at the base of her hand. Pulling back on the plunger, blood swirled into her medicine. Inside, her rush was brewing. She pushed it all in.

4. Damaged Goods

On Saturday, Shelley roused mid-afternoon. She didn't remember driving back from Camden, so it was a relief to find herself in her own flat on Willoughby Road and not in some strange bed or worse, in her working flat. That flat in Belsize Park wasn't meant for sleeping in but after a binge, sometimes she'd wake there and find money she couldn't account for, meaning she'd had clients that she didn't remember seeing. Other times, she'd find a junky she must've brought back from the streets. Though often in need of a wash, a smackhead stranger was more welcome than inexplicable earnings.

From her handbag, she took the white envelope. She recounted her pay from The Lanesborough job and bound the crisp fifties in pairs – one note flat with the Queen's head upright, the other folded over it with the Queen's head on its side.

She hid the cash in the cold bank – a Black Forest gateau box kept in the freezer. For disguise, it was resealed every time it was reopened and stashed amid a plethora of frozen food.

In the bedroom, she wrapped herself in an old duvet. Still in her pyjamas and barefoot, she waddled on the oak floorboards through to the lounge. She switched on the satellite box and her recently acquired Bang & Olufsen television.

Nestled on the claret, velvet sofa, she shot some junk to counter the aching in her bones. The demon inside that drove and controlled her faded, and she settled into the reprieve she'd created.

She did not have a husband of nine years who secretly fathered a child with his cousin. She did not have a pimp who forced her to work in downtown LA and took all her money. She was not begging her woman-beating boyfriend to come back and take care of her and their five children.

No.

The warm blanket of heroin had slackened and in her half-sleep, she'd mistaken the arguments on television for her own. The Jerry Springer show was rubbish, but even armed with this knowledge, she sat up to concentrate. Occasionally, there an American trailer park resident who made her feel less pathetic about her own life.

***

By the time Shelley changed into jeans and a jumper, the effects of her medicine had dissipated. Back in reality, she knew that if she was going to call The Lanesborough, it would have to be done when she went out tonight. If not, it would most likely be too late, and if it wasn't already, it wasn't right for a dead body to be alone in that hotel room.

Her internal board of directors marked the onset of agitation, issuing a shrill warning with their trumpeting. Within seconds, they charged to the front of her mind with fear: she hadn't wiped her fingerprints from the taps in the bathroom.

What else had she forgotten? DNA. Only the other week there was a television programme about it. Why hadn't she thought of it at the time? Would her DNA be in the suite at The Lanesborough? If it was, could it be used to track her down? How would they know it was hers?

Her brain performed a spin cycle and produced the notion that hospitals kept DNA records. They took samples from every person when they took blood for whatever reason. The Royal Free Hospital DNA database would share their records with the police – and that would be how they'd find her.

Another hit was what she needed but she couldn't take one. Shooting more gear wasn't an option so close to seeing family. This evening she was expected for dinner at her Aunt Elsie's house and after last night, she was praying she could keep up the pretence of normality.

To deflect the board's fear-ridden stampede, she busied her mind with a different occupation – vacuuming. Her flat was immaculately clean, having been scrubbed, polished and vacuumed two days ago, but there was always dirt lurking somewhere. Once she'd finished with the Dyson, she rearranged her bookshelf. Currently kept in an unorthodox height system, she switched the books into a conventional alphabetical order. Accomplished, and with still another twenty minutes left before she had to leave her flat, she progressed to her videos. Already stored alphabetically, she reorganised them by genre.

She'd barely made a start on the video shelf when she heard the phone. She knew who it was. Clients calling direct used her mobile, as did the madams she worked for and the girls she worked with. Only the escort agencies had her landline from when she first started working, but they'd long since been eliminated in favour of the higher paying madams. She had fewer friends than she dared count and they rarely phoned. At quarter to seven, it had to be her mother. And if her mother was calling her now, she wouldn't be at Aunt Elsie's tonight.

"I'm sorry, dear." Rita's voice was so quiet that Shelley could barely hear her.

"That's okay." Shelley tried to raise her tone to conceal her disappointment. "Will you make yourself dinner?"

"I'll be fine. I'm not hungry."

"You have to eat, Mum." There was silence as she waited for the distant voice to reply.

"I'll have something later. You needn't worry about me."

But Shelley was worried. She was always worried about her mother.

**

After an aggressive brushing, her hair was eventually untangled. She put on the Tiffany necklace she'd bought herself last week. Then she lifted her jean jacket from the hook behind the bedroom door and went over to the window to ensure it was locked.

Shelley never left her flat without checking it was safe to be left. Once she'd checked the windows in her bedroom, she did the same in the second bedroom, lounge, kitchen and bathroom. Each window handle was pushed in rhythmically in time to her counting aloud. Not believing her eyes, she needed to feel and hear each window was locked. And she needed to feel it and hear it at least twenty times.

The taps were next: a twisting ritual performed in the bathroom and kitchen. Taps, like windows and doors, were counted in four sets of five, but after last night, she kept losing count. Every time that happened, she had to start over from the first set of five.

Finally, she moved on to the six-knob oven. For this, she didn't keep to the four-sets-of-five pattern. Counting to five twenty-four times unbroken – no mind-wandering allowed – was impossible. The oven needed special treatment. Each of the six knobs was patted, as if in congratulations, five times. She worked from the first on the left through to the last on the right. Most days, even with distractions, the six sets of five took no more than a couple of minutes. But today was not most days. For twenty minutes, her feet were fixed on the black and white floor tiles as the waxwork face stared up at her from the glass in the oven door.

**

Shelley entered the terraced house on Queens Grove using her own key. Stopping off at a payphone to call The Lanesborough had added to her pre-existing condition of persistently abysmal timekeeping.

"Come on through." Aunt Elsie's dulcet voice drifted out to greet her, as did the safe smell of musty, old house.

Shelley made her way down the long hall to the kitchen. Her aunt stood by the stove, stirring the contents of a pot chugging away on the back hob. It sounded like a train expelling the same two words on a loop that Shelley heard every time she was a passenger: damaged goods.

Her aunt rested the wooden spoon against the side of the pot, removed her vine and grape patterned apron, and then drew Shelley in for a hug. On releasing her grip, she raised a forkful of fish pie to Shelley's mouth.

Aunt Elsie made the best fish pie with salmon, cod, eggs, potatoes and Shelley wasn't sure what else, but whatever was in it, she loved it. The taste usually evoked happy memories from her childhood. And as those good few were the oldest, they were the rarest recollections.

After three mouthfuls, nothing was recalled. The pot's incessant chanting at her, and her fear of being arrested, prohibited that happening.

"Is something wrong?" Aunt Elsie asked, reinstating the apron as protection over her dusty rose twinset.

Before replying, Shelley ran her tongue over her teeth to remove the particles of fish pie she could feel stuck to them. "No. I'm fine, thanks."

"But that spasm's back on your lip again."

"No, it's not from— I woke up like this. I think I got stung in my sleep."

"Oh, thank goodness. You had me worried." Aunt Elsie clasped her hands together. "You should get an allergy test done. Go to the doctors to be on the safe side."

"I don't know if my surgery does that."

"Well, you can afford to go private." Using her wrist, Elsie swept back the long, red strands of fringe falling over her eyes. "I'm sorry about Mum. We'll have another dinner, the three of us, before you start. I promise."

The family dinner was meant to be celebrating Shelley's offer of a place at university. She'd had a fleeting idea the year earlier to become a mature student. Before the idea fleeted – as all her others had over recent years – she'd acted on it and applied to a number of London universities.

Until the post arrived yesterday, she didn't know if she'd actually be going. She hadn't yet received an offer, and with unspectacular A-level grades and limited spaces for mature students, she wasn't sure she would. The offer from University College London was the one she'd least expected. Failing to get clean in advance of their interview and assessment day, she was sure being high impaired her ability to carry out the reasoning and numerical tests. And even if it didn't, staff from the psychology division would be the most likely to pick up on pinned pupils. That's what she'd thought.

***

After dinner, they took tea in the swirly-patterned lounge. Shelley felt sick as she sat next to her aunt on the brown, velour sofa. It wasn't that the wallpaper, carpet and curtains looked like living, breathing entities – though they did – it was the fish pie.

Apart from croissants and ice cream, Shelley seldom ate. However, she found that most of the time, if she left a few hours from her last fix, she could eat a child-size portion of most food. But tonight, not being like most, the meal wasn't either. She'd had to force down every mouthful so as not to upset her aunt.

Like her living-breathing living room, and every other room in the house, Aunt Elsie was trapped in the seventies. In the three decades she'd lived there, nothing had changed, except once in 1985. The year Elsie's husband left her and the house for a younger woman and a country cottage.

The five-bedroom house was Elsie's compensation. She didn't get any money. She'd been scrimping to save for years with what she earned as a school secretary, and still couldn't afford to redecorate. She could barely afford to heat a couple of rooms during winter. Shelley wanted to give her the money and she'd offered a few times, but her aunt wouldn't accept it.

"I'm so proud of you." Aunt Elsie beamed at Shelley. "Soon I'll have to call you Doctor Hansard."

Shelley looked down at the trip-inducing carpet. "I don't know if my savings will stretch to a PhD."

"If that's what you want, we'll make it happen. You can live here and I'll take in lodgers. I'm not having anything spoil this for you."

"Let's see what happens," Shelley replied, with no intention of allowing her aunt to rent rooms in her house, not after the last time. "I don't know how I'll get on. It's scary. I'm going to be so much older than everyone else."

"What are you talking about? You're practically the same age as the kids going straight from A-levels. Don't worry about that. You'll be brilliant."

Starting university at twenty-two years of age wasn't what worried her, but she couldn't tell her aunt what was really on her mind. That last night she was at The Lanesborough, smoking crack and sucking on some old guy's cock when he died in her mouth mid-fellatio, wasn't confiding-in-Aunt-Elsie information.

"Have you told Foxtons you're leaving yet?"

"Not yet." As the lie left Shelley's lips, guilt rose from her gut. It wasn't vomit she could taste in her mouth. She couldn't swallow it back down, but she tried.

5. The Party

After four days holed up in her Willoughby Road flat, shooting speedballs – her preferred amalgamation of heroin and crack – Shelley was glad to receive a call from Tara. Tara Barnes wasn't her first choice for company. Nicole O'Connell was. But Nicole was in Mustique. A client had flown her out there for a job ten days ago. She was due back tomorrow but for the past ten days, Shelley had no one to confide in. Although she hadn't yet decided if she was going to tell anyone about what happened at The Lanesborough last week, she wanted to be in company where she could be herself, so she accepted Tara's invitation to party at her flat.

'Party' in their terminology wasn't meant in the conventional sense. Guests, or a reason to celebrate, were superfluous. To party for them meant taking drugs. One could just as easily have a party on their own. In fact, Shelley had been partying on her own constantly for the past ninety-six hours, minus the fifteen or so hours of GHB induced sleep. And though she wasn't celebrating it, at some point during the party, her upper lip had returned to its non-twitching state.

On ending the call with Tara, Shelley phoned Jay to place an order for her self-prescribed medicine. She hoped he wouldn't take much longer than the fifteen minutes he said he would, but he was rarely on time.

She cooked up the last of the heroin, mixed in the final few crumbs of crack, shot up and waited. At seven o'clock, an hour had passed, the sun had set and Jay hadn't arrived.

"How much longer are you gonna be?" She tried to conceal the impatience in her tone.

"Soon come," Jay said in his low, soothing voice, but Shelley wasn't soothed.

"How *soon* is soon? You said fifteen minutes and that was an hour ago."

"I'm just pulling into your road now, love." He cut the call.

Thirty minutes passed with Shelley staring out of the lounge window of her first floor flat. Jay couldn't use shortage of parking spaces as an excuse. Shelley had her eye on two spaces directly opposite. She called him back and told him not to bother coming because she had to go out. He insisted he was at the top of her road, and persuaded her to wait for him, which she did.

After forty minutes, he still hadn't arrived. She called him again, and again he tried to convince her that he was at the corner of Hampstead High Street and her road.

"I'm looking out my window. If you're not here in one minute, I'm going out."

"Wednesday's a busy day, love. Give me a break. I'll be fifteen minutes."

"Forget it. I've gotta go now. I'm late for a job," she lied. Why would Wednesdays be busier? Had it been decreed the national giro day?

Although Shelley was craving the next fix and would be unable to use heroin at Tara's, she had to leave her flat. Once it started, this waiting for Jay could go on for hours. His older brother had been the same, before he went to prison and Jay – formerly known as Turgay – took over.

Starting the process again with her other dealer, Ajay, would be insanity. His time keeping was so appalling that in comparison, Jay and his brother, Ali, were as punctual as Big Ben. She would have to make a stop at Camden on the return journey from Tara's and score her gear on the street. Tara could at least score the crack.

***

On the drive to Tara's, Shelley pulled up at a phone box on the Edgware Road. It was the first opportunity she'd had to make the follow-up call with The Lanesborough. The curt receptionist told her the guest in that suite had checked out and she denied knowledge of Shelley's previous call reporting the death. Shelley insisted on speaking to another member of staff but again, she was fobbed off with the same story. They must have been briefed on what to say by the management. The discovery of a dead body wouldn't exactly be something they'd want publicised.

When Shelley arrived at the third floor flat – on a side street off the Cromwell Road – Tara was already high. She was paler than usual, and spots had formed in clusters on her chin, cheeks and forehead. Her thin, mousy hair was loosely tied back in a bun. A failed attempt to disguise its greasiness. She had been an attractive girl but her beauty was deteriorating.

"How much do you want to get?" Tara asked as they walked through the narrow L-shaped hallway.

"A hundred," Shelley replied, following her into the lounge.

Perching on the edge of the navy sofa, Shelley took off her jacket and lit a cigarette. At the other end of the room, Tara stood by the glass dining table, talking to her dealer on the phone.

While they waited for him to arrive, Tara made up a pipe for Shelley from the lilliputian rocks she'd saved. Shelley enjoyed the first hit but it wasn't the same without heroin. The effects subsided rapidly. She was left with the jitters and the craving for another pipe.

In less than an hour, the dealer delivered the crack – and in less than two hours, it was smoked. At midnight, Shelley wanted to get heroin and get home. Tara, however, wanted to score the next batch of rocks.

***

"I haven't got any more cash on me," Shelley told her. The money she had had heroin stamped on it.

Tara insisted on walking her to the cashpoint. They left the flat and went out in the cold night. Shelley was surprised Tara hadn't changed her clothes. She hadn't expected her to go outside wearing the tracksuit that was also functioning as her food diary.

"I won't get my card in," Shelley said, staring at the hole in the wall on Earl's Court Road. "Some idiot's stuck matchsticks in the slot."

"Urgh! That is so council." Tara zipped up her shiny, black bomber jacket and walked on. "This area's meant to be gentrified. What a load of shit."

Shelley stopped after taking a few too many steps in the opposite direction from Tara's flat. "I'm not going far. It's bloody freezing."

"It's only five minutes. Get your car, if you want."

Shelley wasn't willing to walk, nor was she willing to drive. If she was going to get in her car, it would be to score heroin, but she couldn't tell that to Tara. All the call girls she knew – Tara included – disdained smackheads and injecting users. As if snorting cocaine and smoking crack somehow elevated them to a superior plane on a hierarchal structure of drug users.

"I'll give him my laptop for your share," Tara said.

"You've got a laptop? What for?" Shelley had never even seen a laptop. No one she knew had one. She thought she was technologically advanced herself for having the internet on her computer.

"Exactly! What do I want with a laptop?" Tara started skipping along the pavement, back in the direction they'd come from. "I don't even know how to use it."

"You shouldn't sell it," Shelley said, running after her to catch up. "I'm not gonna let you. I'd never sell anything I owned for drugs."

Tara stopped skipping and turned round. "You sell your body. What's a laptop in the grand scheme of things?"

"I can't believe you just said that. How could I sell my body? You can only sell something once. I rent my body and sell my time. What do you think you sell?" Shelley peered through the wide glass window of an all-night cafe, thinking about what she could be doing in their toilet right now instead of traipsing the streets. "I'll go home. We'll have another party when Nic's back."

***

While they were waiting for the dealer, Shelley sat on the navy sofa and lit three cigarettes: one to smoke and two to burn in the ashtray. They needed to stockpile clean ash for when the crack arrived.

She didn't like the thought of smoking Tara's laptop, even more so because it had been a gift from her parents, but Tara had persuaded her. She'd said the Toshiba was better off being traded for something she could actually use and with technology constantly changing, it was best to do it now before it became obsolete and unsaleable.

"Have a shot of vodka. Live a little." Tara returned from the kitchen, carrying two glasses. "You can't have it on its own – it's a child's drink." The glass of lemon barley water clinked with the glass top of the coffee table as Tara set it down.

"No. It's fine as it is."

"How can you smoke crack and drive? It's hypocritical," Tara said, unscrewing the cap on the bottle of Smirnoff.

"Crack makes me more alert. It's not the same thing." Shelley put her palm over her glass, preventing Tara gatecrashing with the uninvited vodka. "I mean it. I don't want any."

Trying to ignore the smudged fingerprints sullying the glass, Shelley sipped her lemon barley sans vodka. She never drank when she was driving. She couldn't, not after what happened to her grandparents. Even though Tara knew this, now and again, she'd try talking her into a drink, forcefully, and interestingly, only when they were alone.

"Do you see your parents often?" Shelley asked. Tara had never spoken of her parents before tonight. Shelley had thought they didn't have contact. There were no pictures of them in her flat. There were no pictures of anyone in Tara's flat.

"Sometimes," Tara said, as she sank into the mountainous armchair.

Shelley slotted three cigarettes between her lips and lit them simultaneously for the same purpose as the previous three. "Do they know you work?"

"Yes, and they're so proud – their daughter, a call girl."

"Why did you tell them?"

"I didn't." Tara stole one of Shelley's left-to-burn cigarettes from the ashtray and took a long drag. "It was one of my regulars. His wife came home and found me tied up in their bed."

"She knew your parents?"

Tara took a gulp from her glass. "I went to the same prep school as her daughter. I hadn't seen them in years but she was still in touch with my mother and blah-blah-blah."

"Oh, poor you. That's awful."

Tara raised her left eyebrow and a half-smile spread from the right side of her mouth. "It would have been, if it'd happened... We're going to Cafe de Paris on Friday. You should come. You won't need any money."

Shelley felt her cheeks warm, part in embarrassment and part in anger. "So, they don't know, then? What do they think you do?"

Tara stood, and then walked towards the door. "Do you want a coffee?" Her voice trailed off as she left the room.

***

The buzzer rang out. Tara answered it. A tappity-tap of high heels resonated up the wooden staircase and into the flat. Shelley was expecting the dealer but unless he'd cross-dressed since his earlier visit, it wasn't him.

Nicole O'Connell strutted into the lounge as if she'd stepped straight off the catwalk. Her runway model looks – usually pale from her Irish heritage – were transformed with a Mustique tan. Defying the British weather, she wore a flowing, strappy dress and her blonde hair cascaded half way down her back.

"You sure there's gonna be enough crack for all that ash?" Nicole smiled. She was as beautiful to know as she was to observe. Shelley leapt from the sofa to hug her closest friend. She took a step back and held Nicole's suntanned face in her hands. She wondered how Nicole managed to look so well when, most likely, she hadn't been doing anything remotely good for her health while she'd been away.

Within minutes, the dealer came to exchange a quantity of crack for Tara's two-hundred and fifty and her Toshiba. Tara brought the booty to Crack Island – the coffee table by the bay window in the front of the flat where they always smoked. Shelley and Nicole were already there waiting, sat on the carpet. Taking turns, they made up their own hits on the shared pipe – another mini Evian bottle abused.

After a few pipes, Shelley and Nicole moved to sit on the navy sofa. Shelley began to hallucinate. She could see the dead john's face staring back at her from inside the glass top of the coffee table. Every time she looked away, she could see it again: on the wallpaper, in the carpet and on the black screen of the television. There was no body, only the head, doing a jig in front of her eyes wherever she looked.

"A punter died on me the other night." Shelley didn't realise she'd verbalised her thoughts until she saw Nicole and Tara gawp at her.

"Are you joking?" Nicole asked, quashing any remaining doubt that Shelley had spoken.

Had the question been posed by Tara, even in her jittery state, Shelley could have probably have mustered a lie, but not to Nicole. She never lied outright to her. "No. I need another pipe."

Nicole made up a pipe, handed it to Shelley, and lit it for her. Shelley sucked hard on the sawn-off biro in the hope it would improve how she felt and what she saw.

"Did he have a terminal erection?" Tara asked.

"I don't think it was his erection that killed him," Shelley said.

"No, I mean did he have angel lust?"

"It's not a damn joke, Tara," Nicole said, taking the pipe back from Shelley.

The context of the conversation was lost in the aftermath of the hit. Shelley was conjuring the image of an angel fantasy in her mind. A request for an angel fantasy had never been put to her, though she'd dressed up for clients innumerable times. She tried to remember if she'd seen an angel costume in Tara's repertoire. She envisaged a transparent, white negligee with curved angel wings of the same material. She spent a while considering how one might lie down in such a costume, or even sit down. She decided the whole job would have to be undertaken with the hooker standing.

Tara walked into the lounge carrying a book in her hand. Shelley hadn't seen her leave the room and wondered how she'd made her exit. Did she fly?

"I wasn't joking." Tara brandished the paperback in front of them. "I was asking if your stiff had a stiffy."

"You're not funny. Can't you see you're upsetting her?" Nicole slipped her arm over Shelley's shoulder. With her other hand, she angled Shelley's face towards hers. "Ignore her. She's smoked too much. Are you all right, love?"

"Can I talk to you later?" Shelley whispered in Nicole's eye.

"Anytime, most precious." Nicole blinked repeatedly.

Tara knelt on the carpet. Using the edge of the blue Rizla packet, she scooped up some fresh ash from the cigarettes Shelley had let burn for the pipe. On top of the ash, she placed the last large rock. She aimed the Clipper lighter at it and taking the deepest of draws, killed it. Only a few crumbs remained on the clingfilm for Shelley and Nicole.

Tara swivelled her body round, stretched her legs under the coffee table and leaned back against the sofa. "I'm sorry if I upset you, Shelley." She looked over her shoulder at Shelley sat behind her on the sofa. "I've been reading about it, angel lust. It's in here, 'Naked Lunch'".

Tara jumped up as if suddenly repelled by her dirty carpet. She waved the paperback in front of Shelley and Nicole. Shelley glanced at the book. So did Nicole. But they both looked away when Tara tried to hand it to them. How could they be expected to start reading now? The words would have wriggled all over the page. Surely, Tara knew that. Regardless, Shelley didn't care for erotic tales, which is what she expected the book contained. That was Tara's interest, for her work at least. Shelley recalled one client in particular. Nicole called him Resident Crack Wrap. Tara had told them he liked to be constrained in clingfilm while she was naked, feeding him crack pipes, and poppers on a cigarette, and reading erotica to him.

Shelley and Nicole tried to prepare their final hits with the few morsels Tara had spared them. Tara, however, distracted them. She flicked through the pages of the open book, blocking their access to the drug paraphernalia they were trying to use on the table.

The last thing Shelley wanted was to try to decipher written words. Being on crack, spoken words were hard enough to follow. With the paperback nearly pressed to her nose, she couldn't help but look. The paragraphs floated up from the page. They flew across the room then out through the closed window. This gave Shelley a new focus – how do words pass through solid objects?

Shelley kept her eyes on the passages of words flying out the window. One sentence bounced off the glass. Perhaps it couldn't get through. The line drifted back in the direction it had come from and paused in front of Shelley. She read the words hovering in the air: *Who can hang a weak passive and catch his sperm in mouth like a vicious dog?*

As quick as that line left, another flew back in. It tapped her between the eyes and back-flipped before stopping long enough for her to read: *And I knew him when, dearie... I recall we was doing an Impersonation Act – very high class too – in Sodom.*

Then all the passages came rushing back inside. Like a frenzied flock of birds, they were soaring round the lounge. Abruptly, they stopped and formed an airborne queue at Shelley's eye-level.

"Enough!" Shelley yelled as she covered her now moist eyes with her hands. "I need more crack," she repeated in between whimpers.

Nicole held Shelley in her arms and rocked her on the sofa. The motion, coupled with the apple smell of Nicole's hair, began to calm her. Shelley leant forwards to the coffee table to make up the one pipe Tara had left her. Nicole pulled her back and told her to wait, lighting a cigarette for her instead.

The intercom sounded. Tara hauled herself up from the armchair and disappeared into the hall. Shelley heard heavy steps, most likely male. She expected the dealer to make his entrance imminently. She hadn't heard Tara phone him but she was aware of her own inattention. The thought of more crack caused her stomach to churn and her heart to beat a racing rhythm all over her body.

***

Nonchalantly, Hugo strolled into the lounge. He didn't deal crack or even take it. Shelley's nervous anticipation deflated and her innards adjusted accordingly, shifting down several gears.

"What's with the serious faces, girls?" Hugo ran his hand backwards through his blond, curly locks. The sound system in Shelley's head played Carly Simon - *You're So Vain.*

"Shelley had a punter die on her at The Lanesborough." Did those words come from Tara's lips or her own head? Shelley wasn't sure.

"Did you fuck him to death, Shelley?" The cad smiled at her with his I-know-you-want-to-fuck-me eyes.

"I bet she fucked his brains out." Tara sniggered.

"Fuck you!" Shelley raised her middle finger in Tara's direction.

"Don't worry, darling. I think they have a morgue in there. They can put it to use."

Shelley was flummoxed.

"How much coke have you done tonight, love?" Nicole asked him.

"Not enough, darling." Hugo swaggered to the dining table where he emptied a bulging wrap of cocaine on the glass top. He began chopping at it with his credit card.

Having elongated what looked like more than a dozen white lines, he bent over the table and snorted two with a fifty-pound note. He passed the note to Nicole, then she to Shelley, then Shelley to Tara.

After their hits had been hoovered, Hugo produced a half-size

36

bottle of whiskey from an inside pocket of his navy blazer. "Get some glasses," he told Tara. Then he stared into Shelley's eyes and she was sure he was reading her thoughts. "So tell me about the dead guy, darling."

6. More Than One Kind of Dead

No one responded to the knocking on the red door concealed behind an overgrown hedge at the top of Hammers Lane in Mill Hill.

"Mum, open the door." Shelley looked up to the bedroom window of the first floor maisonette. "Let me in." She saw the curtains move and knew her mother was home. Although that was really a given as her mother hadn't been out in months. "I know you're up there. I can see you."

Shelley had a key to her mother's maisonette but she preferred her to open the door. If Rita got up to answer the door, she would at least get out of bed. If Shelley used her own key, the chance of that happening was drastically reduced.

A few moments passed and the door opened. Shelley stepped inside the hall. Her scrawny mother stood in her ankle-length dressing gown, slightly hunched and with her head low.

"I'm sorry I didn't come in the week." Shelley hugged her mother, hiding tears of guilt.

Taking her mother's arm, she guided her up the stairs and into the lounge. The curtains were still drawn. It was one o'clock in the afternoon. Shelley pulled them open, letting in the day. The dark lounge transformed into a brighter one, but now the disorder was exposed.

Papers, files and books were scattered everywhere: on the dining table, on the chairs, by the gas fire and on the windowsill. Shelley removed a pile of pink and blue files from the three-seater and directed her mother to sit down.

In the kitchen, Shelley put on the kettle and waiting for it to boil, she washed up the collection of dirty mugs and plates that had accumulated in the sink. She brought her mother a cup of tea in the lounge, then she returned to the kitchen to make her a sandwich. Fortunately, there were still ample supplies left over from the shop Shelley did for her last Friday.

With shoulders slumped, Rita sat next to Shelley on the pale-grey settee. In slow motion, she nibbled her sandwich.

"How are you feeling?" Shelley asked.

"I'm trying not to, dear." Rita put her plate with the barely-touched sandwich on the end table.

"I'm going to Will's grave. Do you think you're up to it to come with me?" Shelley took out a comb from her cream handbag.

"What about work? Don't you have to get back?"

"They're letting some of us go early on Fridays. It was my turn. Will you come?"

"No dear, you know I can't. Not at the moment."

Shelley leant across and gently ran the comb through Rita's long, grey hair. "I'll sit with you for a while before I go."

***

Crime of the Century boomed from the nearly blown speakers in Shelley's Mercedes as she raced up East Finchley High Road. Arriving at the cemetery car park, she lifted the pink carnations from the passenger seat. The coldness of the cemetery air hit her as she opened the door. It always felt colder inside the graveyard.

She walked around her car, counting aloud to five each time she tried a door handle, ran her fingers along the top of a window, and depressed the catch on the boot. What could have been accomplished in twenty-five counts – less than as many seconds – took a few minutes.

On reaching William's grave, she sat down on the ground next to him. She spoke to him quietly. She told him of her plans to go to university, her fears that it might not happen, her dinner with Aunt Elsie and her visit with their mother.

Shelley never spoke to William about work – neither her non-existent job at Foxtons, nor what she really did. So she didn't tell him what happened at The Lanesborough after her visit with him last Friday. She knew he wouldn't judge her, but she didn't want him to worry about her from up in heaven. She wasn't sure if she only knew what she told him or if he saw everything. If he did, he'd already know what happened. In a way, she hoped he was looking out for her, keeping her safe. But in another, she hoped he wasn't, so he didn't have to see how she was living.

Heading back to the car park, she stopped at the double grave of her grandparents. Her mother's parents died before she'd been able to really know them. Shelley was only three years old in 1978 – the year a drunk driver crashed into their Morris Minor on the M1.

Her maternal grandparents were the only grandparents she'd ever known, and the only grandparents she shared with William. Like Shelley, William's father wasn't in his life, although he was back and forth for the first year or so after William was born. After that, his full time job took precedence – alcoholism. William had also known some of his family. Shelley had never met anyone on her father's side, not even the man himself. Apparently, he had his reasons, one of which was being married.

Back in her car, Shelley locked herself in. She put the Supertramp CD on shuffle. From the glove box, she took out the dessert spoon, citric acid powder, gear and her works. Using the water from the bottle kept in the car, she began cooking up a fix.

She sensed someone's presence and looked out her window. A tall man, dressed in a shell suit, with a hat covering a third of his face, was staring at her from the other side of the car park. She recognised him. She'd seen him in the cemetery before. He gave her the creeps. The way he loitered and the way he watched her. Apart from him, the graveyard was nearly always deserted. She rarely saw another living soul whenever she was there and that's how she preferred it.

Once he'd gone, she felt safe to carry on. To be inconspicuous, she bent over with her head down in the footwell. Using a rag conveniently kept in the car, she constricted the blood flow at her ankle. The veins in her feet were thin and easy to burst. She knew she risked losing the hit. Only the other week, she'd caused tissuing in a vein on the same foot. The resulting lump wouldn't massage away. It had given her pain, and restricted her choice of footwear, until it left of its own accord.

Selecting a barely visible vein in which to inject, she slid in the needle. The thrill began as she watched the blood infiltrate the barrel. She pushed in the plunger a little, releasing some of the junk into her bloodstream. Then she pulled out to watch more blood percolate. The next time she pushed a fraction too forcefully. The vein was blown.

She tried to rescue what was left in the syringe, but the blood was congealing. Holding the plastic tube in the air, she flicked it to release the air bubbles. Impetuously, she thrust the needle into her arm. Most of the heroin and coagulated blood had entered her body. However, not all of it went in via the vein. In addition to the new swelling on her foot, she now had another on the inside of her elbow. Of greatest distress was that most of the hit had been wasted. The rush was negligible.

On the drive home, she cranked up the volume. The song that started to play was one that reminded her most of William. She'd heard him sing it countless times in the days he gigged with his band in the pubs around North London. He sang his own version in what he'd described was a blend of punk, ska and reggae.

She part-sung and part-sobbed through *Hide in Your Shell*. She shivered, feeling William's presence. Her tears stopped as he sang to her, "*Why don't you listen? You can trust me.*" It sounded as if he was sitting next to her in the passenger seat.

7. That Palaver with the Blindfold

Flickering light was all Shelley could make out from under the blindfold. Her ability to balance was compromised by her inability to view her surroundings. Her body jolted around on the backseat and she wondered how much longer she could tolerate the motion before surrendering to nausea. She wanted to ask how much time it would take until they arrived. But she didn't, imagining she'd sound like a whinging child.

The car stopped abruptly, lunging Shelley's body forward. Her head smashed on something hard. She knew not to remove the blindfold, so she brushed the back of her hand across her throbbing forehead. She didn't feel any blood.

She heard a car door open, then slam shut. Another door opened. It sounded very close, perhaps the back door of the car. Was that leather she felt wrapped around her arm?

"Sorry about that, miss. Are you all right?" The hand that gripped her hoisted her back onto the seat.

"My head hurts. Is it bleeding?"

The leather glove stroked Shelley's hair away from her forehead. "No, miss. But you've got a little bump, or did you have that already?"

"No... No, I didn't. Does it look bad?"

Leather-clad fingers ran through Shelley's hair, brushing it forward to fall over her face. "Cover it with your hair, miss. He won't notice."

With Shelley returned upright on the backseat, the driver drove on. She berated herself for not asking how much longer they'd be. She'd had the opportunity of conversation and she'd squandered it.

Wearing the blindfold impeded her ability to judge time. In what seemed like half an hour, but may have been much more or far less, the car sharply pulled to the right. It came to a standstill and she heard a door open and bang shut.

Sometime later, something cold was placed in her hands: a plastic bag with little balls inside, tiny little balls.

"Put that on the bump, miss. Might stop it bruising."

"Thank you. That's very kind."

Once again, the car was moving, and again Shelley didn't feel like it was purely a forward motion. Swaying from side to side, and forward and back, she struggled to keep what she imagined was a bag of frozen peas pressed to her head.

The thought of arriving blemished was a worry. She already had plasters adhered to her two existing flaws and stories she'd concocted to explain them. For the lump on the inside of her elbow, a rogue phlebotomist was responsible during her altruistic act of giving blood. The breaking in of new boots had caused the lump on her foot. Uncomfortable shoes had a lot to answer for. Though generally blisters and corns, not lumps – with the exception of bunions – but a man wouldn't know that, she presumed.

She repeated the stories in her head over and over as if she was convincing herself. If she could make herself believe it, then it would sound like the truth when she came to say it.

She heard grinding, as though the tyres were going over gravel. The sound continued. She could tell the car was going slowly. Her body rocked in all directions, but the movements were gentle.

The car rolled to a halt. She heard a door open, then slam. There was a creaking sound close by – the back door opening perhaps. She was right. The leather hand took Shelley's and gently pulled her upwards and forwards.

"Mind the step here, miss."

Shelley tripped on something and fell into a pair of arms. Strong arms, she felt, as they elevated her to a standing position.

"Hold on to me. It's a bit of a way to the house." The leather glove took her hand and wrapped it around the firm arm.

It sounded like stones were crunching and scraping under their feet. And that's how it felt. To avoid damaging the heels of her expensive stilettos, she tiptoed.

"There's steps coming up... Watch it, here's the first."

Shelley counted four steps before her guide stopped. Standing still in the blackness, she heard what sounded like a church bell ring. A door must have opened; it sounded like a door. Her guide told her to mind the step. She lifted one leg, carefully placed her foot on the floor then raised the leg behind her. After a couple of steps on what felt like carpet, there was a thud – most likely the door closing. The blindfold was removed and finally, she could see.

She was in the middle of a gigantic hall, lavishly decorated, and with a ceiling the height of two floors or more. To her right was a mahogany staircase. She looked up and saw a dark-haired man, in a burgundy smoking jacket, strutting down the stairs towards her.

"I'm terribly sorry about all that palaver with the blindfold. My lawyer insists on it. We've had some dastardly girls recently.

Despicable behaviour." He kissed her on the cheek.

"That is terrible." Shelley was blinking, still adjusting to the recent exposure to light. "I'm not like that," she said, patting her collarbone, checking the diamond in her Tiffany necklace was lying centrally.

"I know you're not, sweetie. Marianne assured me." He stroked her hair. "I have a penchant for blondes, but I think they're more deadly. It's always the blondes getting me into trouble. Last time it cost a small fortune, so I have to err on the side of caution. You understand, don't you?" He tilted her chin upwards, looking into her eyes.

"Yes, of course," she said sweetly. Before he released her chin, she took a mental photograph of his face. Following him through the hall, she tried to place him. She assumed he must be someone famous: a celebrity, aristocracy or perhaps a politician. She didn't recognise him. The location of the house must be what gave him away, otherwise what would be the point of the blindfold? Those dastardly hookers must have known who he was in order to blackmail him or sell a story to the papers, or whatever it was they'd done.

Even if she had recognised him, she would never do that. The Golden Rule – to do unto others as she would have done unto herself – was one she tried to live by, as much as she could in her line of work. She'd had several famous clients, though more often than not, they'd had to inform her who they were – in particular the footballers and the lawmakers. Their names as well as their faces were equally unknown to Shelley.

The more-handsome-than-usual client led her into a reception room. The gold-framed portraits hanging on the walls gave him away as a descendant of old money.

"I believe the best place to start is with a drink. So, tell me, Kiki, what's your tipple?" His voice sounded like it had been in the family for as many generations as their wealth.

"Can I have a gin and tonic, please?" she replied, taking a seat on one of the two huge sofas.

He passed her a glass and sat down beside her. From underneath the table in front of them, he pulled out a gilded wall mirror. On the mirror sat a mountain of cocaine, a credit card and a rolled up fifty-pound note.

He took the card and swept some of the white powder away from the rest of the mountain. He milled it down to a finer consistency. Then he ran the card down the length of the mirror eight times, generating eight lengthy lines.

The late-thirties, or perhaps early-forties, male passed her the rolled up fifty. She bent over the mirror and, pressing one nostril down, she inhaled half a line up her other nostril. She handed the note back to him.

"Have some more, sweetie." He nodded his head in the direction of the mirror.

She leant over and finished the line she'd started. As she went to hand the note back, he nodded again, indicating she hadn't finished her turn. Snorting steadily, she succeeded in inhaling a whole line with her one strategically regulated sniff.

She slipped off her stilettos and lay back on the azure sofa. "That's enough for now," she said, passing the fifty to her client.

8. Surviving Life

In the car park at Kenwood House, Shelley prayed the sun would be strong enough to break through and soothe her aching bones. But it didn't look likely. The sky over Hampstead Heath was covered with thick layers of clouds, rolling like hills, like a reflection of the landscape below.

When Nicole arrived – dressed for tea at the Ritz rather than a walk through the Heath – they set off down a muddy track. They came out into a sprawling field scattered with hawthorn trees. Apart from the birdsong and the sound of the wind striking the long grass, they walked in silence, in the direction of Highgate Ponds.

Shelley was conscious that she and Nicole were yet to have their chat about what happened at The Lanesborough. Nicole hadn't brought it up since the conversation last week. Strangely, Tara and Hugo hadn't spoken about it either. She wondered whether the conversation had taken place at all. Crack psychosis confused what was real and what wasn't, and she knew that night it had taken her. Tara was generally one to tease, as was Hugo. So if they knew about The Lanesborough, it was odd for them not to mention it. "Lanesboroughgate," Hugo had called it that night. How could he resist taunting her with that again? If that's what he'd said.

"Are you all right, love? You look tired." Nicole looked concerned.

"I've not been sleeping too well." Shelley couldn't tell her the truth: that she was trying to quit heroin. And what she'd said wasn't a lie. She hadn't slept well in years, not since the nightmares began.

***

She had considered cancelling her walk with Nicole, which had been arranged pre-cold turkey, but she didn't like to let people down. And now it was too late. However hard, she'd have to walk with withdrawal symptoms. Nicole was managing perfectly well in her court shoes.

As they wandered through a third field and climbed up another slope of a hill, Shelley felt a thin layer of sweat forming under her clothes. The wind whispered down the low neckline of her sweater and the coolness of the air against her wet skin caused her to shiver. She hoped Nicole didn't notice.

They left the openness of a meadow and followed a path into a section dense with white-barked, silver birches. Shelley's nose itched and she started to sneeze.

"Bless you, most precious. Maybe you're coming down with something," Nicole said.

"Maybe," Shelley replied, scratching her arm. Although heroin-free, she was itching all over as if she'd had a fix.

***

On reaching Highgate Ponds, Shelley saw the regular ice cream van parked up. She took the opportunity to rest her tired bones by buying an ice cream for herself and Nicole.

Sitting on a mound of unruly grass, they ate their 99s. A loud cry disturbed Shelley and she turned her eyes away from the bare trees surrounding her and toward the source of the noise. On the footpath by the pond, a glaring swan was parading with a biscuit in its mouth. Nearby, in a red pushchair, a crying toddler was being consoled by his mother.

Shelley watched the child. Her baby would have been about that age by now. Purposefully, she turned away, and as she did, the white swan flew past her and returned to the murky water.

"Do you think that swan might eat the chicks?" Shelley asked worriedly, as the swan made a beeline for a brown mallard and its ducklings at the other side of the pond.

"A Resident Killer Swan? I wouldn't think so, love. They all live here together."

Shelley didn't think Nicole sounded too certain and as the swan was now chasing the mallard out of the water, separating it from its ducklings, she dropped the remainder of her ice cream cone and ran over to help.

By the time she reached the other side of the pond, the ducklings were teetering in a line along the footpath, following a large duck waddling up front. She noticed a stranded duckling stuck in the pond, trying to jump out. Instinctively, she grabbed it by the neck and pulled it from the water. She released it onto the footpath and her rescued duckling doddered along and joined the others at the end of the line.

Nicole was on the grass verge on the other side of the footpath. She was stamping her feet near the swan that was still harassing the mallard it had forcibly removed from the water. Shelley went over and together they shooed it away. She watched the freed mallard rejoin its ducklings in the pond before she and Nicole walked on towards Parliament Hill.

***

Shelley tried to concentrate on breathing in the air, which was the purest she was exposed to in London. She thought about the goodness it would be doing for her nicotine-lined lungs.

By the time she'd made it halfway up the steep – and what felt like never-ending – incline to the top of Parliament Hill, she was gasping for breath and lagging behind Nicole. Nicole encouraged her to keep going, but it didn't help. Shelley's legs felt as weak as a pair of twigs. Weakening her further was the wind, so powerful that it was driving the clouds at speed in an anti-clockwise circle in the sky. Whenever she looked up, it felt as though the world was spinning as fast as a waltzer.

On reaching the top of the hill, she joined Nicole on a weather-beaten bench that must have been there for time immemorial. From where they sat, she could usually see right across London, from the tall buildings in the City and beyond to the South. Today, however, the view – from what she called the top of the world – was restricted.

"How's your mum?" Nicole asked. She always asked after Shelley's mother, even though by now she was surely aware there were only ever two answers: she was ill at home or ill in hospital.

Shelley waited for her panting to subside before replying, "She's at home, still the same." She took the box of Benson and Hedges from her handbag. "Has anything happened with the trial? Do you know when you'll be called?"

"Anytime in the next few weeks." Nicole turned her head away, in the direction of the kite-flyers who had congregated at the bench next to them.

"What if they bring up working? Do you know what you're gonna say?"

"I don't think it's gonna make any difference." She turned back to face Shelley. "There's so many others giving evidence as well. And my lawyer says it's really common – most working girls were abused as kids. Not exactly a surprise, I mean, look at everyone we know."

"You're handling it so well, much better than I did." Shelley blinked in an effort to dispel the tears that had surfaced in her eyes. *Fuck off*, she told the stream of intrusive images running in her head.

"Shell, you were much younger than me and I've got Doctor Fielding. I don't think I'd be able to do it if it wasn't for her."

Shelley was pleased therapy was working for Nicole, but it hadn't worked for her. Dr Anne Fielding, the clinical psychologist Nicole had recently started seeing, was the same lady Shelley had seen at the Praed Street Project up until the end of last year. She'd decided therapy wasn't helping her. Although she admitted to herself the fact she'd never been totally honest was most likely a contributing factor.

"She's made me see things differently. It's like I've been wearing the wrong glasses all my life and now I've taken them off."

Shelley nodded as if she understood, but she didn't have a clue what Nicole was talking about.

"I've gotta deal with what happened, go back there again, talk through it, work through it. Somehow I'm gonna move on. I have to."

Shelley took Nicole's hand. She'd never got that far in therapy herself. She'd found out that she suppressed her memories and her feelings with heroin. It didn't stop her. Heroin's what helped her, what made life bearable. This cold turkey business was pointless. She couldn't do life without a buffer. "You're amazingly brave," she told Nicole.

"I'm not, I don't have a choice. I have to do something. The memories are coming up 'cos they weren't buried properly." Nicole flicked open her silver Zippo and lit her cigarette. "Dr Fielding says you can't bury something 'til it's been dealt with. The coke and the drinking, that just pushes everything down – and the working, God it's more fucked up than I ever thought."

"What do you mean?"

"The trial's made it all come back, but it's even worse 'cos I never dealt with it before. I just tried to bury it." Nicole exhaled and sent a puff of smoke into the air. "It's like someone being buried in a shallow grave; it'll only take a dog or something small sniffing around to dig up a bone and then the whole body could be out in the open."

"How's working more fucked up?" Shelley asked her unanswered question a second time while the image of a decomposed corpse occupied her mind.

"I can see why I do it, what's led me into this life. But now that I know, working's so hard I don't shut down like I used to, not unless I'm out of it. And I don't wanna be out of it all the damn time."

Shelley remembered what she'd been told by one of her ex-therapists. That she was a plaster collector, collecting plasters to cover over her pain. The plasters weren't large enough or strong enough to cover the deep wounds she had, which kept her on a journey collecting more. Apparently, she couldn't be helped – or perhaps it was said that she couldn't help herself – until she stopped collecting plasters and removed the ones she'd already accrued.

A hole opened up in the grey and white sky and from a gap of clear blue, a pillar of light beamed down in front of Shelley. The brightly coloured kites that were being expertly flown seemed more alive with the light streaming through them as they bobbed and weaved in the air.

***

Late afternoon, Shelley was still sitting with Nicole on the old bench, watching the kites. The rolling-hill clouds that earlier had dominated the entire sky had transformed into thin ribbons encircling only the perimeter. Though the sun could now warm her, the pain in her bones wasn't touched. The rays weren't strong enough to reach that deep.

Shelley asked Nicole if she wanted to go to a pub. Although her intention for using the lavatory was of far more importance than what she intended to drink. They set off walking down the other side of Parliament Hill in the direction of The Magdala, which was a short walk through the Heath.

With their cars at Kenwood House, Shelley suggested they share a taxi back later. She was too tired to hike back. Frustratingly for her, they were now far nearer her flat than her car.

Parliament Hill was a favourite place. Somewhere she went frequently, but always from her flat. Because Nicole had wanted to see inside Kenwood House, they'd arranged to meet there – only to find it closed, due to a private function.

Shelley felt strange having been on the top of the world and not been on gear. She either went there after a fix or brought one with her to shoot up discreetly in the nearby bushes. She'd sit on an aeons-old bench and switch between looking over London, watching the kites, staring at the sky, and talking to her brother in her head.

"Do you mind if I ask Tara to meet us there?" Nicole asked as they neared the road.

"I thought we were having a quick drink? She'll be ages." Shelley didn't want Tara sharing her time with Nicole, nor did she want to wait for her to arrive in North West London from the West.

"She won't be long. She's staying at Hugo's. They'll probably be in The Freemasons."

While Nicole spoke to Tara on the phone, Shelley wondered why she might be staying at Hugo's. They weren't a couple. She didn't think Hugo liked her that much. And even though Shelley didn't like her that much either, she felt left out that she hadn't been informed Tara was staying in her part of London.

9. Keeping Secrets

Leant against the grubby tiles that clad the outside wall of The Magdala, Shelley and Nicole stood waiting for Tara. Within minutes, Shelley heard Hugo coming. Blaring music – Fugees: *The Score* – and a horn beeping in time to the beat.

On the other side of the road, Hugo pulled over in his red Porsche. Tara dashed from the car. For a second, Hugo waved then he zoomed off up the street.

"Isn't he coming in?" Shelley asked, fiddling with the diamond in her necklace.

"I told him to go back to The Freemasons. His friends are there," Tara said.

Shelley wondered what Tara was up to telling Hugo not to join them. And if he was in fact at The Freemasons, why did he drive to The Magdala when it was just up the road? It didn't make sense.

Inside the pub, as with the outside, time had been at a standstill since the 1950s. The cream paint above the partially wood-panelled walls was yellowed from second-hand smoke. The carpet was threadbare from being walked over for so many years. And the wooden tables and chairs, and the bar and the stools, all showed signs of long-term abuse.

She knew her friends considered the pub a dive, but Shelley liked it like that. She preferred its unpretentious atmosphere, which was nearly dead apart from a handful of alcoholics. Tara and Nicole may have rather been somewhere more vibrant and upmarket but they were in her stomping ground now. They wouldn't go to the clubs that she wanted to in the West End, but at least in Hampstead, most choices were hers.

While Nicole ordered their drinks at the bar, Shelley and Tara sat down at an empty table by a window. Sitting on the padded bench opposite Tara, even through the smoke-filled air between them, Shelley could see that her face was redder than usual. It wasn't just her spots. She looked like she'd been crying.

"Is something wrong?" Shelley asked.

Tara's face crumpled. "I'm having a really hard time at the moment."

Shelley was relieved to see Nicole walking back towards the

table with their drinks. She needed something to soften reality and though not her first choice, alcohol would help.

"What's happened? Have you lost your flat?" Shelley couldn't see any other reason for her to be staying at Hugo's.

"What's wrong, love?" Nicole took a seat next to Shelley on the bench.

"I think I'm going to lose my son." Tara looked at them briefly before lowering her head.

"What are you talking about? When did you have a son?" Nicole asked. From the expression on her face, she was as stunned as Shelley.

"Before I knew you," Tara replied. "I know I should have told you, but I'm not exactly a role-model mother, am I? I didn't want you to judge me."

"We won't judge you," Shelley said, unsure if she was capable of being non-judgemental.

"Max is four. He lives with my parents."

"I can't believe you never told me." Nicole gulped her wine, emptying the glass.

"My— Well, he's not my anything, Max's father is trying to get custody and he's going to take him to the Middle East. I'll never see my baby again." Tara sobbed.

Nicole stretched her arm across the wooden table and took Tara's hand. "I'm so sorry, Tar. If there's anything I can do, anything, love, you let me know."

"Same goes for me," Shelley said, taking Tara's free hand. "I'm sorry I'm such a rubbish friend."

"You didn't know, Shell." Tara squeezed her hand.

***

They spent hours talking in the pub and for the first time, Tara opened up. Shelley realised that she did actually quite like her after all. She made a mental commitment to be a better friend.

Shortly after nine-thirty, Tara received a call on her mobile. While she took the call outside, Shelley took the opportunity to tell Nicole their cars would be locked inside the car park at Kenwood, and they wouldn't be able to get them until the morning.

When Tara returned, Shelley could tell she'd been crying.

"Has something happened with your lad?" Nicole asked Tara.

"It's fucking Marianne. She wants me to do an anal job and I'm not doing it." Tara stood by the table, looking down.

"That's all right. You don't need to get upset over it. She'll call someone else," Nicole said softly.

"The punter wants me. He's seen me before, but I'm not doing it.

I told him last time. Now he's told Marianne he'll pay five-grand and she said if I don't go, she won't give me any more work."

"I'd tell her to shove it up her arse, see how she likes it," Shelley said, cajoling a weak smile from Tara.

"She's such a bitch. She said I'm lucky to still be working for her, earning decent money 'cos I look like a druggie and should be working the streets." Tara wiped one eye with the back of her hand. "I'm too good to be a streetwalker."

"She'll come round. She's all bark and no bite."

Nicole's sympathetic response surprised Shelley. Whenever Tara spoke condescendingly about their counterparts who worked the streets, Nicole – having once been one – always corrected her.

"It's all right for her, she can use her mouth for anal. With a face like a slapped arse, a punter couldn't tell the difference anyway." Shelley smiled, hoping humour might take them off on a tangent, away from the confrontation she was sure was on the horizon.

"She was stunning when she was younger though. Have you seen her pictures?" Nicole said.

"She's shown me pictures but I don't believe it was really her. It could have been any tall blonde." Shelley allowed herself to follow in Nicole's new direction. Perhaps she was letting it slide for the first time.

"She's a disappointment to everyone behind her." Tara sat back down at the table.

"What are you saying? We're gonna look like her in thirty years?" Nicole asked.

"I fucking hope not." Shelley slugged down a quarter of her pint of snakebite and blackcurrant.

"I mean anyone who's seeing her from behind," Tara said. "Like when you see a man from the back, he's got broad shoulders, good build, nice hair, blah-blah-blah. You imagine if he turned around, he'd be hot. Well with her, you see a tall, slim, blonde. You're expecting one thing, but when she turns you're stung by a haggard, old, witch face."

"Maybe that's why she doesn't work any more. She's in breach of the Trade Descriptions Act." Shelley grinned.

"That's mean. Don't laugh at her," Nicole told them. "I bet she's had a hard life."

***

Tara brightened up. She seemed particularly cheerful hearing about Nicole's latest catastrophe. She hadn't realised the clocks had gone forward on the weekend. On the Sunday when she'd arrived at her client's house, the door was opened by his teenage son accompanied by his teenage friends. "I told them I was a Jehovah's Witness," Nicole said. "They only went and asked for a damn leaflet. I said I'd get one out the car, but I just got in and drove off."

They began swapping stories about the clients they'd seen through Marianne. With two years' service, Shelley was a more recent addition to Marianne's girls in comparison to Tara and Nicole, who had both worked for her for three years.

Nicole talked about a job she'd done at The Hilton in Olympia, where she'd handcuffed the client to the bed then mislaid the key and spent three hours searching for it in the hotel room. Tara shared the details of a recent visit she'd had with Resident Crack Wrap, the regular who liked to be bound in clingfilm, and fed a combination of the crack pipe and poppers on a cigarette, while she read him erotica.

They moved on to discussing the bizarre scenes clients wanted them to act out. Shelley shared about her original assumption of what angel lust was. They all laughed, but Shelley stopped abruptly when she realised what she'd said.

She rushed from the table and into the ladies' room. She sat in a cubicle with the seat down and keeping her jeans on. She didn't need to go. She needed to clear her head. If they remembered talking about angel lust then they must remember talking about her dead punter. What had she said exactly? She tried to recall. Had she mentioned that it was Tara who told her about angel lust in the first place or had she just brought up angel lust out of the blue? She couldn't remember, even though the conversation happened minutes ago.

"*This is what heroin has done to you, stupid girl,*" said one of the harsher directors on the board.

It wasn't her short-term memory she wanted erased, it was what happened a long time ago that haunted her the most. If she couldn't remember a conversation that had taken place minutes ago, how would she ever remember anything at university? What was she going there for anyway?

"*You're just a junky whore. You're a slut. Who are you kidding?*" continued the harsh director.

In her handbag, she had a tiny spot of heroin on a small piece of foil. She kept it for emergency use, hidden in the pages of a 1975 edition of *The Escaped Cock* – a short paperback that was a convenient size and weight for living permanently in her handbag. She took out the book, and with a spare section of foil, she rolled a small tube.

Quickly, she chased the molten brown up, down and around the shiny silver. Once she'd finished creating an irregular pattern of burnt out lines, she lit a cigarette to cover any residual heroin lingering in the air.

She felt better, not high, but relaxed. Her achy bones eased a bit too. She looked in the mirror. Her eyes weren't pinned. That was good. Her friends wouldn't notice. She just had to keep herself from scratching and she'd be fine.

Remembering why she was in the ladies' room, she shook her head and laughed aloud at the irony. She'd forgotten why she was in there – and she was in there because she'd forgotten what she'd said in the pub, and the reason she was worried about that was because she couldn't remember for sure if a conversation had taken place at Tara's. And the cause of the problems – well, she'd just had some more.

***

When Shelley returned to the table, the mood was sombre. She could sense it. Had they been talking about the dead punter? She wished they'd just come out and say it.

"Were you raped by the first client Marianne sent to your flat?" Tara asked Shelley.

"Nicole! What the fuck have you been telling her?" Shelley's heart thumped hard in her chest. It was the flight or fight Dr Fielding had told her about.

"Twice might be a coincidence, but not three times. He did exactly the same to her." Nicole nodded her head in Tara's direction. "It's gotta be the same man."

Shelley legs felt strengthless. She put her hands on the table and slowly lowered herself onto the seat. "Was he the first Marianne sent to you too?"

"He was." Tara stood up and walked over to the bar.

In Shelley's mind, the rape replayed. She saw the red, sweaty face above her. Its vicious expression. The soulless eyes rolling back to the whites. She could smell him.

Nicole handed her a lit cigarette. Shelley took a deep pull as if it might push down the pain. The recording continued. Now, she was seeing it from above – out of her body. She could see herself fighting, struggling underneath him, trying to get out. He had her pinned down by her wrists, trapping her under his heavy weight. She was crushed.

She could see the lamp on the bedside table that she'd imagined smashing over his head, but she couldn't reach it. She couldn't get to the knife either. The one she kept under her bed and that she'd pictured herself stabbing him with. She stabbed him again in her head.

She'd wanted to scream, but she didn't want her neighbours to find out what she did for work. She'd only just moved into the Belsize Park flat a couple of weeks earlier. And she'd moved there after an agency sent her a client who raped her in her last working flat. She'd registered with Marianne because she thought that with a madam she'd be safer. Following that first client from Marianne, her three-month wait for a conclusive HIV result started over.

"Marianne's got to have a hand in this," Shelley said when Tara came back with a round of drinks.

"She does." Tara tipped her head back, downing her vodka and coke. "She's making money out of us being raped."

"No way! She wouldn't do that to me." Nicole shuffled back on the bench, shaking her head.

"She fucking did. To all of us, and God knows how many others," Tara said. "I heard her talking to him on the phone. She was fucking talking to him. They're in business together."

"Sick fucking bitch." Shelley lit another cigarette with the end of the one she'd just smoked down to the filter.

"If they were, she's not stupid enough to talk to him in front of you, is she?" Nicole said.

"She didn't know I was there. Matt let me in and I was waiting in the lounge. I heard her on the phone when she came back. I'm telling you, she's making money out of girls being raped."

"I can't believe this." The colour drained from Nicole's face. She kept shaking her head. "I can't fucking believe it."

"It's the truth, Nic. They were talking about money, ten thousand, and she was saying stuff like, 'don't worry she's new, she won't put up a fight... It's her own flat, she won't want any noise... She won't be a screamer.' She's fucking evil."

"How could she do that to me?" Tears were streaming down Nicole's face.

How could Marianne have a business arrangement, a financial agreement with a rapist? "She's a fucking cunt! That's how." Shelley's nails dug hard into the palm of her clenched fist.

"How long have you known this for?" Nicole snapped at Tara.

"Two or three weeks."

"You should've said something then. Why didn't you tell me? What were you thinking?" Nicole wiped her face with the sleeve of her white blouse, leaving a trail of mascara and foundation.

"I'm sorry. I've just had all this stuff with my son and I..."

"I'm sorry, love. At least we know now." Nicole took Tara's hand.

"We can't let this go. We need to do something." Shelley's head spun, thinking of a way to put a stop to Marianne and her rapist client that didn't involve the police. She knew her friends were as unlikely to turn to the police as she was.

The table rocked as Shelley slammed down her fist. "I know how to deal with that cunt."

10. Seething with Loathing

"Nicole... Nicole." Shelley shook her friend's body, as she lay asleep in the bed next to her.

"Hmmm." Nicole rolled over to face the opposite direction.

"Wake up. I need to ask you something." Shelley turned on her bedside light and continued rocking Nicole until she roused. "I'm worried. What if Marianne knows Tara heard her on the phone? Her flat's big, but it's not that big – and if she knows, then she's gonna know Tara told us and then this could all come back on us."

"Calm down, love." Nicole sat up. "She said she didn't know."

"But she can't be sure, can she?"

"Marianne would've said something, you know what she's like, and Tara said she didn't. Anyway, she's been totally normal with me. Has she been off with you?"

"No, she hasn't but—"

"Well then, there's nothing to worry about. What's she gonna do anyway?" Nicole lay down and closed her eyes.

Shelley turned out the lamp on her bedside table. For a couple of hours, she stayed awake, considering the worst Marianne could do. Finally, she fell back to sleep just as daylight began creeping into the bedroom.

***

At eleven o'clock on Friday morning, Shelley was woken by her early-rising guests, and not her nightmare alarm clock that seemed to be set for mid-afternoon. In her striped pyjamas, she walked barefoot into the lounge. Tara and Nicole were sitting on the leather chairs at the circular dining table, eating toast. The bread in her freezer must've been in there for over a year. Keeping that to herself, she joined them and they began going through the names of working girls who might be able to help.

Although they'd listed fourteen names between them – and they only needed to choose one – it wasn't easy. None of them were actual friends. They knew little about them.

"There is one other girl... but she's a bit older," Shelley said.

"They've gotta be young, love. He might only book the young ones." Nicole was waving her arm as if it might encourage the air to dry the wet sleeve of yesterday's blouse. How did she manage to remove mascara and foundation from white silk? She was magic.

"I think she's mid-twenties, twenty-five, twenty-six, but she says she's twenty for work."

"That's too old. I was eighteen when he booked me," Nicole said.

"If she looks twenty, it'll be fine." Tara spoke with a mouthful of toast. "I was twenty. How old were you, Shelley?"

"Nineteen."

"How well do you know her? Can we trust her?" Nicole asked.

"I'm sure we can trust her. But I did only meet her once, on a job."

"Once!" Nicole stopped sleeve-shaking. "You don't know you can trust her if you only met her once."

"I know more about her than these girls." Shelley pointed to their list on the table. "And I've worked with them loads of times, but we never really talk. Me and Angel talked for hours—"

"Where did you meet her, in heaven?" Tara sniggered.

"I just said I met her on a job. The Dorchester isn't exactly heaven, Tara."

"Well, that's a matter of opinion." Tara sipped her coffee. "You've got an obsession with angels."

"It's her working name. We went—"

"You've got your own version of angel lust."

"Shut up, Tara. Let her speak." Nicole glared at Tara.

Shelley tried to keep focused. Now was not the time to be concerned with what Tara and Nicole might know about her dead client at The Lanesborough. "We went to that place on the Edgware Road. You know, where we go sometimes?" Shelley looked at Nicole, who nodded back in her direction. "We were in there talking for hours. No one on that list is better, and it won't be the first time she's done something like this."

"Is she an avenging angel, Shelley?"

"Give it a rest, Tara. This is serious." Nicole pulled a Rizla from the blue packet. "Has she really done this before?"

"Not exactly the same thing... She poured boiling water over her pimp."

"What did he do to deserve that?" Nicole asked, stripping the paper from a cigarette.

"I can't tell you. That's her business, but believe me, he had that coming to him and a lot worse."

Angel was brave doing what she did. She'd had a hard life. She was only fifteen years old when she started working the streets in her hometown – Bristol. Her mother kicked her out because her new boyfriend didn't like her daughter. Angel's pimp was supposed to protect her from abusive punters, but instead he'd taken over where they'd left off – raping her, beating her and stealing her money. At seventeen years old, she fought back and fled to London. She'd been working there ever since, leaving streetwalking for the higher fees paid by the clients of agencies and madams. She didn't work regularly now. Most likely, she'd saved her earnings over the years and didn't need to.

"I'll call her. I'll sound her out first. If it sounds like she's not gonna help then I won't tell her anything. There's nothing to lose." Shelley took out her brick of a mobile phone and brought up her contact list. Angel wasn't stored. She knew she had her number. She remembered writing it down. Angel had asked if she could contact Shelley for other double bookings, so they'd exchanged numbers. Angel had never called though. And although Shelley said she'd call her too, she'd never again had that request from a client – for a pre-operative transsexual.

***

In her bedroom, Shelley rummaged through the discarded scraps of paper she'd abandoned inside more than a dozen handbags. Angel's number had to be on one of them. As she searched, she considered whether to tell her friends about Angel's gender. She decided she couldn't. It wasn't their business. Moreover, it didn't have any impact on the plan. Angel passed for a woman and that was all that was required.

Twenty minutes or so later, Shelley returned to the lounge, exhibiting a serviette with Angel's phone number. "I'll call her now."

"Well done, most precious." Nicole stood up and passed Shelley a joint. "I'm dying for a cuppa. Let me put the kettle on first."

"If you're being mother, I'll have a coffee," Tara said.

Once Nicole had disappeared into the kitchen, Shelley spoke to Tara. "Are you sure Marianne doesn't know you heard her?"

"She doesn't. Why are we whispering?"

"I don't want to worry Nicole," Shelley lied. She didn't want Nicole to think she was paranoid. "Are you sure? You were there when she took the call."

"She doesn't know. She was on the phone in the hall and I was in the lounge."

"What about when she saw you? She must've said something?" Shelley passed the joint to Tara and redirected her fingers to untwisting a knot in her hair.

"She didn't. I had my headphones on. When she came in, I jumped up like she'd given me a fright. You are worried, aren't you?"

Shelley tried not to look worried. What did it matter if Marianne knew anyway? They only needed to keep her onside until the rapist had been dealt with. After that, it didn't matter.

"Shell, honestly, there's nothing for you to worry about." Tara took a pull on the joint. "I'm the only one whose real name she knows, and she knows where I live. If it was going to come back on anyone, it would be me."

"We'll have to keep working for her or she'll know something's up," Shelley said, though she didn't know how she'd be able to speak to her when she was seething with loathing.

"She'll damn fucking know about it when she gets her comeuppance." Nicole came back in with three steaming mugs. "The sooner we deal with that cunt, the sooner we can move on to the sick bitch."

11. Art, Lying and Riding

In the newsagent's, Shelley scoured the papers for a story reporting on the dead man at The Lanesborough. Nearly three weeks had passed and still there was nothing. The cantankerous man behind the counter looked even more vexed than usual. This new daily ritual – on the days she left her flat – looked like it was going to be a long-term project. As such, she decided it would need to be spread more widely than among the three newsagents she currently used.

When Shelley had called Angel on Friday, she was at the airport on her way to Ibiza for a weeklong job. There was nothing they could do until she returned. After seeing her mother on Friday afternoon, Shelley held a solitary party in her flat. Inconveniently, she'd had to break it up twice over the weekend to see clients at her working flat in Belsize Park. Monday was the first time she'd had more than three hours' unbroken sleep and now, on Tuesday, she was going with her friends to see Tara's son.

Outside on Hampstead High Street, Shelley heard a car horn beeping in time to blasting music – Public Enemy: *Bring the Noise*. Shading her eyes from the bright sun with her hand, she saw Hugo driving down the hill in his white Range Rover. He pulled up to the curb beside her and she climbed in.

"Where's the Porsche?" she moaned, turning down the volume.

"Sorry darling, it's a long drive." Hugo tilted the rear view mirror, examining his reflection like a woman checking her lipstick. "Couldn't make the ladies suffer in the back just for you, could I?" He removed his navy blazer, turned the volume back up high, and nodded his head to the music as he sped off down the hill.

"Where's Tara?" she eventually asked, readjusting the volume again.

"She went back to hers on the weekend. Ozzie showed up at mine, brought a few of the old Bullingdon chaps with him – she didn't want to be around."

They drove to Hendon to collect Nicole, then to Earl's Court to pick up Tara. At midday, they finally set off on the long drive to Dorset. Shelley was pleased she'd managed to keep her seat in the front. She was never a good passenger, and even worse in the back.

"You sure it's all right for us to be coming, love?" Nicole asked Tara.

"It's fine, really. Just remember you're my friends from art college and whatever you do, don't slip up."

Shelley hoped she wouldn't be asked questions about art and artists. The names of a few famous artists, and the fact that Van Gogh chopped off his ear, was the extent of her knowledge. At least she had Tara and Hugo on hand. Tara would know enough to keep up the lie, and Hugo's father was an art dealer, so he ought to know quite a bit. They would be able to get Nicole and Shelley out of any sticky moments.

***

Hugo turned off a country lane and stopped the car at a pair of black wrought iron gates. Tara jumped out, pressed the buzzer on the brick wall, then jumped back in again. The tall gates opened and the Range Rover rolled up the long driveway towards the house.

Shelley was amazed. The Barnes family lived in a mansion. A huge, red-bricked, sprawling house. How had Tara fallen from there to how she lived now? Surely, her parents could have given her an allowance.

Mr and Mrs Barnes stood outside the front door, between the two pillars that towered either side. They looked as regal as their house. Mr Barnes, Tom, welcomed them in to an extravagant hall, then through to a massive drawing room that overlooked the back garden. Looking out the sash window, Shelley wondered where the garden ended. It seemed to go on forever, in all directions.

Shelley took a seat next to Nicole and Hugo on the enormous tapestry sofa. With her and Nicole's flowery blouses – their attempt to look like art students – their half was overloaded with a mismatch of patterns.

Tara and her mother, Agnes, had disappeared on their arrival. After a short while, Agnes returned, carrying a teapot and a plate of biscuits on a gold tray. She set it down on the coffee table next to a china tea set. Tom poured the tea and passed round floral teacups on matching saucers.

"Do you ride, Shelley?" Agnes asked. She looked like Princess Margaret, with her hair big and loose in a bun.

"I have but only a couple of times," Shelley replied.

"For a living," Hugo mouthed at her.

"What about you, chaps? Do you fancy going for a ride later, while Tara's with Maxwell?"

"Spiffing." Hugo clapped his hands together.

"I don't know. I've never been on a horse," Nicole said.

"Tom will show you how. Won't you, dear?" Barely moving her head, Agnes peered up at her husband who stood beside her armchair.

"Of course, dear." Tom picked up the porcelain ribbon plate from the coffee table and passed round the biscuits. "Finish up here, then we'll set off."

Tara entered the room with Maxwell, who didn't even come up to her waist. The long sleeves of his white and blue checked shirt draped over his hands, past his knuckles. He shook his arms, perhaps trying to free his little fingers. He looked particularly small, but then Shelley didn't know much about children's heights and ages; she was rarely around them.

A few feet away, he stopped walking. He seemed reluctant to come any closer or for his mother to move farther into the room. He knelt on the carpet with his arms wrapped around one of Tara's legs, clinging on tightly like a trap.

"Come on, sweetie-pie. I want you to meet my lovely friends." Tara bent down and scooped up her son. She rested him on her hip and walked over.

"They're going out riding with Daddy," Agnes said. "Take Max and totter off upstairs."

After the shortest of hellos, Tara followed her mother's instruction and carried Maxwell out of the room.

***

Shelley, Nicole and Hugo followed Tara's father into the garden. At the stables, he handed them each a riding hat. Shelley and Nicole also received tartan body protectors. Tom and Hugo went inside the stables, and came out leading four horses.

Shelley took the reins, gripped the saddle and pulled herself up on the grey speckled horse. Hugo mounted his horse with ease as well, but Nicole struggled to get off the ground. Tom dropped the stirrup a couple of notches. Then he guided her foot in place and pushed her up and onto the horse. Fortunately, this was one of those rare days that Nicole was wearing jeans.

Galloping though the open field, Shelley relished the feeling of the wind in her face and hair. The intrusive memories that dwelled in her head, and charged her in pain for their keep, had been evicted. Only a visit from the bailiff – heroin – had ever been able to do that. This could be better than heroin. There was no guilt in riding a horse. She wasn't hurting anyone, or herself, in the process.

Hugo caught up to ride alongside Shelley. Looking back over her shoulder, she realised they'd covered quite a distance. She couldn't see Nicole and Tom, and expected they hadn't got far. Suddenly, she remembered their charade of being art students. Worried Nicole might be asked awkward questions, she turned around and galloped back to find them.

***

When they arrived back at the house, they returned to the drawing room, where sandwiches and cakes awaited on a three-tier china stand.

"What did you read at Oxford, Hugo?" Agnes asked, sitting down in her armchair.

"PPE."

Shelley looked quizzically at Hugo.

"Philosophy, Politics and Economics." He took a bite of Battenberg.

"And you're an art dealer, Tara tells us. How interesting." Agnes straightened the neckline of her high-collared dress while staring intently at Shelley. "What about you, Shelley? What are you studying at art college?"

Shelley paused, waiting for Hugo – who was a trustafarian and not an art dealer – to come in and help her. But he didn't. "It's very broad, everything really," she said.

"Our wonderful Shelley is an expert in expressionism." Having thrown the grenade, Hugo reclined on the tapestry sofa. To savour the fallout, Shelley expected.

"So you like emotive art." Agnes poked a finger into her colossal hair. "Who are your favourite artists?"

Shelley looked at the ceiling, then at Nicole. "I like Van Gogh... um..."

"She likes all the great ones. You know, Rembrandt, Picasso, Matisse." Nicole smiled sweetly at Tara's mother.

"Shelley doesn't concentrate in class." Hugo leant forward and put his empty plate on the coffee table. "She has a crush on one of the teachers. She's a big distraction for her."

"That's not true." Shelley felt the blood rush to her cheeks.

"He's joking." Nicole smiled at Agnes. "You're not funny." She glared at Hugo.

Later, when they drove back through the giant gates, Shelley felt disappointed. Tara had never come back downstairs with Maxwell. She'd hardly spent any time with him. Although Shelley wasn't keen on being around children, Maxwell was her friend's son and she'd wanted to get to know him. It probably wasn't her first and only opportunity, but with what they had planned for the rapist, and with the issues Tara had with Maxwell's father, it might have been.

12. Pain That Feeds On the Soul

Late afternoon on Wednesday, Shelley was trying to leave her flat to go to Aunt Elsie's house. But she couldn't get out. Her checking had become worse. She knew it was due to increased anxiety. The more paranoid directors on the board were spinning 'what ifs' in her head.

"What if you get caught?"

"What if you go to prison?"

"What if he hurts you?"

"What if he rapes another girl?" she shouted, hoping it would stop them. That was all that mattered. However much fear they instilled in her, there was no going back. She couldn't live with the guilt of more girls being raped, knowing that she could have stopped it. Didn't they know that about her? They were her board. They were in her head.

They didn't stop. And with their constant scaremongering, the fives were constantly interrupted. She had to keep starting over and over and over again. It had been like this ever since last week. Every time she'd tried to leave the flat, it had taken nearly half an hour. It couldn't go on. The situation was untenable; clients often expected her to arrive within thirty to sixty minutes of making a booking.

Unable to quieten the board, she gave up the checking and smoked a cigarette. Still jittery, she took out her foil and had a small chase. She told herself it didn't really count. After all, she didn't shoot it.

The board sedated, she was able to complete the checks. Within five minutes, she was in her 350SL, revving the engine.

***

When she arrived at Aunt Elsie's, she was relieved to smell only the old house mustiness and not her aunt's cooking. She couldn't eat so close to using gear. She'd be sick. Aunt Elsie called from the kitchen and Shelley sauntered down the hall to the back of the house.

Her aunt hugged her then held her back by her shoulders. "You look exhausted. What's the matter?"

"Nothing, I'm fine." Shelley pulled her hair slightly over her face.

"Did you get that allergy test done?"

"I've been too busy with work... I'll get round to it soon."

"They're working you too hard. I can tell."

Shelley scratched her nose. "They're not. They've been very good to me, really."

Aunt Elsie made tea and they sat on their usual white stools at the white, plastic table in the kitchen. Elsie, as always, sat facing the back door and Shelley, facing the hall. From her chair, she could see the picture frames that stood on the hall table. Although she couldn't see the pictures, she knew each one from memory. The pictures were of happier times: baby pictures of her and William, a school picture of William when he was about ten, a school picture of Shelley taken around the same time, putting her at seven or eight, and a picture of them both with their mother before she became ill. That last picture, taken in Brighton in the summer of 1983, was from the last holiday they'd had with just the three of them. Until that year, Rita had taken her and William to Brighton every summer. Neither she nor her mother had been back since, but William had, once.

Shelley gulped her tea and apologised to her aunt for the short visit. On her way to the front door, she stopped at the hall table. It was the missing pictures she noticed. There was no record from that last holiday until she was fifteen years old and William was seventeen. As if those years in between had never existed. Of course, they had. They all wanted to forget them. But how could she erase them when she'd endured them? However much she tried, those years wouldn't stop replaying in her head. That's what caused the rage, the despair, and the excruciating pain that fed on her soul.

At the front door, Elsie put her hands on Shelley's shoulders. "You're a wonderful daughter. If I'd had a child I'd want her to be just like you."

Shelley hugged her aunt. She needed the hug and she needed to hide the tears of guilt she felt forming in her eyes. She was not a wonderful daughter.

***

In her car, the salty tears trickled into her mouth as she sang to Steely Dan - *Fire in the Hole*. Smoking a cigarette had worked to stop the sobbing, but the tears still leaked.

To fill the expanding hole inside her, she needed heroin, but she couldn't have a hit, not yet. She still had to go to her mother's flat, and go shopping. After what she'd found out from Tara last Thursday, she'd arrived at her mother's on the Friday without the groceries.

She swerved into the supermarket car park and pulled into a space. Repositioning the rear view mirror downwards, she inspected the damage. Her eyes were black, and grey tracks marked her cheeks.

She took a tissue from the supply usually used to press on the entry point of a needle and wet it with the water kept in the car for cooking up a hit. As she cleaned her face, she reconsidered making up a shot. She decided against it. She'd save the little she had left for when she got home. Then she could call Jay to ensure she didn't run out completely.

* * *

At the top of Hammers Lane, Shelley tussled with the grocery bags weighing her down. She'd bought more than usual. She needed to make sure her mother had extra supplies. The rapist could be entrapped within days of her meeting with Angel. The meeting was on Sunday.

Looking above the hedge, she saw her mother's curtains were closed, and there didn't appear to be any light peeping through the gaps. At eight-thirty in the evening, Rita may have gone to bed early or perhaps not been up at all.

She lifted the gold knocker and tapped it down hard on the plate. Her mother didn't come. Not wanting to disturb the neighbours at night by shouting, she used her own key. She tumbled over something in the downstairs hall. Steadying herself, she felt in the dark for the light switch.

Under the bright hundred-watt bulb, she saw mountains of files and loose papers stacked up in the tiny hall. One by one, she swung the bags of shopping from outside the front door onto the only floor space available – the stairs.

"Mum, it's me," she called. There was no reply.

Bending like a branch in a gale, she made her way up the stairs, resisting the heavy bags pulling her back down. After she'd dumped the bags in the kitchen, she trudged through to her mother's bedroom.

In the darkness, her mother lay in the bed. As Shelley got closer, she saw her mother's eyes were open. With both her hands, she was holding a picture of William pressed to her heart.

Shelley stroked her mother's hair away from her forehead. "Mum, I'm going to turn on the light now, okay?"

Her mother didn't respond. Apart from her breathing, rapid and shallow, she didn't make a sound.

Shelley switched on the bedside light and sat on the edge of the bed. She wrapped her hands over her mother's hands holding the picture of William. Her head fell, and silently, she cried.

13. Not the Order Life Should Take

"Please, let my mother leave the flat. Please, let my mother leave the flat." Driving up Hammers Lane, Shelley prayed aloud to God. Exactly what she had said to her mother on Wednesday night, she wasn't sure, but Rita had agreed that, on this Friday's visit, she would accompany Shelley to William's grave. She could hardly believe it. If she'd been doing more crack recently, she'd have been sure it was an auditory hallucination. Her mother hadn't been outside in months.

Having set the central locking with the key fob, she looked around, ensuring no one was watching her. Then she circled the car and counted aloud as she pulled on both door handles five times, ran her fingers over the top of both windows five times, and depressed the catch on the boot five times.

She walked between the hedges that concealed the path to the red door. The midday sun was bright. Though it wasn't warm, it looked like a beautiful day; the trees were brimming with blossom.

There was no answer at her mother's door. Rather than using her own key, she tilted her head skywards and shouted, "Mum, open the door."

An upstairs window opened and Rita popped her head out. "Come up. I'm getting ready," she called.

A warm feeling, like the mildest of heroin hits, streamed through Shelley's body. She opened the door with her key. At the top of the stairs, her mother stood in daytime attire. She hadn't seen her like that in months. Like Aunt Elsie, Rita was also trapped in the time warp. But in her blue and green geometric-print dress, she was a vision of beauty to Shelley.

"I'm sorry I'm using up all your holiday allowance again," Rita said.

"You're not. I've got a day off in lieu." Why that came out of her mouth and where it had come from, Shelley didn't know. "You look lovely. Shall I brush your hair before we leave?" she asked.

Shelley hopped up the stairs and followed Rita into the bedroom. The curtains were open and the sun was beaming into the room. Rita sat down on a stool at the dressing table and applied an orange lipstick.

After Shelley had made the bed, she stood behind her mother and gently brushed her hair, all the while, smiling at her in the triple mirror.

"Have you had any breakfast?" Shelley laid the paddle brush on the dressing table.

"Not yet, dear."

"I'll make us some before we go."

Shelley strolled to the kitchen and prepared breakfast. With a tray of toast and tea, she walked through to the lounge and placed it on her mother's lap. Then she went back for her own breakfast tray and joined Rita on the grey settee.

"Have you had a tidy up, Mum?" Reluctantly, Shelley took a bite of her toast. She wasn't hungry but she wanted her mother to see her eat.

"Not really, I just moved things around. That stuff's more in the way up here."

"But you can hardly get in and out with it stored in the hall."

"Don't talk with your mouth full, dear."

Shelley swallowed down her toast a little too quickly and choked. "It's not safe. You need to be able to get in and out."

"I don't need to do that."

"What if there's an emergency?" Shelley guzzled her tea to clear the toast stuck in her throat. "Do you mind if I move it all into the spare room?"

"If you must," Rita replied, shaking her head.

Shelley made umpteen trips up and down the stairs, carrying the files and loose papers into the spare room. She didn't understand why her mother hadn't moved them there in the first place. That room was never used and she'd been asking her mother for years if she could move them in there and out of the lounge. She'd also wanted to sort through it all and throw out the rubbish, which she suspected most of it probably was, but today was not a day for that.

***

"Are you ready, Mum?" Shelley asked, as Rita stood static at the front door.

"I don't know, dear. It's been such a long time since— I shouldn't have left it so long."

Shelley took her mother's hand and guided her over the threshold. After she'd locked the front door, she linked her arm with her mother's and together they walked slowly along the pathway, then down the steep steps that led to the pavement.

As they got closer to her car, Shelley felt as though she was being drawn back to the front door, pulled by an invisible chain anchored in her gut. Because she never allowed her mother – or anyone else – to see her checking, she fought the compulsion with a cigarette.

"You shouldn't smoke, Shelley-Margaret. It's not good for you," Rita said, opening the passenger door of Shelley's car.

"Please don't call me that, Mum." Shelley switched on the engine then drove off, heading to the cemetery in East Finchley.

When they stopped at the red traffic lights at the junction of East Finchley High Road and East End Road, Shelley turned her head to see the familiar pub on the corner. The Bald Faced Stag was the last place she'd seen William and his band play before he died. She'd beaten him at pool that night and she'd felt guilty, and still did, for not letting him win in front of his friends.

Once Shelley had parked in the cemetery, she stretched her arm round to the back of the car and picked up one of the two bunches of pink carnations she'd brought with her. She handed the flowers to her mother, then reached back over for her own.

From the corner of her eye, she caught sight of a man watching them. Locked safely inside the car, she turned her head fully to see him. It was the same man again. It had to be. She rarely saw anyone in the graveyard, and he was the only person she'd ever seen in the cemetery wearing a shell suit. As it always did, his staring made her feel uncomfortable. Though since she'd started referring to him mentally as the Resident Cemetery Lurker, she found it difficult to take him as seriously as she thought she should.

The next time she turned her head, he'd vanished. She stepped out the car and walked round to the passenger side. She held out her hand to her mother. Rita was weeping. Shelley pulled her close.

"They say tears nourish your soul. Like the rain makes flowers grow. You're watering your garden." Though she was unsure it was a fact, Shelley couldn't think of anything else to say.

"It's my fault this happened. It's my fault he's not here. I should have known."

Shelley felt her mother's body shuddering against her. "It's not. He never blamed you. I've never blamed you. It's not your fault."

After a short while, they set off through the expanse of headstones. Shelley felt, as she often did, that the buried souls were there with her in the graveyard. She felt their presence, not individually, but as a collective whole as if she was sensing their parallel world.

She knew there was a heaven and she knew her brother was up there. He wasn't under the earth. His bones were, but not his soul.

That all he was was flesh and bone, Shelley refused to believe. He had to continue to exist. She could think of no other way to explain how she heard him and felt him around her so often.

Rita stumbled over the corner of a grave and as Shelley helped rebalance her, she noticed her mother's hands were trembling. Although she couldn't see her mother's legs for her long coat, she imagined they too were unsteady. They had reached William's grave.

In Loving Memory
Of
William Roderick Hansard
Born September 12th 1972
Died July 19th 1994
A Beloved Son, Brother and Nephew
You Will Forever Live On In Our Hearts

In her head, Shelley could hear Will singing Pink Floyd's *Comfortably Numb*. A song he used to sing with his band and the one that had inspired their name – Numblivion. 'But I have not become comfortably numb,' she told him.

Rita knelt at the headstone and placed the pink carnations on the ground. "My boy, my beautiful boy..." She cried as she laid herself face-down on the grave with her arms outstretched over his body below. "Please come back, son... Please come back..."

Shelley struggled to inhale as she suppressed the sobs firing in her throat.

Holding on to William's headstone, Rita pulled herself up and on to her knees. She looked up to the sky. "God, I'll do anything, just bring back my son. Please God, bring him back. Why didn't you take me? Bring him back and take me..."

Shelley couldn't speak. She wanted to. She wanted to say something to comfort her mother, but she couldn't think of any words. What words could console a mother who had buried her child? It wasn't the order life was supposed to take. So wrong, that a word had never been created to describe a mother who'd lost a child. There should be a word for it. Like there is a word for a child who's lost their parents; they are an orphan. And there's a word for a spouse whose spouse has died – a widow or widower. What of a mother who has lost her child? There should be a word. And there should be a word for a sibling who's lost her sibling. Shelley needed a word. There should be a word. Why was there no word for those left alive when a child died?

Shelley knelt on the grass, beside her mother on William's grave.

She rested her head on her mother's arm. Then she placed her arms on top of her mother's, intertwined and wrapped around the headstone. Shelley and her mother stayed like that for what may have been ten minutes, or perhaps it was twenty or more. It was hard to judge time passing in such a timeless place.

14. Asking For Help

On Sunday afternoon, Shelley meandered along Pilgrim's Lane. Although running late, she couldn't stop herself slowing down to peek through the windows of the grand houses.

Feeling the chill in the air, she tightened the scarf around her neck. The cold found another route to her bones, through the holes in her jeans. She stopped under a cherry tree in bloom and fastened the hook and eyes that were undone on the lower half of her faux-fur coat.

Standing at the door of The Magdala, she saw Angel sitting at a table in the back of the saloon. As she sashayed past the shabby, wooden furniture, making her way over to the corner, she felt as though she'd entered a bygone era. It was more like a Sunday afternoon in April 1957, than in 1997.

She bent down to kiss Angel's cheek and tripped on the leg of her chair.

Angel caught her arm. "You missed."

"You missed out." Shelley smiled. "I'm sorry I'm late. I got stuck on a call with a punter," she lied. Of course, it was her checking that held her up. Due at three o'clock and arriving at twenty past, she was like Railtrack, lacking the commitment to resolve the issues responsible for delays.

Angel picked something out of Shelley's hair. "Very pretty," she said, holding the pink cherry blossom under her nose.

Angel was so obviously meant to be a woman. Had Shelley not met her on a job, she would never have known. She had a delicate bone structure, light brown skin and large brown eyes. Every part of her body curved naturally, with the exception of her breasts, which Shelley recalled felt rigid and rocklike. In contrast to the evening dress in which Shelley had last seen her, Angel was wearing tight jeans and an equally tight, white jumper. Apart from lip-gloss and mascara, her face was bereft of make-up. She was striking.

At the bar, Shelley bought herself a pint of snakebite and blackcurrant, and a vodka and coke for Angel. She joined Angel at the table, and sat on the bench opposite.

During their call a week earlier, Shelley hadn't gone into detail.

She hadn't said anything other than asking Angel a hypothetical question. What would she do if she knew of a madam who was sending a rapist to working girls?

Sat at the corner table in the quiet end of the pub, tucked away from the sparse clientele, Shelley told Angel the situation. She explained what happened to her and to her friends and the call that Tara had overheard.

Angel's expression turned cold. Her soft eyes hardened.

Shelley felt the toxin twisting in her stomach. The pain caused by the rapist piled on top of the pain the other warped excuses for men had caused her throughout the past thirteen years. The poison pushed up to her heart, and when she began to cry, Angel came around to the other side of the table and sat next to her. Shelley cried into her shoulder.

"It'll be all right. We'll put a stop to this, Kiki. I'll make sure of it."

Shelley looked into her deep brown eyes. She felt like she was sinking. She'd be safer in those eyes.

***

After two more pints of snakebite and black, in conjunction with numerous cigarettes, her tears stopped and the conversation veered in a less macabre direction. Shelley asked Angel about her job in Ibiza. Angel told her she'd hardly had to do any work. She'd enjoyed most of the stay on her own even though she was being paid a good few thousand pounds to be there.

"I go away with him five or six times a year. You should come with me on the next trip. He's really nice, not a fascination fuck. He bought me this," Angel said, showing the gold, solitaire diamond ring on her slender middle finger.

"That would be amazing. I'd love to. Thanks." It was the truth, but Shelley knew she couldn't go. She couldn't work through cold turkey, let alone travel through it. She'd have to ride it out in London before she left the country. And with her recent attempts being unsuccessful, she had little hope for those yet to come.

She could have done with the money one high-fee booking would pay. Since The Lanesborough job, she'd been working infrequently and spending her way through her savings, which were meant for university. Even though she doubted she'd be embarking on that plan now, a tiny part of her wouldn't totally admit the idea had no legs. She reminded herself to call the madams when she got home. She had to start putting herself out to work more often.

Once she felt ready, she returned to the subject of their meeting. Quietly, she shared the idea she'd devised with Nicole and Tara.

"You'll need to meet them before we can do anything," Shelley said. "I'll sort it for in the week, if that's okay with you."

Angel nodded, twirling the end her sleek, black ponytail in her fingers. "I'm not sure about the one who uses her real name and address. That madam can get to her any time she wants." She sipped her vodka and coke. "I know she's your girl, but she could be a liability. We can't afford a weak link in something like this."

"She'd never grass us up, I'm sure."

"You need to be. This ain't a small thing. Our liberty's at stake." Angel laid her hands flat on the table. "If she doesn't know exactly what we've done and where we've done it, she can't nark on us."

"She wouldn't."

"Whether she wants to or not, it's irrelevant. That madam or the police could put pressure on her, but they can't force her to tell what she doesn't know."

Shelley tried to reassure her, but Angel wasn't to be assured. She did agree, however, to withhold her final judgement until she'd met Tara herself. And Shelley verbally agreed that Angel had a point about Tara staying out of it, saying she'd mull it over – but really, she wouldn't be mulling anything. The probability of pulling it off successfully increased with the number of them participating.

Shelley took her cigarette packet and her Clipper from the table and put them inside her handbag. "I'm Shelley by the way," she said, standing to leave.

"Hello Shelley." Angel's pink-brown lips swelled into a smile and dimples appeared in her cheeks. "I'll be Angel for a while if you don't mind, 'til I know you better."

As Shelley moseyed back along Willoughby Road, she regretted not sharing The Lanesborough secret with Angel. She felt a need to talk about it to someone, to unburden herself of the fear. But what if it wasn't a secret? Then she could talk with Nicole. But then, if Nicole knew, why hadn't she mentioned it? Perhaps it was because she had enough to deal with. With the court case and now the justice they had planned for the rapist, Nicole didn't need another problem from Shelley.

If she were to tell Angel, it would be useful to have another pair of eyes scanning the newspapers daily. There'd been days she'd missed when she hadn't been able to leave her flat. She didn't want to miss any more. The news might have been reported already and her current efforts could be in vain.

When she got home, she decided to keep it to herself. In time, if she came to know Angel better, maybe she'd confide in her then, but the time wasn't ripe now. She didn't even know Angel's real name. Though she felt an affinity with her, it was foolish to follow her gut instinct. On this, she needed to think and act with her head.

15. Paying For It

Harsh rain pummelled the roof and windscreen of Nicole's TVR Chimaera. It was bringing on a pain in Shelley's head. Her hair was still damp after her shower, and the client they'd just spent the evening with in Belgravia had plied her with alcohol and cocaine – not that she'd objected, but with a cold head and the rain trying to penetrate the car, her buzz was being slaughtered.

"Have you got any puff?" she asked Nicole.

"Check the glove box. There might be a bit in the Silk Cut packet." Taking one hand off the steering wheel, Nicole switched on the overhead light. "Can you believe what's come out about O J Simpson? How the hell did he get off the first time?"

"Money, from what I've read." Shelley foraged for the cigarette box.

"When do you ever read a newspaper?"

"How can you smoke these? They're like smoking fresh air." Shelley waved the Silk Cut ten-pack. "Will you pull over so I can skin up?"

Nicole parked on Eaton Place. Shelley put a Rizla on her lap, broke off part of a cigarette and emptied the tobacco onto the paper. She needed a smoke before they delivered the fee to Marianne. She was dreading looking at her. This was the first time she'd had to see her since finding out what she'd done to her and her friends. How had Marianne been able to look at them knowing what she'd done?

"That cunt makes me feel sick." Shelley crushed the warmed hash between her fingers, sprinkling it over the tobacco.

"I don't think anyone likes a wife-killer."

"I'm talking about Marianne."

"Sorry." Nicole covered her mouth with her hand.

"We need to get moving. I can't keep this nicey-nicey act going much longer. I told Angel we'd all meet up this week and now it's already Tuesday."

"Don't fret about it, love. I'll call Tara tomorrow. We'll get it done this week."

***

The Chimaera roared as Nicole raced down Pont Street, heading towards Marianne's flat. As usual, parking was at a premium in

Cadogan Gardens. Though unlike Shelley, Nicole didn't hide her car around the corner on purpose, she ended up parking there nonetheless.

Shelley wasn't sure if it was one precautionary measure too many, ensuring her car was always parked out of Marianne's sight. Could she really track her down from her registration plate? Although most of the madams Shelley worked for seemed nice enough, she was sure there were bound to be some insalubrious characters amongst them. And as she regularly stole their clients, in the event they ever found out, those were the type she didn't want knowing her real name and address.

Staying out of the rain, they counted Marianne's fee in Nicole's car. Shelley was sickened that not only did she have to see Marianne, but she also had to pay her for the privilege. The job had been a short two-hour stint and, as was often the case, they didn't have sex with the client. In this instance, he was too coked-up to get an erection. That was why Shelley, and most of the other working girls she knew, preferred the cocaine and crack jobs. Generally, they didn't involve intercourse, not with the client.

"Let's get this over with." Nicole released the spring on her black umbrella before getting out of the car. She went round to the passenger side, holding the umbrella over Shelley as she stepped out into the rain.

Turning the corner towards Marianne's building, Shelley heard sirens. Nicole didn't react, appearing not to notice the noise. Though nearly sure that it was in her head, it didn't stop Shelley's heart speeding up and her mind picturing the police arresting her for the dead john at The Lanesborough. Distracted by her thoughts, she skidded on the pavement strewn with mushiness from fallen browning blossom.

Nicole steadied her. "Are you all right, love?"

"I just hate being here," Shelley said. The joint had calmed her marginally, but what she really wanted was to shoot some gear, and that couldn't happen until after they'd paid Marianne, Nicole had dropped her home and she was finally by herself.

Nicole pointed in the direction of Marianne's block, farther up the road, opposite the gated garden. "D'you see that?"

"What?"

"There's Old Bill on sick bitch's step."

***

On seeing the platoon of police stood outside the red-bricked building, Shelley's board called an emergency meeting. Her head was cramped with their voices speaking over one another.

81

"That doesn't mean anything. There's lots of flats in the block."
"It could be anybody. Maybe someone was burgled."
"Maybe the police traced your call from The Lanesborough."
"You're just paranoid from taking cocaine."

The sirens Shelley had been listening to were now so loud they sounded as if they were in the next street. A police car zoomed past, splashing up a colossal puddle and drenching Shelley. She tugged on Nicole's sleeve, signalling her to stop. They stood still, watching from a distance.

Huddled under the large umbrella, the rain couldn't get to them but it was of little use to Shelley. She was now soaked on one side of her coat right through to her dress and her knickers, and her thick hair hadn't dried at all since her earlier shower.

"We look too obvious," Shelley said, shivering. In an effort to appear inconspicuous, she lit a cigarette, although a dog on a leash would have been more appropriate.

After a short while, she saw two police officers marching someone down the steps. From where she stood, she couldn't tell if the figure was Marianne. In the brightness of the security light, she could see that the clothes were overbearingly garish and it did look like blonde hair, but it could have been a pale-coloured hat.

Shelley advised lighting another cigarette and walking closer. With their second round of cigarettes lit, they sidled towards Marianne's building. It only took a few steps for Shelley to see who the police had hold of and were now shoving into a panda car.

"Serves that sick bitch right!" Nicole poked her umbrella in the air.

"Yeah," Shelley said meekly, imagining she was about to be picked up by the police herself for a crime she hadn't committed. How long would the sentence be?

"What? You don't sound very sure."

"I just wanted to deal with her our way." Shelley turned, walking back towards the car.

"They won't keep her for long. It'll be tax evasion or living off immoral earnings. She'll get a slap on the wrist and a fine."

All Shelley could think about was getting home and fixing up, if she managed to get there. It might be her last hit if someone had seen her at The Lanesborough and was able to identify her, if the police had her DNA, if she missed wiping her prints from something in the suite. She had to change her appearance. She had to pray the Royal Free didn't have her DNA. She had to get rid of her working flat. What if Tara told Marianne her real name and address? Her head spun with such velocity it affected her vision.

Her legs quivered. She tightened her grip on Nicole's arm.

"What's wrong?" Nicole asked.

"I'm just tired, maybe."

Nicole stopped under a black street lantern. She unlinked her arm from Shelley's and turned to face her. "I can tell there's something upsetting you. What is it?"

"No, really, I'm fine. I haven't been getting enough sleep, and I think I did too much coke." Apart from the 'no' and the 'fine' that was true, and as such, it wasn't the time to contemplate discussing the dead john. She'd ingested too many chemicals to make a balanced decision.

"Yeah, you were putting it away tonight." Nicole re-linked her arm in Shelley's and set them off walking again. "If something is the matter though, you know I'm always here for you, don't you?" She squeezed Shelley's arm in the crook of her elbow. "You can talk to me about anything. I'll never judge you, Shell, never."

16. A Game of Waiting

Shelley was dying for heroin. She wanted to inject it, but she'd have taken it any way she could if only she could have it. But Nicole had other plans, and hers reigned over Shelley's. She'd insisted on driving straight to Tara's in Earl's Court. She'd said that since they were already practically there, compared to where they lived on the other side of London, it would be "mad not to stop in".

On the King's Road, just before World's End, Shelley asked Nicole if she could roll another joint. Nicole turned up a side street and pulled over. As they smoked, Shelley asked Nicole if she believed Marianne might have been arrested for something more sinister than her previous conjectures.

"Like what?" Nicole asked.

"I don't know. Does she do anything dodgy?"

"Resident Most Precious Pothead, what do you think?" Nicole said mockingly, and she blew smoke in Shelley's face.

Once they'd finished the joint, Nicole drove off, accelerating at her usual breakneck speed. Shelley looked out of the passenger window, watching the yellow light from the street lamps whizzing into one long line of fluorescent blur. She had a feeling that the violent wind behind them could be propelling the car even faster than it was being driven out of World's End.

The rain beating down on the windscreen and roof amplified her feeling of impending doom. She knew once they were at Tara's, they'd most likely end up on the pipe. She didn't like the paranoia and hallucinations that came with it. Nevertheless, it was a price she knew she'd pay to feel higher than the miniscule hit bestowed by the joint. There were no other options open to her in that part of London, and never in the company of Nicole who was a fervent member of the AHF – the Anti-Heroin Front.

***

"You didn't call her, did you?" Shelley said, scurrying along the slippery street, under Nicole's umbrella. She hoped Tara wasn't in. Not only did she want to get home to heroin, she wanted to get into dry clothes.

Nicole pressed the buzzer. They weren't buzzed in. "Damn. We should've called her." She pressed down again, multiple times in succession, but there was no response.

Nicole handed her umbrella to Shelley, then searched in her handbag for her phone. Protecting them from the rain was far harder than Nicole had made it look. Shelley had to fight against the wind that was tirelessly trying to poach the umbrella with a gust.

"Where are you, love?" With the phone in one hand, Nicole used her other hand to assist Shelley in controlling the feral umbrella. "We're outside."

The buzzer sounded and the communal entrance was unlocked. Nicole held the door open while Shelley shook the water from the now concertinaed and containable umbrella. She followed Nicole inside and up the wooden staircase to the third floor where Tara was standing with her door slightly ajar.

"Why didn't you answer?" Shelley asked.

"The intercom's not working properly." Tara hitched up her pyjama bottoms from the waist. They were stained with off-white and brown irregular-shaped splodges, as was the co-ordinating pyjama top. The brown was most likely coffee. But what was the off-white? Milk, yogurt or glue, perhaps, though it looked most like she'd been ejaculated on by a myriad of men.

"Do you want a pipe?" Tara asked, dawdling down the hall in front of them.

"If you've got enough."

"There's enough for one each. Do you want one, Shelley?"

"I can't exactly say no, can I?" Shelley removed her sodden coat and took her place on the navy sofa by Crack Island.

"I'm ordering more. Do you want me to get you any?" Tara said.

"I'll get two-hundred and fifty's worth." Shelley felt anxiously excited and took out her purse. She wanted to use Tara's hairdryer to dry her hair, her wet dress and her knickers, but she wanted the crack first.

Nicole flicked through a wedge of twenties and fifties. "I'll get the same," she said, putting some of the notes on the glass coffee table. The rest, she bound back into the roll she kept secured with a red elastic band.

Tara relocated Shelley and Nicole's cash to the table in the adjoining dining area.

"How much are you getting?" Nicole asked her.

"I haven't got any money." Tara walked back towards them. There was a blankness in her overly wide-open eyes. She looked like the sole survivor of fatal car crash.

"That's okay. I owe you from last time," Shelley said.

"You don't need to." Tara's expression changed unnaturally; she smiled with only half her face. "I'm getting a camcorder's worth."

The good vibe Shelley had been riding from her pleasant feeling of expectance, fleeted. "You can't sell your camcorder."

"There's no need to look at me like that. It's not mine. A punter left it here." Tara took her mobile and made a call out of the lounge. When she came back in, she was carrying wine glasses. She placed them on the coffee table next to a mangy looking bottle of Smirnoff.

Shelley and Nicole were once again left alone in the lounge while Tara disappeared a second time. Shelley stood with her side pressed against the radiator to dry out her wet dress. Twenty minutes passed before Tara returned with a Sony camcorder in hand. Shakily, she set it down on the carpet, and knelt by the coffee table.

Measly portions, hardly worth smoking, Shelley thought, as Tara divided what remained of her crack. Though she knew it wouldn't be much of a hit, Shelley craved it nonetheless. Seeing the pipe being prepared thrust her back into the saddle, riding her vibe again. That once she had the first pipe, she'd be chasing the rush for hours – or possibly days – didn't seem to make any difference to her exhilaration.

Tara lit the rock as Shelley sucked on the misused biro. Just as she was exhaling, she heard Nicole's words and was reminded why they'd come to Tara's in the first place.

"You'll never guess what we saw tonight," Nicole said playfully.

After a couple of failed attempts, Tara said, "I'm not in the mood for this stupid game." She threw her head back and swigged directly from the vodka bottle. "Either spit it out or I don't want to know."

"The sick bitch got arrested, we—"

"We don't know that," Shelley corrected Nicole. "we only saw Marianne being put in a police car. Maybe she got arrested, maybe she didn't."

"What's so good about that?" Tara threw her hands in the air. "How are we going find that scum if she's locked up?"

Shelley was in agreement with Tara: Marianne being arrested was not in their collective best interest. Nor was it in Shelley's personal best interest if Marianne was being questioned about the dead body at The Lanesborough, but she kept that fear to herself.

"Stop fretting. She'll be out in no time," Nicole told them.

"If the police are sniffing around her, we can't do anything," Shelley said, back in her position next to the radiator. "They might be watching us."

Tara chugged down more vodka. "It's a dangerous game, being on the game."

"We're not on the game. No one is. We're sex workers." Nicole tutted. "Game, like it's some fun thing to do. Most of our lives have been littered by tragedy. We adapt or it's a learned behaviour or something. Putting our lives on the line is not a fucking game."

"The same applies for Russian roulette, and that's a game, isn't it?" Tara said.

"No, it isn't." Nicole picked up the pipe Tara had prepared for her and turned Shelley's purple Clipper on it.

Shelley thought longingly about her next round of Russian roulette and in which vein she'd shoot. She lifted her hand closer to her face and examined it for raised blue lines.

"People say it is." Tara looked at Shelley. "What's wrong with your hand?"

Shelley put her hand on her hip and clamped it down with the other to prevent it wandering back up towards her face. "What people?"

"People," Tara said. "Normal people."

"That don't know people like us." Nicole slammed the pipe down on the coffee table, showering the glass top with ash. "This life is a game? Russian roulette would be quicker and I bet it would hurt less."

"What's going on with her?" Tara asked Shelley.

"This life isn't a life. It's a half-life, part existence."

Shelley went to sit with Nicole. "It's not that bad," she told her, though she didn't believe it herself.

"I don't have a real life. I can't, 'cos I don't know who I am, but at least I'm not deluded like you, Tara. Think you're better than me 'cos you've never worked the streets. Let me tell you, it makes no difference, we're all the same."

"Blah-blah-blah..." Tara walked towards the door. She turned back to face them. "Prostitution is a painful business borne out of painful pasts," she recited as if it was a maxim. Then she exited the room.

Shelley willed the dealer to come. She needed to get Tara's last sentence to stop repeating in her head. After another hour and a half of waiting, Shelley urged Tara to chase him up with a call.

"He'll be five minutes. He's just down the road," Tara said, laying her mobile back down on the coffee table.

The minutes amounted to an hour and still he hadn't arrived. The thought of shooting heroin fought in Shelley's head with the thought of smoking crack. The battle would normally be won by heroin. However, this evening was different: she'd tasted a pipe already; had no heroin with her; was stuck on the other side of London with two members, who were currently warring factions, of the AHF; and one of those Anti-Heroin Front members was her means of getting home and so back to heroin.

Shelley coaxed Tara into calling the dealer a third time.

"He's nearly here. He said he'll be no more than five minutes," Tara told them after making the call. Shelley knew the score though. Five minutes could be translated into anything up to, and well beyond, five hours. Yet, she waited.

The coffee, which Tara had kept on constant supply for her guests while she drank the vodka, did not allay Nicole's weariness. Slightly before five o'clock in the morning, Nicole took her cash from the dining table and reunited it with the roll from which it was earlier separated. Then she fell asleep next to Shelley on the sofa.

Shelley was effectively stranded. There was no excuse she could think of to split from her closest friend while they were on other side of London – not one that could be constructed from the truth.

Tara pushed herself up from the armchair. She plodded to the dining table and picked up the pile of notes. "I don't think he's coming," she slurred, handing the money back to Shelley.

With a stop-sign hand, Shelley refused the cash. "Call him one more time."

For the fourth time, Tara phoned the dealer and for the third time he maintained he was just down the road. What a long road it must've been.

"I'm going to bed. Do you want a duvet?"

Shelley declined the offer. She cringed at the thought of using a duvet from Tara's flat. It would undoubtedly be unclean, and possibly inflicted with the same off-white and brown stains that were present on Tara's pyjamas. Having stubbed out her cigarette in the overflowing ashtray, Shelley curled up on the sofa with Nicole and closed her eyes.

***

In the afternoon, Shelley was woken by Tara holding a mug of steaming coffee under her nose. Tara told her the dealer was on his way but judging by his poor performance the previous evening, Shelley didn't think it was likely.

The buzzer sounded on Tara's intercom. Still not convinced it was him, Shelley continued in her endeavour of talking Nicole into taking her home. "If we leave now, I'll have time to get over to my mum's later." It wasn't a lie – she tried to convince herself. She'd only withheld what she planned to do before visiting her mother.

"I need to take the money?" Tara came back into the lounge and held out her empty palm to Nicole. More than twelve hours later than his initial estimation, the no-show dealer had eventually shown. With her camcorder, and Shelley and Nicole's cash, Tara went into the hall to make the trade.

Watching Tara slink back into the lounge, what she had in her hand didn't look enough for five-hundred pounds, let alone five-hundred and a Sony camcorder. "Is that it?" Shelley asked, her tone divulging her disappointment.

"It's good stuff, that's why it's smaller." Tara put the crack on the coffee table and sat down on the carpet.

Shelley looked at Nicole and saw the concern on her face. She knew as with her own concern, it wasn't just that their friend had done them over by either stealing some of their money or holding back some of their crack. Tara may have appeared composed last night while they were waiting for the dealer, but she could disguise her desperation for a pipe. What she couldn't hide, what was undeniable now, was that she was a degenerated crackhead.

Even though Shelley and Nicole had most likely paid for the majority, if not all, of the crack, Tara was controlling the pipe and managing the rocks for their hits. Perhaps she thought she'd get away with it because they were smoking the crack in her flat. Shelley observed her closely as she measured out their hits. Tara's were always more generous.

After smoking yet another of Tara's not-for-Tara sized hits, Shelley's agitation increased. Tara's grip on the pipe was a rock of contention, though at the same time, Shelley sympathised; she could see the grip the pipe had on Tara.

Shelley wasn't far behind her and she knew it. Once she started on the crack, she found it nearly impossible to stop. Some sessions would last for days. She didn't understand what drove her to do it. She didn't much like the feeling it produced, with the exception of the initial high from the first pipe but that was preposterously short-lived. She supposed it might be a matter of not wanting to feel normal, even if it meant feeling worse than she might do otherwise. It was still not her natural state. If she was high on crack and fully focused on thinking about the next pipe, then she didn't have to think about her mother, her brother, the dead client at The Lanesborough, the rapist, Marianne, her mother's ex-boyfriend, her fucked up life.

Shelley felt restless. Her legs were twitching. She felt the need to do something with her hands. The crack was finished, so she lit a cigarette. "Can you call the dealer back?"

"I thought you wanted to get going," Nicole said.

"He's on his way." Tara flashed Shelley a mischievous glance. Her left eyebrow was raised and she did that weird smile thing that spanned only the right side of her mouth.

"But you haven't got any money," Nicole reminded Tara.

"No, but you have." Tara tapped Nicole on the shoulder then took a couple of steps towards the door.

Nicole shook her head. "You fucking—"

"You do want some more, don't you?" Tara leant against the lounge door. Her stained pyjama bottoms hid the foot-sized dent a quarter of the way up in the centre of the door, which Shelley had only realised was there a moment before it was concealed.

Tara explained that she was trying to be helpful by calling the dealer in advance of them running out. She'd known they'd want more and had done it with the best intentions.

"I'll give him the television. I don't watch it anyway," Tara piped in while Shelley and Nicole debated her intent as if she wasn't present.

However cross Nicole might have been with Tara, she sided with Shelley in refusing to allow her to exchange her television for crack. They would both contribute three-hundred pounds each and Tara could buy the crack on another occasion when she was flusher.

When the crack came, Shelley knelt at the coffee table, stealing Tara's position as pipe-master. She made sure they all had equal-looking hits by stashing an additional rock or two deeper in the pile of ash when it was time for her own. Tara had done the same, she told herself, attempting to justify her dishonest behaviour.

Moving to sit on the sofa, she turned her head towards the window. It was night. When did that happen? The last time she'd looked, it was daylight.

Hours must have passed and yet it felt like no time at all. Every second was the same on the pipe, possessed by the thought of the next hit. Even when she was preparing or smoking a pipe, there was no let-up; she was still thinking about the next.

Sirens wailed in Shelley's ears. Her chest felt tight and her breath was short. The police had tracked her down. The hospital DNA database, or Marianne, had led them to her. It must be Marianne. That's how they knew to find her at Tara's. They must have followed her from Marianne's place last night and been staking her out ever since.

She staggered over to the bay window that overlooked the front of Tara's block. Down on the street, she saw police in riot gear.

They were lined up directly underneath Tara's flat.

"Nicole! Nicole! We're under siege!"

Nicole rushed over to the window and looked out. "What are you talking about?"

"Look at all the police out there." Shelley banged on the window then ducked down, kneeling below it, mindful her head was lower than the sill. "Oh my God, what are we gonna do?"

"There's no one there, love." Nicole took Shelley's hands and pulled upwards. Shelley resisted the force. Instead, she managed to pull Nicole down on the carpet with her.

"Where are the police?" Tara's voice quavered.

"Outside. There's an army of them. They've come for me."

Tara crept towards the window. "I can't see anyone. Why would they come for you?"

"Don't be stupid. There isn't a reason," Nicole said, standing up. "She's paranoid, can't you tell?"

"Stop fucking around. I saw them. They're bloody there."

"They must have gone, then." Tara chewed a strand of her mousy hair. "They're not there now."

"There's a fucking row of them on the street." Shelley stood up and pointed out the window. "There— Oh my God, there's one in that tree. Get down! He's got a rifle." She threw her arms around Nicole and Tara's shoulders and plunged them all onto the floor.

Crawling on the unhoovered carpet, Shelley hid behind the armchair. Accompanying her fear was the contaminated feeling on the centre of her forehead. She'd touched the skin with her fingers that had become sticky and collected dirt during the journey on her hands and knees. Although she was in the brace position, she felt the imprint as if her fingers still marked the spot.

"There's no one out there. Get up and sit down. I'll make you a cuppa." Nicole outstretched her hand to Shelley.

Shelley shivered. She looked up at Tara who was also standing above her. "Can you honestly not see them? Swear on your life."

"The street's empty, Shell." Tara bent down and took Shelley's hand. "I think it's the crack."

17. Ch-Ch-Ch-Ch-Changes

With a constant supply of heroin and a batch of new works, Shelley was nearly back to her normal state of mind. Sensibly, she'd laid off the crack since the episode at Tara's the week before and stayed close only to her saviour, heroin.

None of the changes she'd planned to make had happened, and she hadn't been to visit her mother or her aunt. She'd been unable to leave her flat. Apart from calling Angel when she eventually got back from Tara's last Thursday, nothing had been done. She'd been telling herself, just one more hit and then she'd visit her mother to make up for missing last Friday, just one more hit and then she'd call in on Aunt Elsie, get her hair dyed, check the newspapers, terminate the lease on her working flat. But the one more hit had turned into the next, then the next and the next after that.

Lying sideways on the sofa in her lounge, with the curtains still drawn as they had been for days, she cooked up her shot. Again, she convinced herself it would be the last one before making a start on her to-do list. She examined her arms. They were marked with bruises, lumps and scabs. She couldn't work until they healed, and when would that be, if she carried on?

A vein behind her knee was the one she selected. Not out of choice, but necessity. It was cumbersome to manoeuvre her body into such a position that she could see the vein and simultaneously reach it with the needle. Just before her head hit the cushion on the sofa, she realised she'd overloaded the brown powder on the spoon.

When she came to, light was spidering through the edges of the closed curtains. She wasn't sure if it was morning, afternoon or early evening. She looked at the time on the video player – 1.17 p.m. She couldn't remember if it had been day or night when she'd taken the hit. Whether she'd been out for minutes or hours, she didn't know. She'd been at her non-stop solitary party for days and in that world, time didn't count.

The poisonous smell of heroin was emanating from every pore in her body. Reluctantly, she dragged herself into the bathroom. She showered and cleaned out her birdcage mouth. Once she'd prepared her outward appearance to contradict her inner self, she ignored the voice telling her to have a fix and got ready for the final stage of leaving. She took her jean jacket from the hook in the bedroom and went straight to the window.

Essential for completing a round of checks was a quiet mind, devoid of any other thoughts. That was something Shelley didn't have. The bombardment from the board meant she kept losing count. After a few minutes stuck on the same first window, she realised a chase of heroin was essential – it wasn't really a hit. Her mind had to be empty to do the checks. If the act of checking itself didn't instigate the emptying, something else had to be added to the mix.

***

Wrapped in heroin-laced cotton wool, she'd been able to check and leave the flat in less than five minutes. Before she knew it, she was walking past the local newsagent's. She didn't go inside. Instead, she scowled at the cantankerous man through the open door. He might not have been aware of it, but she was boycotting his shop. No longer a source of amusement, he'd begun to rile her. He was unreasonable in taking issue with her reading the papers; she bought her cigarettes from his shop; she was a paying customer. The other two newsagents she used housed equally ill-natured staff, so she took her business out of Hampstead.

In a little shop in Belsize Park, the cotton wool protecting Shelley unravelled. Picking up the first newspaper, she saw that it was Friday. Now it was too late to make up for her missed visit last week, and she couldn't miss another.

She leafed through the papers, finding nothing until she came across a headline tucked away in the middle of the Guardian. Initially, she panicked on seeing the words 'murder' and 'London' but reading on, she realised it was unrelated to her situation.

Although relieved for her own selfish concerns, she was raging at what she'd read. How could the government consider releasing a man who had murdered a child back into society? According to the article, the subhuman could be out as early as next month. What moron made these laws? she wondered, and clearly so did many other people who were pictured on a march to Downing Street. He'd murdered the schoolgirl in 1975 and was being shown leniency a little over twenty years later because he was terminally ill with cancer.

Shelley was sickened. Whether he had seconds to live, or years, it was immaterial. It didn't eradicate what he had done. No longer in the mood for running errands, she used a restaurant lavatory to take a chase of heroin. Calmer, she carried on to the chemist's farther along the road.

She purchased the blackest of black hair dye, which from the back of the box promised to disguise her blonde hair. She wasn't sure if she was being paranoid, but she knew that just because she worried the police were after her, it didn't mean they weren't. Marianne hadn't been in contact since she was taken away in the panda car last week, and that further fuelled Shelley's fear.

Continuing on Haverstock Hill, she turned off a side street lined with white, terraced houses. A few yards up, she entered one and traipsed up the winding staircase to the converted loft at the top.

Her working flat was bare. Some of her clients had called it minimalist. Shelley called it cold. It wasn't somewhere she spent time unless she was with a client, and as Marianne knew she had it, she wouldn't ever be spending time there again. She'd have to use her own flat or rent a new place somewhere else.

From a white envelope in her handbag, she took out one-thousand five-hundred pounds in cash, bound in her uniform style: in groupings of one-hundred pounds, Queen's head sideways on each note folded over securing a pile, and upright on all the others. Although the sum of every group of notes had been verified previously, she recounted the fifteen piles, which consisted of tens and twenties because she'd used the opportunity to rid the cold bank of most of the non-fifties that had made it in. Fifties were best in the freezer as they took up less space.

She addressed the envelope to the landlord and put the money back inside. On a sheet of notepaper, she wrote:

Dear Mr Davis,
I have been called away on urgent business abroad. I do not
know when or if I will be returning to London. I hope the enclosed
£1,500 together with the deposit you are holding will cover the
notice I hereby give.
Yours sincerely,
Mrs Whyte

***

By the time Shelley had trudged all the way up the hill to the corner of Willoughby Road, she realised she didn't have the bag from the chemist's containing the hair dye. She turned the corner into her road and not long after, she was in her car, taking another chase.

She headed north, stopping at Hair on Broadway in Mill Hill to have her hair professionally disguised before going to see her mother. When Shelley arrived at the maisonette in Hammers Lane, she could see the curtains were open. She knocked on the door and heard her mother coming down the stairs.

"Aren't they letting you go early on a— Oh my goodness! You look like that actress from Pulp Fiction. What've you done to your beautiful hair?"

"I just wanted to try something different," Shelley said. "When have you seen Pulp Fiction?"

"I didn't see it, dear. She was on This Morning with Richard and Judy. Something thermal..."

"Uma Thurman." Shelley followed her mother up the stairs. Her head felt lighter. Not surprisingly as she'd lost about seven or eight inches of blonde before the black dye had been applied. She hoped her new style didn't look too much like Uma Thurman's. She'd always thought her black bob looked slightly wig-like.

Rita put the kettle on for tea. She told Shelley that she'd been out shopping with the help of Aunt Elsie. Shelley was delighted. Her mother was the brightest she'd seen her in ages. It had been months since Rita had come to the door without being called, or made the tea.

After an hour, Shelley made her excuses to leave. She still had more to-dos to tick off her nagging list. And most importantly, the sooner she completed the list, the sooner she could have a proper hit. It was the needle she needed.

***

On returning to her flat, she decided what could be put off until the next day, and what couldn't. It was late to be calling Aunt Elsie, so that could wait. But there was one thing she could do now. She compromised with herself to take a little chase. Although she wanted to inject, she knew if she did, this final task wouldn't get done.

She took out her mobile and, leaning on the coffee table, she wrote down the phone numbers of her contacts on an A4 pad. Not many friends, she thought glumly. Even though she hadn't spoken to most of them in years, she still copied out their numbers. On a separate sheet of paper, she wrote out the phone numbers she used more often: her two dealers – Jay and Ajay; the clients she dealt with directly; the five madams she worked for; and the numerous girls she worked with. She consoled herself that three of those working girls were her friends, as was Hugo, to a degree. He didn't fall into any of her categories. As the son of one of Nicole's ex-clients, he was something else entirely.

Once she'd crosschecked the names and phone numbers on paper against the contacts in her phone, she replaced her old SIM card with a new one. Later on, she'd transfer the numbers and contact the people she wanted to know her new number.

Nearly ready for her fix, she filled a glass under the tap in the kitchen. She returned to the lounge, placing the glass on the coffee table and taking her place on the sofa. With her syringe, she drew up the water for her hit and squirted it over the heroin in her spoon. Before cooking up, she dropped her old SIM card into the glass. Marianne could sink on her own.

18. Covering Up

"Kiki! How the devil are you?"

"Hmm..." Holding her mobile in one hand, Shelley used the other to push herself upright on the sofa on which she'd fallen asleep. "Who is this?"

"Sorry if I woke you, sweetie. I—"

"No, no, it's okay. I didn't realise it was you."

"You're not ill, are you? Or were you out partying last night? I want to see you. I'll be staying in London tonight."

How could she see a client when her arms were marked so badly? She selected the 'out partying last night' option, then told him she was booked for the evening already. Unsure what she wanted to do, she said she'd try to cancel the booking or send a friend in her place.

The driver and the blindfold business would be off-putting under most circumstances, but that job was worth feeling sick for a while in the back of a Rolls-Royce. Like quite a few of her clients, he had erectile dysfunction. His ED perhaps caused, or at least worsened, by consuming copious amounts of cocaine. And like most clients with ED, he didn't even attempt intercourse. But there was more to him than what Nicole referred to as a Resident Limp Dick. He also fitted the profile for a Resident Fucked Out My Box – a client who paid them to take drugs. That was Shelley's second preferred category. The Limp Dicks were the first. Those that fell in both camps topped the lot, or they had done until she met him. Resident Dicks All the Boxes was coined by Nicole because he ticked boxes Shelley previously thought couldn't exist within the mode of time-in-exchange-for-money transaction in which she partook.

It was fortunate they'd exchanged numbers. Otherwise, she'd never have had the opportunity to see him again. After what she'd done with her SIM card last night, Marianne was no longer in the position to give her any work. But it wasn't some amazing foresight that had led her to do it. The reason had been the same as it had for every client before him: to cut out the madam's take on her future earnings.

Although she preferred dealing with her clients directly – and not sharing her fee after the initial introduction, or the first few visits –

it wasn't standard practice to share her number with every client (and most didn't share theirs until they were regulars). Dishonesty wasn't the issue; she felt working this way could be justified by the Golden Rule. The reason she had to be selective was for survival, both in terms of her personal safety and in continuing to work for the madams whose clients she effectively stole. Each situation had to be analysed on a case-by-case basis, which wasn't easy when she was with a Fucked Out My Box. She had to weigh up the risks: consider the existing client/madam relationship; their closeness to her compared to each other; the length of time they'd known each other compared to how long they'd known her; their personalities and character traits. Various factors had a bearing on her judgement, but her rule was that whenever it seemed safe, she'd deal with the client direct.

***

Wrapped in her duvet, she sat on the sofa, cooking up her first hit of the day. Once the heroin had released her from the pain in her bones and in her head, she started writing a list on the A4 pad she'd left on the coffee table last night.

Looking at what she'd come up with, none of the reasons seemed plausible for explaining the bandages she might wrap around her arms. If a dog had attacked her, wouldn't it be strange the dog had bitten both her arms and nowhere else on her body? Spilling a cup of tea wouldn't be enough to scald both arms. A hot bath, now that was a ludicrous idea. It would burn one hand or a foot. What idiot would lower both arms into a boiling bathtub? A drunken one, and she didn't want Resident Dicks All the Boxes to think she was a drunk. The best option was a skin condition. She had eczema or psoriasis of which she was so embarrassed she kept it covered whenever it flared up. That way he would be unlikely to insist on seeing the damage, though he might choose never to see her again.

"Hi, it's Kiki," Shelley said, playing nervously with the diamond in her necklace.

"Hello sweetie," Resident Dicks All the Boxes replied.

"I've eventually managed to get another girl on my booking, so I'm all yours."

"Splendid," he said. "I'll send my driver. He'll collect you from the same place. Say eight p.m.?"

The rendezvous was set but looking at the clock, she realised there was only a little over two hours in which to get ready. She threw on an old tracksuit and ran down the road to the shops.

When she arrived at the chemist's, they were pulling down the metal shutter and she was refused entry. However, after the staff heard the details of her dire situation, she was granted access and given one of her four boxes of bandages free. The grey-haired shop assistant identified with Shelley's story of a hypercritical boyfriend. Apparently, she'd married the one she'd been with as a teenager. Still married, forty years later, he was still hypercritical of everything about her, everything she did, everything she wore, everyone she spoke to and everything she said.

"It's been lovely talking to you, but I need to get back." Shelley took a step farther away from the cash desk and the lady standing behind it.

"Don't take up with anyone who won't take you exactly as you are," the lady said. "If he wants to change you then it's not you he wants to be with."

Shelley took another couple of steps backwards and reached for the handle on the glass door. "Thanks for the advice," she called out behind her.

After her shower, she straightened her black hair using a large bristle brush under the hairdryer. Then with her steaming hot curling tongs, she curled under the ends of her bob. Shorter hair took longer to style; she couldn't leave it to air-dry as she had done when her hair was long.

She studied her face in the mirror. Little white bumps had infiltrated her once clear complexion. Worse, there were a couple of angry red spots on her chin. Taking concealer, she covered them over and applied a thick powder foundation, which she hoped would last the night. Her eyes, she made up heavy with purple to draw attention away from her damaged skin. The blush on her cheeks gave the illusion of health, as did the lilac gloss she spread on her lips.

On opening the bandages, she questioned if she could really pull it off, but it was too late to cancel now that she had committed. Having bandaged her left arm, she inspected it in the mirror. Sexy was not a word that came to her mind. Suddenly, she remembered a dress that she could potentially keep on all night and that would mean the client wouldn't come face-to-face with the bandages.

From her wardrobe, she took out the Moschino mini dress. After bandaging her second arm from the wrist to just above the elbow, she slipped her mummified arms into the long sleeves of the black dress. Gold buttons ran the short length of the dress. She fastened them, bearing in mind that she could keep her arms in the dress all night and just unbutton the front when, and if, access was required.

For distraction from her covered arms, she rolled lace top stockings over her legs and attached them to a black lace suspender belt. With the combination of her stockings and her come-fuck-me high heels, she convinced herself she'd get away with keeping the dress on, regardless of the unhelpful comments from the board.

She took a chase of heroin to be sure she left the flat on time. Then she whizzed round the flat counting aloud in fives as she patted, twisted and rattled, the oven knobs, taps and window handles respectively.

She drove the short distance to Belsize Park from where she was being picked up outside her old working flat. Concerned the landlord might see her if he was around, she pulled up outside a row of terraced houses farther down.

At exactly eight o'clock, she stepped out of her car. She completed the ritual that ensured her car's security. Then she walked up the road.

Noticing the Rolls-Royce was already there, she picked up her pace and approached the blacked-out windows. Out of habit, when she opened the door, she was mindful of her nails, but sitting down in the backseat, she realised they were unpainted. Her weekly visits with Nicole to Final Touch had slipped and she'd forgotten to paint them herself.

"Hello again," Shelley said, as a hand reached through the hatch, exhibiting the silk blindfold.

Grateful that she could take her eyes off her unkempt fingernails, she tied the blindfold at the back of her head. Whether it would help take her mind off them too was another matter.

"I nearly didn't recognise you, miss. Is that a syrup on your head?" the driver asked.

"No. Does it look like one?" As the car sped off, Shelley's body was sent flying backwards into the seat. Her Tiffany necklace slapped against her open mouth and the diamond whacked her front teeth.

"I didn't mean no offence, miss," the driver said, as if he hadn't witnessed the collision in the rear. "It's just the boss only usually sees blondes."

19. *Take Me to Your Dealer*

Cocaine and Shelley didn't mix well, and the coke had been unkind to her on the Saturday night she'd spent with her client. Generally, a downer was required to counter the effects and at her client's London townhouse, she hadn't been able to take any. Now, four days after the job, she was still trying to reduce the paranoia with her ally, heroin, but by mixing up her hits with crack, the psychosis-bearing traitor, she was reducing the efficacy of the gear.

She was nearly out, and Jay was unable to deliver her next batch of brown and white. Apparently, he was waiting for a package. On a Wednesday – his busiest day – Shelley doubted that was the case. He was most likely up to something else, like getting his end away. Ajay – her back-up dealer – was also dry, though he was able to refer her to someone else who was holding. Now she had to go out because Ajay's contact, Len, wouldn't deliver to Hampstead. Len assured her that he had what she needed, but she had to go to his house in Ladbroke Grove. She imagined it would be safer to go to his place than to Camden to score from a stranger. Camden was fine for a few twenty bags, but she knew she couldn't hand over five-hundred pounds to a stranger and expect them to come back.

After four days of not bathing or brushing her teeth, she could smell herself. Although she wanted a bath, she didn't want to lie in her own dirty water. While the bath was running, she took a shower and washed her greasy hair until it squeaked clean. With a deep conditioning treatment left in, she pulled back her hair with a clamp then climbed into the bath.

She thought about the call she'd made to Aunt Elsie last week. Her aunt had sounded distant. Shelley wasn't sure if it was because she was cross that she wasn't visiting her or Rita as often as usual, or if it was something else. Also of concern was Nicole. When she'd last spoken to her, she'd seemed different. Shelley thought it was most likely the strain of the court case – she was being called in the next week. Shelley had asked Nicole if she'd heard from Marianne, but she hadn't either. She'd been trying her every day and every time Marianne's phone went straight to voicemail. Shelley had expressed her concern about holding off on their plan, but Nicole said she was pleased Marianne was probably still detained by the police, that it was only a taste of the comeuppance she had coming. Anyway, they couldn't make their move until she'd testified, so at least something bad was happening to Marianne in the meantime. As Shelley tried to relax in the bubbles, she feared the police would be looking for her. She was convinced Marianne wouldn't have been held this long unless it was for something serious.

Once she dragged herself out of the warm water, she brushed her teeth for ten minutes, hoping to counter the damage done to them during the last few days they'd been neglected. After dressing, styling her bob and applying her make-up, she sat on the sofa and made herself a shot – this time using only heroin, as it was all she had left and there was only enough for a minute hit.

She accomplished the checking quickly. Her heart wasn't in it today. So what if the flat was burgled, flooded or went up in flames? She believed she had far bigger things to worry about.

***

Shelley ran to her car, escaping the rain spewing on her from the grey sky. Once out of the storm, she could hear the words 'damaged goods' slamming down on the windscreen. She popped out the *Pablo Honey* CD from its case and put it into the CD player. Her brother had bought her that Radiohead album not long before he died.

In an attempt to drown out the downpour, she cranked up the volume but her mind wasn't silenced by the blast. Her grief, her anger, her fears, her lost hopes, and images, words and phrases painfully etched in her memory competed for attention.

Through her tears, she drove past St John's Wood then into Maida Vale and up Elgin Avenue. She was nearly there and she knew she had to stop crying before she arrived. Taking deep breaths at a set of red traffic lights, she closed her eyes. She imagined herself with her family as they used to be, but it made her feel worse. Her insides felt like they were bleeding out.

As the lights turned green, she kicked down on the accelerator. The low car mounted the curb. She hit the footbrake, pulled the handbrake, then threw her torso over the steering wheel. She roared as if producing the noise would purge her of the pain inside.

After a while she stopped crying and screaming. She gradually edged off the curb. Driving on the road, she realised the car was dipping to the left. She pulled over again – carefully this time. Inspecting the passenger-side front tyre, she saw the deep cut. She didn't know how to change a tyre, so she called the AA. She sat out the wait with Radiohead in the shelter of her car.

Shortly after the rain had stopped, the rescue man arrived. When her tyre had been replaced, she continued on her journey. Part-way down Ladbroke Grove, she turned off and after zigzagging a few times, she arrived at the house on Bracewell Road.

Although the sun had brightened the sky, when Shelley stepped out of the car, the cloud of impending doom hung heavy over her head – and its spawn that resided in the pit of her stomach made her aware of its presence.

It took her five minutes to check her car was locked. Her mind was consumed with worry that she hadn't checked her flat properly. She might've forgotten to close the front door. She couldn't remember closing it. She might've left a window open, a tap turned on, or left the oven, grill or hob on.

***

The front garden of the red-bricked terraced house was cluttered with discarded furniture, remnants of carpet and pots of paint. Shelley thought they might be redecorating, and when the door opened, it looked like a mammoth task. From what she could see down the long hall, the house was a wreck.

The skinny man, who Shelley placed at twenty-eight to thirty years old, led her into a lounge that coordinated with his own derelict appearance. His clothes were stained to rival Tara's pyjamas, laden with the same brown spills – most likely coffee – and the off-white splashes that more closely resembled ejaculate than anything else that came to Shelley's mind, especially as observed against the backdrop of his black, v-neck jumper.

"You got the dough, love?" he said, holding out his open palm in front of her.

"Have you got both?"

He nodded and scratched his hairy chin.

"Brown and white?" She waited for his response but he stared at her, blankly and with closed lips. "Can I have it then?" she asked.

"I'll get it for you." He averted his gaze to the ripped wallpaper and Shelley averted hers to his ripped jeans. Resident Scarecrow, Nicole would have probably called him. "I need to nip out to pick it up."

"I'll drive you," she said eagerly.

"No need. It's only a few houses down. I'll be back in a jiffy," he told the loose hanging strips of wallpaper.

"I'll come with you."

"Nah, love. Can't have you knowing where I keep my stash, can I?" He chuckled. Was he laughing at her or was that her paranoia? "Have you got the readies, then?"

"I'll give it to you when you get back."

"I have to take it now. I ain't up to no thuggery or nothing," he said, grinning. "My mate's holding the parcel and he's taking the money." With a tattooed hand, he gestured to the armchair. "Have a pew."

Shelley remained standing. The armchair, which was the only seat in the room, was smothered with lashings of pet hair and topped with what looked like either food or vomit. Although she hadn't noticed any pets, the house smelt like one might have died. The stink was so rancid that the body odour she'd acquired from not bathing seemed like a delicate fragrance in comparison.

Reluctantly, she took out her purse and handed over the cash: five immaculately presented piles of twenty-pound notes, each totalling one-hundred pounds, the Queen's head sideways on the note acting as the clip over the others which were flat with the Queen's head upright.

As Len tucked the money into an inside pocket of his jacket, Shelley discreetly read the indigo letters across his knuckles. One set of four fingers spelled 'L-U-C-K', and the other, 'F-A-T-E'.

"Laters," he called out, slamming the front door behind him. The bang startled Shelley and as she flinched, she singed her hair with the flame from her Clipper lighter.

Smoking a cigarette, she paced the dual aspect room from the bay windows at the front to the patio doors at the back. She thought it strange that he hadn't counted the money in front of her before he left – checking the cash in the presence of the buyer was protocol.

After ten minutes, she tried to convince the board that he might've got chatting to his friend. Another ten minutes passed and the board had convinced her that he'd run off with the money.

From her handbag, she took out her mobile and called Len. His phone went straight to voicemail a dozen or so times. So, she called the man responsible for making the introduction – her most unpunctual, skunk-smoking, slow-talking dealer – Ajay.

"He's a business associate. I don't know where you'll find him," he told Shelley.

"This is your fault. You have to get my money back."

"This is your beef, not mine. I was doing you a favour, man, init?"

"Losing me five-hundred pounds is not doing me a fucking favour." Shelley kicked the armchair. Several orange and green morsels fell off and landed on her trainers.

"Don't be shouting at me now. You need to mellow, Shello, man."

"I won't be fucking mellow 'til I've got my motherfucking money back."

Ajay didn't reply. She looked at her phone. There was no call. He'd hung up.

***

Thirty minutes had passed and still Len hadn't returned. She told herself another half-hour then she'd have to leave, go to a cashpoint and score in Camden.

Wandering through the house, she looked for money she could take to make up for the cash that had been taken from her. Her ransacking of the place was barely noticeable as every room looked like it had already been burgled.

In an upstairs bedroom, she emptied the contents of a rickety chest of drawers onto the floor. From the heap of dirty clothes, men's toiletries and scraps of paper, a box of two-hundred cigarettes emerged. At least they were Benson and Hedges. But five-hundred pounds for a box of two-hundred Bensons was hardly a good deal.

Continuing her search, she crawled under the double bed. As she shoved around and hurled the lids from the shoeboxes that lay there, the dust caused her to sneeze. It caught in her throat and she choked. In one of the shoeboxes, she found a pair of Nike trainers. Although they had no value to her, she imagined the thief wouldn't be happy if they went missing.

When she stood up, she brushed the dust from her jeans and sweatshirt, and shook out her hair. She flung open the wardrobe and flicked through the hangers of clothes. The only item she could find worth taking was a pair of new-looking Levi 501s. Again, of no use to her – they weren't her size – but at least the crook would miss them.

Having searched the other three bedrooms and found nothing worth taking, she returned to the room with the men's toiletries and clothes. She was certain it was Len's room.

The mattress was soiled with a variety of stains. Some were recognisable as blood, and the rest, quite possibly urine, faeces and food. She wrapped the long sleeves of her sweatshirt over her hands. She took a deep breath and held it while raising one side of the double mattress and flipping it over. The mattress banged against the windowsill as it landed upright on the floor, wedged between the sill and the wooden bed frame.

There was nothing to be seen on the slatted bed frame except for more stains and dust. The dust revisited her throat. She gasped for breath. Coughing and spluttering, she staggered around the bed frame towards the mattress by the window.

Trying to resist her gag reflex, she felt around the mattress for gaps. Something hard was inside but she couldn't find an opening. She took out her keys and stabbed the corner of the mattress near where she imagined the package of drugs or money was hidden. Once she'd made an incision, she used her key to slash along the mattress. She covered her hand with her sleeve and delved into the laceration she'd created.

Her heart sunk as she gazed at the handgun she'd dropped onto the coffee-spattered carpet. Though she knew the thief would miss it, she also knew she couldn't take it. The gun might have been used for a crime and she couldn't have it in her possession. At the board meeting, some disputed her rationale, but she knew they'd only change their minds later if she did take it. They kept her hovering over the gun, goading her to put it in her handbag, but she didn't.

Protecting her hand with her sleeve, she put it back where she'd found it. Then she pushed her body between the mattress and the windowsill, and lifted the bottom of the mattress to slide it back along the slats.

Before she left the room, she pulled the only poster off the wall – a picture of an alien with the sentence, 'Take me to your dealer'. It wasn't a sensible place to be asking that.

With the Blu-Tack from the poster in her handbag, and the cigarettes, trainers and jeans tucked under her arm, she went to the front door. The door didn't open. Frantically, she pulled at it but it wouldn't budge. It was locked. She rushed through to the back of the house and tried the patio doors. She was locked in.

***

Every window she tried in the downstairs and upstairs of the house was nailed shut. She needed to find another way out, but she was wary of breaking glass in case a neighbour heard and called the police.

Under the stairs, she noticed a small door, which she expected led to a basement but she hoped might also lead to an exit. She couldn't remember seeing a garage or a lower level to the house when she arrived, but she had been inattentive with her mind focused on scoring.

She tried the small, gold handle but the door was stuck. Using all her strength, she yanked it towards her. Putrid air rushed out to greet her. Despite retching, she climbed down the narrow staircase and entered the dark room. She felt her way to a light switch. A single bulb lit up the damp cellar. It was completely bricked in.

She sprinted back up the creaking stairs and rushed out the cellar door straight across into the pestiferous kitchen. The slimy vinyl caused her to skid and she fell. Pushing herself up from the floor, she felt the stickiness on her hands. While the taps ran, she searched for something to clean them with. Soap or washing up liquid would have been ideal but she couldn't find anything, not one bottle of detergent. In the absence of a cleaning agent, she rinsed her hands under the hot tap, wincing as the water scorched them.

Having dried her hands on her sweatshirt, she pulled open all the kitchen drawers until she found the cutlery. She took a knife, a fork and a spoon and returned to the front door. She tried with each utensil to use them as a lever to open the door, but the cutlery didn't work. The gap between the door and the frame was too narrow and too short to get leverage.

Deflated, she tramped through to the patio doors at the rear of the lounge where she tried with the cutlery. First she used the knife but, as that had been misshaped during her attempt at the front door, it didn't work.

Before she went to get another, she tried with the fork, pushing it in the gap where the two glass-panelled doors met. The fork was too curved to fit right through, although she noticed the doors moved slightly when she jiggled it. There was no point in trying the spoon; the fork was too curved, and she could tell that the handle of the spoon would be too fat.

Back in the kitchen, she rummaged for a long-bladed knife. In a drawer housing an abundant supply of every imaginable kitchen utensil, she found three. She took her finds into the lounge and laid the blades on the grimy carpet by the back doors.

The first knife she managed to get right through the gap, but it wasn't strong enough to pull the doors apart. She put another knife farther down, below the lock that held the doors together. That knife also went right through the gap.

For about five minutes, she twisted and pulled on the knives, causing the doors to rattle as they jarred back and forth. The lock was still holding the doors together but the gap between the doors was increasing with each pull. She moved the knives closer to the lock: one just above and the other just below. With all her strength, she pulled with the knives angled in opposing directions. The doors opened inwards. With her handbag over her shoulder, she picked up the swag and walked into the garden.

She looked around for a way out but the garden was fenced in. There were no side exits. Of course, it was a terraced house, she remembered. She stepped up on the low wall that bordered the patio and looked over the fences on either side. All she could see were rows of more fences.

She ran to the rear of the garden to see if there was a way out of the back. There was nothing to stand on that allowed her to see over the fence, unless she climbed a tree. She was not in the mood for tree climbing. The only thing she wanted to do was get out and get her drugs.

Heading back towards the patio, she heard voices from the garden next door. She approached the fence and pulled herself up, clinging to the rough wood with her hands.

"Excuse me, please," she said, with her head peeping over the fence. "My boyfriend's locked me in by accident. Would you be able to help me get out, please?"

"Oh, you poor thing," said a grey-haired lady from next door.

Shelley began to cry.

"Don't worry, sweetheart. My husband's gone to get the ladders. We'll have you out in no time."

Shelley jumped down and examined her hands for splinters. Within a few seconds, a ladder was being passed over the top of the fence.

"Thank you so much," Shelley said, reaching up and taking the silver ladder. She opened it and set it on the grass, next to the fence. As she stood on the platform at the top – about six-feet high – she stalled, unsure if she could manage the jump down into the next-door neighbour's garden.

"Come on, love, it's okay, I'll catch you." The old man from next door opened his arms in front of her.

Shelley threw over the jeans, trainers and cigarettes. She leapt in his direction and he caught her. As he steadied her to stand on the grass, she started crying again.

"You know we hear how he talks to you, sweetheart. You really shouldn't stand for it." The lady put her arm over Shelley's shoulder. "There, there, it'll be all right," she said, patting Shelley on the back. "Come on, I'll take you out."

Shelley picked up the swag from the grass and followed the lady through her house. The decor reminded her of Aunt Elsie's and part of her wanted to stop there for a cup of tea.

"Thank you ever so much." Shelley stood on the doorstep. "You've been so kind. I really appreciate it."

"That's no bother, sweetheart." The lady smiled. "Don't you go back to him now. A lovely girl like you needs to set her standards, you hear me, and higher than him."

20. Stolen Goods

Fresh works, a boulder of crack and a heap of heroin lay on the coffee table in front of Shelley. The spoon, the glass of water and the bag of citric were lined up neatly. Everything was ready for her solitary party. Jay had come through with the drugs in the end. When she'd told him what had happened to her yesterday, he'd asked for the address in Ladbroke Grove and offered to help her recover the stolen money. He'd been so concerned that when he'd delivered her medicine, he'd come in and made her a cup of tea – the cup of tea she was still drinking.

The five-hundred pounds worth of heroin and crack that Shelley now had in her possession had cost her a thousand pounds. Her savings, supposed to see her through university, were diminishing at an unsustainable rate. Her client list was shrinking, and she was working infrequently. Somehow, she'd pulled it off with the bandages and had been paid the other night. Although Resident Dicks All the Boxes seemed sympathetic about her skin condition, she wasn't sure he'd be calling her again.

Earlier in the afternoon, Shelley had called Ajay who'd been the one responsible for the introduction to Len, the thieving connection, but Ajay told her he couldn't get hold of him. She'd called Len countless times herself during the night, but to no avail. She was about to try again – but first, she needed a fix.

Having got her itch on, she sat back on the sofa, scratching at her face and neck. Later, as the effects lessened, she picked up her phone to call him again. This time he answered.

"I'm the girl you locked in your house, fucker. I want my money back."

"What are you on about?" he replied. "I never locked you in. I came back and you was gone. You nicked the Blu-Tack off my poster. What the fuck did you do that for?"

"You can have it back. And your two-hundred Bensons and your five-o-ones and your Nikes when I get my motherfucking money."

"It's all right, love. You can keep 'em."

"I don't want your shit. I want my fucking money back."

"What about what you done to my back doors? It was like sleeping out in the Antarctica in here last night."

"It's your own fucking fault." Shelley leant forward to prepare her next hit on the coffee table. "I want the money or the drugs today. If you don't sort it, someone's gonna be paying you a visit – and believe me, they're gonna fucking get it."

"There's no need to do that. I weren't up to no skulduggery," he said, softly. "It's a misunderstanding, that's all. Just gimme a few days and I'll come up good."

"No. Not a few days. Today."

"I can't do it that fast. I need a bit of time."

Shelley could tell the conversation was going nowhere, so she put down the phone. She thought how desperate he must have been for a fix that he'd steal from someone who knew where he lived.

After a few moments, an idea came to her mind. Whether he came through with the money or the drugs, or he didn't, it didn't matter any more. She'd thought of a more useful way he could pay her back.

21. Sick Leave

On Sunday, when Shelley's supply of drugs had dwindled to an unacceptable level, she got back on to Jay. She knew to allow up to a day for his arrival. Even when he said he was down the road, it could take up to twenty-four hours to get to her flat. Fascinatingly, the same journey could also take fifteen or twenty minutes, although that had only happened on a handful of occasions. She imagined how it would be if she ran her business like that. She'd have no clients. But then, there's no client more desperate than a junky – that she knew too well.

Shelley picked up her ringing mobile. "Sick bitch is back in business," Nicole told her.

"Do you know what's going on? Why did the police take her?" Shelley sat upright on the sofa and popped a pinch of heroin into her spoon.

"No. She said she'd been away. I couldn't let on that we saw her getting arrested."

"Did she say anything about me?" Shelley sprinkled in the citric.

"She's been calling you. She asked if you had a new number."

"You didn't give it to her, did you?"

"Of course I didn't. But why don't you want her to have it? We're supposed to be acting normal."

"I know but I can't bear talking to her, keeping up the nicey-nicey act." Shelley balanced the phone in the crook of her neck as she added water then cooked the contents of the spoon. "You told her I was on holiday?"

"Yes, everything you said. Are you coming to Final Touch with me this week?"

"Maybe next." Shelley tried to ignore the dirt under her uneven fingernails. "How was court?" she asked.

"They're gonna be sentenced... It's over and I'm not gonna let those cunts in my head again."

With Marianne back and Nicole finished with court, they could finally move on with their plan for the rapist client. They arranged to meet up later in the week, which gave Shelley time to enjoy her private party a little longer. Inconveniently, it would need to be broken up at some point though; she'd managed to drag herself out the flat on Friday for a visit with her mother, but she hadn't seen her aunt for over three weeks.

Shelley had her fix, then lay back on the sofa. She flicked through the channels, stopping at the brawling on Jerry Springer. Watching the show, she decided her life could, in fact, be worse.

Her last hit had been too weak. Leaning forward, she dragged the wooden coffee table closer towards the sofa to cook up the next. As the quantities of heroin and crack were dangerously low, to ensure she didn't run out before Jay arrived, she first measured doses for a twenty-four hour period. Less crack was required than heroin; although the initial high was stronger with more, the hallucinations were also increased.

Cautiously, she selected a good-looking vein on the inside of her elbow. If the weather was pleasant, she'd use her skin condition excuse for wearing long sleeves. Lying to Nicole would be hard, but she didn't want to keep blowing the veins in her feet and the veins behind her knees required contortionism for which she couldn't muster the energy.

She wrapped a belt around her arm and waited for the vein to bulge. When it looked ripe, she pulled the orange cap off the syringe and slipped in the needle. Drawing back, she watched her blood unite with the brown liquid in the barrel. The thrill of the needle consumed her. Gently, she pushed in the plunger and felt herself hurtling into the other dimension.

***

The buzzer sounded and Shelley roused. Slowly, she opened her eyes. The flat was bright with sunshine. She raised her partially dead arm from its dangling-off-the-sofa position and swung it up onto the coffee table to reach for her phone. A needle was hanging from the inside of her elbow. She plucked it out.

From her mobile phone, she could see that it was 10.02 a.m. on Monday. She deduced that she'd passed out sometime the day before. She didn't know what time, but the fact that the curtains were open led her to believe it was before dusk. Passing out didn't concern her; it was regular occurrence. What was most irregular was someone at her door so early in the morning.

"Who is it?" she asked over the intercom.

"Why aren't you at work? Are you not well?"

"Auntie Elsie! What are you—? Come up."

Shelley slammed down the receiver, ran through to her bedroom and ripped off the stinking tracksuit she'd been wearing since Friday night. As she changed into her pastel-pink, long-sleeved pyjamas, her mind raced with reasons why her aunt had arrived unannounced.

There was a knock on her front door. "Coming," she called from the bedroom at the other end of the flat.

In the hall mirror, she caught a glimpse of herself. Her complexion was pale, uneven with spots, and her eyes didn't look like her own. Reluctantly, she opened the door. "I don't want to come too close. You might catch it."

"I thought you'd be home." Aunt Elsie leant forward to hug her. "I know you're not one to skive."

"Has something happened to Mum?"

"Not yet. I'm going over there later to try and make something happen. Something has to change." Aunt Elsie took off her fuchsia anorak and marched through to the lounge then into the kitchen.

"Why are—?" Shelley began, then realised her question could be rephrased more politely. "What are you doing in Hampstead?"

"You weren't at work." Elsie held the kettle under the running kitchen tap. "Where've your teacups gone?"

"There's mugs in that one, there." Shelley pointed to the cupboard above the sink. As she lifted her arm, she felt it tremble. "How did you know I wasn't at work?"

"Because you weren't there. That's why I came here."

Adrenaline surged through Shelley's body. She felt electrified. "You were in Foxtons?"

"I had a good mind to have a word with your boss too, swanning around like—"

"Did you? What did you say?" Shelley thought her time with the borrowed eyes was up. They felt ready to launch out of her sockets and into the sink where she'd averted them.

"I bit my tongue this time, but if he keeps it up, I won't be doing it next time. They're working you too hard. I knew this would happen. Look at the state of you, you poor thing." She rubbed Shelley's shoulder. "It's not catchy what you've got. You're run-down. It's exhaustion. What did the doctor say?"

"What did you say to them?"

"What did the doctor say is wrong with you?" Elsie asked, not looking at Shelley but at the poster with black lettering, sellotaped to the side of the fridge. "Oh, this is good, positive thinking. Choose life. Choose a—"

"What did you say in Foxtons?"

"Not a lot." Her aunt continued looking at the poster. "This isn't nice at all. It's full of swearing. Go in the lounge and I'll bring in your tea."

Shelley wouldn't leave the kitchen. She couldn't because her quivering legs had taken root through the tiles. "What happened in Foxtons?"

"Calm down. Don't worry. I didn't get you into any trouble." Aunt Elsie shunned the poster and looked at Shelley. "I only spoke to the receptionist. Is it legal to employ people that young? Being new isn't an excuse either, not to know who you are – it's ridiculous. You have been to the doctor, Shelley?"

"Not yet. What did she say to you?"

"You have to see the doctor. Call him." Aunt Elsie removed the lid from the cream tin labelled 'tea'. "And I bet you haven't had that allergy test done, have you?"

"Not yet, but I will... What did she say?"

"Who's she?"

"The receptionist. What did she say?"

"You mean he. Haven't you met him yet? How long have you been off?" Elsie poured boiling water into the purple mugs on the work surface.

"Only today." Shelley thought quickly. "He must be a temp."

"Call the doctor. Please, for me," Elsie said.

When her aunt walked past her, Shelley's formerly entrenched roots retracted from the black and white floor tiles. She followed Elsie into the lounge. Her shaking hadn't abated and tea splashed out of her mug, leaving a puddle trail on the floor. She kept her eyes straight ahead, pretending not to notice as she walked over to the couch. She saw a needle lying underneath the coffee table. Before sitting down, she kicked it under the sofa with her bare foot.

Aunt Elsie sat next to her on the sofa and picked up Shelley's brick-like mobile phone from the table. "Make an appointment. I'm worried about you," Elsie told her.

"I'll do it later. I promise." Shelley convinced her aunt that it wouldn't make any difference whether she called now or in the afternoon. The doctors' surgery was always booked up so far in advance that she'd probably be better by the time she got an appointment.

Aunt Elsie went to make Shelley some toast. Thankfully, Shelley had brought herself some new bread for the freezer. The cold bank was well hidden in the sealed Black Forest gateau box, so Shelley didn't fear its discovery – not until her aunt called out from the kitchen that she'd disposed of all the food past its best before date.

Shelley rushed into the kitchen and opened the tall, silver bin. Inside she saw her savings – thousands of pounds – buried under a box of frozen burgers and a bag of frozen chips, topped with two leaking teabags. The Black Forest gateau box, she hoped, would provide shelter enough to keep dry the hundreds of pairs of fifties inside. The notes would need to be left out to air to remove the bin-odour they'd be acquiring in their current habitat. And the cold bank container would need to be replaced – she'd been using the same one since she'd started working in 1994, just after Will died that summer. The cake had been bought for him, but he'd never got to eat it.

"I'll replace your food." Aunt Elsie rubbed Shelley's arm, causing pain around the areas of blown veins and lumps. "Don't be upset. I'm sure lots of people forget to throw out their old food."

A tear rolled down Shelley's cheek to the corner of her mouth. A cardboard box was a stupid thing to be sentimental over, she told herself.

After Shelley ate her toast and drank a second cup of tea, she followed her aunt's suggestion of having a bath and changing her clothes to make herself feel refreshed. She didn't waste any time relaxing in the bath as she'd been directed; she worried what her aunt might find if she continued her mission of reorganising the contents of her flat.

"Are you trying to be a Uri Geller?" Aunt Elsie asked when Shelley returned to the lounge.

Sure that she'd misheard, Shelley pushed the baby-blue towel covering her wet hair away from her ears and walked closer to where her aunt sat on the sofa. "Am I what?"

"Your dessert spoons are all bent." Elsie waved her index finger at Shelley. "Really, at your age, you should know better." She laughed.

In the kitchen, Shelley left the cold tap running while she checked her cutlery drawer. There were no dessert spoons – the single, essential piece of cutlery for an intravenous addict. She lifted the lid on the bin and there they were. Her silver spoons now joined the cold bank and the other rejects from the freezer, topped with several soaking teabags.

Shelley carried a glass of water into the lounge and sat next to her aunt on the couch. Inside she felt like a furnace. She needed a hit. As she fantasised about the fix, she suddenly remembered Jay was on his way, as he had been since she called him yesterday. Now that it was midday, he would most likely be awake, though when he'd turn up, it was impossible to know.

"I'm really tired. Do you mind if I go to sleep?" Shelley faked a yawn and stretched out her aching arms. *I am tired. I will be asleep, in a way.*

"You have a nap, and I'll have it all tidy in here for you when you wake up." Elsie smiled. "Then we can go for a walk and get you some lunch. You really should get some fresh air."

"I'll be fine on my own. You go and enjoy your day." As Shelley stood up from the sofa, she knocked off a velvet cushion and exposed a bloody syringe. "How come you're not at work?" she asked in an effort to distract her aunt while she grabbed the cushion from the floor and replaced it over the needle.

"There was a fire at the school. Didn't Mum tell you? They're saying it was arson. You should see the mess. We're meant to be off for a week, but I can't see how they'll have it ready by then. At least I'll be around for a few days to look after you."

There was no chance for Shelley to have a hit in her aunt's presence. Moreover, she worried what her aunt might find if she persisted with the tidying, how she would deal with Jay's arrival if he came and how she'd retrieve his money from the bin. Staying in the flat was no longer an option.

"It's a lovely May day. Let's go for a walk now, then I can have my sleep after," Shelley said enthusiastically. "You don't need to hang around here. You should be enjoying your time off." She picked up her handbag, this time being careful not to move the cushion when she stood up.

"I don't have to go to Mum's today." Elsie picked up her fuchsia anorak from the back of the dining chair. "You need looking after too."

"No. You should see Mum. Don't let me stop you." Shelley wiped the sweat from her forehead with the back of her hand. She was dying to roll up the long sleeves of her red blouse, but she couldn't expose the war zone on her arms.

"If you eat something, I'd feel better about leaving. I'll treat us to lunch at The Coffee Cup," Elsie said.

Shelley agreed. If her aunt saw her eat, she'd be more likely to leave – and while she was in the restaurant, she could sneak to the ladies' room and call Jay with her request that he delay the delivery.

22. Shutting Down

Shelley tried to ignore the painful feeling of her face and hands chapping in the wind. For early May, the weather had been mild but in the depths of the graveyard, she felt the cold. She sat on a grey bench a few feet away from Nicole who stood at her mother's grave.

By the time Shelley stood up to leave, her body was stiff. Every bone felt like it had been replaced with ice. She struggled as she threaded her frozen arm through Nicole's.

"Does this cemetery have a Resident Lurker?" Shelley asked as they followed the twisted paths that crisscrossed between the gravestones.

"What's that when it's at home?"

"When it's in the cemetery, you mean." Shelley smiled. "There's a creep I keep seeing when I go to see Will."

"Like a flasher?" Nicole asked.

"No, otherwise he'd be a Resident Flasher and this one doesn't flash. He only does lurking."

"Maybe you just haven't seen him."

"No, he couldn't. He wears a shell suit. You need a raincoat to flash, otherwise how do you get it out?" Shelley shivered, and she didn't think it was purely due to the cold air. For warmth, she drew Nicole closer, pulling tighter on the link of their arms. "He stares at me, like he's looking through me. He really creeps me out... I don't know why I'm making a joke out of this."

Nicole steered them onto the main path that led back to the car park where she'd left her Chimaera. "You were trying to cheer me up... and it's a coping mechanism."

"I was trying to give you a coping mechanism? How very generous of me." Shelley grinned.

"No. Well, actually, yes, but that's not what I meant." Nicole tucked a few rogue strands of blonde hair back underneath her black beret. "It's your coping mechanism."

"Crack is for coping." *Thank fuck I didn't say junk.*

"Crack's what happens when your coping mechanisms internally stop working. You look for others, externally. But then they stop working too, and that's when you're really fucked."

117

"That's me," Shelley said, half joking. She pulled out the box of Benson and Hedges from her handbag. "You're talking very textbook. Is this what you're doing with Doctor Fielding?"

Nicole nodded. "I've got inappropriate coping mechanisms."

"Is that what she told you?" Shelley stopped to light her cigarette by a gravestone so worn by the elements the lettering was illegible scribbles, and so overgrown that it looked like it hadn't been tended to once during the twentieth century. "That's not very nice of her to say that."

"She's being honest, that's her job. Some are choices I made – crack, working, sex, food, spending – what I do to myself. But what's happened to my mind, shutting down, I didn't choose that."

"It's a learned response to past experience. I remember she used to say that. But I think it's a good thing. It's like your mind's got its own way of protecting itself." Shelley held her purple Clipper under Nicole's cigarette.

With her cigarette lit, Nicole carried on walking. Shelley tucked her lighter into the front pocket of her handbag and tottered along the path behind her friend. Once she caught up, she slipped her arm through Nicole's and slowed down their pace.

"I hardly remember anything nowadays and what I do... it's just snippets, unfinished," Nicole said.

"There's not much that happens that I wanna remember."

"I wanna remember normal things, like what I did last week." Nicole took a deep breath. "For some people, some things might be too painful to remember, but it's not helpful when it happens on everything. Sometimes I don't even feel like I'm in my own body."

"I like being absent, dissociated enough that I can't feel. Automatic protection in advance, just in case it's needed."

"I don't wanna be a machine. I'm a human being." Nicole untangled her arm from Shelley's. She stamped her cigarette into the ground and shoved her hands into the pockets of her red coat. Without Shelley slowing her down, Nicole returned to taking her standard long strides and Shelley couldn't maintain their walking in sync. To keep up, she had to jog.

"It's like I get told a white lie to protect my feelings." Nicole stopped by the black obelisk, the memorial for the Katyn Forest massacre. "Actually, it's not. I don't even get a lie. I just don't get the truth. And it doesn't protect my feelings 'cos I still get them anyway, the fucked up emotions, and they're fucking up my mind, only with less information."

Nicole's eyes were shining. Shelley took a tissue from her handbag and passed it to her. As Nicole wiped her eyes, Shelley read the sorrow the vandals had graffitied on her friend's face.

"The fear, the anger, the dread, the pain, I've got it all," Nicole said, her hands now out of her pockets: one holding the white tissue, both gesturing in the air, "but I don't know all the facts. It's like my mind rejected them, or stored them in my subconscious because it would've been too shocking to know, to really know, to fully remember everything."

"Some things are best left unknown," Shelley told her.

***

The plan was to drive from the cemetery in Gunnersbury to Tara's in Earl's Court, so they could work on what they had in store for the rapist. To Shelley, it didn't feel right to be doing it on a day when Nicole was clearly distraught. Shelley tried to talk her round.

"He could be out raping other girls. We can't just leave him to it," Nicole said.

Having strapped on her seatbelt, Shelley took out one of the pre-rolled joints from her cigarette box. She lit up as they were driving out the cemetery. She hoped the dope would satisfy her enough that she wouldn't end up on the pipe. After the conversation in the cemetery with Nicole, her heart wasn't in the meeting. Even more so, because it was at Tara's where they always ended up on the pipe. Although she wanted a hit, she didn't want it to be crack, not on its own without heroin and a needle. Shelley was adamant that today there would be no crack at Tara's.

"My dad's been in touch," Nicole said, as they zoomed down Chiswick High Road. Nicole explained that she'd received a letter from him before the trial, but had only just decided to reply. Shelley was upset that Nicole hadn't confided in her sooner, but then – like Shelley – Nicole never spoke of her absent father. They'd only ever had one conversation on the subject and that had taken place in 1995 – the year after Shelley started working and had met Nicole.

"Do you want to see him?" Shelley asked.

"I don't know. I'll speak to the others first. I don't want anyone upset." Nicole took a deep drag on the joint Shelley passed her.

Unlike Shelley, Nicole knew her father. Though he had abandoned her too, he was present for the first few years of her life. He'd left Nicole's mother for another woman when Nicole was young. Shelley couldn't recall the exact age, maybe six or seven. She'd told Shelley that from the day he left, he'd never come back to see her or her younger brother and sisters. He'd had a new family. He'd remarried and had more children. So she had more than her three siblings but she didn't know the names of the others, their ages, if they were boys or girls, or how many of them there were. Shelley wondered if Nicole would be able to forgive her father. Nicole's mother had blamed him for her alcoholism, which is what sent her to an early grave. Briefly, Shelley asked herself the same question, but it was a waste of time.

***

On a side street off the Cromwell Road, Shelley and Nicole stood waiting outside Tara's building. Was her intercom really broken or was there someone she was avoiding? Again, Tara didn't answer.

Eventually, she buzzed them in after Nicole phoned from her mobile. Walking up the stairs, Shelley recalled the state of Tara last time she'd seen her. On entering the airless flat, Shelley noted there was no improvement today. Her dirty clothes consisted of a well-worn, grey tracksuit top and baggy sweatpants. In her imagination, Shelley added an orange bib and pictured her friend in prison.

As soon as their feet were on the dirty carpet in the cramped hall, Tara asked them to buy some crack. Surprising herself, Shelley declined. She'd planned not to take crack – but usually her plans not to failed. Her fix in the morning to stave off the sickness must've given her willpower a boost – though her mood could have still benefited from some tweaking.

Not happy with Shelley's answer, Tara tried to sway Nicole. But Nicole stood her ground. "We need to keep our heads clear," she told Tara.

Nicole led the way into the lounge and took her usual spot on the navy sofa. Tara sat on her armchair and Shelley stood awkwardly by the door. She was thirsty but she didn't want to drink from a vessel kept in the filth-pit that was Tara's flat.

"Can I wash my hands in your kitchen?" Shelley asked.

"If you like, or use the bathroom," Tara replied.

Shelley turned back into the lounge. Something was different. Tara no longer had a television. Shelley felt pity for Tara as she walked through to the kitchen. Tara had most likely sold her television for crack.

With the tap turned on, Shelley carefully leant over the pile of pots and crockery in the sink and drank from the flowing water.

"I'll get you a glass."

Shelley flinched. Her chin narrowly missed the faucet. She hadn't realised Tara had come into the kitchen. Tara took a glass from the cupboard and passed it to Shelley. Before filling the glass with water, Shelley rinsed it a few times under the hot tap.

When Shelley walked back through to the lounge, she took her place in her usual seat, next to Nicole on the sofa. In front of them was the glass coffee table – Crack Island – on which they usually prepared their pipes. Shelley had that feeling she was missing something, or had forgotten something. She guessed it was the crack.

For a second time, Tara asked if they'd join her in buying a rock, and Shelley expected that she too had the same 'missing' feeling. Following the second rebuff, Tara stormed out of the lounge, leaving Nicole and Shelley alone.

After a while, Tara returned. Her eyes were slightly bloodshot and not quite looking in the same direction. "Oh my God, Shelley, you've changed your hair!"

"Resident Unobservant, surely it hasn't taken you this long to notice?" Nicole said.

"Your mind's on a pipe, isn't it?" Shelley pulled a cigarette from her twenty-pack and held it out to Tara.

"Fuck you." Tara's nose screwed up as her face contorted and reddened. "I was about to say you looked really nice but I won't bother now."

"Calm down, love. She didn't mean it."

"No, I did mean it." Shelley put the cigarette she'd earmarked for Tara in her own mouth and lit it. "You've got a problem. You sold your laptop and now your TV's gone. What's gonna be next?"

"My TV's getting fixed at the shop. Anyway, it's not your fucking business."

"I'm gonna make a cuppa." Nicole stood up. "When I get back, I want you ladies on your best behaviour." Nicole smiled at Tara as she walked out of the lounge, and from the hall, she shot a wink in Shelley's direction.

Guilt and anger tussled to find their order in Shelley's head. She was angry with Tara for her outburst and also cross with herself. Her honesty she knew could be brutal. And when it was directed at someone for whom she cared, she tended to feel guilty. That she hadn't mentioned Tara's son and the reason he didn't live with her was some consolation. Though she'd thought it, thankfully, she hadn't converted the thought into spoken words. Reflecting on her intention, she knew it wasn't to hurt Tara's feelings. She had wanted to make her see that she couldn't go on as she was.

"I'm sorry I upset you, Tara. I didn't mean to," Shelley said.

"I'm sorry too. I haven't had a pipe today and I'm climbing the walls."

Shelley was stumped for what to say. She didn't want to get into another argument but she was quite sure Tara had taken a pipe since they'd been in her flat. She wanted one herself, but she couldn't let Nicole down and get high with Tara, not today. Perhaps Tara had taken something else in place of crack that had a similar effect on her eyes. In case she was strung out, Shelley took a fifty-pound note from her purse and pressed it into Tara's palm.

"Thank you," Tara said. Her face crumpled as if she was about to cry, but she didn't. Her head rocked a little, and her slight smile looked forced.

When Nicole came back through with the tea, Shelley examined her mug closely. It didn't look clean, but she decided it appeared more coffee-stained than dirty, so she took a chance and drank from it.

"Let's get started," Nicole said. With a writing pad on her lap and a pen in her hand, she looked as if she was responsible for taking the minutes.

"You can't take notes, Nic," Shelley said. "You're making evidence."

"I'm trying to be organised, in case I forget anything."

"Like an organised criminal?" Tara sniggered.

Nicole turned her back on Tara and spoke to Shelley. "I know we've gotta be mindful of the police, but whatever's going on with sick bitch or not, we can't stall any more."

"I think we should wait, let things cool down a bit," Tara said.

"Another girl could be being raped right now for all we know. I can't live with that," Nicole said forcefully.

Tara stood up from her armchair and walked out of the lounge.

Nicole shook her head and looked up to the ceiling before returning her attention to Shelley.

"I'll call Angel from the car," Shelley said.

"Thanks, love. Shall we go back the North Circ way, then we can check out those empty houses?"

"No. There's too many squatters," Shelley said. "I think I can sort something else."

On the way downstairs, Shelley reflected what a waste of time it had been having their meeting at Tara's when she'd been absent for most of the conversation. As she reached the front door of the building, she imagined Tara telling Marianne about the change in her appearance. She clambered back up the stairs.

When Tara finally responded to her knocking, Shelley reminded her of the holiday Marianne thought she was on, and that she shouldn't share her new phone number. Casually, Shelley added, "And don't mention my new hair."

"Your cut and colour is safe with me," Tara said, breathing vodka over Shelley.

23. The Message

Shelley was feeling weak and craving her next fix, but she was unable to go straight home. On the drive back from Tara's, she'd been talked into eating dinner at Nicole's. Not being able to lie meant she couldn't excuse her urgency to leave. If she couldn't lie about that, she worried how she'd ever cover her tracks wearing long sleeves in the summer.

Nicole handed her a cup of coffee and sat down next to her on the black leather sofa. "What I told you before, it's happened with my Mum as well," Nicole said. "I know she's dead, but I'm not processing it."

"That's normal, there's a grieving process. Everyone goes through it." Shelley tried to sip her coffee but it was too hot and burnt her tongue.

"There is, but I'm not allowing myself to grieve properly. I'm running away, escaping through punters, getting stoned, smoking crack."

"We haven't done crack today." Shelley rubbed her tongue on the roof of her mouth in the hope it would ease the pain.

"It's stopped working, Shell. I don't even— None of my crutches work any more. I'm falling and they're not keeping me up. If anything, they're pushing me down." Nicole lit a cigarette and took a deep pull. "I want it to feel different. I want to be able to move on, make Mum proud of me, do a better job with helping the family. I'm not— I'm not doing life. Not how I want to be."

"Time heals, Nic. It'll be okay."

"Time... right, that hasn't healed you either, has it?"

"No, not yet, but maybe it will." Shelley felt the onset of tears. Nicole sounded angry, but it wasn't with her, she told herself. "I know Will's watching me, and your mum will be watching over you."

"If she is, I don't want her seeing me living like this and I'm sure Will wouldn't want to see your life wasted."

"Like he wasted his," Shelley muttered as Nicole headed to the other side of the room.

Shelley fought the envy emerging inside her as she listened to the never-ending stream of messages play out from Nicole's answer

123

phone. Far more people cared about Nicole than her. Lying back on the sofa, Shelley tried to resist her eyelids closing as the tranquil voices of Nicole's family (her brother, Enda; her sisters, Milly and Susie; two aunts) and her friends (Shelley had lost count of how many) washed over her.

The sudden rant booming from the machine shocked Shelley out of her near-hypnotised state. From her horizontal position on the sofa, she sat upright. Her eyes were now open wide.

"What the fuck's that about?" Nicole stomped back into the room and replayed the message. Perhaps she couldn't believe it either. "Why's she blaming me? I wasn't even there."

"You were. It was the day you got back from Mustique."

Still as a picture, Nicole stood by the answer phone.

"It's not your fault, Nic. She's off her head. She's probably been on the crack since we left, sold something else and now she's looking for someone to blame." Shelley felt guilty; Tara had probably started off with the fifty she'd given her.

"Why me? It doesn't make sense. I've only ever been nice to that girl." Nicole hovered by the sofa. She looked as though she was about to sit down next to Shelley but, after bending her knees, she straightened back up then walked over to the dining table. She picked up her keys and threw her red coat over her shoulders.

"Where are you going?"

"I'm gonna put that bitch right. I'm not having her treat me like this."

Shelley persuaded Nicole it was best left until Tara had sobered up, that it wouldn't be possible to reason with her given the unstable state she was in.

Angel had been right. Tara was a weak link, a liability - not only for what had been discussed earlier in the day, but also for the secrets Shelley was trying to hide from Marianne.

***

To avoid running dry, Shelley had called Jay on her way home from Nicole's. Surprisingly, he'd arrived at her flat before she'd made it back herself – and he'd sounded annoyed on the phone when he'd called asking why she wasn't there. The turning of the tables was unintentional and she hoped this wouldn't result in his return to tardiness.

Had she not spent half an hour in the twenty-four hour store at Hendon Central, she would have been there by now. The man in the shop had been amiable and didn't seem to mind her reading the papers. He may have been under the impression her interest lay in politics; the newspapers were still focused on the new Labour government. But their landslide win in the election a few days earlier, and the independence they'd given the Bank of England, was neither of interest nor relevance to Shelley.

As she pulled up in Willoughby Road, she caught sight of Jay leaning against the wall of another split, Victorian house a couple of doors down from the one she lived in. With him watching her, she couldn't carry out her usual leaving-the-car ritual. She'd have to rely on the central locking working, her eyes seeing the door locks depressing and her ears hearing it happen. The boot was on its own.

She did it, and although she felt uncomfortable, her anxiety waned after a director in her head told her she could go out and do it properly once Jay left.

The dour expression on Jay's face became obvious as she rushed towards her flat. She made rolling-wave motions with her arm and he walked up the road.

"Sorry I'm late. I didn't think you'd get here so soon."

"Don't let it happen again." He cracked a smile and closed Shelley's front door behind him.

Standing in the shadows of the communal hall, their deal didn't have much light. Both bulbs in the hall had blown and none of the residents had replaced them. Their only illumination was a yellow glow from a streetlight shining through the stained glass panel in the front door.

"How's Ali?" Shelley asked, as she counted the cash from her purse that had already been organised into groups of one hundred pounds when it was originally folded.

"He's doing all right. They've moved him to the Isle of Sheppey. He's teaching himself to play the drums. He says it's like a holiday camp compared to Brixton."

"That sounds good." Shelley slipped the money into Jay's hand.

Jay delved inside the front of his jeans and from somewhere near his bulging crotch, he pulled out a drawstring pouch. "I can't find your man in Ladbroke Grove. I've been round that yard nuff times but no one's ever in and there ain't nothing to rob – it's like a squat in there." He took two clingfilm wrapped parcels and slid them into Shelley's palm. "I'm back again tonight. I'll see what I can do."

Shelley pushed the parcels into the front pocket of her jeans. "I think there's another way I wanna sort this, but thanks for what you've done. I really appreciate it."

"That money's heading for my pocket anyway, love."

If her using carried on at the same pace, every fifty from the freezer would be heading that same way too.

Through her weakness, she ran up the stairs, which were unlit until the first landing. She didn't return to her car. She was being pulled in that direction, but the pull to have a fix was more potent.

After closing the door to her flat, she checked it was locked eight times – forty counts. The rhythm of pushing down on the handle while counting aloud in time to the tapping engrossed her. Three of her senses were involved – sight, hearing and touch – and they nourished the sixth. The pull to her car faded. In her stomach, neck and shoulders, she could feel the tension ebbing away.

Sitting on her usual spot on the sofa, she cooked up the first shot. Only heroin for the first because she still had to call Len. An early night was required as well, so somehow she'd have to take the control away from her drugs and not stay up partying for hours. Her commitment to support Nicole at Tara's the following day was something she couldn't shirk. The confrontation that she anticipated would be awkward. She was furious with Tara and committed to defending Nicole, but she'd have to curb her anger. If she didn't restrain what came out of her own mouth, then Tara would be less likely to restrain what came out of hers in Marianne's company.

24. The Revelation

"Thanks for picking me up," Shelley said, stepping into Nicole's Chimaera.

"You look as tired as I feel." Nicole gave her a slight smile. "I couldn't sleep thinking about what she said. I don't know how I've managed not to call her."

"You haven't though, have you?" Shelley could hear the concern in her own voice. They'd agreed nothing should be said until they got into her flat. If Tara knew Nicole had already listened to the message, it would be obvious that Shelley would know about it and then most likely Tara wouldn't let her in.

Shelley was exhausted. The weakness bestowed by a junk habit partly caused her tiredness but it was also due to the call that had disrupted her sleep at seven o'clock in the morning, only two hours after she'd put herself to bed. Resident Dicks All the Boxes had wanted to see her for a full day booking. She'd had to ask for a rain check due to her prior obligation to Nicole and, as it was Friday, she was due at her mother's maisonette some time before dusk. The money she could have earned would have had a nominal impact on increasing her ever-decreasing savings in the cold bank – the Black Forest gateau box that had cleaned up beautifully after she rescued it from the bin at the beginning of the week. Nevertheless, the extra cash would have been enough, perhaps, for a week's supply of heroin and crack, and looking at it from that angle, it was substantial for a day's work.

As they passed through Kensington, Shelley became aware that Nicole's rage was intensifying. Not only was her once soft and lyrical voice now loud and brash, but her predisposition as a fast driver had crossed the line into dangerous. When Nicole swerved off the Cromwell Road, Shelley had to grip the central console to stop the force pulling her upper body into the door.

"Take it easy, Nic," Shelley said, as they parked up. "I know you're angry, but if we say too much, she might grass on us."

"That tart needs to apologise, and I'm not gonna stop until she does." Nicole's face was reddening and Shelley admired the vein in her neck as it throbbed. It would have been a great vein to shoot in if it didn't lead to a stroke or paralysis. "Are you listening to me?

Snap out of it."

"Sorry, I thought there was a spider on your collar," Shelley replied, trying to take her eyes off the vein but, of their own volition, they kept returning.

"Argh! Get it off. Get it off." Nicole grabbed at her blouse and shook it as she jerked her body in an effort to dislodge the spider. "Where is it? Has it gone? Can you see it?"

"I can't see it now. It must have gone." *That wasn't a lie; I can't see it now.* Engrossed in her vein fixation, she'd forgotten Nicole's arachnophobia. She could feel a guilty blush in the warmth of her cheeks. There could be no escaping that first statement was a lie.

***

Tara's lack of response to the intercom was no shock to Shelley. What was, however, was the immediate buzz in that followed the brief call she made to announce her arrival. Naturally, she hadn't mentioned Nicole was accompanying her, but she had still expected an interrogation of sorts.

Nicole tiptoed up the wooden staircase, as advised by Shelley who was skilled at listening for footsteps and knew how loud the reverberations were from Tara's flat. Shelley motioned towards the corner, near Tara's front door. Nicole hid, and within seconds, Tara was at her door.

"Do you want to get a rock?" Tara asked.

"Not today." Shelley followed Tara down the first section of the L-shaped hall. She could feel the heat from Nicole's body behind her. The door slammed and Shelley flinched. Tara didn't seem to notice. She didn't even turn around. Perhaps she thought Shelley was responsible.

Nicole rushed past Shelley, causing her to teeter. Her legs knocked into a low table at the corner bend. As Shelley tried to regain her balance, Nicole grabbed hold of Tara and rammed her up against the wall in the hallway.

"If you've got something to say, say it to my face you evil—"

"What the fuck are you doing? Put me down you mad bitch."

"You're fucking mad." Nicole shook Tara's shoulders, causing her head to pound on the wall. "Why the fuck did you leave that message? I want a fucking explanation. Now."

"Stop. You're hurting me."

"You've fucking hurt me, more than you'll ever know." Tears were falling down Nicole's cheeks, but her grip on Tara remained, as did the hammering of her head against the wall.

"What the fuck is wrong with you?" Tara cried.

Nicole threw Tara down on the floor and stood towering above her. "You've fucking lost it, you stupid fucking crackhead. I'm done with you." Nicole turned and walked toward the front door. Her face was a picture of sadness. Shelley had never seen Nicole so enraged. She imagined her sympathy for Tara had been diminished due to the poor timing of Tara's accusations. And Shelley knew that as well as the pain Tara had caused with her verbal assault, Nicole would feel guilt for her own physical assault.

"Hold on, Nic... Wait." Shelley reached for Tara's hand and helped her off the sullied carpet. "Get in the lounge," she told her.

Once Tara had vacated the hall, Shelley put her arms around Nicole and hugged her. She brushed Nicole's blonde locks out the way and in her ear, she said, "I know what she's done is terrible and there's no excuse, but we need to sort this. We can't afford to leave it this fucked up."

"I've got nothing to say to that crackhead tart."

"She might have something to say, an—"

"There's nothing she can say. I'll never forgive her for this."

"Well at least get an apology."

"I don't care any more. It's not gonna change anything. Nothing will change how I feel about her. Nothing."

"Wait for me here. We can't leave it like this." Shelley walked through the hall and into the lounge. The fight or flight feeling was on her. Her breath was short and she felt her ribcage vibrate with the force of her beating heart.

What Shelley wanted to say she knew she could not. She wondered if with a soft tone the same words would be any less cutting. This was a time she did not want to hold back.

Tara sat in the armchair and looked up at Shelley. "I didn't—"

"You need to shut the fuck up and listen."

Tara snivelled.

"Yesterday, as you fucking well know, Nic went to her mum's grave. Then we came here and we were talking about one of the most horrific experiences she's gone through, bar the fucking court case she's just had to testify in and talk about the sadistic cunts that molested her.

"You can stop your fucking whimpering, it's her that's upset. She had nothing to do with you selling your fucking laptop for crack. You did it 'cos you're a fucking crackhead, and until yesterday, I felt sorry for you but now I can see you're just some spoilt cunt that hits out when she can't get her own way." Shelley's heart was still thumping, but her anger had been laced with a sliver of pity; Tara was a wreck.

"You don't know what my life's been like. You don't know what

I've gone through. I've—"

"Remember we've seen how you lived, your lovely house, your family, your fucking horses. If I'd had your life, I wouldn't be in the fucking state you are."

"'Cos I lived in a nice house that makes it all right does it?" Tara's nostrils flared as she looked up. "It was a private school, well that's all right 'cos I had a smart fucking uniform, a nice dormitory and it was fucking paid for by my parents." Tara howled as if she'd just been notified of a loved-one's death.

Shelley swallowed back her tears. She squeezed in on the armchair next to Tara and held her tightly. She felt as if she might snap – the wisp that Tara had become.

"I'm so sorry, love. I had no idea." Nicole stood above them, her hand outstretched to Tara.

Tara clasped Nicole's hand in hers and pulled her onto the overcrowded chair. "It's my fault," Tara said. "I don't talk about anything, nothing that matters."

25. Estate Agency Business

Emotionally exhausted, Shelley slept until a nightmare woke her late afternoon. Swaddled in her favourite duvet, she shuffled along the cold, black and white floor tiles in the kitchen. She poured a glass of water and took it through to the lounge. She landed herself on the sofa, then picked up one of her new, sparkling dessert spoons and began cooking up her fix.

What she'd heard from Tara yesterday shocked her. Not that another call girl would have a past like that, most of the hookers she knew did. The shock was that Tara knew what she had gone through as a child, yet hadn't confided in her. Was it her fault Tara had never been able to tell her? Possibly not – Tara hadn't told Nicole either. But Shelley knew she could have been a better friend. There were things she could have done differently, things she could have said differently, and things she could have not said at all. She remembered the cruel words she'd spoken the day before.

Guilt grew from her gut and permeated her body. Her breathing shallowed. This had to be a big hit. It would take more heroin and crack than usual to change this feeling. This feeling on top of her grief, her anger, and her fears had done more than add to them. It felt as if they'd all been amplified. The noise had to be muted.

The speedball she'd prepared was overgenerous but essential. She needed to get to nirvana. Without a tourniquet, she squeezed her wrist and went straight for a visible vein in her hand.

She fell back on the sofa and thought this time she might die. This was overdose territory. She lost control of her body as she convulsed. She tried to scream for help but no words came, not recognisable words. She could hear herself babbling but couldn't tell if she was making those sounds or if they were coming from inside her head.

When she came to, it was nine o'clock in the evening. She wasn't sure what time she'd taken the hit but it had been light outside, she remembered that. Cautiously, she prepared another, this time using what remained in the filter from the near-lethal shot from which she'd only just recovered.

What had been left provided an explosive high. She wondered

131

how she'd survived the earlier hit. Though Shelley knew she was dicing with her life, she didn't want to die. That wasn't an absolute truth. She did want to die. She wanted it all to be over, but she didn't want to leave her mother without any children alive. So, although inside when the pain became too much, she fantasised about taking her own life, suicide was not an option.

Once she was able to walk, she went through to the kitchen to make herself a cup of tea. Instead of her usual two sugars, she added honey to soothe her sandpaper throat. Her stirring was disturbed by her ringing mobile. Returning to the lounge, she hoped it was Resident Dicks All the Boxes who yesterday she'd postponed.

"Shelley?" a man said. Confirmation it wasn't a client.

"Who are you?"

"It's me, Len. I only just picked up your message. I've got that thing I owe you. Only a little but I'll get the rest soon, I promise."

"I don't need it any more." Shelley took the phone into the kitchen. "There's something else I want instead."

"Nah, no can do. Sorry, love, but I've got a girlfriend. I can't—"

"Not that, for God's sake." Shelley scooped out the teabag and dropped it in the sink. "I can't talk on the phone. You need to come here."

"I ain't got a car."

"Well get a fucking bus. You owe me big time." Shelley returned to the lounge with her honeyed tea. With her mobile nestled between her shoulder and her ear, she gave Len her address while preparing a fix.

Putting the mobile down on the coffee table, she looked at what remained from her stockpile of drugs. It was plain to see the stash was depleting just as rapidly as her savings that were being spent maintaining it. With her income reduced by the mess she made with the needle, she knew something had to change. Either her using would need to reduce, or she'd end up working the streets. The dilemma was beyond deliberation. She found both equally unpalatable.

***

The buzzer woke Shelley at three o'clock on Sunday afternoon. Still dressed in yesterday's clothes, she untangled herself from the duvet. She staggered to the intercom and on hearing Len's voice, she pressed the buzzer to open the main entrance.

Before he arrived at her door, she scuttled into the bathroom. She appraised her appearance in the mirror. There'd been no reason to adorn her face with make-up yesterday, so she didn't have panda eyes to tackle. Because she didn't have the time to brush her teeth, she smeared on toothpaste using her finger. She swallowed down the surplus and gagged as it stuck in her throat that had been delivering an odour as foul tasting into her mouth, and felt as dry, as she suspected Marianne's retired, fallow fanny would.

"So you came then?" she said, tripping over her stray boots in the hall.

"Said I would, didn't I?"

"That was yesterday." Shelley stumbled backwards from the door and into the lounge.

"It was the middle of the night, love." Len pulled out a chair and sat down at the circular dining table.

"Do you want a cup of tea?" Shelley felt a shooting pain in her temple. Her legs wobbled and she held onto the chair to keep herself erect.

"I'll do the tea," he said. "What's up with you? You look awful."

"I just get a bit dizzy sometimes." Shelley smiled, still bent over the back of the chair. "I probably need a hit."

"That usually does the trick." His thin lips widened. Shelley noticed that he'd sacked the beard that had been masquerading as designer stubble. His eyes were a racing-car green and he was handsome, unconventionally. The greasiness was gone from his mousy hair, which today looked soft and with his jacket on, he looked like he had a good build, although Shelley knew he didn't.

***

While she was making her fix in the lounge, she watched him from behind as he made the tea in the kitchen. She didn't think he could be deemed in breach of the Trade Descriptions Act – his face would have been a fair defence.

"How do you know I take two sugars?" Shelley asked as she sipped her perfectly sweetened tea.

"I know, love. We all do. Something to do with the gear." He sat down next to her on the sofa. He took a long, black wallet from a pocket in his leather jacket and opened the zip. Inside the wallet were his works, all neatly stored under elasticated hoops. "I took a spoon out your kitchen. Hope you don't mind."

"You can share mine. There's always shitloads left in my filters."

"Nah, love, I can't. No offence, but I dunno what you've got."

"What are you trying to say?" *Does he know I'm a hooker?*

"Nothing bad. I didn't mean to upset you," he said. "It's not only you. I've got Hep C and I don't wanna give it to you."

"I'm not gonna get it. We're not having sex."

"Back up. Back up," Len said, bowing with his hands. "I mean catch it off the spoon."

Shelley looked at him nonplussed.

"Don't you know you can catch stuff sharing spoons?" His voice became quieter. "My mate's dying of AIDS. I've been lucky to get away with Hep C." He added heroin and citric and then the water before lighting the underside of the spoon.

Shelley considered the number of spoons she'd shared over the past three years. "I haven't got anything. I know I haven't. I get tested all the time," she said defensively, remembering she needed to get her throat seen to. Then she realised admitting to being regularly tested might lead him to a conclusion she didn't want him to reach.

Len took the belt off his jeans. He wrapped the leather strap around his bicep then put one end between his teeth. While he was tapping for a vein in an area Shelley deemed too high up his arm, she couldn't find a viable vein on her own. They were either concealed by lumps or had collapsed. She looked at her hands instead. Where was the map of blue veins?

"Your arms are a right mess. You need to be careful those lumps don't turn into abscesses."

"That's never happened. It's just a pain. I can't see what I'm doing with double vision," she said. It hit her that as she was not speedballing alone, someone else would see her drug-induced cross-eyes.

"Come 'ere." Len removed the belt from his teeth. It unravelled around his arm before falling to the floor. He took Shelley's hand on his lap, and with his 'L-U-C-K' and 'F-A-T-E' fingers, he examined her arm.

"You need to give that one a rest, make sure it don't get infected." He switched arms and repeated the process. Tapping on a vein, he said, "I can get this one for you. Do you want me to do it?"

"Please, yeah," Shelley replied.

He took the belt and wound it around her arm, halfway between her wrist and her elbow. Then he took her syringe and expertly administered her fix.

"Thank you," she croaked, lying back on the sofa. Her eyelids half-closed and she felt every part of her body hum – internally and externally. It felt as though the nastiness she housed was being buzzed out of her. She knew what she had put in was nasty too, but it was a different form and one she had invited.

From the corner of her eye, she could see Len back in his position with the belt around his upper arm. He pierced his skin with the needle and then he was lying back on the couch with her.

For a while, there was silence but Shelley didn't feel it was awkward. Even if she had, she couldn't have filled it, not with words.

"Do you want some crack in there?" Shelley asked as they took their second cup of tea, which again had been made by Len.

"Don't take this the wrong way, love, but why are you being so nice? You don't even know me and I owe you a monkey?"

"I need to ask you a little favour, that's all." Shelley took her empty syringe, drew up some water from the tumbler on the coffee table and dropped it onto her spoon. "So are you having some crack or not?"

"If the lady doth insist." He grinned and scratched his hairless chin. "So, how come you got all this dosh then? You got a sugar daddy or did you marry some rich cunt?"

"I've got a good job. That's what I want to talk to you about actually." Shelley removed a rock from the cluster on the clingfilm and deposited it on his side of the table. "I run an estate agency and I'm trying to close this deal, but the couple want to see more houses in the area before making an offer on the house I'm trying to sell them. I need to show them some properties so they can see what the market has to offer in their price range."

"Lardy dardy, hark at you," Len said, looking at the spoon in which he was pulverising the crack with his plunger.

"I'd like to show them yours." Shelley smiled at him, using her eyes as well as her mouth because she knew that came across as more authentic.

"That's not a little favour. I'm not selling my gaff?"

"I'm not gonna sell it. I'm just gonna show it," Shelley replied, trying to hide her irritation behind a reassuring tone.

26. The Meet

After an early evening visit to her aunt, Shelley returned to her car. She drove father along Queens Grove then onto Queens Terrace. Parking up a few yards past a low block of flats, she prepared a shot.

Having transferred the junk into her body via a vein on her wrist, she sat back in the driver's seat and closed her eyes. *This is too much responsibility.* Trying to look after herself was hard enough, but she had her mother to take care of, Aunt Elsie to check up on, and now she had to stop a serial rapist.

Cramming this much into one day was draining. She preferred leaving her flat as seldom as possible, so in order to spend the weekend at home, she'd arranged all of her plans for today – Monday. But she knew this couldn't go on. There was so much to put in place this week. She'd need to be out another two or three times at least. The crack would have to be reduced, or cut out, or she'd never make it.

In her weakened state, she feared toppling her wall of lies. Keeping track of the various stories she told was hard, problematic when drugs were added, and at its most complex when drugs were combined with her two lives on the same day.

Perhaps it appeared even more challenging because she'd been disheartened on seeing her mother on Friday. When she'd arrived at the maisonette around lunchtime, the curtains were drawn and her mother was still in bed. She was despondent every time Shelley tried to engage her in conversation. She ate little of the toasted sandwich Shelley made for her and watching her favourite film – *It's a Wonderful Life* – didn't yield the smile it usually did. The progress Rita had been making evaporated, and it had happened so suddenly, like a death, as if Shelley had dreamt it. Now everything had returned as it was before, possibly worse.

When she'd left her aunt's house earlier, Elsie was stressed and Shelley felt responsible. She'd told Shelley she needed more help with Rita, that with her own commitments and work, she couldn't visit more than three times a week. Shelley suggested increasing her visits, which had slipped from daily to weekly, and recently from weekly to fortnightly, but Elsie said she'd find another way, that she didn't want Shelley's life taken over by her mother. But there was no other way – Shelley knew that. And her failure as a daughter and the guilt she experienced from the storytelling of her imaginary life was gnawing at her conscience.

It was her own fault that her visits had slipped. The blame didn't lie at the door of her fictitious demanding boss at Foxtons. She was a poor excuse for a daughter. She was undeserving of the pride her aunt showed for her.

She took the syringe with a needle too blunt to use for a fix, and ran it down the inside of her arm. The blood that fountained was unexpected. Quickly, she found the rag and pressed it to her arm. How would she explain away blood seeping through her sleeve?

Stupid junky whore. Stupid junky whore. Stupid junky whore. The mantra repeated in her head. She looked at the gash on her arm.

"*You deserve it*," said one of the harsher directors on the board.

With only a miniscule amount of junk in her blood stream, her arm throbbed as she drove from St John's Wood towards Hampstead. A decent hit was unfeasible as she had yet to attend the meeting with Angel, Nicole and Tara.

Whether or not she was wise to have invited Tara concerned her. The decision had not, and could not, be made with her head. Nicole and Shelley accepted Tara had become more unstable, but she wanted to be involved. How could Shelley take that away from her? An opportunity for revenge on a man who'd raped her. Somewhere buried under the heavy rubble crushing it was Shelley's heart.

***

On her arrival at The Magdala, Shelley saw Angel sitting at the same corner table in the back. As she manoeuvred her body past the battered tables and chairs, she scanned the smoky saloon; Nicole and Tara weren't there.

"Are you incognito?" Angel whispered. She stood up and kissed Shelley on the cheek. "What's with the wig?"

"It's not. It's my hair." Shelley combed her fingers through her hair that was not a wig as if proving its authenticity.

"Sorry, babe, you just look so different." Angel smiled. The dimples in her cheeks surfaced.

While Angel stood at the bar buying Shelley's drink, Shelley took out her mobile and phoned Nicole. Nicole informed her that a punter had kept her longer than she'd anticipated but she would be there soon. Before Shelley could phone Tara, Angel had returned and handed her a pint of snakebite and blackcurrant.

"Your girls are gonna show, babe, aren't they?" Angel asked.

"Nic's on her way. Tara, I don't know." Shelley wished her

friends would hurry up so she could get home. She could feel the crusty blood cracking on her sleeve every time she moved her arm, and she was sweating from keeping on her coat.

Someone tapped her on the shoulder and she turned her head and gaped as she set her eyes on Tara. Although in three days, Tara hadn't lost the spots or put on any weight, she looked nearly beautiful again. She wore a maroon dress, her shoulder length hair looked clean and silky, and make-up covered the spots that plagued her face.

"Why can't we go to The Freemasons? It's much nicer in there," Tara said to Shelley as she bent down and kissed her on the cheek. "This has got to be the most council pub in all of Hampstead."

Shelley smiled, hiding her disapproval of Tara's snobbishness. "We need somewhere quiet," she said.

On taking Tara's order for an orange juice, Shelley went to the bar. Tara never took non-alcoholic drinks, with the exception of coffee, and the orange juice wouldn't be to do with not drinking and driving because Tara used taxis; she didn't have a car. Perhaps she was making changes. Shelley hoped she'd stay clean-smelling too. For the first time in ages, she hadn't smelt like a mountaineer after a week trekking the Whiskey route up Kilimanjaro.

As she returned to the table, Shelley caught the end of what must have been a conversation about Tara's son. It had taken Tara two years to tell Shelley about her child, and Nicole even longer, and there she was telling a stranger. Shelley plonked Tara's drink on the table then sat herself down on the cushioned bench next to Angel, opposite Tara.

"My clit's the size of a small penis," Tara announced, obviously not as sober as Shelley had thought.

"My clit is a small penis," Angel whispered. Was she always this frank?

"Not that small, from what I remember," Tara replied.

Shelley pointed at them alternately. "Have you two...?"

"Yeah, we've done jobs together." Angel nodded. "Took me a while to recognise you though. You've lost a lot of weight, babe."

"And what's with the name change? I like Destiny better." Tara sipped her orange juice. "What do you think it could be? It's itchy as hell and it's huge."

"Could be tight jeans, washing powder, could be anything. You're always safe aren't you?" Shelley spoke with some concern for Tara's clitoris, but more for her sanity and sobriety. This wasn't like her, talking uninhibitedly about personal matters.

"Of course, I'm safe."

"Get checked at the clinic just in case," Shelley told her. "I'll come with you. My throat's been feeling really rough."

"Then go to a doctor like a normal person." Tara sniggered.

"We're not normal people," Angel said.

Shelley saw Nicole standing at the door of The Magdala. She stood up and waved to get Nicole's attention. In her fitted black dress and with her hair in large curls, Nicole reminded Shelley of a taller and slimmer, but equally stunning, Marilyn Monroe. Contributing to the 1950s vision was the decor that looked like it hadn't been updated since David Blakely was shot and killed outside the pub. Forty-two years on, the bullet holes that Ruth Ellis had been blamed for still remained on the cream-tiled exterior wall.

Nicole kissed Shelley on the cheek. "My Resident Most Precious," she said. Her breath tickled in Shelley's ear. Nicole turned to the others and began to apologise for her tardiness, but Shelley took her arm and stole her away to the bar.

"There's something not right with Tara. She's being very strange," Shelley told her.

"She looks a damn sight better though, doesn't she?"

"You know what looks can be."

While they were waiting for Nicole's wine, Shelley deliberated whether she should tell Nicole about Angel's gender. She decided against it. It wasn't her secret to tell, and perhaps Tara would think the same way – if they both were fools, or great minds.

When they returned from the bar, Nicole took a seat next to Angel. Shelley reluctantly moved her pint glass across the table and sat down beside Tara.

"Is everything all right with you?" Nicole asked Tara.

"Top of the world, me." Tara released a stench of vodka as she poorly mimicked Nicole's slight Irish accent. "Apart from a cock-sized clit, I'm fucking sound."

27. Moving On

On Draycott Terrace – a road running parallel to Marianne's – Shelley sat waiting in her Mercedes. She untangled the knots in her hair with her fingers. Part in fear and part in excitement, her heart was thumping. Their ensnarement of the rapist had advanced from talk to action.

Angel had called Marianne last night, saying that she was recommended to her by a girl she'd met. She'd said it was a while ago and couldn't recall her name. As expected, Marianne pushed her, and as agreed, Angel had described a tall blonde, which covered over half of Marianne's girls.

The tap on the window caused Shelley to jump. She turned her head, saw Angel and unlocked the door.

"How did it go?" Shelley asked.

"I'm in." Angel fastened her seat belt. "She knew I wasn't twenty though, but she's put me down as twenty-two."

Shelley thought Angel looked younger with the bare make-up and casual clothes in which she'd seen her most recently. In broad daylight, with full make-up, she looked older, and her face lost some of its soft femininity. The taffeta cocktail dress she wore wasn't something Shelley would have chosen either.

Shelley worried whether Marianne would send the rapist to someone older. They'd all been twenty or under. Did he want to see all her girls or just the younger ones? Although she was concerned, she didn't want to say anything blatant in case she offended Angel. And would he only book white girls or would he also see mixed race girls? They'd have to wait to find out.

"Did she mention any regulars she's going to send you?" Shelley asked.

"Just to keep my phone on and she'll call. She was talking about you though, babe."

"What did she say?" Nervously, Shelley rubbed the diamond in her necklace.

"She asked if I knew a girl called Kiki from Belsize Park. She described you but I told her most of the girls I work with are tall and blonde."

"Thanks."

"You don't need to thank me, babe, we're in this together." Angel twirled her ponytail. "But she's pissed at you. Do you know that?"

"Did she say why?"

"She said you owe her money."

Shelley didn't owe Marianne money, unless she'd found out about any of the clients she'd stolen from her. If it was The Lanesborough, which is what Shelley feared, she'd hardly be likely to tell Angel, "I was arrested for a crime committed by Kiki." No, she wouldn't say that.

Shelley drove off headed for Tufnell Park to take Angel home. She needed a proper hit when she got back to her own flat. All this using the bare minimum to stave off withdrawal symptoms was no good for her sanity. She needed more than just maintenance.

"Don't worry about her. She can't do anything."

"Tara knows my address though." When the words passed her lips, she realised she'd spoken a thought that she didn't mean to share. She didn't want to remind Angel of her original concerns about Tara. She tried to relax her face in case the lines on her forehead had given her away.

"That girl won't grass on you. I know."

She wondered if Angel was trying to make her feel better or did she know Tara well enough to make that judgement. Shelley wanted to believe the latter. When this was all over, she might move to another part of London and start again, or another country if necessary. She didn't hold out much hope of studying psychology after this. She snorted at the irony.

"Did I miss something?"

"No, just something I was thinking about." It was either that or crying, Shelley thought.

At the junction by Camden Town Tube station, Shelley took her usual route towards Chalk Farm. Just after she'd passed the lights, Angel informed her she'd taken the wrong exit, but it was too late. They were jammed in the one-way traffic and there was no way out.

As the car crawled along, on her left, Shelley caught sight of Inverness Street. She looked up the road and saw the futuristic public toilet in which she'd injected with the stranger on the night her client died at The Lanesborough. The dead client's face invaded her mind. Would the face of the rapist do the same to her? Even if it did, it couldn't be any worse than the image already tainting her memory. That mark he'd left was unerasable, and she'd rather have a picture of her own making.

"Traffic's moving," Angel said.

"Sorry, I was in another world." Shelley drove on, narrowly missing a couple of tattooed, mohicaned pedestrians crossing Camden High Street. The weather was becoming milder and she noticed most people were wearing T-shirts. She worried how much longer she could keep herself in long sleeves. At least she had the one good vein Len had shown her. She planned to use that one in different areas and let the rest heal. Then she could get back to working properly again. There were only two madams she could work for now instead of the previous five with whom she had been registered. Although she'd chosen to drop Marianne, the other two had dropped her at the beginning of last week. She'd been sent away from a couple of jobs, which she should never have accepted with damaged arms, and they'd found out why – her track marks.

Once they were out of the one-way system, Angel directed Shelley through the back streets. They emerged on Kentish Town Road where they joined another traffic jam. Within moments, Shelley heard sirens. The wailing was in the distance but it was getting closer. Her fear that had lain dormant was stirred. She told herself not to worry. It was hardly irregular to hear sirens in London.

"Take the next right," Angel said.

Concentrating on what she hoped was a poker-face expression, she followed Angel's instruction.

"I'm sorry I won't be able to invite you in," Angel said. "My place is a total mess."

"I don't mind. I can help you tidy up, if you like." Shelley tried to smile.

"It's not that kind of mess. I've been packed up to leave for the last month, but since you called I couldn't go, not after what you told me."

"You're not moving out of London, are you?"

"I'm leaving England, babe. I've bought a place in Manhattan... Don't look so worried, I'm not leaving you and your girls. I'm not going anywhere 'til we've done this, I promise."

After another turning, the sirens were louder. In her rear view mirror, Shelley saw flashing blue lights on top of a police van that was a few cars behind. She felt her hands trembling and her palms sweating on the steering wheel. On checking the mirror again, only a red Fiesta separated her car and the police van.

The sirens became deafening. She watched in the mirror, helpless, as the Fiesta pulled over and the police van raced towards the rear of her car. This is it – it's all over, she thought, pulling up to the curb.

The van didn't stop. It passed her by and sped up the narrow road ahead. As the wailing trailed off into the distance with the flashing lights, she wiped her sweaty palms on her jeans, then lit a cigarette. She joined the end of the line of cars led by the red Fiesta, and Angel guided her through a maze of back roads towards Hilldrop Crescent. Once Shelley finished her cigarette, the shaking in her hands subsided and she hoped it hadn't been obvious.

28. The Boxer and the Quidnunc

On one of her grandparents' wooden folding chairs that she'd brought with her, Shelley sat in Len's front room. She prepared a shot while listening to Simon and Garfunkel's *Bridge Over Troubled Water*. The music soothed her, diminishing the usual urgency for a hit. Less haste, she hoped, would result in greater accuracy when it came to getting her vein, which in turn would lead to cleaner arms – if she could keep it up. And if she could, it would increase her earning potential, therefore enabling her to keep up with her habit.

"Eww!" Shelley flinched, then lifted her foot, realising it was rested on a dirty, discarded sock. "You need to clean up in here," she told Len as he darted out of the lounge.

"I'm sorry, love. I'll be right back," he called.

"What the fuck are you doing?" Shelley yelled, as Len hurled a second tomato at her trainer. "Stop! That hurts," she cried, after her foot was hit with a potato.

"It's okay. I think I got it."

"You fucking did get it." Shelley tossed the prepared syringe into her cream handbag and stomped across the room to where Len was standing, holding a plastic container of mouldy-looking vegetables. "And you can buy me another pair, you idiot," she said, stabbing the air below with her finger. "These are TNs. Do you know how hard it is to get Nike TNs in the UK? They only sell them in Foot Locker."

"I'm sorry. I've been after that bastard for ages."

"Just pick it up like a normal person and put it in the wash."

"Put it in the wash? Are you tripping?" Len raised his eyebrows. "I'm taking it out with the rubbish." He walked over to the wooden chair and bent down by the brown sock. From the back pocket of his jeans, he took a shiny, silver fork and held it over the sock.

"Just pick up, for God's sake. I wanna have my hit."

"I can't do it. They make me feel sick." Len's hand hovered in the air, holding the fork above the crusty sock.

"It's your sock. Just do it."

He cocked his head to the side, and looked across the room at Shelley. "Come over here, love."

"Holy fuck!" Shelley leapt on top of the vomit and fur-coated armchair. "Get it out! For fuck's sake, get it out!"

"That's what I'm trying to do." Len prodded the rat's body with the fork.

"Not like that. It might not be dead."

"It's not moving. Look, it's dead." He flicked the rat with the fork, rolling it over one-hundred and eighty degrees so that it was lying on its back, face up to the ceiling.

Shelley screeched as she watched the fork coming into contact with the rat's swollen stomach. "Stop! Its insides will explode everywhere if you do it like that. Get a bag."

"When I've picked it up I'll put it in a bag, but I'm not touching it." He rolled the rat back over on its stomach. "I can't do it with it looking at me like that."

"Get a bag and pick it up like a poo." Shelley explained the concept of an inside out bag for scooping up dog shit and Len dealt with the rat without the fork.

When he returned to the lounge, he knelt on the floor next to the Kenwood hi-fi and fast-forwarded through the tracks on the Simon and Garfunkel CD.

Shelley retrieved her pre-prepared syringe from her handbag and held it upright, flicking out the air bubbles. There was only heroin present in the syringe; she was saving the crack for when she got home.

This second time entrusting Len to score had gone far better than the first, notwithstanding the rodent intrusion. She'd insisted no money would change hands until the drugs were in her possession and he kept to his word. In fact, she wondered if he'd given her more than the three-hundred pounds worth she'd paid for.

As she pulled Len's belt around her arm, *The Boxer* played. She listened to Len sing the words. Once she'd injected her fix, she leant back on her chair, gouching out. She could still hear him singing. She sensed vulnerability in his voice, as if he had conviction in those words.

The next time her eyes were open, there was a mug of tea on a lopsided table in front of her. As he wasn't in the room, she took the opportunity to carry out a thorough inspection of the mug. There were no marks on it at all; no stains around the rim, nor did it have any chips. Maybe it was new, she wondered, sipping her tea.

Taking the mug with her, she went over to the front window and looked out. Len was in the garden, tidying up, and from what she could see, he'd made a good start. About half of the clutter was gone.

She checked the time on her phone – 5.07 p.m. Around two hours had passed since her hit. After lighting a cigarette, she meandered out of the house.

"I'm so sorry. I must've fallen asleep." Shelley raised the clean mug to her lips.

"You were dead to the world, love." Len picked up a white chest of drawers and leant it against his shoulder. "I'm sorry about ratty. You all right to help now?"

"Are you replacing my TNs?"

"I'll give 'em a clean. They'll come up good."

Shelley shook her head. "What do you need me to do?"

"Can you lift these?" Len pointed to the pots of paint that were stacked like a shop display pyramid.

Shelley lifted one and, as it wasn't too heavy, she took another in her other hand then followed Len into the house. They walked through to the lounge, and out of the damaged patio doors. In the back garden, a pile was accumulating, reminiscent of that which had previously been in the front.

"My neighbours are gonna love me." Len inserted a cigarette into the side of his self-satisfied smile.

"I wouldn't go that far." Shelley grinned.

When they returned to the front of the house, the old lady from next-door was walking down her front garden towards the street. As Shelley went to collect the next load of paint pots, the lady walked past Len's garden and tutted in their direction.

"What now? You fucking interfering old biddy!" Len hollered after her.

"That's a bit strong, isn't it?" Shelley said, expecting the tut was due to her getting back with her boyfriend – as she had assumed Len was – as opposed to disapproval over the clearance of the front garden.

"You don't know what I have to put up with from that one. Bloody curtain-twitcher. She's always up in my business."

"She's an old lady," Shelley informed him, as if he might not have noticed for himself. Although she liked the lady, it worried her how much of an interest she might take in her business. A quidnunc next door was the last thing she needed.

29. Unhappy Birthday

A shiver ran down Shelley's spine as she sat on the grey settee between her mother and Aunt Elsie. On 17th May – her birthday – for the third year, she had a feeling the day was incomplete. The family was incomplete without her brother. In a way, it was as if her birthdays didn't pass at all and she stayed at nineteen, the age she'd only just turned before William had died.

"Can I get you some more cake, dear?"

"I'm not hungry, Mum." Shelley walked through to her mother's kitchen and put on the kettle. She'd felt tears coming and wanted to cry on her own. When she couldn't control her sobs, she went into the bathroom.

She looked in the mirror and thought what a broken mess she'd become. Her judgement of Tara may have been correct, but it applied equally to her. From the bowl on the white vanity unit, she took a piece of cotton wool and tipped the jar of moisturiser onto it. Then she wiped her face while she breathed slowly, trying to calm herself.

This year had been hard to live. She had survived past the twenty-one years her brother had not. Now she was in an age unknown at twenty-two. In some ways, she still felt like a child, but in others, she felt far too old.

With her face clean of wandering mascara, she wandered through to the lounge and took her seat between the two sisters. On lifting her cup of tea and seeing it empty, she remembered the kettle boiling in the kitchen. She picked up the brown teapot and stood up.

"Stay where you are. I'll do it." Aunt Elsie took the teapot and went into the kitchen.

Shelley sat down again and looked at her mother. "Are you okay?"

"I don't know, dear, all these changes. You know Elsie's got me going to this counselling person?"

"How's it going?"

"They just want your money, those quacks, but she's making me do it."

"She's trying to help you, Mum, we both are." Shelley took her mother's hand.

"We'll see. I don't feel any different yet."

"She's only been once," Elsie said as she came back through, carrying the teapot. She filled Shelley's cup and then Rita's before sitting down. "There's not a quick fix, Rita, you know that. You can't expect to feel better in a week, or even a month. It's taken years to get where you are, so it'll take some time to get you better."

"She's got me in a bleeding self-help group as well. Did she tell you that?"

"That sounds lovely, Mum." Shelley picked up her teacup.

"It's a bereavement support group. I'm going too. You could come with us," Elsie said.

"I don't know... I've got a lot on." Shelley looked at her aunt's encouraging stare. "I'll think about it," she said, considering the power grief had to age. Her mother, at fifty-one years, was nearly four years younger than Elsie, but her withered skin and grey hair belied her as the older sister – over the past seven years, she'd aged a couple of decades.

"Have some cake, dear." Rita put a slice of the Victoria sponge birthday cake on Shelley's plate and handed it to her.

"I don't—"

"You should. You're looking too skinny nowadays," Elsie said.

Reluctantly, Shelley ate her cake. She didn't even like Victoria sponge but she'd never told her mother or Aunt Elsie, one of whom always made that cake on her birthday. Rita had been the one to bake it until Shelley's fifteenth, after which time Aunt Elsie took over – not only the cake making, but all the things her mother used to do. So what if she didn't like the bloody cake? What the fuck did it matter?

"How's work?" Elsie asked.

"Same old, same old."

"You still look tired. I can tell they're working you too hard." Elsie pushed her long, red fringe away from her eyes.

"Not really. I've got a bit more responsibility now I've been there so long."

"I think they're taking advantage of you. I'd like to give your boss a piece of my mind," Elsie said.

"What are you talking about, Elsie? It's my fault she's so tired, running around after me. Isn't it, dear?"

"No. It's no one's fault. I'm just not good managing my time. I'm not even here that often now, am I?" Shelley felt warm tears on her face. She hadn't realised she was crying again.

"Now look what you've done," Elsie said.

"What do you mean, what I've done? You started it." Rita put her arms around her daughter and rocked her as they sat on the settee. Shelley couldn't recall her mother comforting her in a long time. Their roles had been reversed and she'd been the one providing comfort to her mother.

Being held like that, Shelley felt like a little girl – but a safe little girl in the arms of her mummy, and that wasn't a feeling she was used to. She remained in her mother's embrace until Rita released her, and when she did, Shelley felt the heroin-shaped hole inside her expand.

"I better get going." Shelley picked up her small, cream handbag.

"You've not been here that long," Elsie said.

"She'll need an early night. She's got work tomorrow. Haven't you, dear?"

"No, she hasn't," Elsie said. "It's Sunday tomorrow."

"I'm going in for a few hours to catch up... I'll be back in the week, Mum." Shelley kissed her mother goodbye.

Aunt Elsie walked with Shelley down the stairs to the front door. As they stood together in the hall, she said, "Tell me you've been for your allergy test."

"I don't think I need one." Shelley knew what she was allergic to. She injected it daily to make living bearable. And it would probably show in her blood if she went for an allergy test.

"Well, maybe next time you're at the doctors, you could ask about it." Aunt Elsie patted Shelley's arm. "Make sure she doesn't give up on this counselling. Keep encouraging her, won't you?"

"Of course I will. I can't believe you got her to do it."

Elsie put her hands on Shelley's shoulders and looked directly into her eyes. "I told her if she wants you to make something of your life, she needs to get herself together. There's no way you can get the grades you need at UCL if you're still being her carer."

"Thank you, Auntie."

Although Elsie's hands were no longer on Shelley's shoulders, they'd been replaced with the heavier weight of guilt. She kissed her aunt on the cheek, and called out, "I love you," as she dashed to her car.

***

Wrapped in the safety of her duvet and the warm blanket of heroin, Shelley's guilt eased. Although she was delighted her mother was at last in therapy, Aunt Elsie's explanation of how she'd coaxed her caused Shelley to question herself. Initially, she'd felt remorseful as the thing most likely to ruin her grades at university was drugs,

149

that's if they didn't stop her going in the first place. But then she decided the reason didn't matter; the fact that her mother was in therapy at all was all that mattered.

Knowing the awkwardness of birthdays, Shelley had ensured a decent supply of heroin and crack. She stretched over from the sofa and prepared her next fix. The pain she felt was mainly due to Will's absence but there were also other factors. Even when Will was alive, for both of them, their birthdays had been difficult. She wondered if it wasn't just her but that perhaps her mother, and Will too, felt guilty about celebrating anything after what they'd lived through.

Maybe next year Shelley would do something different, a holiday possibly. Without fail, every birthday she'd spent with her mother and Aunt Elsie, and of course William when he was alive. Now that she was older, surely it was time for a change.

Though the day had been hard, it wasn't the worst. Her sixteenth had been. That birthday she'd spent in the psychiatric ward of Barnet General Hospital. Her mother had been held on a twenty-eight day section following a suicide attempt. She knew her mother still felt regret over Shelley's absence from school during that period, and blamed herself that her daughter hadn't achieved the GCSE grades she'd been predicted.

With her speedball prepared, Shelley found a spot untouched on the one vein she was using. She tied a chiffon scarf around her arm and carefully inserted the needle. She drew back the plunger, watching her blood dance with her medicine in the barrel. She pushed it in gradually. The commixture of comfort and chaos engulfed her. This was the way to utopia.

30. Little Policemen

After forty-eight hours with no sleep, no food, and regular intravenous transfusions, Shelley's medicine was making her ill. In an old, pink nightdress, she staggered to the dining table. She tried to pick up a pen but it kept slipping from her fingers. She wanted to write a list to stop the worries multiplying any further in her head. If she could get them on paper, they might stop increasing and she might be able to make sense of them and make a plan to calm the panic.

The recent periods of hibernation had ruined her daily ritual of examining the newspapers. Although she hadn't seen anything on the news, not everything was reported on television – or the papers. But what if it had been, and she'd missed it?

She pictured her face in a wanted article, her mother and her aunt's reactions. But if it had been printed, and if they had seen it, they would have phoned. Perhaps they hadn't seen it yet. A friend or neighbour would take a clipping and show them. Any time now, she'd be found out. Her head felt compressed at the temples, creating pressure on her skull as if it might crack.

Still unable to lift the pen with her hands, she laid her chest on the table and pressed her face over the nib of the pen. With one hand pushing the other end, she forced it into her cheek to lever it up. Finally, the pen was in her hand but she couldn't remember how to hold it. Her fingers weren't working properly. With the pen gripped in one fist, she used her other hand to slide a white envelope from the opposite end of the table closer towards her.

She fell back on a chair. "Ow," she screamed. Her bony backside broke her fall and as the leather chairs were thinly padded, it hurt.

Her double vision meant that she couldn't tell if she was writing on the glass table or on the paper. The exercise was futile. She stood up. Her head felt heavy. She couldn't see anything apart from shadows. Then, emerging from the shadows were the shadow people. Her legs went. Her body tilted forward then slapped down onto the wooden floor.

"Ow," she cried again.

Diminutive policemen – the size of garden gnomes – were rolling out from under the dining table in droves. "You're a bad girl, Shelley Hansard. We know all about you," said one.

"Leave me alone." Shelley hit out with her arm, but her hand was grabbed. A bantam policeman squeezed it. He stomped over her as he yanked her arm high behind her back. "Get off. You're hurting me." Shelley moaned in pain. "I didn't do anything, I promise."

"We know what your promises are worth, Miss Hansard," a shrill voice said.

"The worthless promises of a whore," said another.

She felt the tiny policemen climb onto her back, and with the weight of so many, she was pinned down on the floor. She looked around as far as her head could turn. She couldn't see the shadow people. At least she was alone with the police.

"I didn't kill him. He just died. It wasn't my fault." She sobbed. "Please, I'm telling the truth."

"You were in Sodom," one said, and they all jumped up and down on her back. "You think you're high class. You're a fucking whore."

"Why are you being so cruel? I've never hurt anybody. I don't deserve this."

"High-class call girl, you're still a whore girl. High-class call girl, you're still a whore girl. High-class call girl, you're still a whore girl." Their high-pitched voices sung so loudly that Shelley feared her neighbours would hear.

"I haven't done anything. I haven't hurt anyone. I'm not like that."

"High-class call girl, you're still a whore girl. High-class call girl, you're still a whore girl."

"Stop it! Please stop," Shelley begged, but they continued to sing. Preternaturally rage replaced her fear. "Shut up! Shut up!"

Unrelenting, they kept on.

"Shut the fuck up, you fuckers!" With all her strength, she pushed herself up from the floorboards and as she did, the miniature policemen rolled back under the table. She bent down on her knees to see if they'd disappeared, but they had not. They stood together in a line, holding their lilliputian shields and batons.

"Get out my fucking flat!" She banged her hands on the hard floor hoping to scare them. The tiny policemen bounced up and down.

"You have to come with us." Two by two, they marched out from under the table and formed an orderly line. Their numbers had increased to maybe thirty or more.

"Where do you want to take me?" Shelley's voice quavered.

"To the place where girls like you belong," one said poking her in the cheek with his baton.

"Where's that?"

"Hell," they said in unison.

Shelley rushed into the kitchen and pulled out a bag of rice from the cupboard. She ran back to the table where the policemen stood and poured the rice over and around them. She watched as they tripped and stumbled, falling over each other on the oak floorboards.

"You're not helping yourself, you stupid whore," one said.

"We'll get you, Shelley Hansard," said another.

"No crime goes unpunished," said a third.

The urge to run from her flat was intense. However, the fear of what might be outside was greater. She tried to move, but what she was telling her brain wasn't being relayed to her legs. Her knees could move but her feet were glued to the floor.

She bent her knees and lowered herself down. Turning her head, she saw the policemen wobbling on the rice and shaking their batons at her. She looked away. She lay flat on the floorboards and used her arms to drag her body from the dining table by the entrance of the lounge to the coffee table in the centre.

Holding on to the wooden coffee table, she pulled herself up to kneel. The table appeared to be flooded. Her drugs, the works, the scarf, the spoon, the ashtray, her phone, everything floated on top of the river. She glanced over to see if the policemen had left. They hadn't.

Apprehensively, she dipped in her hand. To her surprise, it didn't feel wet. She blinked a few times and then squinted. All the items were still afloat. As they bobbed up and down and shifted around, she found it hard to keep her eyes on her ever mobile, mobile phone.

Swishing her hand in the dry water, she finally grabbed her phone. On bringing it towards her face, she couldn't make out the buttons. With one hand, she covered one eye and her vision from her seeing eye became clearer. Her clumsy fingers eventually brought up the short contact list and she called for help.

***

"I need to go back and pay the cab," Len said, standing at her front door.

"Of course." Shelley clung to the door handle to stop her body from falling. "My bag's by the sofa. Can you see it? I can't see straight. My purse is in it. Take what you need."

She heard Len's light footsteps on the stairs. Although she hadn't noticed him leave, he must have passed her; she was sure she hadn't moved from her position by the front door. Her arm was getting tired holding the handle, so she pulled the door inwards and leant against it.

Suddenly, she was catapulted up in the air and floating through the hall. She flew into the lounge, past the dining table and chairs, and landed on the sofa. The ride had been exhilarating and she was disappointed it had come to an end.

"Let's get you some fluid. Have you been drinking?" Len stooped over Shelley where he'd placed her on the sofa.

"No, I haven't, I promise – just speedballing."

"I mean water. Have you had any liquids?"

"I had some tea, or maybe that was yesterday. I don't know."

Len handed Shelley a glass of water, which she tried to pour into her mouth. Though she felt some go down her throat, she also felt her face and legs get wet. Len disappeared for a while then she saw him come back with another glass.

"Sip it slowly." He raised the glass in his 'F-A-T-E' hand and held it to her lips, tipping it at an angle as she swallowed the water. "Sit up, Shelley. Sit up. You're gonna choke."

"I'm okay. I think I need a hit," Shelley said in between coughs.

"You need a rest, love. That's what you need."

"I need a bit of gear to bring me down and I'll be fine."

"We'll see. First, you've gotta eat." He stood up. "What've you done to your Chevy?"

"What do you mean?"

"You've got biro all over one side of your face."

While Len was in the kitchen, Shelley could smell burning and she expected it was her food, though what he might be cooking, she had no idea. She hadn't shopped for herself in ages and Aunt Elsie had cleared the kitchen of everything that was out of date, which was everything she had.

She watched Len walk out of the kitchen, holding a dustpan and brush. He swept up the rice from under the dining table. As she looked over, she was relieved to see the policemen had gone. She hoped they'd actually left the flat and weren't hiding somewhere. She would ask Len to check before he left.

He went back into the kitchen, and she heard the rice being poured into what she imagined was the bin. What would she use if they came back again?

Following the scraping noises that had come from the kitchen, Len sat down beside her and handed her a slice of toast. Shelley couldn't grasp it. He raised it to her mouth and she took a bite.

"I'm so sorry. I usually manage okay on my own," she said, with her mouth full.

"It's all right, love. We all get fucked up sometimes. Like they say, shit happens, don't it?" He fed Shelley another mouthful of toast. "What happened to you?"

She knew she wasn't close to reality yet, and she told herself to watch what she said. There were a few matters of which she'd need to be mindful.

31. Never-Ending Benders

Fifty-seven hours wasn't long enough for Shelley's paranoia and hallucinations to dissipate. Although during that time, she hadn't used crack, the junk she'd injected along with the joints she'd smoked were unable to return her to a non-psychotic-but-pleasantly-drugged state of mind.

The policemen had gone, but from time to time, she could still see the shadow people following her around. The words 'damaged goods' were being spoken by an ever widening range of objects, which were also saying, 'high-class call girl, you're still a whore girl'.

From the passenger seat, she turned her head to look in the back of the Chimaera. At last the shadow people had gone.

"Have you lost something?" Nicole asked.

"No, I was just stretching my neck." *I did stretch it.* Shelley tried to convince herself it wasn't a lie.

"I think you'll make it worse if you keep doing that."

How many times had she looked backwards already? The rising urge to keep checking behind her would need to be suppressed. The sirens in her ears kept on relentlessly and she told herself not to look round. They'd been blaring on and off for days, and most times an emergency vehicle was nowhere in sight. With the visions and sounds, she knew her mind was playing tricks. She prayed it would end soon.

Shelley didn't want to leave her flat, but Nicole had phoned earlier in the day and insisted she come to Tara's that afternoon. Neither Nicole nor Shelley had heard from Tara since the meeting with Angel in The Magdala. Nicole was concerned that Tara's phone was going straight to voicemail; she'd tried Hugo, but her attempts to contact him were equally unsuccessful.

Though Shelley didn't always speak regularly with Tara, Nicole did. For Nicole, ten days with no contact was a long time. The three of them used to go nightclubbing at least once a week but since February, Shelley had managed to excuse herself from most of those nights with various versions of the truth. Nicole and Tara liked to go where they were known, and given special treatment and VIP access. But Shelley didn't like the feeling she got in Cafe de Paris and those other upmarket nightclubs where everyone knew she was a hooker. Admittedly, some might have fallen for the model story, but she'd rather go to Freedom where she felt secure that no one knew anything about her.

Trying to get out of the visit, Shelley had proposed that Tara might be staying with her parents or on a holiday. Nicole wouldn't believe it. "We're waiting for Angel to call. She wouldn't go AWOL on us now," Nicole had said.

Shelley wondered whether Tara had an issue with Angel, but it didn't make sense. They'd got on so well at the pub and seemed pleased to be reunited. Tara's problem wouldn't be that. Her problem would most likely be the same problem she always had – crack.

"You know she won't answer the door," Shelley said, as Nicole was turning off the Cromwell Road.

Nicole slowed the car down, looking around for a parking space. "I'll call her."

"You told me she's not picking up her phone." Shelley shook her head – wasn't she the one whose thinking was supposed to be skewed? "You'll never fit in there."

Having reverse-parked into the space Shelley deemed too small to fit the TVR, Nicole stormed ahead to Tara's building. Shelley caught up and, as she'd anticipated, there was no reply from Tara's flat. Nicole took out her phone and called her. Shelley already knew there'd be no answer. She was right.

"What are we gonna do now?" Shelley lit a cigarette.

"Wait. What else can we do?"

"Get a coffee?" Shelley had in mind a specific use for the lavatory of an eatery.

"Damn! You can be so selfish sometimes." Nicole put her hand in Shelley's handbag and helped herself to one of Shelley's cigarettes. "Aren't you worried?"

"She'll be on a bender."

"That's why I'm worried, you stupid tart."

Still recovering from her own bender, it wasn't the time to argue with Nicole. "I'm sorry, Nic. I'll call Hugo."

"Haven't you been listening? His damn phone's not picking up either."

Shelley felt tears come to her eyes but she managed to blink them away. She knew she was more sensitive than usual. If only she could have a fix; she needed a public convenience.

"I need a wee," Shelley said.

"Go and find a toilet then."

Shelley kissed her angry friend's reddened cheek. Then she headed to the main road towards Earl's Court Tube station to find a lavatory. While she walked, she felt the sun warm her back. She wanted to take off her cardigan to cool down, but she couldn't.

She went inside the first place she found, a run-down cafe, and asked to use their ladies' room. A scraggly haired woman dressed in a gingham uniform denied her request.

"I'm sorry to ask, but I've a problem with my bladder." Shelley rubbed her stomach and hunched her shoulders.

The lady showed her through to the back where the lavatory was. Shelley locked the door, put down the seat and sat on the toilet with her jeans on.

Frantically, she cooked up a hit. Using the ribbed sleeve of her cardigan as a tourniquet, she pulled it tight around her arm, just above her elbow. The vein on the inside of her elbow was now restored and it was the easiest one to get when it was present.

"*Straight in, pull back, shoot up, and get out,*" a wise voice on the board advised her. It was true; there was no time to indulge her needle fixation. She'd have to be quick or the staff would get suspicious.

"You've been ages." Nicole stood with her hand on her hip, looking angrily at Shelley walking towards her.

"Sorry. I've got a dodgy tummy," Shelley said, hoping Nicole wouldn't notice her pupils, which she imagined were now pinned. Lying to Nicole was easier than she'd expected, but the sickening feeling with which it came tasted as vile as when she lied to her mother and aunt.

As their wait outside continued, Shelley lit a cigarette. Nicole asked her for another as she'd finished her pack. Shelley already knew that before, yet on her expedition to have a hit, it hadn't once entered her mind to buy her friend a new box. Nicole was right: she was selfish.

"I don't wanna upset you but if Angel doesn't get that call, we need to find someone else."

"Shouldn't we give it another week?" Shelley looked down at the grey paving stones.

"A week and that's it." Nicole took a pull on her cigarette. Puffs of smoke escaped from her mouth as she coughed. That was Shelley's fault for not getting her a pack of her own brand.

"I'm not putting off my punters any more," Nicole said. "She'll just have to stall him."

"You can't do that." Shelley scratched at the itching skin on her ribs. "We need to be available all the time."

"It doesn't need four of us. Three's enough to get started. Then we can take turns to— Resident Handyman."

The communal door of Tara's building opened as a man dressed in denim overalls and a yellow checked shirt walked out.

Shelley jammed her foot in the door to prevent it from closing. "I'd say he's more of a Resident Lumberjack," she said quietly to Nicole once the man was out of earshot.

"And I don't care," Nicole added lyrically, and indiscreetly, which was the opposite of Shelley's planned subtle entrance.

***

Although they were now inside, they still had to convince Tara to open her front door – if she was in. While Shelley struggled to climb the stairs, she heard banging and assumed Nicole, fit as she was, had already reached Tara's flat.

Shelley's legs were aching by the time she eventually made it to the third floor and once there, she discovered that Nicole had been responsible for the noise. How much longer she could stand with the weight on her feet, she didn't know, but she knew that she wanted to sit down. And how much longer she could bear the banging on the door, she didn't know either, but she expected it would be around the same amount of time it would take for Tara's neighbours to come out and complain.

"There's a fire. Get out. Open this door," Shelley said gruffly in the lowest voice she could muster.

Finally, Tara's door opened. In fear of it closing, Shelley barged inside, thrusting herself into the flat. Tara ran from her, down the hall. Shelley chased after her, dashing into the lounge, which neglected had aligned itself to the style of Miss Havisham.

Tara threw herself on her knees. She picked up tiny pieces of crack from the glass coffee table. "Tell them I'm coming," she shouted.

"What's going on?" Wearing only a pair of red checked boxer shorts, Hugo appeared in the lounge.

"Resident Handyman or Resident Lumberjack?" Shelley whispered to Nicole as they stood together at the bay window.

"Not the kind of resident I'd like to be lumbered with," Nicole replied.

"Don't you ladies know it's rude to whisper?" Hugo sounded vexed.

Nicole swept Shelley's hair back behind her ear. "Good with his hands though, wasn't he?"

Tara combed the carpet with her fingers. Shelley knew she was looking for crack, though it would be impossible to decipher the crack from the dirt. The carpet still sported the same non-vacuumed look that was worsening with every passing season.

"You're not going to find my laptop down there." Hugo walked towards Tara.

"I can't look for it now." Tara stroked the carpet. "The building's on fire."

Hugo peered out the window. "There's nothing to see out here. Is the assembly point in the back, Tars?"

"How would I know?" Tara replied.

"There isn't a damn fire. We've been worried about her." Nicole knelt on the carpet next to Tara, who was still down there searching for crack.

"It's my fault, darling. Don't be angry with Tars." Hugo sat down on the sofa.

Shelley glared at him – he'd stolen her seat. Then she glared at Tara – she'd quite possibly stolen his laptop. Although she was furious with Hugo, he was still a friend, and her other supposed friend, Tara, had most likely exchanged his laptop for crack: crack that she'd smoked, some of it in Hugo's presence. She'd partaken in the smoking of Hugo's Toshiba in front of him. She felt terrible.

"We've had quite a party. You should've come over," Hugo said.

If they'd wanted her or Nicole present, they would have taken their calls. She wondered what Hugo was doing there. He never used crack, yet there he was setting up a pipe. In disbelief, Shelley watched as Hugo lit the rock and sucked in through the hollow pen. He sat back and, after a short while, blew out the smoke. In that instant, Shelley felt overwhelmingly sober. She took Nicole's arm and dragged her out into the hall then through to the kitchen.

"What are you doing?" Nicole said.

"She's taken him hostage."

"I know she's a fuck up, but you can't just blame her." Nicole reached into Shelley's handbag and took out the gold cigarette box. "He's got his own mind."

"Yeah he has – and a lot of money. I bet that was his laptop."

Nicole switched on the gas hob and lit her cigarette over the blue flame. "You don't know that for sure," she said.

"I don't know why you're defending her. No one has a laptop. Why would her parents have bought her one?"

"It can't be very interesting talking about me." Tara walked into the kitchen.

Shelley looked up at her then looked away, saying nothing. She knew a conversation with Tara on crack would be wasted. Nicole kept quiet too as she filled the kettle.

The three stood in a silence unbroken until the kettle whistled. Nicole poured the boiling water into four cups containing teabags. Shelley assumed this was her passive-aggressive way of letting Tara know she was riled – neither of them ever made tea for Tara; she only took coffee.

With a look of disgust, Shelley handed Hugo his tea and with reluctance, she sat down on Tara's armchair. Tara was already at Crack Island, putting a pipe together. Within seconds, Tara was aiming the lighter at the crack that was resting on the ash-covered foil. Having taken in the hit, she immediately placed another rock on the blackened and crusty ash. In her desperation to get a hit, she was wasting the crack. The ash needed changing before putting on a new rock. Shelley was aware she did the equivalent when injecting: each time she rushed it, causing a vein to pop, and when she reused the same blunt needles too many times because she couldn't get it together to go out for new works.

Perhaps Shelley was better able to hide how fucked up she was, except when she was psychotic like the other night with Len. She hoped she hadn't let anything slip that night. She didn't think so, but she couldn't be sure because she'd been so far gone.

"You better not have called that lowlife who stole my camcorder," Hugo said when the buzzer from the intercom sounded. "The girls will know another dealer."

"How many times do I have to tell you? I don't score from him any more." Tara walked into the hall. "You need to go. I've got a punter," she said, looking back at Shelley and Nicole.

Shelley followed Tara into the first part of the L-shaped hall. She imagined the sort of punter who'd want to see a hooker in the state her friend was in. What sort of friend was she anyway? The type who'd steal your electrical items, blame a dealer for the camcorder she thieved from you, and help you look for a laptop she knew would never be found because she'd already stolen it and sold it on. She thought about her own dishonesty. Maybe she ought to look at herself a little before pointing her finger, too judgementally perhaps, in Tara's direction.

A door creaked open and soft footsteps became louder. "Mummy, what's going on?" Maxwell rubbed his eyes with his tiny fists.

"Get back to bed, sweetie-pie. It's still naptime." Tara shooed her son down the hall and he retreated.

Shelley remained silent, feeling the heat of her anger flush her face. "What the fuck are you doing?" she finally asked, having waited to hear Maxwell return to the bedroom at the other end of the flat.

"Just go." Tara turned towards the front door.

Nicole raced around her and stood with her back against the door. "You think I'm gonna leave a child here, while you're doing crack and there's a punter? Are you out of your mind?"

"I need the money."

"Get rid of him. Now." Nicole looked to Shelley. Shelley raised her hand to the button on the intercom.

"No, don't, please." Tara stepped in front, blocking Shelley's access.

Shelley nudged her out of the way and pressed the button to talk. "Fuck off," she yelled.

"But I've got an appointment."   A man's voice boomed out the box.

"Wait," Tara shouted.

"Fuck off or I'm calling the police," Shelley re-advised him.

"Give me your parents' number." Nicole sprinted into the lounge. Tara chased after her. As Nicole made a grab for Tara's mobile phone on the table, she knocked over the pipe. Crumbs of crack snowed down on the carpet.

"Why are you doing this to me?" Tara got on her hands and knees and crawled around, scrambling for the crack.

"You've fucking lost it. You can't smoke that shit around your son." Nicole looked at Tara's phone as she hit the keypad. "Don't you realise the danger you're putting him in?"

"Stop it, Tara. Get up." Shelley put her hand out to Tara but it was ignored.

"You're off your fucking head, having strange men here. Even you can't be that stupid." Nicole held the phone to her ear.

"What the fuck are you doing with my phone?" Tara looked up at Nicole.

"What someone should've done for me... I'm calling his grandparents."

32. Impossible Proposal

Shelley was glad to be back with Resident Dicks All the Boxes even though it was inconvenient to be seeing him on a Friday night. Due to oversleeping until the afternoon, she'd had to postpone her mother's visit until Saturday.

He leant forward and pulled out the gilded wall mirror from under the coffee table. Near the centre was the mountain of cocaine and on one side, the roads: four colossal lines spanning the length of the entire mirror.

Although Shelley's nose had acclimatised to the lines he made, her mind had not. She was aware that she needed to restrict the amount she sniffed – unlike the last time when she'd seen him at his London residence. Having only just recovered from her last bout of crack-induced psychosis, she didn't want another attack inflicted by cocaine.

He rested the mirror on the rectangular table in front of them and handed Shelley a rolled up fifty-pound note. "It's all yours, sweetie."

"I'm taking it easy tonight, remember? Just one for me." Shelley stayed sitting on the azure sofa. She bent over the mirror and snorted one line.

She rested her head in his lap. He stroked her hair from her temple to her neck. It wasn't like being on a normal job. If she didn't need to keep the cold bank refilled, it might not have been a job at all because she'd be in a position to see him for free.

"Can I get you another gin and tonic, sweetie?"

"I'm okay for now, thank you." She smiled up at his narrow face. From that unfortunate angle, she could see right up into his nostrils, all the little hairs.

Her arms felt uncomfortably constrained in the bandages but she'd have to bear it a while longer. Oddly, he didn't seem to mind that she kept her long-sleeved, button-down dress on. He was sympathetic to her predicament and had told her that this time, she'd be getting a little extra to buy herself a few similar dresses while her psoriasis was active.

"I've got a little something for you." He repositioned her head on the sofa then left the room.

Unlike her, Resident Dicks All the Boxes hadn't given a false name. It would have helped if he had. Because she was referring to him mentally as Resident Dicks All the Boxes, she worried saying the name aloud while she was high. Convinced it would slip out, she started calling him John in her head. After all, that is what he was – her favourite, but a john nonetheless.

Where was he? Shelley wondered, feeling uneasy. Just before panic set in, she saw him at the doorway. He'd returned with a gift-wrapped parcel.

"Happy belated birthday, sweetie." He put the square package in her hands. "I hope you like it."

"Thank you." Shelley was stunned. Clients had given her gifts before, but never a present for her birthday. This was a first.

"Well, open it." He smiled.

She pulled on the bow, neatly unfolded the wrapping paper and revealed a black velvet box. She opened the box, which was lined with cream silk or satin (she wasn't sure which) and resting on that was a gold necklace with a red, pear-shaped pendant.

He took the necklace out of the box and sat down on the sofa next to Shelley. "May I?" he said. Then he turned her round to face the opposite direction. He removed the necklace she was wearing before fastening the new necklace at the nape of her neck.

"Thank you so much," she said, staring down at the clear, red stone. "I love it... It's perfect."

"You're perfect, perfectly sublime, and rubies are special, Kiki, like you." He looked into her eyes. "They're not as hard as diamonds," he said, passing her the other necklace.

Shelley felt a warmth come to her cheeks. She hoped she wasn't as blood red as her new pendant. She couldn't understand why he liked her; she was no longer a blonde, she had bandaged arms and she kept her dress on all night.

"There's something I want to ask you," he said. "In the summer I live in America. I have a house in South Beach, in Miami, and I usually have a girl or two come to stay. I was thinking that maybe you'd like to come. I'll be over there for two months, but you don't have to stay the whole time. You can come for a week or a few weeks, whatever you like."

"That's very kind of you, but I don't think I can." The job would be worth thousands, but Shelley couldn't go. Going abroad was impossible with a heroin habit. Even if she went cold turkey, she still couldn't leave her other responsibilities.

"I know what you're thinking." He placed his hand on her arm and patted it lightly. "Don't worry, it's okay. I spoke to a friend of mine, he's a top dermatologist, and apparently, the sun can heal your psoriasis. Even the sea could help."

Shelley didn't have anything to say. What excuse could she give now? She tried to think of a lie but nothing came. The truth – she'd have to tell the truth, but only a small portion.

"It isn't that." Shelley turned her head towards the fireplace. "I look after my mum and I can't leave her."

"I'm sorry, sweetie. Is your mother ill?"

"Kind of, she's got depression."

"Well she's very lucky to have you taking good care of her." He placed his arm around her slumped shoulders. "Can't you ask someone to stand in for you?"

"There isn't anyone. Just me and my aunt, and she can't do any more than she does already."

Grief coursed through Shelley's body. Her eyes stung with uninvited tears. *There was someone else but he's gone.* Perhaps the truth hadn't been such a good idea after all. Crying wasn't in her job description.

33. The Missed Turning

In her head, Shelley lay on South Beach under the azure sky, the sun warming her from the outside in. The art deco buildings that were behind her housing the restaurants, bars, and nightclubs were where she'd eat, drink and dance later. At night, she'd sleep in her own private annexe and in the morning, her breakfast would be brought in by the staff. The next day she might spend around the house, read a book by the pool, and perhaps call in the beauty therapist for a massage and a facial. Resident Dicks All the Boxes had done a good job on her; she was sold.

Shelley looked out the window to the grey sky that coordinated with the grey settee on which she was sitting. "God, it's bleak out there." *This is England, cold and bitter.*

"There's beauty in the bleakness, if you look, dear." Rita sipped her tea. "Only a week or so and it'll be summer."

What did that mean? The summer in England was a con. This could be the driver she needed to kick her habit. Surely, her aunt could pop in on her mother an extra once or twice a week, her psoriasis could be miraculously cured before she left, and she could be in Miami for July.

"What's wrong with you today? You're not yourself."

"Why do people say that? Who else am I gonna be?" Shelley snapped. "Oh Mum, I'm sorry. I didn't mean— I'm just a bit stressed."

"That's a nice necklace, dear. Is it new?"

"Yes, I got it yesterday. Did you know rubies aren't as hard as diamonds?"

"More likely to break then. You better look after it. Don't you ever think having all this money to spend is a waste if you're going to burn out earning it?" Rita said. "I have to agree with Elsie. I think she's right. They're working you too hard. You need to tell that boss of yours you can't do so much."

"I have to work, and they've been very good to me." Shelley thought of the long lunch breaks Foxtons allowed her so she could visit her mother, and the time off that they'd granted her whenever Rita was ill.

"But you're burning out, dear. I've seen it happen to people."

"No you haven't. Who do you know who's burnt out?"

"Not people I know, dear – on the TV. It was a documentary," Rita said. "I don't think you're looking after yourself properly. You're so pale, and skinny. You need to put some meat on your bones and get a decent night's sleep."

Although in a way she'd been scolded, Shelley was touched by her mother's concern, until her guilt stole the comfort from those words and replaced it with remorse.

"You have to tell people how you feel or they won't know how to help you."

This from a woman who's shut herself away from the world for the past seven years - Shelley looked quizzically at her mother.

"Communication, it's essential for relationships to work. You need to let them know your limits."

"What else have you been watching?" Self-righteous Silk, Shelley presumed.

"That's not from the television. I've been writing things down to help me... I'll show you." Rita walked out the room then quickly returned with a mauve notepad in her hand. She took her seat next to Shelley on the sofa. She opened the notepad and read aloud her handwritten notes, or as she told Shelley, the pearls of wisdom that were apparently gifts from her new counsellor and the bereavement support group.

Although Shelley wanted her mother to make progress, her behaviour was disconcerting. Walking around in the flat was manic for Rita, let alone entering into talking therapy, which she had always been against. Within a week, suddenly, there she was reciting phrases that were contradictory to her actions of the past few years. Shelley worried exactly what Aunt Elsie had enrolled her in – some kind of brainwashing, possibly.

"When you're at UCL, I want you to be at UCL, not worrying about me. I've enough regret to last a lifetime already. I don't want any more."

"It wasn't your fault. You know I've never blamed you."

Hiding her own regret, Shelley hugged her mother. Her mobile rang out from her handbag but she wasn't ready to break away. The ringing persisted and after letting three calls go unanswered, Shelley reached for her phone. She was a second too late and the caller had hung up. As she looked at the list of missed calls and saw the phone number, she knew she had to leave her mother's immediately.

***

As she raced back towards Hampstead on the A41, Shelley made the three calls from her mobile to put everything in place. The car screeched as she pulled a sharp right onto Willoughby Road. Her open handbag fell from the passenger seat, emptying its contents into the footwell.

She parked at an angle in a space too short for her long car. Leaning across, she picked up her purse, mirror, lipstick and the syringe that had fallen out. Without checking the car was locked, she sprinted to her flat.

From the bedroom, she grabbed her beige suitcase. She searched through her work paraphernalia for the specific accoutrements required for the job: blindfold, handcuffs, whips, GHB, Rohypnol. She bundled some casual clothes on top, then rummaged in the drawers of her dressing table. She found her curling tongs and packed those.

She took off her jeans and sweatshirt, exchanging them for a red silk blouse under a black skirt suit. Finished in the bedroom, she ran through to the kitchen and picked up the cardboard box of beers, wines and spirits. From the cupboard under the sink, she lifted the air freshener, clingfilm and parcel tape. Finally, she went back to the lounge to pack her gear and a needle.

With her case packed, she sat on the sofa. She couldn't leave without topping up her opiate level. From her black patent handbag, she took out her heroin. There was no time to inject, so she sprinkled some on a piece of foil and quickly had a chase. To save the leftover heroin, she folded it inside the foil. Then she hid the foil between the pages of *The Escaped Cock* – the slim paperback that was ideal for carrying and concealing in her handbag.

The compulsion to check the windows, taps and oven was on her. She tried to resist the pull of the obsession, but an authoritarian voice from the board relentlessly commanded her not to leave without checking. She had no choice but to succumb.

She managed to keep to the minimum counts for all her subjects. She scooped up her fake-fur coat from the sofa and rushed to the front door. Having locked it behind her, she allowed herself to slow down again, this time for the four-sets-of-five that were essential in ensuring her flat was safe to be left. Succeeding in keeping her concentration, she completed the task in twenty counts.

When she got to the car, she threw the box of booze, her case and her coat in the boot. She sped off down the back streets. Her foot shook against the accelerator as she drove. She worried she might crash if she couldn't control it. Hoping to calm her nerves, she lit a cigarette and broke the silence with Capital Radio.

As she approached the main road at Swiss Cottage, she hit traffic.

Making use of the time, she pulled out her foil and tube. She bent over her lap for a quick blast. She hoped no one in the surrounding cars would notice. Although it was early evening, the sun had made a belated appearance and transformed the sky to a brighter shade of grey.

A horn sounded. On looking up, she realised the traffic was moving. When she put her foot to the pedal, she noticed the shaking had stopped. After a short stint on the main road, she returned to the back streets, heading straight over Edgware Road then onto Elgin Avenue.

While she'd regained her external composure, her insides heaved with nervous anticipation. Her stomach turned as if a hit on a crack pipe was imminent and she felt queasy; though amid that, she recognised a splash of excitement.

Preoccupied with scenarios of what might lie ahead, she missed the turning for Ladbroke Grove. By the time she realised her mistake, she'd nearly reached Kensal Green. She decided it wasn't worth turning back and continued on Harrow Road, taking the scenic route down Scrubs Lane.

Falling back into a reverie, she smiled. She bit her bottom lip between her front teeth. If it was him, then this Saturday night would be like no other. A snigger escaped from her mouth, but there was no reason to laugh except in hysteria.

34. In the Twilight

Turning into Bracewell Road, Shelley scanned the street for Nicole's blue Chimaera. It wasn't there. She parked up farther down the road. Stepping out of the car, she shivered. Tomorrow would be a good day, she thought as she gazed up at the red clouds that were populating the sky.

She took the box and her beige case from the boot. She placed them on the pavement while she wrapped herself in her warm coat. Then she walked round the car, counting aloud as she used her hands to feel what she didn't trust her eyes to see – that it was secure and safe to be left.

Approaching Len's terraced house, she noticed the next-door neighbour's lights were on. Through their net curtains, she saw the couple sitting in their front room, watching television. They'd have to keep their noise to a minimum, she thought.

The wrought iron gate squeaked as she pushed it open. She paused to look at the immaculate front garden. She noticed the three red rose pot-plants in front of the bay window that replaced the mess previously residing there.

Her heels clicked on the multicoloured mosaic embedded in the path that led to the front door. Walking up the three stone steps, her heart quickened. When she took the key from her black patent handbag and turned it in the lock, she realised the shaking had returned.

A light shone down the hall from the kitchen in the back of the house. Nervously, she advanced towards it. The germ-ridden kitchen was empty. With boiling water on a tea towel, she wiped down the Formica worktop. On it, she placed the wine and beer bottles. To the side, she arranged a display of the spirits.

She checked the lounge. The same filthy, and possibly flea infested, armchair was still the centrepiece of the dilapidated room. Thankfully, leaning against the ripped wallpaper were her grandparents' folding chairs, which she'd brought on her last visit for a clean place to sit.

From her case, she took the can of air-freshener. Heading upstairs, she sprayed as she walked. She checked the four bedrooms, which had retained their après-burgled look. Where were her friends? She took her mobile from her bag and checked the time – 8.22 p.m. He was due at the house at half past. If her friends didn't arrive, she'd have to manage on her own.

Eight minutes to prepare was all she had. She went back down and yanked open the little door under the stairs. The cellar reeked. The fetid odour stuck in her throat. She was convinced there was a dead rat, or two or three or more, somewhere in that room. Her footsteps creaked down the narrow staircase. She switched on the solitary light bulb. There were no dead rats. Maybe the vermin lay above her, under the floorboards in the hall, or perhaps they were among the boxed-in pipes for the central heating; it was too late to do anything about that now.

Returning to the lounge, she unfolded one of her grandparents' wooden chairs. There was only five minutes until the rapist's arrival. She needed a chase. If the others smelt anything, she could blame it on the tenants. She shook the paperback to free the silver square from its pages. Then she took the foil tube and her Clipper out of her handbag.

As she sucked in the fumes from her third run on the foil, she heard a knock on the front door. She folded the foil, put it back in its hiding place and stuffed the book and the tube back inside her shiny handbag.

Calmness enveloped her. She wondered if it was not from the heroin, as she hadn't taken much, but perhaps the finality of the situation.

Approaching the front door, she tried to make out the figure on the other side of the glass. The shape was too long and wide to belong to her friends. It was a man, but was it the rapist? For a moment, fear infused her calmness.

Her hand was on the lock. The ordeal he'd put her through played out in her head. Hot rage permeated her body. She hoped it was him and not a random punter. Her heart pumped in her chest. It was a different feeling to that when she wanted to flee. This wasn't the flight with which she was familiar. This must be the fight.

***

Shelley stood at the front door, facing the demoniac who'd raped her. In the radiance of the twilight, she smiled at him. To other people he was probably an ordinary looking man: a businessman, a husband, a father with a young family, but Shelley could see the evil in him. She looked past the pretty lashes, disguising the malevolence, and into his dark, sunken eyes. She could see the sickness in his soul.

"Come through. Let me take your coat." Shelley helped him take off his navy suit jacket. She hung it over the banister.

"Where's the black girl? I didn't book you."

"She's making herself beautiful for you. She won't be long." If he saw the lounge, he might not stay so she led him into the kitchen, explaining they were in the middle of redecorating.

"Can I get you a drink?"

"No thank you. Will she be long?"

"I don't think so." Shelley had to get him to drink in order to get him drugged. Although her hair was different, she worried that he might recognise her face or her voice. If he did, he might leave, and either way he might rape her.

"You may as well have a drink while you're waiting. What do you like, spirits, wine—?"

"I don't want a drink. Can't you hurry her up or something?"

Shelley walked to the bottom of the stairs and shouted up to her friend who wasn't there. While she was opposite the front door, she lingered for a minute, listening out for a car. Where were her friends? Her eyes welled. She took a deep breath to suction the tears back from whence they came.

She returned to the kitchen and noticed his impatient glare. She knew she couldn't stall him much longer. She poured herself a gin then took the glass round to the fridge. Hiding behind the fridge door, she added the tonic, GHB and pre-crushed Rohypnol. Stirring it, she tried to avoid the teaspoon coming into contact with the glass. The whole thing was risky, but she didn't see another option.

She closed the fridge and turned to face him. She raised the glass to her mouth and took a sip. "She's very bad to keep you like this but she's worth the wait, I promise." Shelley walked closer to him and undid the top two buttons of her red blouse. "I'll look after you," she whispered in his ear and through gritted teeth, she forced herself to kiss his neck.

With both his hands, he grabbed her buttocks and lifted her up on the work surface. "I think you're the bad girl." He pulled her hair and pushed his tongue into her mouth. Shelley fought the urge to bite it. She gulped back the vomit that shot up her throat. However much it hurt, it would be worth it.

"Your mouth is dry." She held the glass of date rape drug to his lips and as she tilted it upwards, he swallowed it down. All of it.

35. Not Again

Her skills in the art of shutting down and zoning out were of no help as the rapist groped her. The horrendous images of his last attack wouldn't leave her mind. In an effort to change the pictures of the past to those of the future, she tried to concentrate on what she planned to do to him.

She was physically revolted as he sucked on her breast but with his eyes off hers, she took the opportunity to look at the clock on the kitchen wall. It was approaching nine o'clock. Anytime now, the GHB would take effect and not long after, the Rohypnol would kick in. Then their roles could be reversed.

Shelley heard a knock on the door. "I'll be back in a minute," she said, breaking away. She swallowed down the vomit that rose into her mouth.

"No you won't. I'm not done with you yet." He seized her from behind as she neared the kitchen door. He wrestled her down to the sullied vinyl. "Take off your skirt."

"I can't…That's my friend…We're going out."

"No you're not. You're not going anywhere." He lay on top of her, gripping her wrists. He raised her arms above her head, pinning her to the floor.

"Stop. I'll call Destiny for you. Dest—" Her scream was cut off as he shoved his yellow tie into her mouth. With the hand he'd released, she grappled for the tie but he snatched her wrist and threw her arm back down. Both her narrow wrists were constrained by one large hand. With his other hand, he pushed the tie deeper into her mouth.

Trapped under his heavy frame, she writhed in an effort to free herself. Her flailing arms were hampered by his grip. She kicked her legs and tried to raise her torso off the floor but she was crushed by his weight. She couldn't get away.

"There is no Destiny, is there?" He forced his hand under her skirt and tore into her knickers. "I thought I recognised your face, and now I remember. You want some more, don't you?"

Shelley told herself not to cry, that it wouldn't be long until he was knocked out. The incessant knocking at the front door echoed in her ears. She pictured Nicole standing on the doorstep. If only she'd given the other key she'd had cut to Nicole and not to Angel.

When she felt him invade her, she shrieked, but her call for help was muffled by the tie. The sick that she'd previously managed to keep down crept up her throat and into her mouth. She choked as the dam of the tie forced it back down.

Her heart journeyed to her head – perhaps for its protection – and in there it thumped. The feeling of suffocation gripped her as particles of puke caught in the back of her throat and clogged her nostrils. She struggled to breathe. Her internal feeling of dying became accompanied by an external death; perhaps this is how it felt to drown. She agonised how her mother would cope without her, identify her body, and bury her only living child. Through the pain, guilt gripped her as she pictured her mother and Aunt Elsie's faces. She felt her windpipe shut down and blackness descended.

She was startled by coughing that was confined within her chest. Her eyes opened. From her nose, vomit splattered onto the rapist's white shirt.

"You disgusting, dirty whore." He spat on her. She felt his saliva spray her forehead.

To avoid his baleful stare, she turned her head. She felt the tears that had brimmed in her eyes trickle across her face, over the bridge of her nose, and into her hair. In her head, she prayed to God to save her.

Ideas to escape fired in her mind. However hopeless, there was a determination inside her. From the corner of her eye, she saw a pot of paint and pictured herself ramming it into his head, his blood gushing from the wound. But in reality, she couldn't reach the pot. She recalled the long knives in the kitchen drawer that she'd used to break out of the house. In her mind, she drove a knife into his chest repeatedly. Blood fountained from the lacerations. But she couldn't get to the drawer. She thought about head-butting him. She could do that. She tried, but she was unable to raise her head off the floor.

"Is it hurting?" He panted.

Shelley nodded. Unable to make a sound, she screamed for help in her head.

"Good. I know this is how you whores like it, don't you? This is what you want."

Fighting for air, she took short breaths through her nose. Vomit stuck in her windpipe. The tie stifled her choking. *Hail Mary, Mother of Mercy, to thee do I cry ... mourning and weeping in this valley of tears.*

"Tell me you like it. Tell me, you little whore. This is what you want."

Shelley shook her head. She widened her eyes. *Jesus, save me. God, save me...*

"This is how you like it, isn't it? Ask me for more. Say it. Tell me, you slut."

Will, help me. Get him off me, please.

The soulless eyes in the red, sweaty face above her rolled back to the whites. She slipped one of her wrists free. She grabbed the tie out of her mouth. The repugnant face hanging over hers received a vomitus bespattering.

"Whore," he said, wiping the debris from his face.

With her free hand, she slapped him on the side of the head. She dug her nails in behind his ear and planted her thumb deep into his eyeball. He bellowed as he tried to prise off her hand but her grip was firmly entrenched.

Suddenly, he fell silent. His head fell, face-down next to hers on the vinyl. His body was still. She presumed he'd fainted from the shock or the pain, or the GHB had kicked in. She rolled out from under the dead weight and straddled its back. From the crown, she grasped a clump of short, brown hair and she pummelled the face into the hard floor.

***

"Fucking hell." Angel was kneeling down next to Shelley. In her frenzy, Shelley hadn't heard her come in.

Shelley relinquished her grip. The rapist's head thudded on the floor.

"Oh my God. I'm so sorry." Nicole rushed over to Shelley.

Shelley felt a coldness from the air on her chest. She realised her blouse was gaping open. She lowered her gaze to fasten the buttons. She tried not to look at her torn knickers and the savage next to them on the vinyl. "Where the fuck have you been?" she said.

"Ladbroke Grove was gridlocked. The police blocked everyone in," Angel said.

"I dumped my car and ran here." Nicole glared at Angel. "What were you doing sitting in the damn fucking traffic? If you'd been here—"

"I couldn't go anywhere. I was right by the police," Angel replied.

"Why didn't you answer your fucking phone?"

"I would if I'd had a signal. You think I wanted this to happen to your girl?" Angel shouted. "I care about her too, you know."

Angel held her hand out to Shelley, who ignored it and pushed herself up from the dirty floor. She stumbled to the sink. Holding onto the draining board, she put her face under the tap. Once she'd rinsed off the residual puke, she gargled with water.

Nicole came over and handed her a pack of tissues. Shelley expelled the vomit from her nose. She crossed back to the other side of the kitchen and replaced her shoes, which she'd lost during the attack. She approached her assailant and began kicking into his ribs.

"I'm so sorry, love," Nicole said.

"It's too fucking late." Shelley drove the heel of her stiletto into the rapist's ear. Blood trickled out and down the side of his head.

There was a knock on the front door and Angel left the kitchen. Nicole wiped her eyes then took her cigarettes from her bag. She put one in Shelley's hand. As Shelley raised the cigarette to her mouth, she became aware of the tremors in her hand. Then she realised her whole body was afflicted. Though she wasn't convulsing, this was how it usually started.

"I'm sorry, Shell," Tara said, walking towards her. "I've been stuck in the station... I think someone got shot."

Shelley stormed out of the kitchen and into the lounge. She picked up her handbag and case. She ran up the stairs on her unsteady legs and went straight into the bathroom. With the door locked and the shower running, she knelt on the cold tiles and took out her works, heroin, citric, spoon and lighter. She swallowed hard, trying to steal back the tears; a little longer and the only friend she could rely on would take away the pain.

She tried to control her shaking as she prepared the hit, but the spoon wobbled under the tap. As she added the heroin, some of the precious liquid spilt. With the spoon resting on the tiles, she put in a pinch of citric and when she precariously held it for cooking, she prayed not to spill any more.

She carefully dropped in the filter, took her syringe and drew up the elixir into the barrel. There was nothing in the room to use as a tourniquet so she selected a recently healed vein on her wrist. So what if her friends noticed? While applying pressure with her other hand, she noticed her pulse – something she'd never paid attention to before.

"Come out, love. I'll make you a cuppa." Nicole tapped on the bathroom door.

"I don't want fucking tea. I just wanna be on my own."

"I tried, Shell. I couldn't get round the back. I'm so sorry... There was nothing I could do."

"Just fuck off!" Shelley listened to Nicole's footsteps retreat down the stairs; she heard what she thought was Nicole sobbing.

As Shelley had kept a tight hold on her wrist, the feeling in her hand was nearly numb. If only that numbness would pervade the rest of her, she wished.

Taking deep breaths, in the hope that she'd steady herself, she inserted the needle into her vein. Having pulled back a little on the plunger, she pushed in. The abhorrent images were purged from her mind as she crossed the threshold into the refuge rendered by heroin.

36. Darkness

When her eyes opened, the shower was still running. She could barely see through the steam in the bathroom. The needle hung from her wrist and her blood stained the off-white floor tiles. She didn't know how long she'd been out, but she had to take a shower and remove the tainted clothes touching her flesh. If the rapist came to, her friends could deal with him. After all, they hadn't been there for her when she'd needed them.

Having removed her blouse and skirt, she braved the scorching water and stood under the weak jet, still in her nightmare for a while. Inside she was crying but on the outside, there were no tears. *It feels like my insides are being shredded. There's a vandal inside and he's ripping me up with razor blades... He's killing me.*

Using the men's shampoo she found on the side of the bath, she scrubbed at her scalp for several minutes. After rinsing off the foam, she washed her hair twice more before scouring her body. By the time she was ready to come out, the outer layer of her skin felt like rubber.

Once dry, she became aware of the masculine scent left on her from the shampoo and shower gel. Even though it smelt clean, it repulsed her. Taking the perfume bottle from her case, she doused her body and hair with Obsession.

In her toiletry bag, she found the toothbrush she'd brought with her. With lashings of toothpaste, she brushed her teeth over the sink. Before long, the white foam that fell into the basin took on a pink hue. Though her mouth was sore and she tasted the blood, she continued to brush vigorously: her teeth, gums, inside her cheeks, the roof of her mouth, her tongue, and as far as she could reach down her throat.

Dressed in the casual clothes she'd brought with her, her body still felt besmirched. However hot the water was, and however much soap she used, the feeling of contamination remained. Eventually, on the outside, it would fade – she knew that's what happened – but she also knew, on the inside, it would mar her forever.

***

With her hair still wet, Shelley went downstairs. She put her handbag and small suitcase in the lounge before going through to the kitchen. The room was empty. Her friends weren't there and the rapist's body had gone, along with his blood that had pooled on the vinyl. They must have started without her.

She turned the gold handle of the cellar door and light beamed up the staircase. When she reached the last step, she felt satisfied to be setting her eyes on the sight she'd been waiting for.

"When did you move him?"

"A few hours ago," Tara said. "How much did you give him? He's been out cold since you went up."

"Only two roofies, and half a bottle of GHB... maybe a bit more."

"Are you all right, Shell?" Nicole asked.

"I don't wanna talk about it." Shelley walked back up the stairs and into the lounge. She took out her curling tongs and plugged them into the socket. Having picked out the items required from her case, she carried them down to the damp cellar.

"Have you been in here this whole time?" Shelley asked.

"Me and Nic have. Angel went for a nap after we dragged him down."

How her friends could bear the stench of dead rat or sleep in the filthy house, she didn't know. She hadn't seen Angel in the lounge, so she must've been sleeping in one of the bedrooms, but how could she do that? The mattresses in every room were rank.

Shelley unpicked the edge of the roll of clingfilm. She walked towards the subhuman where he lay naked at the opposite end of the room. The feeling of fleas crawling over her skin intensified. As she got closer, she inspected the damage she'd inflicted after the rape. His face was battered.

Shelley handed Nicole the loose end of the clingfilm. Nicole bent down and wound it several times around his toes. She held it steady while Shelley began binding his feet together with the industrial-size roll of plastic wrap. With his feet secured, Tara and Nicole kept his legs raised as Shelley bound them in transparent layers.

"How are we going to do this?" Tara asked. They were stuck at the top of his fat thighs and unable to raise him. Shelley sprinted up the stairs, grabbed a folding chair from the lounge then came back down to the cellar.

They wedged the curved back of the chair under his buttocks. Her friends levered him up, enabling her to continue the mummification. They jiggled the chair along underneath him as Shelley worked her way up his body.

On reaching his stomach, Shelley removed the handcuffs from

his wrists and folded his arms over his torso. She bound them straitjacket-style, then continued the swathing up to his shoulders. Tara and Nicole lifted his head as Shelley wrapped his neck and then his face.

"Can you poke your finger in?" Shelley asked Nicole, because she couldn't bear to stick her finger up his nose.

"I can't. Can you do it?" Nicole asked Tara.

Tara tried, but she couldn't break through the clingfilm. Shelley unravelled the film covering his nose while Nicole went to fetch a knife from the kitchen. Taking the blade from Nicole, Shelley pierced two holes for his nostrils. As she rewrapped his face, she watched the blood ooze from his nose and spread out underneath the transparent cover. At the top of his head, she tore the clingfilm then stepped back to admire her handiwork.

"Do you wanna get some sleep, love?" Nicole asked Shelley.

"No way, I couldn't."

"I just thought after what happened, you—"

"She said she didn't want to talk about it," Tara said. "You need to learn when to leave things alone."

***

Shelley went upstairs to the lounge and sat on one of her own chairs. She didn't want to be in that house. There was no escape from her mind there after the rape. The scene replayed in her head. She saw it occur as if she'd been removed from her body and watching from the ceiling.

Added to the pain were the practicalities. She'd need to pay a visit to the Praed Street Project to be tested for sexually transmitted diseases. After he'd raped her the last time, she'd been clear of STDs. However, over the course of two years, a serial rapist with his modus operandi would most likely have contracted something.

She was distraught with fear over what diseases he might have passed to her. Though she'd have most of the results within a few days of an intrusive examination, it was a few days too many to wait. And the three-month delay before she could obtain a conclusive result on HIV filled her with dread.

A week or two of lone speedballing at home was what she wanted. Her body began to crave, but she hadn't brought any crack with her – she couldn't afford psychosis mid-abduction.

Taking her handbag, she returned to her sanctuary upstairs in the bathroom. At least she could have some gear. She looked in the mirror to check her pupils. She wondered how her friends hadn't noticed their near absence because the pinhead-sized, black dots were retracting through the centre of her blue eyes.

37. A New Day

Through the mottled bathroom window, Shelley watched the moon glowing in the blackness of the sky. She heard her name being shouted. She crouched on the floor, bundling her drug paraphernalia into her handbag, then she rushed downstairs.

"He's awake." Angel stood at the top of the stairs that led down to the cellar. She looked well rested. Shelley wondered how she'd been able to sleep on a grimy mattress.

"I'll be one minute." Shelley darted into the lounge, suddenly remembering that she'd forgotten to unplug her curling tongs earlier. They must have been on for a couple of hours and, as there was no fire, she worried they might have broken.

After dumping her handbag, she unplugged the tongs. They were steaming. Holding the handle low down to eschew the heat, she walked with her arm outstretched as she carried them to the cellar.

"Are you all right?" Nicole squeezed Shelley's free hand as she entered the dark room.

Shelley nodded. Of course, she wasn't all-fucking-right, but at least she was less wrong than last night.

"Do you want this?" Tara held out a torch.

"Will you hold it for me?" Shelley asked.

Tara shone her torch on the rapist. Under the stream of light, his clingfilm-encased body glistened. The sound system in Shelley's head switched on REM - *Shiny Happy People*. The mental recording of last night's rape that had been running on a loop ceased. She felt as though some of the fleas on her skin had fled.

When she got closer, she saw the purpleness of his swollen face and the patches of dried blood that had formed under the plastic. He could have been any of the men that had raped her, but there was only one she would have traded him for – her mother's ex-boyfriend.

She concentrated on the lyrics of the song – *happy, happy* – and pumped up the volume. After a minute had passed, the music had the desired effect of drowning out the rerun of another rape, which was attempting an infiltration of her mind.

By his side, she stooped and put her mouth next to his clingfilm-covered ear. "I've got something for you... It's just a little thing, to say thank you for everything you've done to me."

The music in her head was disturbed as the bull in the slaughterhouse bellowed. The cocoon she'd created muffled the noise. As she heard him cough, she hoped he'd be sick. He could experience the feeling of suffocation he'd imposed on her.

"I bet you're always the giver, aren't you? Well, I like things to be fair... fair and equal. So it's only right that you have your turn now. This is your turn to receive." Shelley pressed the top of the fiery, cylindrical tongs against his ear.

He howled, floundering on the concrete floor. Tara, Angel and Nicole rolled him flat onto his stomach and held him down while Shelley seared a hole with the tongs through the plastic coating on his arse. The smell of dead rat commingled with the fumes from the singeing clingfilm. When the dancing smoke had dispersed in the air, she inserted the tongs. He cried like a man on fire.

Shelley laughed. Then she said matter-of-factly, "This might hurt a little. Hopefully a lot, and it's exactly what a sadistic cunt like you deserves. Do you recognise my friends?"

He shook his head, bawling inside his plastic shroud.

"You raped two of them. You can't remember? It's a slow death, and that's what you're gonna have." Shelley wrenched the tongs, showing no mercy to his smothered cries. "Is that what I wanted, then? That's what you think – that I wanted that? Well I think... I think you want this. You really fucking want it, you motherfucking, twisted, evil cunt."

Screaming, he squirmed on the floor. With Nicole and Tara sat on his back, and Angel holding down his legs, he wasn't going anywhere. Now he knew how it felt to be violated, powerless, unable to escape.

"Have I killed him already?" Shelley said, noticing he was silent and no longer moving. She rested the tongs on the floor and helped her friends flip him onto his back.

"He's alive. Look, his chest's moving," Angel said.

"That's a shame." Tara booted him in the groin.

"Are you on another planet? This isn't meant to be quick," Nicole told Tara. "I'm gonna put the kettle on." She crossed the room towards the stairs.

"Will you watch him?" Shelley asked Angel and Tara, as she wiped the sweat from her forehead. "I want a drink ready for that cunt when he wakes up."

***

In the sharpness of the Sunday dawn, Shelley sat on the low wall between the patio and the grass in the back garden. From the

Benson and Hedges packet in her handbag, she took a cigarette. Once lit, she took a hard draw. Nicole floated towards her and handed her a mug of tea. Shelley became entranced by the evaporating steam swimming up into the air and then vanishing.

She tilted her head to the cloudless sky. She had been right, it was going to be a good day, but there was nothing good about what she felt. Although the rapist deserved his punishment and she didn't have a choice in taking part, she wondered if the fact that she had done it made her a worse person. A voice in her head told her it didn't.

"If we only stop one more girl getting raped, we've done the right thing." Nicole put her arm around Shelley's shoulders. "I don't like it either, but it's a catch twenty-two, isn't it? I'd rather live with this than knowing I did nothing to stop him."

Bewildered, Shelley realised she wasn't having a debate with the board of directors in her head.

"And this is different... we planned it, and for a damn good reason. What happened at The Lanesborough, that wasn't your fault."

Shelley raised her cigarette to her mouth, but the gap between her fingers was bare. From the gold packet next to her on the wall, she took another and sparked up.

Aftershock from being raped the night before had cast her into oblivion. Everything seemed surreal and she didn't feel like she was alive. Was she actually in the garden? Did Nicole really just mention The Lanesborough?

She touched the stone wall with her fingertips and felt its coldness. She took a drag on her cigarette and waved her hand through the smoke she exhaled, watching it disperse.

"Ow," Nicole said, as Shelley prodded her. "What did you do that for?"

"I'm just checking I'm really here."

"Aren't you meant to pinch yourself for that?" Nicole smiled.

"I'm checking you're here too." Shelley spread her open palm across her collarbone and pressed the ruby into her skin.

"What you've said, Shell, it sounds like you might have post-traumatic stress. I know I'm not an expert but after what happened to me, I know a lot about that stuff."

Shelley wondered what else she'd missed. How did a conversation about The Lanesborough and post-traumatic stress disorder materialise? She didn't have PTSD; that was something her mother suffered – and she was nothing like her mother.

"Flashbacks and nightmares are part of it - I have them. I don't have the checking, but I think that's you trying to stop something bad from happening again. I think that's why I work." Nicole took a pull on her cigarette. "I've been trying to recreate situations where I've got control... but I don't."

Staring at the dewed grass, Shelley was confounded. She'd never told Nicole – or anyone else – about the constant stream of haunting images that she relived in her head, nor the nightmares, nor the checking. Had she been reading her mind or had Shelley spoken unknowingly?

"The heroin's part of it too." Nicole took Shelley's hand and pushed back her sleeve. "You're trying not to feel, but you can't."

***

"Fucking hell, babe. What've you done to yourself?" Angel appeared on the patio.

The secret that Shelley had meticulously kept with her carefully planned hits and her long sleeves was no more. It wasn't good that Angel knew, but what was most disconcerting was what Nicole would think and whether they'd remain friends.

"You can't leave Tara alone with him," Nicole told Angel.

"It's okay. He woke up but she's knocked him out again." Angel directed her eyes on Shelley. "Babe, you got a problem. You can't—"

"She knows and she's gonna stop. That's what's taken us so long," Nicole said.

I don't want to stop... I'm not stopping... It's what keeps me going. Had she made a promise to give up heroin or was Nicole appeasing Angel? She couldn't recall divulging her junk addiction, let alone committing to abstain.

"I'm making Tara a coffee. That girl needs to sober up. She's not in a good way, you know."

"She's a fucking crackhead. I've tried with her, haven't I, Shell?" Nicole flicked the contents of her mug over the grass. "She's beyond help."

"No one's beyond help with that stuff, never. Don't give up on her. She needs her friends right now." Angel reached out and took Nicole's mug from her hand. Then she took Shelley's mug and went back into the house. Nicole followed her in. Shelley remained sitting on the wall, wondering if her closest friend wouldn't be any more, now that she knew she was a junky.

Shelley lit a cigarette and stared at the empty space that Nicole had left on the low wall. She tried to picture her friend in her mind, attempting to recall their conversation. Part of it suddenly entered her head: she'd been talking about her maxim – the Golden Rule.

Nicole had said that she was treating the rapist how she'd want to be treated herself. If she were he, culpable of raping countless women, she would want to be stopped whatever that took. Then she remembered another part of the conversation: how she'd breached the rule with the lies she told to her mother and aunt. If she were her mother, she wouldn't want her daughter to lie to her, and far less to prostitute herself. There was no justification she could cook up for that.

Shelley lit a cigarette with the one she'd just smoked down to the butt. She dropped the butt on a terracotta paving stone and stamped it out with her trainer. She gazed at the void on the patio wall, feeling her own internal void expand. It spread upwards from her gut and created an emptiness only heroin could fill. Consumed by that feeling and the craving for a hit, her effort to evoke the conversation with Nicole was fettered.

***

When they returned to the garden, Angel handed Shelley a purple mug and Nicole filled the space on the wall. As Shelley looked at her closest friend, she tried to conjure more of their earlier tete-a-tete, but nothing came. She averted her gaze to her own hand and became fixated on a vein.

Even though Nicole and Angel were now aware of her junk addiction, Shelley didn't want them to know she was using in their presence. Her pain needed numbing, so she excused herself from the awkwardness on the patio to return to the solitude of the bathroom.

As Shelley stood to make her exit, Angel grabbed her arm. "You're playing with death, you know that, girl? You're on a path of self destruction."

"I know. I told her to leave him, but she didn't listen. He's hurt you again, sweetheart, hasn't he?" In her dressing gown, the lady from next door looked down at them from the top of the fence. She must've been standing on a ladder, making her nearly seven feet tall.

"What's she talking about?" Nicole whispered in Shelley's ear.

"No, it's not him. We're fine thanks." Shelley looked up at the giant old lady. What was she doing in her garden this early on a Sunday morning? How long had she been eavesdropping on them?

"I don't think so. We heard you fighting last night. My husband was this close to calling the police." She gestured with her thumb and forefinger. "You can't expect us to hear that and do nothing. If something happens to you, sweetheart, I'll never forgive myself."

"We're fine, really. You don't need to worry."

185

"Denial, that's what you've got. I'm telling you, sweetheart, wake up. You shouldn't be here."

Shelley walked through the patio doors and headed upstairs.

38. The Search

In her muddled state, Shelley saw only one solution to the problem posed by the lady next door. Having packed the foil, tube and lighter into her handbag, she left the bathroom and walked through to Len's room.

Oddly, as she approached the mattress, her aversion to dirt didn't ignite the urge to vomit. Perhaps it was due to the state of obliviousness, which was causing her to feel absent from her own body.

She studied the corners of the double mattress for the rip she'd made previously. She saw nothing. In case her eyes were unreliable, she pressed around with her hands, but having checked every corner, both feeling and seeing, she concluded there were no tears.

Perhaps her memory had failed her and she'd made the cut on a side. She checked the sides but found nothing. After scanning the top of the mattress, she climbed on and stroked it, feeling for something her eyes couldn't see.

In case she'd made the rip on the underside of the mattress, she flipped it up. It thumped as it landed upright on the floor between the windowsill and the bed frame. There were no visible tears so she walked up the tight space to check with her hands. There was nothing to feel. It couldn't be the same mattress.

Her head spun but tumbling on empty, the output was nil. Her heartbeat quickened and her hands trembled, causing her to feel partially present. She wasn't yet ready to return and regretted having a chase instead of a fix. The latter would have kept her away from reality. There wasn't time now. She'd told Nicole and Angel she'd be a couple of minutes and by her estimation, she'd already been fifteen or more.

A thought dropped into her empty drum: perhaps the mattress had been swapped, and the one she was looking for had been moved into a different bedroom. She left Len's room to look in the others.

Fuck this. I need a hit. On the hall landing, she was sucked back into the bathroom. After what she'd been through, withholding a fix wasn't cruel, it was torture, and she wasn't the one lured there for that.

Injecting was messy with shaking hands. Following numerous misaligned needle insertions, her wrist resembled a section of dot-to-dot puzzle. On realising the cause of the problem – aiming a quivering needle at a trembling target – she hit a vein in her ankle and successfully delivered the shot.

With the junk riding in her blood, she felt ready to check the other bedrooms. There were single mattresses in two of the ransacked-styled boudoirs but in the fourth, a dirty double mattress lay on the floor. Having pushed aside the clutter of clothes and papers, she checked the corners. When she stumbled on the hole, she looked up to the ceiling and she whispered, "thank you."

Using her sleeve as a protective cover for her hand, she delved inside. Unable to feel anything, she pushed her hand in deeper until she was in halfway up to her elbow, but the cavity was vacant. This might be a different tear. There could be another. Unwilling to accept there were no other holes, she rechecked the four corners. She found nothing.

The mattress was heavy to overturn, especially being on the floor, but after struggling for a while, she managed to lift it and lean it upright against her body. She pushed it forward and as it banged on the carpet, dust was stirred into the air. Tiny specks flew into her eyes, causing her to blink profusely.

When her eyes stopped watering, she studied the mattress then ran her hand over it – the final place the tear could be. It wasn't there.

Perplexed, she walked back into the disarray that was Len's bedroom and stood by the window, staring at the coffee-spattered spot on the carpet where she remembered seeing the handgun the first time. For a better view, she elevated out of her body and watched herself standing there, looking at the gun on the floor.

The memory was clear, but she wasn't certain that it had in fact happened. Although she was sure she didn't have crack psychosis on that day, it could have been an hallucinatory flashback.

***

"What do you mean you can't find it?" Tara threw her hands in the air then appeared to lose her balance, wobbling backwards perilously close the cellar stairs. Nicole, who was nearest, grabbed her arm and pulled her away from the edge.

"That I can't bloody find it. It's not there. It's gone. Vanished. Moved. Stolen. I don't bloody know, but it's not where I thought it was," Shelley said.

"What are we going to do now?" Tara slurred.

"Well, you can stop drinking for a start," Nicole told her.

"Blah-blah-blah-blah-blah-blah-blah." Tara waved her middle finger close to Nicole's face. "I'll do what I like. It's your fucking fault anyway."

"It's my fault you neglected your kid." Nicole swiped Tara's finger and bent it back. "Really? What did you think I was gonna do, you crackhead bitch?"

"Don't do this now, please." Shelley shot them both a disapproving look, and Nicole released Tara's finger. "I'll think of something. Maybe we can search the house. But please, stop drinking, it's not helping," she told Tara.

"She's ruining my life. Tell her to stop." Tara swayed as she walked down the stairs, muttering what sounded like, "Then I won't need to drink."

Shelley clasped Nicole's hand and led her into the shipwreck lounge. "What the fuck are we gonna do with her?"

"You know what she's like. You shouldn't have asked her to come." Nicole proffered her Silk Cut packet.

Shelley declined. She sat down on one of her wooden, folding chairs and lit one of her own stronger brand. She knew why she'd asked Tara to come, and she knew Nicole did too. Although she was aware there would be awkwardness, she'd thought they'd put their differences aside. And earlier there wasn't a problem. It had only started once Tara was drunk.

***

"He's awake. I need his drink, babe?" Angel came running into the lounge.

"Oh shit, I forgot. I'm on it." Shelley stubbed out her cigarette in the black, stolen-from-a-pub ashtray and got to her feet.

"Why don't we make him overdose on roofies? Do you think we've got enough?" Nicole asked.

"I don't know. I don't know how many it takes."

"Give him what's left and see what happens." Angel walked towards the door then added, "Can you bring it in? I can't leave Tara on her own again. She's out of it."

Shelley walked down the hall and into the kitchen where the early morning sun was streaming through the window above the sink. She didn't want to let him go so early. *He won't suffer if we do it like that.*

"It won't take your pain away," replied a voice from the board.

Having selected the grimiest mug she could find, she looked by the bottles of alcohol for the Rohypnol. She couldn't see it, so she shuffled them around on the work surface. Within moments, it became apparent that the paper wrap, which she'd made to store the tablets, was missing.

"Have you seen the roofies?" She shouted to Nicole while widening her search to the sink and the rest of the work surface.

Nicole came into the kitchen. "Yeah. They're on the side, in front of the bottles."

"They're not. Look. It's not here." Shelley turned her palms. "Where the fuck I have put it?"

"It's there. I saw it when I made the tea. They were in that wrap, weren't they?" Nicole took over from Shelley shifting the bottles around on the worktop.

"Yeah, they were, but where the fuck is it now? What the fuck have I done with it?" Shelley drove her fingers into the hair at her temples.

In order to look in the cardboard box, which she'd used to carry the drinks, Shelley had to crouch on the dirty vinyl. As she did so, she glanced to the side and there she saw her body trapped under the rapist.

Agony poured into her from the dark cloud hovering above. Then the feeling of suffocation returned until she remembered to breathe. When she got to her feet, she felt shorter. Shorter and thinner. If only she could disappear like that.

***

Shelley and Nicole abandoned their search for the Rohypnol mid-morning and returned to the cellar. The rapist's muffled groaning echoed in the room. In Shelley's mind, it took over from her own internal screaming.

The malodour of dead rat seemed to mingle with something even more offensive. When Shelley approached the rapist, she realised what that was. In her anticipation of the proceedings, she'd omitted to factor in bodily eliminations.

"Where's his drink, babe?" Angel asked.

"I can't make it. We can't find the roofies." Shelley retched and backed off to stand farther from the rapist and closer to the staircase. "This is gross. I can't stay in here."

"You're not the one who's been breathing this in for hours. I swear it's damaging my lungs," Angel said.

"Let's fix him more secure and get out. This has gotta be bad for our health." Shelley walked over to the brown tape that lay on the concrete near the rapist. She held out one end to Nicole.

"I don't think he's going anywhere, love."

"There's no point risking it, is there?" Shelley said.

Bound in the wide, brown tape on top of his shiny wrapping, the rapist looked like a parcel. Shelley walked over to the stairs where Tara was asleep on the floor with a bottle of Stolichnaya clutched to her chest.

"Wake up." Shelley shook Tara's shoulders, mindful her friend's face didn't rub against the splintered step it was resting on.

"Tara...You fucking crackhead, wake up," Nicole shouted in her face.

"Stop. You'll scare her." Angel pulled Nicole away.

"You sort her out then. I'm done with her." Nicole stomped up the creaking staircase.

"Has she said anything to you?" Shelley asked Angel once she heard Nicole's footsteps walking over the hall above them.

"What do you mean?"

"I don't know. She's in a weird mood, that's all." What a stupid thing to say! Why did those words come out? Of course, she's in a weird mood. Angel didn't look concerned by Shelley's comment, but what she'd really wanted to ask was whether Nicole knew that she'd lied to her about Angel's gender, but she wasn't confident to ask either of them outright. She was aware that Nicole's mood could easily be justified by the current situation as it was – discovering her best friend was a junky who had no Rohypnol and couldn't find the gun.

Shelley slipped her hands under Tara's armpits and Angel lifted her feet. With Angel walking forwards and Shelley backwards, they carried her up the stairs and into the lounge. Shelley scanned the carpet for a clean section on which to deposit Tara. There were none, so she opted for an area under the bay windows where the intensity of stains, dust and dirt was closer to that found in Tara's own flat – not yet as bad as Len's house.

"I bet she's fucking taken the roofies." Nicole pointed at Tara.

"No, she didn't. She wouldn't," Angel said. "She's drunk, that's all. She's polished off a whole bottle."

"I wouldn't put it past her. Look in her pockets." Nicole went over to Tara, knelt down beside her and reached for the pocket of her jeans.

"You can't do that." Angel took Nicole's hand and gently guided it away from Tara. "Believe, she wouldn't take them."

"We have to do something. What about GHB? He could overdose on that. Or heroin. You could inject him," Nicole suggested.

"The GHB's finished and I haven't got enough heroin."

"What about bleach? We could inject him with that." Nicole said.

"There isn't any," Shelley replied.

"Something else, then. Flash, Mr Muscle, whatever." Nicole

threw her hands in the air.

"There's nothing. Fairy Liquid, shampoo and shower gel."

"Would that kill him?" Angel asked.

"Probably, but if it clogs the needle, we're fucked. I've only got one."

"Suffocation. That'll be—" Nicole began.

"Too quick and peaceful for that cunt," Shelley said.

While Nicole and Angel discussed ideas, which kept leading them into dead ends, Shelley wondered when she'd be able to speak with Nicole about what she'd said in the garden. She needed to know how much Nicole knew of what happened at The Lanesborough. How much had she told her? And while they were on the subject, she may as well find out if the conversation she recalled at Tara's had ever occurred. If it had, she couldn't think of a reason why Nicole had never mentioned it before.

As her thoughts wandered, she recalled the girls she'd met on jobs through Marianne, and others she'd met in Marianne's flat. The thought that Marianne had sent that animal to all those girls – it was incomprehensible.

"I'll do it... I'll stab him," Shelley said.

39. Dressing Up

On the bathroom floor, Shelley measured out her remaining heroin. There was enough, most probably, to kill the rapist but she'd have to use it all. Therefore, there wasn't enough because she'd need a hit before administering his lethal injection and she'd need one after, before embarking on the onerous task of removing his body.

Would there be enough to kill him and leave her with one hit? She remeasured. No, she'd need to use all of it to be sure and it would be a waste of her heroin if she gave him any less and he didn't die.

She took the works, spoon and citric from her handbag and began preparing a shot. As she heated the underside of the spoon, her mind was invaded by the tape that had been recorded last night. Although stabbing him would be unpleasant, because of the risk of being spattered with his blood, there could be some satisfaction to be had.

With the filter in the spoon, she pressed her needle against it and drew up the brown liquid. She pulled her sock halfway down her foot and inserted the needle into a skinny vein, which was the fattest she could find. Too much pressure had been applied and the vein blew. Part of the hit was wasted.

In the knowledge she only had enough gear for two more hits, she cooked up another. When the syringe was full, she looked for the best vein. None were ideal. To avoid another accident she decided to go for the vein on the back of her knee that hadn't been touched for a while.

She pushed herself off the cold, bathroom tiles and stood with the syringe in her hand. She twisted at the waist, bent at the knee, and bowed sideways. Fighting the pain caused by contortion, she manoeuvred her arms lower in position to insert the needle.

Her impersonation of a gnarled tree made it awkward to pull back on the plunger, but she managed. Then, as she slowly exerted pressure, she felt the power behind the rush of her penultimate hit.

***

When Shelley roused, she was still in a half-dream; she was walking around wearing jumble sale clothes. Genius idea, she thought as she opened her eyes and reached for her cigarette packet.

She took a few puffs then flushed the cigarette down the toilet.

In the hall, she looked through the doors of the bedrooms until she found the room with the double mattress on the floor and the sea of papers and worn-out clothes.

On finding an oversized and holey white T-shirt, she pulled it over her head. Then she picked up a pair of over-washed, black cotton trousers. Once the trousers were at her waist and falling off, she realised they weren't a good idea and slipped out of them.

Rummaging further through the pile, she found a greying-white men's shirt. With that buttoned up over the T-shirt, it would provide a shield for the holes.

Using another T-shirt, she covered her hair and face. Although, after trying it for size, she took it off. Before it was operational, she'd need to cut out spaces to see.

On the bedside table, she found a biro. She poked two holes through the T-shirt for her eyes, one for her nose, and a fourth for her mouth. She put the tight neck of the T-shirt over her head and tied the wide hem in a knot in the position of a high ponytail. After some minor adjustments, widening the holes to reach their required positions, she was ready.

The dilemma of what to do in relation to protecting her own jeans remained. She went into Len's room to check his wardrobe. There was nothing of any use hanging up, but among the heap of clothes on the bottom of the wardrobe, she caught sight of a black belt poking out.

Wearing a pair of stonewash jeans too wide and too long for her, she threaded round the plastic-imitating-leather belt. At its tightest fastening, she realised there weren't enough notches in the belt. To secure it, she tucked the free-end under a section on the side of her waist. With the hems of the jeans rolled up a few times, she was ready to go down.

***

"Are you planning on haunting him to death?" Tara asked Shelley in the lounge.

"I don't think you're in a position to say anything. What the fuck were you thinking getting drunk like that?" Nicole looked angrily at Tara.

"I needed a drink. That's what I was thinking."

"Was it just the vodka or did you take the roofies? Tell me the truth, Tara." Shelley took a seat on a folding chair near the bay windows where Tara was sitting upright on the carpet in the same spot Shelley had left her sleeping a few hours ago.

"How can you even ask me? I expect that from Nic, not from

you."

"Where else could they have gone?" Nicole shouted.

"Don't start on that again. She said she didn't take them and I believe her." Angel walked into the lounge and sat on the folding chair to the other side of Tara.

"It's just odd, isn't it? I mean where—" Shelley was cut off.

"For the last time, I didn't fucking take them and I'm not staying around for you to pick on me." Tara glared at Shelley. "You're the one who's fucked up. They're aiming a rifle at me! We're under siege! You imagined you fucked your punter to death."

"That wasn't my—"

"Leave it, Shell." Nicole stood in front of Shelley, took her hand and dragged her into the kitchen. "Don't talk about that with her."

"What are you on about? She was out of order." Shelley took one of the clean glasses she'd brought with her and poured herself a gin.

"You don't need to talk about that punter with her. She doesn't know. She thinks you were hallucinating."

"What the fuck? Who the hell is that?" Shelley walked out of the kitchen and peered around the corner to see the front door. There was a shadow through the glass of someone too big to be the quidnunc neighbour, but it could be her husband. It could be anyone. Shelley's blood felt like it was panicking as it raced in her veins.

She heard what sounded like the clunking of keys. Then she watched as the door was pushed open. She ran back to the kitchen to hide, but there was nowhere.

"Shhh." Shelley stood by the fridge. She put her index finger to her lips and looked at Nicole with wide eyes. Tapping footsteps crescendoed in her ears.

"What the fuck are you doing here?" Shelley shouted.

"I was down the Grove but then I fucking— Why am I telling you? I don't need to tell you. This is my fucking gaff," Len slurred.

"Yeah, and you're not supposed to come back until I say."

"Chill out, Shelley, man. You ain't no estate agent, are ya?" he said, coming so close she could taste the beer on his breath. "If you wanted a fancy dress party you only needed to ask."

"This is a private matter." Shelley put her hands on his chest and gently pushed him out of her personal space.

He staggered backwards out of the kitchen and stopped partway down the hall. "By the way, I want my jeans washed and ironed before I have 'em back."

Shelley was surprised he'd noticed. Not only was he clearly

drunk but also his wild eyes indicated drug use, and the darkness around them, that he hadn't slept. The palm tree sprouting from his crown, however, and the mud stains on his jeans and leather jacket could betray a night spent in a park, possibly inclusive of a fall from a bench.

40. The Gun

Two hours later, at five o'clock, Len was still asleep upstairs and Shelley and her friends trapped in limbo in the lounge. The revised plan was for Shelley to talk Len into leaving the house with her, so that one of the others could kill the rapist. However, the improvised blood-splatter protective clothing, which Shelley had been wearing, lay on the lounge floor unclaimed.

The problem was posed by the final part of the plan – body disposal. Firstly, it would have to be undertaken in the middle of the night and as none of them knew the length of time it took for rigor mortis to set in, there was consensual concern regarding its potential to prevent, or at best hinder, the malleability and manipulation of the body. Secondly, it required four of them to carry the body; it had already been established that with three, the body could only be dragged. Therefore, Shelley had to come up with a scheme not only to get Len out of the house, but also to keep him out and allow her to return.

"Can you hear him?" Shelley picked up her faux-fur coat.

"You don't need that. Look outside." Nicole pointed to the window. "Just go."

Shelley listened to the footsteps getting closer. She walked into the hall, carrying her handbag. Even if she couldn't get him out, it would be a good time to visit the bathroom.

"How long's this party going on for?" Len asked Shelley by the foot of the stairs. "I've got stuff to do."

"We had a deal. Five-hundred pounds for one night, isn't what it was."

"Something happened... It was coming on top. I had to come back."

"What happened?"

"I didn't mean— It's nothing. Look, Shelley, man, this is my—"

"Can you score for me?" Shelley grabbed the sleeve of Len's brown leather bomber jacket and pulled him towards the front door.

"Back up, love. It's in my pocket." At the front door, Len pulled his arm free from Shelley and then lurched his way into the kitchen.

Shelley chased after him. "Not here. Not in front of my friends."

From his position by the draining board, Len curled his hand around the edge of the worktop and propelled himself out of the kitchen, gaining velocity from his swimmer-like push-off. He stopped at the undersize door opposite, his fingers on the gold handle.

"I don't wanna go in a fucking cupboard. For God's sake, come upstairs." Shelley walked to the staircase, hoping Len was behind her. When she turned, she saw that he wasn't. "Come on. Hurry up."

"Shut up."

"Don't fucking speak to me like that." Shelley retraced her steps until she was outside the kitchen. In front of her, she saw Len kneeling. His head was cradled sideways in his arms and his arms were resting, opened flat, against the small door.

***

"Listen, can you hear that?"

"I can't hear anything," Shelley said. "You're tripping. Have you seen the state of your eyes?"

"There's something down there and I know what it is." Len turned the handle. "I'm going in."

"There's nothing there. Come on." Shelley tugged at his sleeve, but he didn't move.

"Unless you wanna see ratty's mate, you best go in the lounge," Len warned. "This is the fucker that won't die with poison."

Shelley sprinted into the lounge and frantically waved her arms in the air, signalling for her friends to come close. Huddled in the centre of the room, she whispered into the space between them.

"I'm not leaving you," Nicole said.

Shelley heard the squeaking of the cellar's wooden steps.

"Say hello to my little friend." Len's unconvincing American accent drifted into the room.

"What the—" Nicole started.

"He thinks it's a rat. Just get out. Go. I'll sort it."

Shelley's friends stayed where they were. The cellar stairs creaked and as the sound became louder, Shelley knew Len was on his way up.

"Shelley. A word. Now," he yelled.

Before she left the lounge, she turned to her friends and vigorously poked her arm in the direction of the window. She listened as she made her way slowly down the hall, but she didn't hear them make a sound. They weren't leaving, at least not yet.

In the kitchen, Len stood in front of the work surface near Shelley's bottle display. She kept her gaze high as she walked in, trying to avoid looking at the vinyl. She fought the images that were firing in her mind, and went to stand next to Len. She couldn't look at him either. The spot where he stood marked the area of the work surface where the rapist had...

"Give me a minute." She took a deep breath. It wasn't the time to suffer now. She had to be composed. She needed to come up with a lie, an excuse, an explanation, but nothing came. Nothing, except the intrusive images.

"What kind of fucked-up freakery is going on in my cellar?" Len slurred.

Shelley raised her hand. "I need a moment," she said. To escape the heat from his stare, she faced the worktop. And to escape her mind, she picked up the green bottle of gin, took a glass and filled it halfway. The internal burning she felt from downing the half-glass of neat Gordon's allayed the razor-wielding vandal inside her. Having poured herself a second measure, she put the glass to her mouth, tipped back her head and slugged it down until the glass was empty. With her third glass of gin in her hands, she turned to face Len. "I'm sorry," she began. "I was... we've been…"

"You're taking me for a cunt. Mi casa, si casa, I said, but not for this." Len gestured vividly with his arms, more accurately Mediterranean than his words were. "A fucking show home, you said. A fucking show home. You never fucking asked to host the fucking Torture Garden." He dipped his hand into the pocket of his leather bomber jacket and pulled out a handgun.

"That's where it is." Shelley's thought escaped from her mind and into her mouth from where it departed.

"Nah, love, it ain't. My cellar ain't a venue for your fucking S and M party." With the 'F-A-T-E' fingers of his right hand, he placed the gun on the work surface.

"What are you doing with that?" Shelley edged her hand along the Formica, closer to the gun.

"Sometimes I have to— Fuck this." Len slammed his hand down next to Shelley's and his arm nudged the gun into the bottle of gin. "That sadist cunt's gotta be out of my house in the next two minutes. End of party. Capiche?"

41. Going in Circles

Shelley found herself being dragged around the circumference of the lounge, held upright by the human crutches flanking her – Nicole and Len. Her sweatshirt clung to her back, chest and arms. She felt cold and realised her clothes were wet against her skin. With her eyes less than a quarter open, she was able to see that it was still daylight. She assumed it was the still the same day – Sunday. She lowered her head; it rocked and remained unsteady as she gazed down at her stumbling feet. The dark blur of the carpet caused her to feel dizzy. How did she end up like this? The last thing she remembered was sitting in the lounge with Len.

"How could you let this happen?" She heard Nicole say. "She's my dearest friend. I fucking love her."

"Don't put the dairy on me," Len replied. "I never made her take it."

Of course, she'd had a fix. But the last of her heroin wasn't enough to cause her to go over. Then she remembered – she'd had help. Len had been complicit, although unwittingly. Had he known she was in possession of her own heroin, he most probably wouldn't have parted with any of his. For a better high, she'd lied, and he'd given her enough for a reasonable hit. She'd added his contribution, as well as a scoop she'd discreetly stolen from him, to what she had left.

After circling the stinking armchair innumerable times, she realised Nicole and Len hadn't noticed she'd woken. Remaining silent, she took the opportunity to eavesdrop on their conversation, but her mind wandered. She recalled Len kneeling beside her as she sat on one of her grandparents' chairs in the lounge. He had his belt pulled tight around her lower arm and she was handing him a syringe. The image changed to another: tears streaming down her face, Len with his arms around her. What had she told him? She tried to remember, but she couldn't.

"Are you really sure about this?" Nicole asked.

"Nah, but there ain't no other way round it," Len said.

On hearing that transaction, it became apparent that her snooping skills were impaired. Although she tried to concentrate on what was being said, it mostly sounded like gobbledegook with only the occasional word or phrase in English.

Unable to decipher the majority of the conversation, it took what felt like an age until anything made sense. Eventually intermittent words, and strings of words, started to connect. Nicole had been the one who found Shelley and she was responsible for her drenched clothes, which had been caused by the water she'd thrown over her in an attempt to bring her back.

What remained unclear was what, if anything, Len knew about the rapist and the reason he was in the cellar. Not only was she unaware of what Nicole might have told him, but she couldn't remember what she'd said on the subject herself. And if she had, would it have been the truth or a lie?

Even though her body ached like a low-scoring boxer who'd gone the distance – and the laps of the lounge exacerbated the pain and exhaustion – she couldn't stop. She had to keep her consciousness covert until she knew how to act, and to do that she needed to know what Len knew.

42. Keep Quiet

When Shelley opened her eyes, everything had returned to normal – as normal as it had been before she'd gone over. Angel, Nicole and Tara sat talking in the lounge. Her friends and the room had stopped swaying. And to her relief, once again, she understood English.

"You've decided to join us, then?" Tara sipped from a purple mug.

"I'm really sorry. It was an accident."

"Oh, so the needle injected you itself, did it?" Nicole's tone was cross, but she spoke through a smile. "I thought you were dead. Don't you ever do that to me again." Nicole took Shelley's hands and pulled her up from the chair. She hugged her tightly and whispered in her ear, "You're my most precious friend and I love you. You've gotta start taking care of yourself."

Shelley nestled her head into Nicole's apple-scented hair and squeezed her eyes shut. She felt another pair of arms wrap around her.

"And you had a go at me for drinking," Tara said in a gentle voice that Shelley hadn't heard her use before.

"Have I missed anything?" Shelley asked, sitting back down on her chair.

"No, we're still fucked. He's upstairs, sleeping," Nicole said.

"That's a rock bottom, you know, babe. OD'ing like that." Angel moved her chair next to Shelley's and rubbed her back. "This can be where you get off. There's groups you can go to."

Shelley went over to the CD player and put on Len's Simon and Garfunkel CD. She closed her eyes for *I Am a Rock*. After the CD started again from the beginning, halfway through *The Sound of Silence*, she became aware that her clothes felt less clingy. They'd progressed from being drenched to damp, and although they were still far from dry, she wasn't going to change; the only other set of clothes in her case were tainted – the ones she'd worn the night before.

Through the nicotine-stained net curtains, she watched as the twilight stole the day. Faced with reality, the dark cloud that housed her fears, lingered over her head. She worried if they'd be able to move quickly enough to get Len out of the house, and even if they did, she'd yet to devise a scheme that would keep him out and allow her to return alone.

***

Having insisted that Shelley eat, Angel went through to the kitchen with Tara to make her a sandwich. Shelley hadn't realised that Angel had brought food. When she'd made her own list of essential items for the job, food had never crossed her mind.

Unusually for Shelley, she did feel hungry, and she finished all but the crusts of the ham sandwich prepared by Angel. As she drunk the strong, bitter coffee – courtesy of Tara – she stood up and turned off the music. On returning to her chair, she listened carefully for any noise coming from above.

"What does he know?" she finally asked the question to which she'd been dreading hearing the answer.

"That we're making a porno... and he bought it," Angel said. "That reminds me, Tara, how's your cock of a clit?"

"Back to normal now, thank you. How's yours?"

"Still the—"

"He must be really off his head to swallow that," Shelley cut in, trying to steer the conversation away from Angel's pubic area. Was Tara the fool or the great mind taking them there? Whichever one she was, Shelley was not.

"Maybe we should leave," Nicole said.

"I'm not leaving. He's a good bloke. It's not fair to leave that cunt to die in his cellar," Shelley told them.

"I bet he'd forget about it," Angel said.

"Yeah, until the house starts stinking of rotting rapist." Tara smirked.

"This has gotta get sorted tonight. You are still in, aren't you?" Shelley looked to her friends and although they agreed they were, she wondered if what she sensed was reluctance.

***

After a cigarette, and still no sound from upstairs, Shelley walked out of the lounge and into the hall. She looked on the banister for Len's jacket. It wasn't there. She returned to the lounge to recheck the room, but the jacket wasn't in there either.

From her handbag, she took another smoke and then braved the kitchen. As she trudged through, she caught sight of the yellow tie in the bin. In her head, she repeated – *a rock feels no pain, an island never cries*. To hold back the tears, she took deep pulls on her cigarette. Her head felt squeezed, as if magnets on either side of her temples were being drawn together.

"What do you think you're doing?" Nicole positioned herself in front of the bottles on the work surface, securing the area with her outstretched arms.

"I'm looking for something. Get out the road." Shelley manoeuvred her arm around Nicole's, pushed her out the way and looked among the bottles.

"Don't you go doing a Tara on me, Shell."

"I'm not. How could I? The fucking roofies are gone."

"I didn't mean that. She's too awake now anyway. I don't think it was her."

"Oh right, she's never had to get over a sedative before. She could have taken some and stashed the rest. If it wasn't her, who was it?"

"Maybe they're lost. Anyway, Resident Most Precious, what are you doing in here?"

"Looking for the gun," Shelley told her.

***

At the foot of the stairs, Shelley kicked off her trainers. She looked through the glass panel in the front door and noticed the twilight had been replaced with darkness. The glow of a streetlight shone into the hall and created a rectangle of brightness on the dirty carpet, illuminating its flaws.

In her socks, she slowly tiptoed up the stairs. At least if she could find the gun, she'd avoid any further contact with the rapist's blood. Halfway up the stairs, she heard creaking, but it wasn't in time with her own light steps. She turned her head to see Nicole behind her.

"What are you doing? Get your fucking shoes off," she whispered through clenched teeth.

"Come back. It's too risky." Nicole pulled Shelley's hand.

"Get off, for fuck's sake." Shelley shook her hand free from Nicole's and crept up to the top of the stairs. On the landing, she looked down and saw Nicole at the bottom of the staircase, motioning for her to come back.

Ignoring her friend, Shelley tiptoed farther into the hall towards Len's bedroom. Gently, she pushed open his bedroom door. Before she had a chance to peek inside, she heard someone bounding up the stairs. She darted into the room next to Len's and hid behind the open door.

From where she stood, she could see nothing, but her ears relayed the activity from outside. There were footsteps in the hall, although she couldn't tell if it was one of her friends or Len – his footsteps were soft; she'd noticed that before and attributed it to malnourishment.

She heard what sounded like a door opening. Then the footsteps became quieter. A moment later, the footsteps were louder. It sounded as though a door was dragging against the carpet. It was close, perhaps the door next to the one she was hiding behind.

"Shelley, where are you?" Nicole's voice called.

"Shhh." Shelley slithered out from behind the door and slunk into the hall. "What the fuck are you doing?"

"It's too risky. What if nosey Nora calls the Old Bill?"

"What if Len clocks on to what we're doing? If you wanna go, just fucking go, but I'm not."

"Don't be silly. I'm not leaving you."

"Well stop making so much bloody noise."

With Nicole tailing her, she walked through Len's open bedroom door. He wasn't in there, and neither was his jacket. She searched the other three bedrooms, the bathroom and the airing cupboard, but she didn't find Len or his jacket.

"You said he was sleeping up here." Shelley looked puzzled at Nicole.

"I thought he was. He went up a few hours ago. I haven't seen him since."

"Did you hear him leave?"

"Don't be stupid. I would have said."

"Well he must've done... He's probably gone to score." With her hand resting on the banister for balance, Shelley flew down the stairs. "I'm gonna sort that cunt."

The obsession to have a hit pervaded her, but she refused to succumb to the compulsion. She couldn't try to score now. The possibility of Len returning at any time meant the opportunity to finish off the rapist couldn't be squandered.

She flung open the kitchen drawer and rummaged for the sharp knives. She pulled out one but it was bent, and then another – also bent, most likely of her own making from the escape through the patio doors.

A whisk, a ladle, a can-opener, a corkscrew and various other kitchen utensils piled up on the work surface as she searched for a knife with a straight blade. Something sharp pricked the tip of her middle finger. She pulled her hand from the drawer, saw a bead of blood and popped the sore finger into her mouth.

Using her left hand, she sifted through the drawer and found the culprit. She held its thick, black handle at eyelevel and observed a slice of her reflection in the serrated blade.

***

"Let's go," Shelley hollered as she stomped out of the kitchen.

"Are you sure about this?" Angel stood at the cellar door and passed Shelley a T-shirt.

"You got a better idea?" Shelley laid the knife on the carpet then looked at the T-shirt. It was the one riddled with holes to be worn on her body. She pulled it over her head.

Angel held out the stonewash jeans and Shelley put them on over the top of her own. With the belt pulled tight, she secured the loose end by tucking it under the section on her waist.

"You don't have to do this," Nicole pleaded.

"I do." Shelley slipped her arms into the greying-white men's shirt and fastened the buttons.

"You need gloves," Nicole said.

"I'll look for some." Tara walked away down the hall towards the stairs.

"We can all go. It'll be quicker." Nicole took Shelley's hand and led her a few steps in Tara's direction.

"There's no time," Shelley said to Nicole.

"But your hands—"

"They were covered in that cunt's blood this morning. Len could come back. This is wasting time," she told Nicole. Then she shouted up to Tara, "It doesn't matter. Come back."

"I'm sure I've seen a pair of Marigolds," Angel said as they reconvened at the cellar door. "Hold on, babe." She darted into the kitchen and a moment later, returned with a pair of bright-yellow rubber gloves.

Shelley's aversion to rubber caused her to cringe as she slid her hands into the gloves. The squeaking noise was worse than the sound of chalk scratching a blackboard. A hand gently clasped Shelley's wrist. She looked up from her gloves and saw Tara stood next to her. In Tara's other hand, she was holding a knife.

"It's a bit bent, Tar." Shelley clasped Tara's bony shoulders.

"I'll be able to get him from another angle," Tara said with a weak smile that spanned only the left half of her mouth.

"Shout if you hear anything," Shelley told Angel and Nicole as she rolled up the long shirtsleeves that fell below her fingertips. She bent down to pick up her knife. With her fingers wrapped over the gold door handle, she turned to Tara. There was fear in Tara's eyes. "You don't have to come. I'll be okay on my own." Shelley tried to keep her face from crumpling to look like she meant it.

Tara put her hand over Shelley's and twisted the handle. The door opened and a dim light revealed the edges of the wooden steps.

Angel switched on two torches, passed one to Tara then held the other out to Shelley. Her blade gleamed and its long, dark shadow was cast down the cellar stairs.

Following the light brighter than the solitary bulb in the cellar, Shelley made her way down the creaking steps. She could hear Tara behind her and at the same time in her head, she heard whispering – not words, just a low humming sound that echoed.

At the bottom of the stairs, she became aware of her racing heart. She recognised it as the fight in her. Suddenly, she remembered the T-shirt to protect her face. She'd forgotten. She couldn't go back. There wasn't time. She had to get this done before Len returned.

She raised her torch. The stream of light found the plastic-encased rapist. Tara joined her, aiming her torch in the same direction. The second light exposed a person sitting on the concrete floor, next to the rapist.

43. Coming Clean

Shelley wondered if the shadowy figure sitting in a hunched position on the floor was an hallucination. She turned to Tara with the intention of whispering the question, but seeing Tara's dropped jaw and bulging eyes, she got the answer without the asking.

"What the fuck?" Shelley's body shuddered.

Caught in the light, the figure spun round. Len's pale face was illuminated. "I'm doing this for you."

"What are you doing for me? What do you think this is?"

"I know, Shell. I'm putting it right for you." Len held the handgun to the rapist's head.

"Cover his fucking face. What've you done? This is nothing to do with you." Clasping her knife, Shelley approached the vermin on the floor. "I said cover his face!"

"Let me go," the rapist groaned.

"Shut the fuck up, cunt." Shelley pressed her blade against his neck. The purple face of the pernicious man, even though barely recognisable, started the replay. The magnetic force pulling her temples together increased. It set off a shooting pain behind her eyes.

"You have to believe me. They're the scum of the earth these whores. Don't listen to them."

Shelley increased the pressure on the knife and drew blood.

"Look, it's all right, love. I've fixed it." Len shoved a scrunched-up wad of clingfilm into the rapist's mouth.

"No, it's not all right. It's all fucking wrong. Why did you do that? I don't want to see his face. I don't have to... Fucking sort it!" She pulled off the yellow Marigolds, tossing them onto the floor. Her revulsion to the rubber was unbearable. She stood over Len, watching his fumbled attempts at rewrapping the savage's face. "I can still see the cunt. You've fucked it up. It was all tidy. Why've you messed it up?" She jabbed the knife in the air.

Len fiddled with the clingfilm, but his 'F-A-T-E' and 'L-U-C-K' fingers couldn't return it to the state of tight binding that Shelley hands had originally perfected.

Fleas scurried, crawling their way up her legs, to her chest, her neck, in her hair, down her back and over her arms. She was swarmed. She hurled the torch. It crashed on the concrete. Shards of glass scattered across the room.

"Give it to me." She threw out her free hand in Len's direction, catching her nail on his cheek.

"No, love, I'm gonna do this... for you."

"You don't know me. What are you gonna do for me?" She swooped down and seized the gun from his hands. With the walnut grip in her shaking fist, she edged away and aimed the gun at the rapist's head.

"Not yet. It's too early," Len said, rushing to his feet. He picked up the pillow he'd been sitting on and placed it on top of the face that was torturing Shelley.

"What do you know? If you knew... it's too fucking late. That's what it is. Too fucking late!"

The fleas entered her blood. The itching transferred from the top of her skin to underneath. With a gun in one hand and a knife in the other, she was unable to scratch. Her eyes twitched, then her nose and her chin. She jerked her head, her arms and her torso. She stomped her feet on the hard floor and it hurt.

"Why is he here?" Shelley looked at Tara, stood by the stairs, providing their only light. "What's going on?"

"I've got no idea, honestly, Shell."

"I'm carrying on where you girls left off."

Shelley pointed the gun at Len. "What does that mean?"

***

"Nicole! Get the fuck down here now!" Shelley's hot tears felt like spikes against her tingling face. "Bring my fags."

The stairs creaked as Nicole walked down to the cellar. Shelley passed her knife to Tara then snatched the box of cigarettes from Nicole's hand.

"What are you doing with a—" Nicole started.

"Shut up and gimme a light." With her trembling fingers, Shelley put a cigarette in her mouth. She grabbed the Zippo lighter from Nicole's hand. "You gonna tell me what he means by carrying on where we left off?"

"He knows." Nicole looked guilty.

Shelley pulled deeply on her cigarette. Her tears stopped flowing but her temples still felt compressed. "You told him?"

Nicole nodded.

"Everything?"

"I had to, love. I thought you were dead. I didn't know what to..." Nicole started to sob.

Questions reeled in Shelley's mind, though none came out her mouth. Watching her friend cry stumped her words, but it was worse because she was dying for a hit and for the itching to stop and nothing could happen until she'd dealt with the man who'd...

She marched to the other end of the cellar, stopping four or five feet from the rapist. He was worming on the floor. His moaning infuriated her. She aimed the gun at his head.

"Get out," she shouted at Len.

"Give me the gun." He stood next to Shelley and looked into her eyes. "Let me do this. I'll do it with the pillow."

She turned away and stared at her target. She lowered the gun, levelling it at his groin.

"Give him the damn gun," Nicole cried.

"He'll do it, Shell. You don't have to," Tara called from her position by the stairs.

"Why should he?" Without moving the gun, Shelley turned to face Tara. "He doesn't know me. He doesn't know any of us." She looked at Nicole. "How can he know what you said is the truth?"

"He does. He said he owes you," Nicole answered.

"I do, Shell, big time. More than you—"

"Yeah, you fucking do. But if you knew that, why did you come back? Why didn't you fuck off when I said?"

"C'mon love." He reached across and placed his hand over Shelley's on the walnut grip. "Go home. This ain't for you."

"I'm not a fucking idiot. You're gonna risk going down for me?" Shelley shook him off.

"What else is he gonna do? This is his house," Nicole said.

"How do you know it's his house?" Filled with fear, Shelley turned to the board. They couldn't be certain this was Len's house. What junky kept a wider variety of kitchen utensils than the cookware department in John Lewis?

"This is mad, Shell. I live here. It's my place. Do you want ID or something?"

"Don't move." Shelley glanced at Len. If she let him leave, he might call the police. No one could leave, not yet. She kept the gun pointed at the glistening, plastic-wrapped target.

In her head, the song started up again – *happy, happy*. It made her smile. Then a wave of warmth similar to mild heroin hit washed over her. It washed away the creeping fleas. Her shaking stopped.

Holding the gun steady, she lined up the sights with the rapist's chest. The process of estimation reminded her of shooting pool, looking down the cue to judge her shot. Most of the time, she was a good judge and she was a good shot.

"It's not even midnight. My neighbours, Shelley, they'll hear."

"Fuck your neighbours!"
"*Pull back, shoot the cunt, get the fuck out.*"

44. Altering Reality

"It's never gonna work," Shelley shouted to Len, running after him up the cellar stairs. At the kitchen door, she barged past Angel and followed Len into the kitchen. From the cupboard under the sink, he grabbed a vintage tin box. Then he bolted into the lounge and out through the patio doors with Shelley behind him.

When she reached the garden, she stopped running and stood still. Her chest heaved as she took deep breaths, filling her lungs with the crisp, night air. She felt lighter, and a sense of relief. The sky was clear and she took a moment, looking up at the stars.

"Thank you," she whispered to William. "I'm sorry."

The others came out and joined her on the patio. Nicole passed her a cigarette, but she couldn't touch it, not with her dirty hands. She went back inside and washed them with Fairy Liquid under the hot tap in the kitchen. The room was dim, lit only by the light creeping in from the hall. It was better that way, not to see. And the burning on her hands didn't allow her thoughts to drift.

Through the yellowed net curtains at the window above the sink, she could see out into the garden. Tara was shining the torch at the back of the lawn and Len was setting up the fireworks. When her hands could bear no more of the scorching water, she went back outside.

On the patio, Nicole handed her a cigarette. She'd meant to pick up her own from the lounge when she'd gone back in but she'd forgotten, so accepted the fresh-air smoke from Nicole.

"Are you all right, love?" Nicole said, holding her Zippo under Shelley's cigarette.

Shelley shook her head and smiled weakly. "It wasn't supposed to happen like this."

"I need some help," Len called from the lawn.

"Don't we all," Angel replied.

The three of them walked over to the back of the garden where Tara and Len were standing. Tara shone her torch on the row of fireworks as the others bent down lighting the fuses.

"Is it safe to be this close? Shouldn't we have those long sticks or something?" Shelley lit her second airbomb battery.

"Hurry up." Len burned the fuse of another.

From the corner of her eye, Shelley noticed Angel and Nicole were gone. Tara grabbed her wrist and they ran to the patio.

Striking white flashes raided the sky, simultaneous to the succession of bangs as loud as gunshot. The explosions charged her body. She felt exhilarated.

Within minutes, it was over. Time for a hit. Six hours had passed without any junk entering her system. Len and Tara walked back inside the house. Shelley took the opportunity to leave Nicole and Angel by following the others.

As she crossed the threshold, she heard Nicole speaking in her posh voice. Something wasn't right. She turned back to see Angel shining the torch at the top of the fence next door. The spotlight shone on the elevated, dressing-gowned quidnunc.

"That better be the end of it. If you start up again, I'm calling the council!" The old lady squinted.

"I'm ever so sorry we disturbed you. We won't do any more, I promise," Nicole said.

"I don't want to be a killjoy. It's nice to see her having fun for a change, and I like fireworks just as much as the next person, but not this time of night. Scared me half to death, it did." She fiddled with her hairnet, tucking in a straying roller above her ear.

"We're sorry. We didn't realise the time," Angel said.

"I thought it was a bomb that first one, so did Lionel. The house was shaking. We were too scared to go out. We thought it was the IRA."

"I'm sorry we scared you," Shelley said.

"We're going in now. We won't disturb you again," Nicole said.

"Good night." Shelley looked up at the old lady and waved.

"You enjoy your party, sweetheart. God only knows what he did to you last night, and at least I can see for myself you're having fun now. Next time you need a costume mind, give me a knock. I can lend you something better than that get-up."

***

In Len's room, Shelley sat on the edge of the bed with her drug paraphernalia balanced on a sturdy magazine. The red bulb in the bedside lamp provided barely enough brightness to measure out her hit. It was just after midnight and finally she was close to having her fix.

"I told you it'd work, didn't I?" Len smiled.

"I can't believe she thought it was a firework. That's a classic," Shelley replied enthusiastically, though she felt some guilt for scaring the old couple.

With his 'F-A-T-E' fingers, he tipped the heroin into the spoon held by the hand that read 'L-U-C-K'. "You all done with your paranoia now?"

Shelley nodded as she held the lighter under her own spoon. She wasn't done with her paranoia, although it had been redirected. Now that she felt calmer, she had regained her mask, which enabled her to hide it.

"That cunt's never gonna fit in your boot, you know that?"

"Give it a rest, will you? It's deep. He will."

"He won't, I'm telling ya."

"You haven't seen my boot. You don't know."

"I do, love, trust me. I can have that van here in an hour and you girls can go."

Shelley wanted to enjoy her hit, not contemplate the removal and disposal of the rapist's body, nor argue about it. In truth, she wasn't sure that it would fit in her boot and she knew that Angel and Nicole's cars had even smaller boots than her own. But she wanted to deal with it herself to ensure it was taken care of properly. Len's suggestion of calling in a favour from his friend was ludicrous to Shelley. There was no way she would accept anyone else being involved, no less a stranger.

With the heroin and citric dissolved in the water, she added a small section of a cigarette filter to the contents of the spoon. She pressed the needle into the filter and drew up the hit into her works. She rested it on the bedside table. Under the red glow, it looked like a blood-filled syringe. She pushed back her sleeves.

"Do you want me to get you?" Len asked.

She placed her hand in his lap. He seemed able to find veins in her arms she didn't know existed. He tied his belt around her lower arm, constricting the blood flow. She passed him the syringe.

"We've gotta be out of here in a couple of hours, no longer." He slipped in the needle.

"I know. Can you just let me enjoy this first? Please."

"Don't go nodding out on me. I want that body out of here tonight." He pulled back on the plunger. Shelley watched her blood flow into the barrel. The two shades of red united.

Len injecting her mitigated the risk of blown veins, but it left her feeling deprived of the chance to indulge her needle fixation. She watched intently, trying to take what little pleasure she could.

His 'F-A-T-E' fingers pushed in the plunger and she felt the junk rippling through her body. When he removed the needle, her eyelids half closed. At last, she was transported.

45. Meanwhile Gardens

Shelley dipped her fingers into her handbag that lay on the soiled carpet in the lounge. She pulled out a cigarette from her packet, reminding herself to clean the surfaces of her bag and case when she got home.

"I don't think he's coming back." Shelley returned to her seat.

"He'll be back. He said he would." Nicole walked into the lounge, two purple mugs unsteadily balanced in each hand.

"When did he leave?" Shelley repeated the question she'd been asking ever since she'd found out Len wasn't in the house.

"Don't fret, love. He's only been half an hour," Nicole replied, passing the mugs to Angel, Tara and Shelley.

"You really think he's coming back?" Shelley took a sip and burnt her tongue.

"No doubt, babe." Angel smiled, her dimples making a fleeting appearance.

"He's a nice chap. I'm sure he'll come back," Tara said. "I don't understand why you didn't tell us about him before."

"Have a ciggie. It'll calm you down." Nicole winked at Shelley as she held out her Zippo and lit the unlit cigarette Shelley had been holding.

Shelley took an extended pull. She couldn't comprehend how her friends had made an immediate assessment of Len's nature, even more so because he was a smackhead and two of them were members of the AHF. How were they so sure he was going to come back?

She was furious, both with herself and with Len. Herself, because she'd gouched out after her fix and managed to lose an hour, and Len because during that hour he'd taken an action following a discussion in which a decision had been reached on the disposal of the rapist's remains without her. Granted, none of them had taken into consideration the size of their sports car boots, but there could have been another way. It didn't mean they could reach an agreement in her absence. Although she was pleased she wouldn't have to sell her car as she'd intended, it would be of no use to her in prison. Len wasn't meant to be involved. And now that he was, he embroiled someone else she didn't know at all, so the risk of getting caught would increase. How this didn't appear to worry her friends, she couldn't fathom.

If he'd walked down the road thirty minutes ago to pick up the van, why wasn't he back? A director told her it was most likely the same reason as the last time he'd disappeared. She hadn't forgotten that on that occasion, he hadn't returned.

***

After an hour and a half with Shelley in a state of anxiety, Len staggered into the lounge. He approached Shelley's chair. He jangled a set of keys in front of her face. She shook her head and tutted. Not only had he been doing something to which she objected, but he was also late in returning, drunk, possibly stoned and he'd definitely had more gear.

"Where the fuck have you been? It's three a.m," Shelley said.

"It's the perfect time to move a body, init?" Len slurred, scratching his stubbly chin.

"You still think this is a good idea?" Shelley looked angrily at her friends.

"I'm an expert at villainery. I know about these things." Len grinned.

"He's got a van and it probably is the best time," Tara said.

"You're not driving." Shelley glared at him and walked out of the lounge.

"You better watch it. He doesn't have to help us," Angel warned her by the cellar door.

Inside the damp room redolent of dead rodent, Shelley inspected the body. She wondered if she'd be able to help move it. The damage from the shooting was revolting. She reminded herself it was not as repugnant as the man had been alive.

Len stumbled down the cellar stairs then joined the others by the monstrosity at the opposite end of room. He unravelled a roll of black bin liners and struggled as he tried to detach them. Having successfully separated a few from the roll, he passed them round to the others.

"What are we doing with these?" Nicole asked.

"Put his body parts in 'em after we've chopped him up."

"What are you on about?" Shelley said.

"I can't do it. I'm sorry, but I can't cut up a corpse." Nicole backed away.

"How else are we gonna feed him to the pigs?" Len slipped over sideways, landing hard on the concrete.

"We're not doing that. Look at him. He's off his head. If we were gonna cut him up, we would have put him in my boot," Shelley

216

said.

"I'm having you on, love. 'Course we're not butchering him." Len chuckled as he pushed himself off the floor. He picked up a heavy-duty bin liner and ripped it down the middle, creating an irregular shaped sheet. From the floor, he picked up Shelley's wide roll of brown parcel tape and brandished it in the air. "We're gonna gift-wrap the cunt."

***

The Ford Transit van swerved out of Bracewell Road and onto North Pole Road. There was a jolting sound from the back. Either Len or the body had collided with the interior of the van, or perhaps each other.

On the next turn, into Scrubs Lane, Shelley strived to control the vehicle. She'd never driven anything larger than a jeep and felt nervous at the wheel. Driving a van would have been a worry in itself under any circumstances – but in this instance, the pressure was increased. She couldn't afford the appearance of an erratic driver and worse still, a crash.

"Has he fallen asleep?" Shelley looked to her friends who were squeezed next to her on the front seat.

Angel turned around. "You can't see into the back, but he'll be all right, babe. Just keep your eye on the road."

"How much longer?" Tara asked when they reached the junction of Scrubs Lane and Harrow Road.

"We've past Meanwhile Gardens already but I've gotta drive round. I only know one way in," Shelley said.

"Why don't you ask Len?" Nicole suggested.

"The state he's in. What's the point?" Shelley replied.

"I heard that. Where the fuck are you? We should be there by now," Len shouted from the rear.

"We're on Harrow Road."

"You're mental! There's always Old Bill down here. I told you to go the back way. You've gone right round the houses. Fucking hell."

Eventually, Shelley arrived on Golborne Road. She pulled up at the side of the Brutalist, concrete high-rise block – Trellick Tower. Though it was quiet, they were not alone. Other junkies and hookers seemed to favour the location.

Shelley turned off the engine, opened her door and jumped down to the street. She walked to the back of the van and swung open the doors. Len was sitting up, holding a lighter under a spoon. She climbed inside, kicked the rapist's body out of the way with her Nike TNs, then sat down.

"Tell us when they've gone," she shouted to her friends in the front.

"That's for me," she mouthed to Len as she pointed at the spoon and then to herself.

He took out a syringe. "I ain't got another spoon," he whispered. "Not my problem."

"You have got a fucking problem. I'm doing you a favour and you're being a cunt."

"Keep your voice down. What do you expect? You weren't supposed to come back."

"I wouldn't have unless I had to."

"Why did you have to?"

"It's a long story and I'm not fucking whispering it here."

"Save me some." Shelley opened the doors and slipped out of the back. She rushed around to the front.

"We shouldn't be hanging round here. By the time they've gone, there'll be more people going to work," Angel said.

"Give it a few more minutes and see what they do." Shelley picked up her handbag from the footwell.

"It'll be daylight if we leave it much longer," Nicole said as Shelley was closing the door.

Clutching her handbag to her chest, Shelley ran around the van and returned to the rear. Once inside, she took out her thin paperback and found the foil. She held it out to Len and he sprinkled on some heroin.

While he injected his fix, she used the tube, which she'd saved since her last chase in the bathroom the morning before, and sucked up the fumes.

"Who let one go? It stinks in here," Angel said.

Shelley looked wide-eyed at Len.

"Mine don't smell like that," Nicole said.

"I don't fart," Tara added.

"Don't be stupid. Everybody farts," Nicole replied.

"Someone's been eating some weird shit," Angel said. "I'm not breathing in any more crap today."

Shelley heard one of the front doors open. Worriedly, she looked at Len and he began packing his tools into his long, black wallet. She folded her foil and hid it in *The Escaped Cock*. The back doors were opened, and just in time Len slid his wallet into an inside pocket of his jacket.

"Which one of you was it?" Angel waved her hand in front of her nose before stepping back. "They both look guilty as sin."

***

Inside Meanwhile Gardens, it was deserted. The five of them carried the dustbin liner and parcel-tape bound cylindrical package through the undergrowth. The fellow hookers and junkies didn't seem to have paid them any attention when they'd left the van, donning balaclavas and carrying the parcel, which was probably distinguishable as a body. Perhaps they too were fellow killers, though it was more likely that their minds were consumed by the customary junky and hooker preoccupations.

"What if someone sees?" Nicole said as they came out from the copse and onto the footpath by the Grand Union Canal.

"We can't walk any farther. It's nearly light." Shelley looked over at the blocks of flats with their balconies backing on to the other side of the canal. With the sky paling, she could see the colours of the clothes, the bedding and the towels that were hanging over the washing lines. "Do you want to go? We can manage," she said to Nicole.

"I've got no idea where I am," Nicole replied. "Can't we just get it done quickly?"

Len directed them to lay the parcel on the grass. He rushed off, then reappeared, carrying bricks.

"Where did you get them from?" Shelley asked.

"I stashed them here the other day."

"You do know that sarcasm is the lowest form of wit," Tara said, with one hand resting on her hips. "But I like it." She giggled.

Len knelt on the grass, placed a brick on top of the body and secured it with parcel tape. "Gimme a hand then." He looked up at the others.

They all crouched down and within minutes, they'd attached numerous bricks. Shelley wondered if the tape would hold once it was wet.

When they lifted the body, Shelley struggled; it was far heavier with the added weight. They walked the few steps across the path then dropped the body into the canal. There was a huge splash and something louder, a thump. They ran back into the bushes.

"How deep's the water?" Angel asked, looking at Len.

"I don't know. I don't usually go swimming here."

"This ain't no joke, man. What are you on?" Angel said.

Shelley gave Angel an I-told-you-so glance.

"Do you think anyone saw us? It's so light," Nicole said.

"No one will recognise us like this," Tara replied.

"What'll happen to the parcel tape in the water? Won't it stop being sticky?" Shelley asked as they walked back to the van.

"I ran some tests in the lab. Don't worry ma'am, everything will be fine."

"This isn't funny. You need to stop fucking around," Angel told Len as they approached Trellick Tower. "What about your mate's van? Is there CCTV that could pick up his plate?"

Shelley felt the onset of an episode of shaking. She hadn't thought of CCTV. She should have done. Recently, she'd noticed new cameras appearing in previously unmonitored streets. They'd also been popping up in some of the shops she used regularly and some of the hotels she worked in. Would there have been CCTV at The Lanesborough?

46. Smackhead Kitchen Klepto

"Who do you think lives in a house like this?" Len said in a plummy accent as the Transit van turned onto Bracewell Road.

"A smackhead chef or a kitchen-klepto." Tara sniggered.

Shelley yanked the steering wheel. The Transit van jerked and ran up on the curb. She heard the impact in the rear. Under most circumstances, she would have been pleased to see Tara happy, but the inappropriateness of the situation riled her. Moreover, they were blatantly having a laugh at her expense.

Shelley kicked open the driver's side door. Standing in the Monday morning light, she remembered they were supposed to be keeping a low profile. She looked around. Apart from the parked cars, the road was empty and all the houses had their curtains drawn.

Maintaining her vigilance, she walked to the back of the van and opened the doors. Tara and Len slithered out onto the street.

"We'll clean up. You get yourself home and get some kip, love," Len said, patting Shelley on the back. He curled his arm around Tara's waist and the two of them sauntered up the road towards his house. "Laters," he called out, turning round to wave at Shelley and the others.

"Nighty night." Tara turned and waved. They looked like an unfortunate couple walking off the set of *Blind Date*. Cilla wouldn't need a new hat for them.

Angel reached for Shelley's hand. "Don't let her upset you, babe. She doesn't mean to. It's just her way."

"I'm surprised he's not too fucking council for her," Shelley said.

"Do you want me to stop at yours tonight?" Nicole lit a cigarette.

"I'll be waking in a couple of hours to get to Praed Street. We won't get much sleep."

"I don't think I could sleep now anyway," Nicole said.

Shelley turned to Angel. "Do you wanna come with us?"

"If you want me to. I feel so bad about what happened. I'm so sorry. If I could've done something different..." Angel wrapped her arm around Shelley's shoulder.

With Angel on one side of her, and Nicole linking her arm on the other, Shelley walked with her friends down the road towards her car.

"What if we were seen on CCTV?" Shelley asked, opening the door of her 350SL.

"I doubt it, babe," Angel said.

Angel followed behind Shelley's car. Shelley dropped off Nicole to her Chimaera where she'd abandoned it on Saturday night. Then they drove in a convoy heading for Hampstead.

Alone in her car, Shelley felt apprehensive. Fear pervaded her about being caught on tape at Trellick Tower and at The Lanesborough, and the depth of the canal, and whether parcel tape remained effective in water.

She blasted her Pink Floyd *Dark Side of the Moon* CD to drown out the noise in her head, but it didn't work. A hit was required to stop that – temporarily providing a break from caring. But how would she score and manage to use in her small flat with both her friends present?

***

As soon as they arrived in Shelley's flat on Willoughby Road, Nicole disappeared into the kitchen to put on the kettle. From not wanting to be left by herself, Shelley was now anxious to be without her friends. Although they knew about her habit, she couldn't call Jay while they were there, and she had no heroin left. There was nothing except the skunk Nicole had.

After bringing the tea to the other two in the lounge, Nicole rolled a joint. Shelley glanced at her phone – 6.57 a.m. Even if she were to call Jay, she couldn't do it until she'd gone to the clinic. Once she had heroin, the chance of her actually going to Praed Street was close to nil.

"What time does the drop-in open?" Shelley asked.

"Ten, I think." Nicole passed Shelley the joint. Shelley took an extended toke. Added to her concern for the lack of 'A' class drugs was her fear of attending the clinic. The staff would know something was wrong because she'd only recently been checked. Usually she could lie: blame a split condom with a punter, or an overenthusiastic boyfriend – not that she ever had any boyfriends, but she could tell a story and tell it well. In this instance, however, lying would not come easy. It never did after a rape.

Shelley took a hard pull on the joint and held her breath for several seconds before exhaling. She averted her eyes to her wrist. The dot-to-dot puzzle she'd created was scabbing over. Farther along, in her hand, she saw a plump, blue vein. In her mind, she pictured a syringe full of heroin and crack; the needle sliding in; pulling back; watching the blood percolate in the barrel; pushing in;

feeling the rush.

"Are you all right, love?"

"Yeah." *No, I'm desperate for a hit.* "I think I wanna be on my own now though. I'm sorry," Shelley said, offering the joint to Angel.

"You shouldn't be on your jacks, babe." Without taking a toke, Angel passed the joint to Nicole who sat between them on the sofa.

"I'm not letting you go to the clinic by yourself and I don't want you going back on the heroin when I've gone either."

"For fuck's sake, Nic. What do you expect? I'm a junky."

"I know that's why you want me to leave." Nicole jumped up from the sofa. "You'd rather be with your heroin than with me. Is it a better friend? Am I that bad that a damn fucking powder is better?"

"It's not like that. I'll get ill," Shelley said, looking up at Nicole who was standing in front of her.

"I know. I've seen it, but you have to stick it out."

"She's right. I know a few girls who've done it. You go cold turkey," Angel said. "And there's meetings you can go to. Step programmes."

"I don't believe in all that self-help bollocks."

"What else are you gonna do? You've been cold fucking turkey loads of times but you just give up."

"What do you know about it?"

"I've seen you. Shivering, sweating, disappearing for ages in the loo, coming back with your eyes pinned, scratching. I'm not an idiot. I'm your friend, Shelley, supposed to be your best friend, and you don't even confide in me. What does that say about me?"

47. Getting the Sack

Nicole dropped Shelley off outside her flat after she and Angel had accompanied her to the Praed Street Project earlier that morning. Nicole seemed to accept the inevitability of Shelley scoring, though she'd insisted they meet later in the week to discuss her getting clean.

Added to Nicole and Angel's proposals of assistance were those of the Project – a referral back to Dr Fielding, a treatment centre, or the option of a methadone prescription. Going in with her friends had led to the truth being exposed, of not only her junk addiction, but also the rape. Why Nicole needed to be honest in that respect, Shelley didn't know. Did she want to report it, they'd asked, offering to support her. Reporting a rape committed by a man she'd since murdered wasn't pointless, it was madness. Thankfully, Nicole's honesty didn't stretch to the whole weekend.

Shelley sat on the sofa and took her mobile from her handbag to call Jay. On seeing the record of the thirty-six calls she'd missed on Saturday between 8.25 p.m. and 9.42 p.m., she reset the settings to delete them.

"When can you be here?" she asked Jay.

"Soon come," he said in his velvety voice.

She made a joint from the skunk Nicole left her and poured herself a glass of neat gin. His 'soon come' could mean anything. Although she'd stressed the urgency – without divulging the details – that most likely meant nothing. Any junky desperate for a fix would say anything to hurry a dealer.

"Are you running an express delivery service?" she asked when Jay entered her flat twenty minutes later.

"My days! I knew something was up. What's happened to you?"

"Nothing." Shelley turned away from him and walked over to the sofa. He went into the kitchen and she heard the kettle boiling. What was he up to with this newfangled tea-making business?

Shelley rolled another joint. She didn't yet have her real drugs from Jay, but it wouldn't have made a difference; she never shot up in front of him. He wasn't a user himself, just a dealer, and since taking over from Ali two years ago, he'd clearly made a success of it. To be a nineteen-year-old boy driving a BMW M3 and not be a trustafarian or a joyrider was quite a feat.

"Are you doing this for all your customers now?" Shelley asked, taking the steaming hot mug from Jay's hand.

He sat down beside her. "I'm not serving you up no more," he told the oak floorboards by his feet.

"You are joking." The tea in Shelley's mouth sprayed back into her mug. Using the long sleeve of her pyjama top, she dabbed her wet chin. "What did you come here for, then?"

"To see how you're doing... and you're ill," he said with some hand-wringing.

"Of course, I'm ill. If I wasn't sick, I wouldn't need any gear."

"It's more than that." He swivelled his baseball cap one-hundred and eighty so the peak was at the back of his head. He turned to look across at her. Was that pity in his eyes? "You need help... You were a stunner when I first met you, and now..."

"So I'll put on some make-up." She took her lipstick and compact from her handbag.

"And some weight. You're anorexic."

She opened the compact and looked in the mirror. "How would you know? I could be bulimic."

"With an empty fridge."

Mid-application, her upper lip twitched, causing the red to smear outside her lip line. "If you're not gonna sell to me, what are you here for?" She threw the closed compact on the table and as it made contact with the wood, she knew inside it had shattered.

"So I'm only your dealer, not your friend?" He spoke softly. "I've known you since I was a kid. You're not just some random skaghead, not to me and Ali." He stood up from the sofa and turned his cap back round the right way.

"If I don't score off you, I'll only be spending my money with someone else."

"I can't stop you," he said. "But I'm not gonna be the one who kills you."

***

"When your dealer won't sell you drugs, that's when you know you're proper fucked."

"I don't need your take on what he said. I need you to bring me some fucking gear," Shelley yelled down the phone to Len.

"We're still cleaning up here."

"Well stop for a bit and bring me some. I'll pay your cab. Two-fifty of each. Come now, please. I can't wait."

Shelley rolled another joint. Why was the universe conspiring against her? And today of all days. Finding a viable vein was usually the more awkward element of her drug taking than finding a viable dealer – with a few exceptions, most notably being robbed and locked in Len's house, although that had proved serendipitous.

She looked out of her window. Was Nicole hanging around outside? Had she spoken to Jay on his way in? Her car wasn't there. She phoned her mobile.

"Don't be stupid. You have given me an idea though."

"I'm calling your flat. You better pick up." Shelley redialled Nicole's home number.

"I told you it wasn't me," Nicole said.

"What kind of dealer won't sell you drugs?"

"I don't think you should be saying that on a landline."

"Now who's paranoid?"

"Call me if you wanna get clean, otherwise I'll see you Friday. And remember, I do love you. I'm trying to help."

***

Shelley poured herself another gin and switched on the television. She watched the news to check if a body had been pulled from the Grand Union Canal. Tomorrow, once she'd had some gear and some sleep, she planned to visit the library to see if she could find out the depth of the canal. And in the meantime, she continued to think of a place she could go, or someone she could ask, to ascertain the stickiness of parcel tape once submerged in water.

"The man shot dead outside Ladbroke Grove station just after eight p.m. on Saturday has been identified as sixty-seven year old Peter Langton. Langton was sentenced to life imprisonment in 1975 for the murder of schoolgirl, Kimberley Wright. Despite the recent public outcry, he was given an early release following a diagnosis of terminal cancer. Witnesses are pointing to a single gunman, but the police are investigating whether the attack was instigated by a vigilante group. The gunman has been described as..."

Shelley turned off the television. She had imagined, being Ladbroke Grove, the shooting that held up her friends had been gang or drug-related. There was some comfort in the knowledge she'd suffered for that subhuman to be killed. There was justice sometimes, just not always delivered by the system designed to dispense it.

She wondered if the body in the canal had been found, but part of her didn't want to know, not until she had junk in her system. Until then, she wasn't ready to deal with the repercussions if it had.

***

At five o'clock in the afternoon, Len still hadn't arrived at her flat. She thought of calling Ajay, but on top of all the waiting she'd done already, throwing his tardiness into the mix would be a recipe for disappointment. She considered going out to score on the street. Although the risk didn't bother her, she couldn't score a large quantity from a stranger and, even if she were to buy enough for a few hits, she didn't feel she had the strength to leave her flat again or to be outside alone.

When the phone rang, Shelley answered in anger, screaming, "Len, where the fuck are you?"

"Kiki, is that you?"

"Oh, my goodness, I'm so sorry. I thought it was someone else."

"Is everything okay, sweetie? You sound troubled." It was Resident Dicks All the Boxes.

"Yes. I am a bit." Shelley looked around. Her flat was a mess. "My builder keeps letting me down. The flat's a tip."

"All the more reason to come to Miami. I'm leaving a week on Wednesday. I can still get you a ticket."

"Thank you, but I can't come." *Or can I?*

"*No, you can't*," a director from the board told her.

"*You can't leave your mother.*"

"*You can't go with a habit.*"

"*You can't leave your friends.*"

"Call me if you change your mind. It'll be so good for your psoriasis... You'll be brand spanking new."

"I won't... I mean, I can't. I want to, but it's just not possible. I'm sorry 'cos I'd love to come."

"You can always fly out later in the summer. I'll be there until the end of August."

"I won't see you for three months." The thought Shelley had been holding in her mind came out of her mouth unplanned. Why did that happen to her? Escaping words. Surely, it didn't happen to normal people.

"I'll miss you. I'll miss the... the contentedness I feel when I'm with you," he said quietly. "Next summer. I hope you'll come with me then. It's an open invitation. I mean it. You're a very special woman, Kiki."

48. Audacity

Len came through with the drugs on Monday night, but he didn't bring the quantity of crack Shelley had requested. Apparently, it was a strategic move on his behalf taken to avoid her becoming psychotic. His strategising had worked. It also enabled her to leave the flat and visit William's grave the following day.

The usual cemetery coldness that was always there to greet her wasn't present. Tuesday brought a beautiful afternoon with a clear sky, and a bright sun that shone down on Shelley as she walked around her car in the car park, checking and checking and checking again that her car was locked.

Shelley pointed at her head. "I'm mad," she shouted, staring back at the woman who was staring at her. "It's called O-C-D."

When the woman finally walked away, Shelley resumed her checking. After a few minutes, she turned to leave the car park.

Walking through to the graveyard, she noticed a sign she hadn't seen before. She went closer and read the words: *Lock all your windows and doors whilst visiting your grave.* She smiled. Even she didn't think her vigilant checking would be necessary in the afterlife, nor was she likely to have a car.

As she wandered through the sea of headstones, her body felt uncomfortably warm. Even though there was no one around, she kept on the long-sleeved, burgundy sweatshirt that she wore unzipped over a T-shirt. It would have been disrespectful to bare her war wounds in front of Will. And in the face of the other souls who no longer had life, it wouldn't have been right to flaunt that she flirted with death.

On reaching William's grave, she sat down next to him on the ground and laid the pink carnations by his headstone. She looked around to ensure there was no one present before speaking to him.

"I'm so sorry for what I've put you through," she whispered. "I know you probably understand, but I'm still sorry you might've seen it..." Shelley heard footsteps behind her. She swung her head around brusquely.

"I want to talk to you," said a man with a northern accent, walking towards her. Shelley raised her hand above her eyebrows and held it there for shade as she watched the man approach. A barren scalp shone in the sun. The long strands of dark hair swept across had failed to disguise its baldness. He was in a suit; perhaps he was there for a funeral.

"Do I know you?" she asked as she pushed herself off the ground and got to her feet.

"You can't keep ignoring me, doll." He stood next to her, leant towards her and stroked her cheek with his hand.

Shelly flinched. Her brain sent the message to her body to run, but her body wouldn't cooperate. She was rooted in the soil, her feet frozen still. Her legs were shaking so uncontrollably she felt as though they were about to surrender to gravity.

"I really am sorry," he said.

"I've got a knife and I'll fucking use it," she yelled in the man's face. Was he the creep who usually wore a shell suit? Fear sent adrenalin pumping through her body and provided the catalyst to dislodge her entrenched feet.

As she sprinted on unsteady legs, in the direction of her car, she heard him panting behind her. She tried to pick up her pace, but she couldn't run any faster.

"Fuck off," she screamed in the hope that someone would hear. But it wasn't likely. The graveyard was nearly always empty. Today was exceptional but unfortunately, the woman who'd been staring at her earlier had been on her way out, not in.

"Stop, Shelley. It's all right. I'm not gonna hurt you," the man called out.

She didn't reply nor did she turn around. How did he know her name? Was he the Resident Cemetery Lurker? Was he stalking her and not the cemetery? Although her legs felt even more unstable, she continued to run.

"I'm on the wagon. I'm sober."

Shelley kept running along the narrow path that weaved through the headstones, but she stopped dead when she heard him say, "Don't you think you at least owe it to Will to hear me out?"

After he'd caught up with her, she stared at him, studying his face. He was the man she'd seen before, she was sure of it. And now that she looked at him closely, she could tell that he was William's father. His face didn't have the same look as William's – kind and open – but the resemblance was there.

His face was chiselled like William's, but it was hidden underneath skin that hung as loose as a housewife pillowcase stuffed with a bolster cushion. High cheekbones were concealed by eye-bags merging into sagging cheeks. What would have been a strong jawline was obscured by a number of dangly jowls, as well as a succession of chins in residence beneath the main one. The one that was there first. The one in which Shelley spotted the central dimple. William's central dimple.

***

In the Bald Faced Stag on East Finchley High Road, Shelley sat waiting at a window table while William's father, Jim, stood at the bar. The windows didn't let much light through and although outside it was a glorious day, inside the run-down pub it was gloomy.

As Jim carried their drinks over from the bar, Shelley watched him closely. His swagger created a slight twist in his shoulders every time he took a step closer to the window table where Shelley was sitting. The way that he walked reminded her of Will; he'd had that same gait.

The square table wobbled as Jim set down her pint of snakebite and blackcurrant. When he slumped into the high-backed, wooden chair opposite, he reminded her of Will again. The way he sat with his shoulders rounded, and the way that every now and again he jutted out his chin and bottom lip – a nervous habit or twitch, Shelley had thought, but now she knew it was hereditary, though perhaps a hereditary habit or twitch nonetheless.

"How's your mother keeping?" Jim asked.

"She manages." Shelley looked at his hands – the shape of his fingers, and his fingernails, were identical to Will's.

Jim supped his pint of Guinness. Maybe that's what turned him into a thin, fat man – fatness in his stomach and face. He had the red nose and cheeks of an alcoholic.

"Am I imagining it, or did you tell me five minutes ago you were sober?"

"I am, doll, have been for years now," he replied.

"I don't think so." Shelley gestured to the pint glass cradled in his hands. "There's only one kind of sober and you're not it if you're drinking that."

"No, I still am. The Guinness doesn't count." He raised the glass to his mouth. "It's for keeping in good health. You know, medicinal purposes and that malarkey." He smiled at her, perhaps apologetically or in embarrassment, but his eyes didn't smile. William's eyes had always smiled. William's eyes, so light a blue they were nearly transparent, were expressive. She knew where she stood with those eyes. Although the eyes of this man were an exact colour match, they were shifty, and the baggage they carried was obvious. The hoods were as heavy as the bags underneath.

Shelley took the packet of Benson and Hedges from her handbag and lit a cigarette. What she really wanted though was a fix. If only she could get to her car, but she couldn't, not yet. She owed it to Will to have a conversation with the pathetically coiffured man across the table. Will never had the chance to have his questions answered by his father and Shelley was sure he was watching them now. Although she resented the man whose company she would have to endure, this was something that she could do for her brother.

"Why didn't you come back and see him?" she asked.

"Times were hard for me in those days." In one quick movement, his bottom lip and chin protruded. "It was complicated. There was a lot going on."

"He needed you. He really needed you." Shelley took a pull on her cigarette. "Do you even know what happened to us?"

Jim responded with a nod then began shaking his head vehemently. "That was a terrible thing... an absolutely God-awful thing. No kids should have to go through what..." He took a gulp from his glass. "I really am truly sorry for you, doll."

"You should've come back. He might still be alive if you had."

"Whoa, hold your horses right there. You can't lay that at my door. That was your mother's job. She should've protected him properly. And you. Both of you. She was the one with responsibility for your safety."

The heat of Shelley's rage imbued her face. "If we didn't have useless, fucking fathers that cunt wouldn't have picked my mother."

"Shelley-Margaret, I might not have been around in William's life but you cannot pin what that nonce did on to me. And I will not have you use that language in my presence."

To calm herself, and hold down the urge to slap Resident Comb-Over, Shelley took several long draws on her cigarette. She lifted her black patent handbag onto her lap, took out her mobile phone and checked the time. How much longer could she bear his brazenness?

She turned her head away from the familiar stranger and instead stared at the pool table. The pool table on which she'd played her final game with William, and where now, under the light of the green, low-hanging lamp, a game was being played by two men dressed in white overalls.

"He wanted to know why you never came back." Shelley returned her gaze to Jim. "Why you never called, sent a card on his birthday, at Christmas. You broke his heart. Do you know that? Have you got any idea how much pain you caused my brother?"

Jim stared into his pint glass. Did he think the answer was in there?

After a short silence, he spoke. "It was a difficult time, made harder by your mother. You've got to remember it was her that took him away. She should've told me where she moved to. I didn't know where to find him."

"You could've found him easily." Her upper lip curled in contempt. "Mum had the same friends, she was in touch with the old neighbours – they'd have given you our address. There's pictures of you taken in Aunt Elsie's house, the same bloody house she still lives in. There's no point lying to me. You abandoned your son. You could have found him anytime you wanted but you didn't."

"You kids have no idea what it was like back then. Thatcher was closing all the pits and—"

"For twenty-one years solid? I don't think so. And when were you ever a miner?"

"My whole life, doll, apart from when I lived in the South. Look, I know you're hurt, but—"

"Hurt?" Shelley stared at him incredulously. "I've been fucking destroyed. Will was destroyed, and where the fuck were you? Mining somewhere. Fucking mining. Well that explains everything. Now it all makes sense."

"I've come back to make it up. I'm here now because I want to put it right." A chin and lower lip jut interrupted Jim's words. He smiled at her, unauthentically. It caused Shelley no surprise that as the sister of this man's departed son that was the smile she was given; it was more of a smile than her brother had received in two decades.

"You wanna make it up? How's that gonna work?" Shelley threw her handbag strap over her shoulder and got to her feet. She walked around the table to Jim's chair. She lowered herself with her face up close to his. "You're too fucking late. He's dead. Your son is dead."

She stormed towards the exit. As she reached the step that led to the door, she felt a hand on her back and turned around. "There's nothing to say," she told Jim.

"If you think of something..." From a pocket in his suit jacket, he pulled out a scrap of paper and pressed it into Shelley's palm.

She pushed the silver bar, opening both the wide double doors and for a moment, the glorious day, the sunshine, the brightness of the sky, came pouring into the pub and washed away the bleakness, killing the darkness with light.

"You can call me any time." He rested his hands on her

shoulders. "I want to put things right if you'll let me. I'm not too late, doll, not for you."

49. A Not So Different Generation

"He was full of excuses, pathetic excuses. He's a fucking loser. I don't even look like the cunt. He can't be my father."

"Shelley, stop swearing or I am not having this conversation with you." Aunt Elsie sipped her tea as they sat having breakfast outside The Coffee Cup.

"Why did Mum tell me I had a different dad? It doesn't make sense." Shelley was trying to keep her voice low. There were other customers seated at the tables nearby and although it was early, an endless stream of shoppers and workers were walking along Hampstead High Street, a few feet from their table.

"You mustn't judge your mother. Things were different back then. She did what she thought was right." Aunt Elsie patted Shelley's hand.

Shelley wondered if she'd done the right thing telling Aunt Elsie what William's father had told her, or even that she'd met him. Her to-do and to-worry lists had grown exponentially in the three days that had passed since they'd dumped the body. She'd yet to visit the library to establish the depth of the canal. She had to research the stickiness of parcel tape. She had to make enquiries to ascertain if there was CCTV at The Lanesborough. She barely had enough crack for another couple of hits. Her friends were hassling her to get clean. Her checking had become overwhelming. And to top it off, she was having breakfast with her aunt at nine o'clock in the morning – a time when she should have been asleep.

"I don't understand. Why did she lie to me?"

"You know you mustn't discuss this with her. She's just started taking steps in the right direction, but she's still so fragile. This will really set her back. Promise me you won't tell her you met Jim. You won't tell her anything about it. For a while at least, keep it between us."

"I won't. I wasn't going to. That's why I called you," Shelley whispered. "Do you know why she lied to me?"

"It wasn't so much a lie. She didn't know the truth. Back then you were stigmatised for being a single mother. If you didn't know who your child's father was... well, you can imagine."

"You mean she doesn't know who my father is?"

Elsie nodded.

"So what she told me about him being married, that's a lie?"

"Not exactly. Things aren't always black and white; there's shades of grey." Elsie took a bite of her raisin toast. She chewed for nearly a minute before carrying on. "There was a man and at the time, he wasn't married, not when they were together. Will was a baby – he was going to take him on as his own. He proposed to Mum, but it wasn't long after they were engaged she caught him cheating. Mum left and she got back with Jim. That's when she found out she was pregnant with you, but she didn't know which one of them was your dad. Jim and her didn't last, they never did. She didn't tell you, she didn't want Will to know anything bad about his father but..." Elsie paused.

"What? What did he do?"

"He was a drinker, and he'd take it out on Mum when he was drunk," Elsie said. "Look, it wasn't that bad. He shouted mostly. He only hit her a few times."

"That doesn't make it right."

"No, I'm just saying, people change. I've been told he's been sober for quite some time."

"He's not."

"You could give him a chance. It was the best thing he could have done for you, leaving when Mum was carrying you. It wasn't right for Will to live like that and thank God you never had to see it."

"What happened to the other man?"

"Vincent... By the time you were born, he was married. Mum told him about you but— She had to say it was one of them. She had to choose. We all knew Jim was long gone and probably for the best. She thought, we all thought, in time Vincent would—" Elsie's eyes welled with tears. Shelley shuffled her chair closer and leant over to hug her aunt.

Shelley interrupted the board meeting in her head. She didn't look like Jim, she told them. She hadn't inherited his mannerisms like Will had. But how had her beautiful brother, the gentlest spirit, come from such a callous man? And now she knew that she either came from that same coldness, or another equally as harsh.

Once her aunt released her, Shelley pushed her emotions down, temporarily and not deep enough, with a cigarette. She survived the next hour with the certainty that she'd be having the later billed, blockbusting, solo, intravenous, feeling-killing extravaganza.

50. An Explanation

The fleeting taste of British summertime in spring had passed. On Friday, as Shelley traipsed through Hampstead Heath, the sky had returned to an overcast grey. At the top of Parliament Hill, she slumped on a bench that had taken a battering from the elements. To protect herself from them, she pulled her jean jacket tighter around her.

This was the first time she'd been out of her flat since the Wednesday morning breakfast with her aunt. She'd been busy with her friend, heroin, anesthetising her pain. She hoped that today she'd actually make it to the library.

She lit a cigarette and sat back, listening to the chatter of the birds and looking over London from her favourite spot at the top of the world. In the distance, near the foot of the hill, she noticed Nicole strolling effortlessly up the steep gradient towards her. She looked like a 1950s movie star in her black trouser suit teamed with a headscarf, her blonde hair curled out at the sides and a pair of oversized sunglasses shielding half her face.

"Sorry I'm late. Were you waiting long?"

"It's okay." Shelley smiled. She stood up and wrapped her arms around Nicole. "Will you do it? I want to get it over with." Shelley held out her mobile phone, too scared to be delivered the bad news by a stranger.

"Go on then. Give it here." Nicole joined Shelley on the bench and made the call. "Good afternoon. I'm calling on behalf of my client and I'd like to ask you some questions before making a reservation . . . He's an international celebrity and I need to book him into one of the very best hotels in London . . . It's about security. We've had issues in the past so this is exceptionally important . . . Do you have CCTV? . . . Where do you have it? . . . Thank you for your time."

"They have it, don't they?" Shelley was horrified. She looked anxiously at Nicole.

"In the entrance hall and the corridors, but it doesn't mean anything. They might not even monitor it and you look totally different now anyway. Don't worry love, really. I look more like you than you do."

Shelley forced a smile.

"No more secrets, my Resident Most Precious." Nicole hooked Shelley's pinkie finger with hers and shook it.

"No more secrets. There aren't any left."

"I hope so." Nicole smiled. "And by the way, it doesn't include other people's secrets."

Shelley slipped her finger from Nicole's and took a cigarette from her box.

"Angel told me. That's about the only secret I can think of that you were right in keeping from me."

"Why didn't you tell me?" Shelley asked.

"I only found out when we took you to the clinic."

"Why didn't you ever talk about The Lanesborough?" Shelley clasped the ruby pendant on her necklace.

"I wanted you to trust me, Shell. To be honest with me, not because you were off your head and didn't know what you were saying, but to confide in me. I'm supposed to be your best friend."

"Oh." Shelley drained her cigarette as she watched the kites – expertly flown as they always were on the top of the world – breathe life into the dull sky with their primary colours. "I'm sorry. I'm not good at trusting people, but I always trusted you the most."

Now she didn't need to ask why Nicole had never mentioned her heroin habit. She had the answer. She looked at Nicole and felt tears welling in her eyes. She tried to blink them away. She had the most wonderful friend, the most caring, loyal, forgiving and understanding friend, and yet she'd felt unable to trust her. Nicole had asked what that said about her, but it was no reflection on Nicole. It spoke reams about Shelley.

***

"How's it going with your dad?" she asked Nicole as they wandered out of an open field, heading into the woods. Shelley scratched her nose, looking up at the tall, white-barked birch trees. She was always itchier there. She wondered if she had an allergy.

"I'm seeing him on Sunday. He's bringing my other brothers and my sister. It's sad Enda and Milly won't see him but Susie's gonna come." Nicole retied her headscarf. "Even if Jim's not your dad, he is Will's dad. You could keep in touch."

"I hate him." Shelley smiled at the old lady walking towards them.

"You'll feel better if you forgive him. You're the one being hurt by the anger you've got for him. You could go back to Dr Fielding, work through it."

Open-mouthed, Shelley stared at Nicole. "Forgive him? How could I?"

"It doesn't mean you're saying it's all right what he did. It's not right to abandon your kid. But you can forgive him for who he is now, not who he was then."

She wouldn't forgive Jim. Not for being her absent father, if he was. And even more so, not for leaving her brother. It would invalidate the pain Will suffered – the rejection he felt, the inadequacy – like it didn't matter, like it never happened. Had Jim been a proper father, Will would still be alive.

***

Having ambled for an hour, they approached the edge of the Heath. As Shelley walked on the shorter grass, parallel to East Heath Road, she gazed up into the lacklustre sky. She needed a hit but they were headed to The Magdala where later they were meeting with Angel. Now that she knew Nicole and Angel could tell when she was high, she hoped she could wait until she got home to have her next fix.

As they walked towards the street, Shelley caught sight of The Freemasons Arms on Downshire Hill, which reminded her of the library. She was sure it was on a road in that direction, although during the two years she'd lived in Hampstead, she'd never been.

While they carefully navigated their way down a sloping grass verge that led to the pavement, Shelley asked Nicole to accompany her to the library.

"Not this canal and tape thing again. There's no point. If the canal's shallow or the tape stops sticking, we can't do anything about it, can we?"

"I just wanna know, that's all. So I can stop thinking about it." Shelley lit herself a cigarette and passed one to Nicole.

"You know what? I don't even care." Nicole stopped walking. She turned to face Shelley. "You do things the right way and you get jack shit. Look at the sentences those fucking nonces got. They'll be out in a few years, free to do it all over again, fucking up more kids' lives. At least that rapist can't rape anyone again."

"It's all so fucked up, the law, the judges. It's all so wrong." Shelley took a hard draw on her cigarette. She watched the school-run traffic. The noise resounded in her head.

"Getting justice is a farce," Nicole said.

51. Never Too Late To Learn

"What the fuck's happened to you?" Shelley asked Hugo. He'd been unrecognisable from a distance when she'd first seen the unkempt man sitting on a bench outside The Freemasons Arms. It wasn't until she was farther along Downshire Hill, barely more than an arm's reach away from him, that she realised the man in the beer garden was Hugo – her friend with the rugged good looks. But now the goodness had gone and only the ruggedness remained.

"Tars happened." Hugo spoke like he was possessed and he looked like he had been too – by a tramp who'd ousted his suave style. "Do you have a spare cigarette?"

Shelley passed him a cigarette then lit it with her purple Clipper. "When did you last have a wash?"

"Wednesday... or was it Tuesday. The day Tars came back."

"Are you still stopping at hers then?" Nicole sat down on the wooden picnic bench next to him.

"My dad's banned me from my own flat. Can you believe it? I'm disowned until I go into treatment." He pulled his woolly hat lower over his ears and forehead. His blonde locks were still able to find an escape route down the sides and the back of his neck.

Shelley took a seat on the uncomfortable bench. "Maybe you should go."

"That's rich coming from you, love," Nicole told her.

"Look at him. He's fucked."

"Thank you, Shelley, darling, I am here you know." Hugo gave her a crooked smile as well as a nasty waft of decay. "I am going, I just haven't decided when. You should see the place... swimming pool, five-star food, luxury private rooms."

"You might wanna have a bath first," Shelley said, smiling at him.

Nicole leaned forward over the picnic table, in Hugo's direction. "Did you ever find your camcorder and your laptop?" she asked him.

"How would I? Tars's lowlife dealer pilfered them."

"What make was your laptop?"

Shelley cringed. She hoped the conversation wouldn't result in Nicole disclosing the crimes she already knew with certainty Tara had committed.

"Toshiba. Why?"

"And your camcorder?" Nicole continued investigating.

"Sony," Hugo replied. "Do you know something about this that I don't?"

"Don't be silly. I was just wondering what the good makes are."

"Do you know if Tara's all right? I can't get hold of her." Shelley picked up her handbag and in one smooth manoeuvre, the strap was over her shoulder.

"You think I'm in a bad way?" Hugo raised his eyebrows and they disappeared under the rim of his hat. "You need to see her."

"Tell her to call me, please. I'm worried about her." Shelley motioned with her head for Nicole to leave.

"You're off so soon," Hugo said to Shelley as she stooped by the bench to kiss him on the cheek. Their faces brushed, and he whispered in her ear, "Have you got any crack on you, darling?"

**

From Downshire Hill, Shelley and Nicole turned into Keats Grove. After a few steps, Shelley tried to sneak a look through the window of a grand house. She tripped on the uneven pavement. Nicole steadied her, preventing her fall.

"Are you sure it's down here?" Nicole asked.

Shelley had thought it was a library she'd driven past on the leafy street countless times before, but now she was walking, and not driving, she wasn't as certain. When she caught sight of the black iron gates, she changed her mind again. Through those gates, she believed was a path that led to the library. Having walked under the iron arch and down the passageway, they reached their destination.

Once inside the old building, she stopped for a moment, gazing up the stained glass, domed roof. She imagined how beautiful it would look with the sun shining through it. Her brief dreamlike moment was brought to an end by Nicole's clonking footsteps on the parquet floor behind her.

"Shhh." Shelley put her index finger to her mouth and glared at Nicole. Faces looked up at them from the tables scattered across the room. Shelley disregarded the disapproving stares and continued towards the books. She studied the section titles. She was at a loss where to look for the information she required. It would be quicker to ask the librarian. If she didn't, she might not find what she needed before the library closed.

As she made her way across the floor to the enquiry desk, she concocted a story to explain why she needed to know the depth of the canal. Her boss had bought a barge and instructed her to come up with a route for his first trip. She repeated it to herself to make it more believable when she spoke.

"Can you help me with something please?" Shelley called to the stout woman behind the desk who stood with her back towards them. While she was being ignored, Shelley took the time to develop her second lie about parcel tape.

"Yes, dearie. What do you need?" The woman turned around. Shelley realised he was a man.

"It might sound a bit strange but I'm trying to find out the— What are those?" Shelley pointed to the floor by the cupboards behind the enquiry desk. The librarian's eyes followed.

"Newspapers. You have seen—"

"What newspapers are they?"

"Local and national. What is it that you need, dearie?"

"What about the canal?" Nicole whispered in Shelley's ear.

"When are they from? Are they recent?" Shelley attempted to wink at Nicole when the librarian turned his back, but she could never wink like Nicole could. Instead, she simultaneously shut both her eyes.

"Very recent. We only store a few weeks' backlog here." The librarian looked down, fiddling with the books on his desk. "You might be better off at Swiss Cottage. They're bigger than we are," he mumbled.

"Can I see them, please?"

"Which ones do you want to see, dearie?" He didn't look up, but Shelley could hear the impatience in his tone.

"All of them," she said defiantly.

52. Pilgrim's Lane

***FROM COMA TO CORNERED** – Lord Richard Sears Caught in Drug-Crazed Sex Romp*

Lord Richard Sears, 54, was discovered yesterday morning in a coma at one of London's most exclusive hotels, The Lanesborough in Knightsbridge. The Old Etonian hired a luxury suite for a night of drug-fuelled sex with 23-year-old call girl, Mia Anderson. In the early hours, Anderson reported his death to the emergency services, however, on arrival, paramedics found Lord Sears in a coma with respiratory depression and a low pulse believed to have been caused by Gammahydroxybutrate (GHB). The disgraced peer was taken by ambulance to St Mary's Hospital, Paddington from where he was later discharged in good health. The police have confirmed that crack cocaine was seized at the scene and an investigation is underway.

Shelley sat on the cushioned bench, opposite Angel and Nicole, tucked away in their quiet corner in the back of The Magdala. Laid out on the shabby table in front of her was the photocopy of the Daily Mirror article from Saturday 19 April 1997, which she'd found at the library. She stared at the picture. That was him. Her greying-blonde john. And he wasn't the dead john she'd thought he was ever since she'd left him that night at The Lanesborough in March.

"You look like the cat that got the cream. Did you have a vendetta with that Mia or what?" Angel asked.

"No, I don't—" Shelley began.

"She's someone we know from a few years back," Nicole finished.

***

For over half the day, Shelley had been holding out for her next hit. She couldn't leave it until she got home. She was desperate, so she slipped off to the ladies' room. She sat on a toilet with the lid down and with her jeans on, as she usually did, and heated the underside of the spoon bearing her medicine.

Although she felt a lightness from the burden that had been removed, she was still weighed down by her fears about the canal and the parcel tape. They didn't have time to investigate those issues at the library because it had closed minutes after their extensive trawl through the newspapers ended in success.

When Shelley returned to the saloon, she hoped her eyes wouldn't give her away. To avoid looking at Angel and Nicole who were sat opposite, she stared blankly into her pint glass. After a while, she picked up the drink and drained what was left of the snakebite and blackcurrant. Empty-handed, she was left studying the scratches on the wooden table in front of her. She took out her cigarettes and lit one. As she replaced the packet in her handbag, Angel grabbed her arm and pushed back the sleeve of her jean jacket.

"What are you doing?" Shelley said, pulling her arm free.

"You're arm's a mess! You're fucking high! So much for quitting." Angel shook her head.

"I said I'd try, not that I was doing it now, but I will... There's the whole summer."

"You won't cope at university on that poison, believe," Angel said. "You can do it but you have to want to."

"I do want to... Part of me wants to, just not all of me."

"You have to stop, please, Shell. You're gonna kill yourself." Nicole leaned forward, resting her elbows on the table. Shelley sensed both her fury and her sympathy.

Angel lifted Shelley's chin, which – like her eyelids – was falling south. She tilted Shelley's face towards hers. "A friend of mine says some people don't stop 'til the pain of their using gets worse than the pain they're running from."

With a cigarette resting between her lips, Shelley contemplated what Angel had said. Was her drug taking causing her more pain than her past? No it wasn't – not yet. But how much worse did it need to get before it was?

***

"When's your flight to New York?" Nicole asked Angel.

"Monday." Angel took a sip of her vodka and coke.

"So this is the last time I'll see you?" Shelley asked. *I'll miss you*, she thought.

"You can come and stay anytime, both of you."

"I will. If that punter still wants me in Miami, I'll be out next summer." Shelley tried to conceal her shame by averting her gaze. She looked at the veins in her hands. The only way she'd make it to America is if she could get off the junk.

"You promise to look after Tara when I'm gone?" Angel asked.

"I can't. You do know she's blanking me?" Nicole picked up her bottle of wine and poured the last of it into her glass.

"She's in a bad way, babe. It's not your fault Max is gone. She'll come round."

"She's never gonna see him. It's the bloody Middle East. If I were her I wouldn't talk to me either." Nicole downed her glass of wine and as she looked up, Shelley saw the sadness in her glazed eyes.

"You did what you thought was best, Nic." Shelley smiled weakly.

"But it wasn't best, was it? Not for Tara. Not for her boy. Who was it best for?"

"You did the right thing. You didn't know that was gonna happen." Shelley walked round to the other side of the table. She perched on the end of the bench and took Nicole in her arms. "It probably would have happened anyway, even if you hadn't called her parents." Shelley gently rocked Nicole.

Shelley hadn't seen Nicole drunk in a while, and she didn't like it. For a moment, she imagined Nicole's perspective: how she felt about Shelley's heroin habit. And for the briefest moment, she considered rethinking her options – not giving up junk, but possibly counselling and a methadone prescription. Then the thought left her.

***

At closing time, outside The Magdala, the air was cool. "See you in Manhattan," Angel said, hugging Shelley.

After saying goodbye to Nicole, Angel took a few steps up the road, then turned round and called out, "I'm Lucy. Don't be a stranger."

Shelley set off walking towards her flat with Nicole. She looked up to see the stars, but the night sky bore the effects of a hangover from the overcast day; the stars were invisible, hidden behind the dark clouds.

With her arm linked in Nicole's, they hobbled along as a pair down Pilgrim's Lane. Shelley slowed down each time they passed a house lit up from the inside, extending her glimpse at life through the naked window of a stranger.

As she stole a final peek at a hybrid townhouse-castle, she noticed a figure watching them from an open window upstairs. Her heart rate quickened and she tightened her link on Nicole's arm.

"Slow down. You're gonna pull me over," Nicole said, as Shelley dragged her along, causing her to totter.

"Sorry, it's just creepy round here." Shelley glanced back over her shoulder to check if they were still being spied on from the castle of a townhouse, but it was too distant now and she couldn't tell.

They walked on a little farther before stopping by a Victorian street lantern. Under the dim light, Shelley searched in her handbag for her cigarette packet. "Will you call Marianne tomorrow?" she asked Nicole.

"She won't turn up at Len's house. What would she say?"

"That's not what I'm worried about. He can handle her – he's a Resident Master Bullshitter – but we still need to stay close." Shelley pulled two cigarettes from her gold twenty-pack and passed one to Nicole. "You keep your friends close and your enemies closer."

"Now who's the master of bullshit?" Nicole puffed on her cigarette to catch the flame that Shelley was keeping alight for her. "I'm not calling. I won't be speaking to that sick bitch again."

"You have to. How are we gonna—"

"Find another way. I'm finished with her, with all of them." Nicole hurled her mobile phone, sending it smashing into the road.

"What the fuck are you doing?"

"Cutting ties," Nicole said, throwing her arms in the air. "I'm not working any more. I'm done."

"What are you gonna do?" Shelley stared at her friend's shadowy face in the dusky light.

"I don't know, it doesn't matter, as long as it's not this. I'm repeating the pattern of what those perverts did to me for years. What I let them do."

"You didn't let them. You were a child." Shelley's heroin-smudged vision of Nicole blurred further with tears. "You were selfless, protecting your little sisters. I know it's fucked up, but you did it out of love for them."

"They took a chunk of my soul and I let them." Nicole stamped her foot on the pavement.

"You didn't. They just took it."

"On every job I've done, I've lost a bit more, given away a bit more." A sad anger contorted Nicole's mouth. "We might not sell our bodies but we're selling our souls."

"We're not."

"We are, Shell, and I'm trying to hold on to the little bit of me that's left before there's nothing... I'm sick of it, being used like a sex object. In this life, everyone wants to fuck you. They don't wanna know you. They'll never love you. They just wanna fuck you."

53. The Ripple Effect

Nicole's words were still resonating in Shelley's head two days later on Sunday 1st June during the train journey to Brighton. The board, with its existing armoury of powerful, negative mantras, didn't need a new one with which to flog her.

She looked out the window to give herself a break from the conversation with her aunt and mother, who were sat opposite on the blue seats. She reached to the empty seat beside her and picked up the bunch of pink carnations. Holding them to her body, she inhaled their scent. "I'll never forget you," she said silently in her head to Will.

Rita and Aunt Elsie appeared outwardly to be far more emotionally ready for the day than Shelley felt within herself. She continued to remain silent as the two sisters chatted about matters as important as flowerpots.

This was the first time she would be back in Brighton since the last family holiday they'd taken with just the three of them – Shelley, William and Rita – in the summer of 1983. It was also the first time her mother would return. But William had been back, once. He'd been a ten-year-old boy on his penultimate visit, and he was a twenty-one-year-old man at the time of his final trip in July 1994 – from which he returned in a body bag.

Aunt Elsie maintained her belief in the possibility it had been accidental. But Shelley and her mother had no doubt it was deliberate. Shelley thought that perhaps her aunt only voiced that supposition to allay her sister's guilt. There had been too much spoken, too many times, for the incident to have been a random accident.

Shelley excused herself from her aunt and mother's company and walked to the rear of the carriage. Cool air gushed through the open windows where she'd taken a seat in the smoking section. She stood up and closed them all except one that was stuck. Still feeling a chill, she buttoned up her red cardigan that she wore as a cover-up over her cream, linen dress. Protruding under the tight sleeve was a lump that she'd noticed had been increasing in size. She stretched the material to ensure it wouldn't be visible to anyone else.

The train chugging, 'damaged goods,' could still be heard over the noise of the rowdy wind rushing through the window. To drown out the talking train, she put on her headphones. Listening to her Hue and Cry – *Bitter Suite* album often soothed her, but today her mind was in turmoil and her body equally so. There was drilling in her head; her stomach cramped; and she felt twitchy and sweaty. It wasn't withdrawal symptoms because she'd had a fix before leaving her house that morning. Though not enough to be noticeable, it had been enough to hold her and she still had the itch, which told her it was still in her system. Although she didn't have Jay any more, for the price of his cab fare, Len had been willing to come over yesterday to replenish her supplies. This time he'd been more generous with her allowance of crack. She hoped the arrangement would work long term; waiting for Ajay was like waiting for a block of ice to melt in a Siberian winter.

After stubbing out her cigarette, she remained seated. Isolated in the stormy, smoking area, she listened to the third track – *Shipbuilding* – on repeat. The dark cloud that hung over her rained down, drenching her in melancholy. She thought about the ironic system that planned, allowed and paid for the destruction of souls. The system that had parents building ships on which their children were taken to their death. The system that bore the cost of her family's case and supposed recovery – and seven years later was still paying out – yet next year, that same system would be sending that same child rapist back into the world to reoffend. It was a farcical strategy she couldn't comprehend because once again – as if on a loop – it would facilitate the destruction of more souls. The system paid for everything, financially, but what it couldn't meet was the cost on every other level – that was borne by Shelley and her family. For William, the price had been his life. It was nearly too high for Rita and though Shelley was adept at disguise, she knew in her marred heart that she couldn't pay. Heroin bought her time, and heroin kept her from going under, but she'd begun to see heroin came with its own price. It was costing her more than money.

***

On King's Road, between Ship Street and Middle Street, Shelley sat outside a cafe with her aunt and mother. She stared out to sea, breathing in the salty air carried across the road by the zephyr. In the clear sky, the sun looked powerful, but its looks were deceiving; the cool sea breeze weakened its warmth.

The grandeur of the Regency, white-stucco townhouses in Brighton reminded Shelley of Belgravia, which led her to think of The Lanesborough. For a couple of seconds, her breathing shortened until she remembered that was something she no longer needed to feel anything about. The guilt from that night was gone. If only the rest of the guilt she carried could vanish as rapidly. William had been burdened with guilt that wasn't his too. He had nothing to feel guilty for. A voice in Shelley's head told her she didn't either. It sounded like Will's voice – was he on the board? Although she could agree with him in her head, she couldn't accept it in her heart.

Having eaten a croissant, she lit a cigarette to smoke with her coffee. She hoped the caffeine would make her feel more awake. She felt so exhausted in body and mind that if a bed was wheeled into the road, she could have lain down and slept in the bustling street.

"Are you ready, dear?" Rita asked Shelley.

"I don't think so, Mum. But you feel ready, don't you?"

"It's something we've got to do, dear. We've got to stop living in the past."

Shelley watched Aunt Elsie take Rita's hand across the table. When Elsie turned to smile at her, Shelley saw there were tears in her eyes. "Are you okay, Auntie?" Shelley asked.

Elsie picked up a napkin from the table and dabbed the corners of her eyes. "It's not a sad tear," she said, "not completely. It's healing for me being here. It'll be healing for you too." She shuffled her chair backwards then stood up, holding her bunch of pink carnations.

Rita got to her feet and as she picked up her bunch of flowers, she looked over to Shelley and gave her a knowing nod. Fighting against her instinct that told her to stay where she was, Shelley forced herself off the chair.

Carrying her pink carnations, Shelley crossed the road to the seafront with her aunt and mother. They sauntered along the promenade, heading towards the white, Victorian pier, which from a distance looked like a horizontally stretched and vertically challenged palace on stilts.

Behind a bus stop, Shelley noticed a break in the turquoise-painted balustrade that was separating them from the beach. They left the hard concrete and ambled down the slope to walk the rest of the way in the sand.

***

"We're here," Elsie said as she stopped walking, one-hundred yards or so from the pier. Although it was Rita and Shelley's first time back since William had died, it wasn't for Elsie. Shelley wanted to ask about her previous visits, but today she was stuck in the pattern of keeping things to herself. The questions she really wanted answered could not be asked. They would have been addressed to her mother, but as agreed with her aunt, she would hold off for a while.

They sat in a circle on the sand. In the empty triangle in the centre, Shelley laid her pink carnations on top of the other two bunches.

A white Alsatian, dripping wet and ignoring the recall of its owner, flicked sand and shook water over everyone in its path, including Shelley. She brushed the sand off her dress and cardigan, then lit a cigarette.

The beach wasn't deserted as Shelley had pictured it every time she'd imagined being there. Disappointingly, her time reliving the past was disrupted by the people around her living in the present. There were families picnicking and there were couples frolicking. Children played noisily in the sea and on the sand, rattling buckets and spades, throwing balls, digging holes and making sandcastles as she and Will had done years earlier.

She stubbed the butt of her cigarette into the sand that was already rubbish-ridden with ice-cream wrappers, bottles, cans and plastic bags. Having removed her shoes, she stood up and took a deep breath. Her legs wobbled. Her knees felt near to giving way, but she managed to bend down, pick up her bunch of flowers and get herself back into an upright position.

Clutching the pink carnations to her chest, Shelley fixed her gaze on the horizon in front of her. She staggered across the sand towards the sea. Even though it was the sea that had taken her brother, she knew it wasn't responsible for stealing him from her. The blame for that lay at the prison cell door, which contained the man their mother had met in Brighton at the end of that last summer holiday in 1983.

Waves brushed over her bare feet as she navigated her way across clusters of egg-shaped stones in the wet sand. At first, her clothes were only lightly splashed as she trudged out into the sea. As she walked deeper, the hem of her linen dress became drenched. Walking on, the arms of her long-sleeved cardigan were soaked up to the elbows.

She stopped once she was waist deep in the ocean. Her dress danced in the water. Standing perfectly still, she noticed the noise that had been dominating her ears suddenly sounded dulled down. Louder was Pink Floyd - *Shine on You Crazy Diamond* playing on the sound system in her head.

In the sea peopled with strangers, Shelley felt alone. Everyone around her appeared blurred. She was in her own world as if she'd crossed over into another dimension.

"I'll never forget you," she chanted, tossing the pink carnations, one at a time, into the sea.

She felt as though Will had walked through her. She shivered. Now he was standing beside her. With her hand in his, she watched the sun reflecting on the waves and her flowers, coaxed farther out by the current, floating away on the sparkling surface.

54. The Uninvited Guest

When Shelley set off from her mother's home back to her flat, it was six o'clock in the evening. Her clothes were still damp, her skin was itching, and a rash had come up on her chest. In an effort to dry herself, she set the heating to the hottest temperature at the highest power. Finding it hard to breathe, she kept her window ajar. With the air making so much noise, she cranked up Capital Radio because the air alone didn't clear her thoughts.

She wanted to escape and America would have been far enough had she been able to go. A voice from the board reminded her that she could be there next summer if her mother was well enough. But really, as with everything else she might be able to do, it hinged on whether she was ready to let go of what Nicole called her coping mechanism, and what she preferred to call her crutch – because somehow that didn't seem as bad – heroin.

There was a big part of her, probably most of her, that didn't want to stop. She couldn't imagine a life without it. Her mind needed to be cleaned out and the only way she knew how was with heroin. Heroin drained the bad memories, although it was only temporary and the whole solution brought with it a new set of demons.

Considering the strength her mother had shown today, Shelley wondered if the best way to clean a contaminated mind was to wash it and not to drain it. If reciting words that were not her own meant feeling better, then perhaps it wasn't such a bad thing. Earlier, her aunt had again suggested that she attend the bereavement support group and again, Shelley told her that she'd give it some thought, but in truth, she couldn't imagine sitting in a room full of strangers talking about how she felt, which apparently was what they did.

As she turned off Hampstead High Street and onto Willoughby Road, she drove slowly, looking for a space to park. There was none. Sundays, at this time, were always busier. Shelley suspected it was due to a local evening class, and a few times, she'd considered exploring it in case she might be interested in attending, but because of the junk that hijacked her time and her life, it had never progressed past consideration.

She drove up and down the street, hoping someone would move

their car so she could nab their space. On nearing the junction with Hampstead High Street for the umpteenth time, among what looked like a congregation of druggies, she saw Len. He'd been over yesterday with a delivery of heroin and crack and hadn't mentioned coming back today. He was only ever willing to come to Hampstead if she paid his cab fare. He'd never mentioned knowing anyone who lived there.

***

Dried, and dressed in her thermal pyjamas, Shelley wrapped herself in the special duvet. She waddled out of her bedroom to have a hit in the lounge. As she passed though the hallway, a director insisted she check the front door because she might not have locked it properly when she'd come in.

Even though she could see a section of the gold bar between the lock and the doorframe – which would indicate the door was locked – she didn't trust her eyes alone, and neither did the board. She began the checking, but her skin was irritated from wearing wet clothes and she was compelled to scratch it. Every time an itch interrupted her counting, she had to start over. Although her anxiety was increasing after standing at the door for several minutes, the craving for a hit was stronger than the compulsion to check and she withdrew from the hall.

She switched on the television, then lay sideways on the sofa and prepared the heroin required for a speedball. She hoped Len hadn't seen her. She wasn't in the mood for company but for a few minutes, at the junction, she'd been stuck in traffic feet away from him and had he seen her, she wouldn't have known because she'd kept her head turned in the opposite direction. So as not to increase the risk further, she'd made her re-entrance to Willoughby Road through the back streets and parked at the far end.

She added a rock of crack to the heroin she'd cooked in the spoon. As she picked up the syringe to grind it in, she glanced at the changing patterns moving on the walls. With the sun streaming in, the white walls looked alive.

Inside Shelley felt nearly dead. She wondered if she was wrong wishing Jim not to be her father – because if he was, then Will would be her full blood brother. Surely, she should want that. But she didn't think she did, and she didn't know if it mattered; it wouldn't change her love for Will.

She pushed back the long sleeve of her pastel-pink pyjama top and scanned her arm for a vein. The damage wreaked on her limb was severe. There were bruised and reddened lumps of varying sizes. One, she worried, could be an abscess – the one she'd had to stretch her sleeve for. It was growing in size rather than shrinking as they usually did, and it had been causing her more pain than the others.

With her right hand, she grasped her left wrist and stopped the blood flow. On finding a thin vein near the base of her thumb, she removed the orange cap of the syringe with her teeth and then slid in the needle.

As she pulled back on the plunger, she told herself that after this hit she'd go back out and drive herself to the accident and emergency department of the Royal Free. She'd been denying it to herself, but now the lump was half the size of a golf ball, she had to admit it. If left much longer, and if it was an abscess as she suspected it might be, it could burst leading to septicaemia and death. However convenient that would be for her, she couldn't leave her mother.

***

When Shelley heard the buzzer, she was filled with dread. She wasn't sure if it had sounded in her head or in her flat. If it was the flat, it could be the police. Maybe they'd found the body.

She checked the time on her phone. The buzzer went off again. It was nearly midnight. She'd had a few hits during the course of the past few hours, and it had been a while since she'd crossed that invisible line with crack - the one where rather than building up over time, psychosis was able to kick in after one hit, picking up from where it had left off the last time.

Being paranoid, it was with difficulty that she talked herself into answering the intercom. "Who is it?" she said, trying to sound normal.

"It's me, Len," said a meeker version of his voice over the intercom.

Shelley pressed the button to open the street door. She heard his clambering footsteps. It sounded like he was running up the stairs. His footsteps didn't usually sound this heavy. In case it wasn't him, she kept her front door closed, waiting for the knock before opening it.

"Who is it?" she asked. She needed to hear him speak for confirmation that it was his voice she'd heard over the intercom and not someone else or something in her imagination.

"It's me, Len. Let me in."

The voice sounded similar to Len's, but she wasn't absolutely sure it was him. Perhaps someone else was pretending to be him and was outside her door waiting to hurt her. She sprinted into the kitchen then returned to the front door carrying a bread knife. She attached the chain before opening the door a fraction.

"Are you gonna invite me in or what?"

"I was just checking it was you." Shelley removed the chain, letting Len through the door. She pinched his arm as he walked into the lounge.

"What the fuck are you doing?" He turned back to look at her. "My God, Shelley, what the— put the fucking knife down!"

"I'm not gonna hurt you. Not if you're real." Shelley held the wooden handle of the knife tightly in her hand.

"Can I sit down?" he asked, hovering by the sofa.

"Have you got ID?"

"Of course I ain't got I-fucking-D. Generally, I don't get asked to show it when I visit my mates." Len sat on the sofa. "Put that knife down. For fuck's sake, you're losing it, love. How much of that crack have you done?"

With the knife in her hand, Shelley took a seat on the couch next to Len. She studied the 'L-U-C-K' and 'F-A-T-E' tattoos on his fingers. Surely, her mind couldn't be projecting the image of eight tattoos onto someone's hands. And if the man next to her was entirely an hallucination, then in reality, she was safe.

He laid his long, black wallet on the table. She picked it up and opened it. She rubbed her fingers over the elastic loops that held the syringes in place. Feeling the elastic and watching it move in response to her touch, she was sure – as sure as she could be – that the man sat next to her was indeed Len and that he was there in person rather than in projection.

Having returned the knife to the kitchen, she sat down next to him and prepared her fix. Her anxiety over him faded. She remembered that she didn't know why he was there. He must have come to see her for a reason. He'd never turned up uninvited to her flat. He'd only been there a handful of times previously and the last visit was only yesterday.

"Is something wrong?" she asked, believing the question was neutral without appearing rude. What she meant was: What the fuck are you doing here?

"I need a favour." Len balanced his spoon of brown liquid on the coffee table. He turned to face Shelley. His eyes were sad. She suddenly noticed they were red, as if he'd been crying. They must have been like that when he arrived. She'd not heard or seen him cry since he'd been in the flat.

"What's the matter? What do you need?" She felt her forehead crinkle. She wasn't used to being in the company of a man showing any emotions other than lust or anger, or both.

Soul Destruction: Unforgivable

"It's a big one this, Shell."

"Don't worry about that. I owe you now, big time, after what you did."

"No, Shell, you don't. I owe you. I've been trying to tell you."

"Not any more you don't. As long as that cunt's body doesn't float." Shelley grinned. "What do you need?"

"Can I stay here?"

"How long for?"

"I don't know yet... a while I think."

"That's all right. You can stay in the spare room. Has something happened to your house?"

"My gaff ain't the issue, but I can't stay there no more," he said. "There's something you need to know... I'm not gonna blame you if you chuck me out."

"I'm not gonna do that." Shelley dropped a bitten off segment of cigarette filter into her spoon. Through it she drew up her fix into the syringe. With her hit ready in the barrel, she turned to face Len. "What's wrong?" she asked.

She heard the television, which had remained on, but gone unnoticed for hours. "...If you recognise the gunman from this CCTV picture, you can call anonymously on the number below. He's a white male, mid to late thirties, five-foot eight with short, brown hair. On the night of the shooting, he was wearing pale blue jeans with a brown leather jacket..."

Len turned off the television. He stood, frozen, looking at Shelley. Mentally, she compared the image of the man's face she'd seen on the television to the face she saw in front of her eyes.

"That's what I've been trying to tell you, Shell. It's my fault your friends were held up. It's my fault they didn't get to you in time. It was my fault you were —"

"Don't say it!" With shaking hands, Shelley put a cigarette in her mouth and lit it. She took a rapid succession of pulls to stop the tears she felt rising from spilling over her lower lids.

"It was me, Shell. I'm scared they're gonna find me."

"He was child-murdering scum. He fucking had it coming."

"She was my sister... Kim was my big sister." Len fell to his knees, covering his face with his hands.

Shelley dropped her syringe on the coffee table. She rushed over and knelt down next to him on the floor. She held him in her arms. "You did the right thing," she told him, as Nicole had told her.

She thought about Nicole – what she'd said and how she'd acted last Sunday evening in Len's house. Nicole had known Len was in the cellar when she was looking for the gun. Maybe she knew about the shooting as well.

He pulled back from her and rested his hands heavily on her shoulders. "You sure you still want me to stay?"

"You can stay as long as you need." Shelley stood and outstretched her hand. She took his and pulled him up.

They sat down on the sofa. Shelley pushed back her sleeve and placed her hand in Len's lap. "Can you find a vein for me please?" she asked.

"What the fuck have you done to yourself?" Len leapt from the sofa. He threw on his jacket. "We need to get you to A and E. You need to get that lanced."

Shelley looked up at him. "Let me have a hit first." She waved her works in the air.

"When did that rash come up?" he asked, ignoring her advance with the syringe.

"I'm not going anywhere without a hit."

"Have you got it anywhere else?"

"No, it's nothing to do with that. I got wet in the sea."

He darted out of the lounge and returned with her fake-fur coat. "Get up and put this on."

"I don't need a coat. It's too hot. I just need this, then I'll get dressed and I'll go, I promise." Again, she held out her works to him, but her request was disregarded.

"Where's your keys?"

She picked up her handbag and threw it at him. Grabbing her wrist, he pulled her off the couch. He wrapped her in the warm coat as he dragged her out the flat.

"I need to lock the door." She tried to turn back, but he was holding her hand, pulling her towards the staircase. "I need to go back. It's not the gear. I need to lock up properly."

He didn't reply with words. He held her hand tighter and galloped down the stairs, towing her behind.

"We can't go yet." She looked at the syringe in her free hand as they walked out onto the street. "I wanna go back. Please. The door's not locked and I can't go without a hit."

He didn't talk. He hauled her towards her Mercedes at the end of the street. Using the key fob, he released the central locking and let himself in the driver's side.

Stood on the pavement, Shelley was shivering in her thermal pyjamas. She fastened the hook eyes on her coat. In her particular manner, she sat sideways on the passenger seat, keeping both TNs on the pavement. She raised her legs then rotated her body ninety degrees, swinging her feet into the footwell.

He revved the engine. She squeezed his arm, trying to prevent him from driving. "I need to have this." She held her filled syringe in his line of vision. "Just one. That's all I'm asking."

He swerved out of the tight space and accelerated onto Willow Road towards the Royal Free Hospital. The velocity hurled Shelley back in the passenger seat. Her skull collided with the headrest and the ruby from her necklace smacked her centrally in the forehead. She lost her grip on the syringe, which went flying from her hand and disappeared into the darkness.

Lightning Source UK Ltd.
Milton Keynes UK
UKOW04f2052311013

220195UK00005B/347/P